JILL TRESEDER was born in Hamps
in sight of the sea on the Solent and
Wales. She now lives with her husb
River Dart.

After graduating from Bristol wi
lowed careers in social work, manage   ... and social
research, obtaining a PhD from the School of Management at the
University of Bath along the way. For the last decade she has focused
on writing fiction.

C000091445

PRAISE FOR *THE HATMAKER'S SECRET*

'*An original and imaginative novel, which bravely confronts head on the issue of racial prejudice and its corrosive effects on relationships. It also takes a refreshingly honest look at the ambivalence of the bonds between parents and their adult children, and the emotional uses and misuses of parental power. For all the weightiness of these themes, however, the personal stories engaged me in their own right.*'
Christa Laird

'*There is a profound wisdom to Jill Treseder's fiction, worn lightly as befits this subtle, engaging storyteller, but always there, always thought-provoking, and always enlightening.*'
Peter Stanford

THE
Hatmaker's
SECRET

JILL TRESEDER

SilverWood

Second edition published in 2017 by SilverWood Books

SilverWood Books Ltd
14 Small Street, Bristol, BS1 1DE, United Kingdom
www.silverwoodbooks.co.uk

First edition published in 2013 by Gold Wind Ltd

ISBN 978-1-78132-624-4 (paperback)
ISBN 978-1-78132-625-1 (ebook)

British Library Cataloguing in Publication Data
A CIP catalogue record for this book is available from
the British Library

Page design and typesetting by SilverWood Books
Printed on responsibly sourced paper

In memory of my mother Eve
in all her complexity

The Hatmaker's Family

The Silking Family in the Early 20th Century

The Hatmaker – Marjorie Dorothea Silking, known as Marge, and
later as Thea

Flo Silking – her mother

Dick Silking – Flo's second husband and Marge's father

Nora and Edna Porter – Flo's daughters by her first husband, Charlie

May Silking – Marge's younger sister, known as Binnie

Henrietta Silking – Dick's mother and Marge's grandmother

Rose Day – Flo's sister, married to Jim; Marge's aunt

Lucy Day – daughter of Rose and Jim; Marge's cousin

Maudie Thorne – another cousin

Later Generations of the Family in the Early 21st Century

Thea Stanley (née Silking) – now 93, married to Ted

Vanessa Harris – daughter of Thea and Ted, married to David

Kate Ward – daughter of Vanessa and David, married to Daniel

Jack and Flora Ward – children of Kate and Daniel

Lisa Harris – Kate's younger sister

Roz Ward – Daniel's mother, married to Blake Taylor

1

1913

'I never did like delivering on a Good Friday.' Miss Mulvaney slammed the front door and stamped down the passage, blowing on her hands and leaving crusts of snow on the lino.

Dolly Best sighed. 'Why's that, then?' As if she didn't know the answer.

'Day of death.'

'Don't you go talking like that upstairs.'

'People have to take me as they find me. They can't do without me, that's for sure.'

Dolly ignored that remark. She'd been unofficial midwife to the neighbourhood for years and she wasn't sure Mary Mulvaney, much as she respected her, was any better for all her qualifications.

She attempted a more optimistic note. 'It's the first day of spring.'

'Spring, my foot. Wicked wind blowing off the harbour. And the snow's settling. Coming down quite thick.'

Dolly gave up. 'I'd best be getting back up to Flo.'

'How's Mrs Silking doing?'

Dolly smirked at Mary's professional formality. For heaven's sakes, they'd all been at school together. She dropped her voice with a nod towards the door at the end of the passage. 'Not going too well for her. Exhausted, she is.'

On cue, the door to the back room opened and a dark-haired man leant into the hallway. His folded arms seemed to be holding his spare frame together and his hand shook a little as he removed a cigarette to speak. 'I heard the door.' He held the butt close to his mouth, ready to replace it at the earliest opportunity.

'It's Miss Mulvaney, Dick. Just going up to see to Flo.'

'Anything I can...?'

'Put the kettle on. We'll be needing more hot water.'

Mary toiled up the stairs after Dolly, her ample hips brushing the walls on either side. The front bedroom was dimly lit and Flo was half-squatting at the side of the bed, moaning. She'd gone into labour the day before and it was now two o'clock in the morning. Together they helped her back on to the bed and examined her.

Then Dolly excused herself to go and check on another mother who lived a few doors down.

'Elsie Chapman? 'Twon't be anything. Not yet. Shouldn't waste your time.'

Dolly pulled on her coat and made for the stairs. 'I know. But 'tis her first and she thinks she's started.'

Mary Mulvaney said she'd give her at least another two weeks and Dolly let her have the last word. She was right, of course, but there was also such a thing as neighbourliness that tended to go out of the door when qualifications came in. Dolly kept her opinions to herself.

Dick heard Dolly tap down the hall and let herself out. He had no desire to go up to Flo, not now that strange woman was there. Or at all, if he was honest. The whole thing put the fear of God in him, especially now he carried responsibility.

'A man has no place,' he murmured to the kettle as he lifted it off the stove.

It had been bad enough when his little brother was born when he was only a nipper – his mother crying out in that crowded little quarter in Gib, and being told to put the kettle on. The next time, he remembered, he'd been the eldest at home, but his sister Ada had taken over. She was only eight, but that was Ada. He'd ended up boiling water that time too. Seemed it was all men were fit to do.

Father had made sure he was never in the house, and now Dick thought that was probably the way it ought to be. He added a small knob of coal to the fire and a sprinkling of dust which flared into yellow flame and died away. They'd had to eke out the coal to light a fire in the bedroom. Dreadful time of year to bring a littl'un into the world in this climate.

He gave the heart of the fire a poke and watched the fireflies eating the soot on the back of the grate. So he was going to be father of a child. He'd had nearly nine months to get used to the idea, but it was only in the last few hours that the reality started coming home to him. It wasn't the family life he'd dreamed of, but as Father always said, 'Where's the use in all that dilly daydreaming, boy?' He'd struck lucky with Flo. She wasn't the love of his life, but theirs was a good partnership. They might have married for practical reasons, but their affection was growing and deepening. Or so it seemed to him. Maybe it was turning into love. Maybe it was better that way. Better than having a passion that faded away. He'd never know the answer to that one.

Dick was roused by a wail from upstairs. It wasn't the sound he'd been waiting for and was followed by a thud and footsteps above his head. He took the stairs two at a time to intercept Nora as she went looking for her mother. He didn't want the little maid to be scared. He took her back to bed, cuddled her up and told her a story.

This was the room where he'd started life in this house, being treated formally as the lodger. He could make out little Edna asleep at the other end of the bed, her half-clenched fist on the pillow with the thumb still extended where it had fallen from her mouth. She'd sleep through anything. Dick had often thought Edna was deaf in her left ear, but when he'd asked Flo whether she'd always been like that or whether something had happened to cause it, she'd looked at him in puzzlement. She didn't seem to know what he was talking about. Poor Flo. She never seemed to give herself time to look at her children, let alone notice very much. Their clothes got more attention than they did. Always clean, ironed, mended. Respectable. That's what women were good at. It didn't make her a bad mother. Probably it made her a good mother.

He didn't know much about the first husband, the local hero nobody mentioned. Rumour said he drank, and Dick knew what that could do to a man. Flo had taken it hard, that's for sure. They'd had a good life, running a shop. Parties and so on. Nice clothes. All that had come to an end.

Nora was back under the covers now with heavy eyes. He sung her the song his mother used to sing with the words he didn't understand, waited for her breathing to soften and padded from the room.

The door to the front bedroom was ajar. There was a bundle on the washstand. It stopped his heart to see it. He couldn't move. He wanted to rush and pick it up but he couldn't cross the threshold. There was a musky, musty smell hanging on the air. A woman smell. He could hear murmuring, the creak of the bedsprings, the hiss of the gaslight and the midwives moving about. Dolly Best must have come back. Then the door swung to and he turned away, stepping down the tunnel of the stairs, uneasy. He realised he'd been waiting for certain sounds that hadn't come, a pattern of events that must have imprinted itself in his brain from the times, both remembered and unremembered, when he was present in a house at the time of a birthing. Something was wrong.

He took a small black prayer book from the dresser drawer and sat with it on his knee, open at the first page where there was an inscription dated *September 1894* and signed *Almira* in a flowing hand. He continued to sit by the dwindling fire, still except for one finger, which moved back and forth across the signature.

As Mary Mulvaney sponged Flo and made her preparations, she wondered about Flo's marriage to the quiet-spoken soldier smoking downstairs. It had been remarked upon that none of his family had come to the wedding and it was rumoured he'd been born in foreign parts. Not that there was anything unusual in that for an Army family. Dolly knew more than she was letting on, that was for sure. Personally, she thought Flo had done well for herself. A woman with two children couldn't afford to be choosy, and if the lodger was prepared to make an honest woman of you, it was a chance not to be missed, even if he was a soldier. She was better off now than with that first husband of hers. Local hero, my foot.

Mary wrestled with Flo through a difficult delivery. The woman was deep-down tired, had no reserves for the work of pushing. Mary was all too aware of the skin tone of the baby as she delivered her, and the fact the head was turned backwards. She placed her carefully in a towel on the washstand, thinking perhaps it was for the best this one would not survive. Flo absorbed all her attention. She was dehydrated and bleeding heavily. When Dolly returned she told her briefly, 'It's a blue baby. We must look to the mother.'

It was fully half an hour before Dolly was able to turn to the bundle on the washstand. 'Oh, my Lordie,' she muttered to herself. This wasn't the typical hue of a baby who wouldn't survive. So Flo's worst fears had come true. She'd confided in Dolly when Dick wanted to marry her. Dick's mother was evidently 'not one of us'. Flo had asked her what she should do? Dolly told her straight, better a roof over your head and food on the table for your girls than sticking out for a man who might turn out like Charlie.

Dolly shook her head at the memory of Charlie. Flo was crazy about him from the first time she saw him leading out the horses. He'd only been the groom at the Mother Shipton, and his mother no better than she should be, but that didn't worry Flo. Dolly had to admit he had charm, but that wore thin, even with Flo, once the drink took hold. Well, he came to a sticky end, God rest his soul. Flo brought the little girls to her that dreadful night. And then she'd helped Flo concoct the story, for the sake of the children mostly, and to save a bit of face with the neighbours.

Dick didn't touch drink, Flo said, which was down to his mother. She'd seen to it that all her boys took the pledge. He was quiet, reliable. What more could you ask of a man? And what man wants to take on two little girls? Dolly reckoned all people were made by the same God and what did it matter what colour your skin was? She ended up saying to Flo, 'Where do you think you got that hair from yourself?' For Flo had hair like wire wool, and she'd always thought old man James had a very wide nose for a white man. You saw plenty like him in Portsmouth, what with it being a seaport.

Then Dolly thought she'd spoken out of turn, for Flo went very quiet and she added, to soften it, 'You might not have any children anyway. So where's the worry?' And Flo had gone away and accepted him. What could she say to Flo now? What troubles might lie ahead for such a child?

For all the while Dolly was having these thoughts she was working on the baby girl who was cold rather than lifeless. She turned the head around, beat the little body with the towel to get the circulation going and then cuddled her into the blanket warming on the fireguard. She took her to Flo, nestling her into her arm and propping it with a pillow. Flo opened an eye and smiled down at her daughter.

2

1918

My eyes are full of sunshine so I can't see inside the carriage at first. But I can smell. Underneath there is a fusty pong like dust and the seats where old ladies have been sitting. But over the top comes a whiff that teases my nose like feathers. Not quite sweet, not quite peppery, not quite like humbugs. It comes from the direction of a smile which hangs in the far corner of the carriage. The smile has a calm voice like honey, which invites me in and says I must be Marjorie. 'Marjorie Dorothea,' I say grandly. The voice repeats it, making my name sound like a song. I can see the lady now and, my, is she a lady. Not that she is grandly dressed, except for the veil on her hat and her long gloves. It's the way she inclines her head, just like a queen. I make a little bob like we were taught at school for the visit of the Lord Mayor and the Lady Mayoress with all the gold chains round their necks. She smiles again and pats the seat beside her. Next thing we are clip-clopping along and chatting like we've always known each other. Every now and then she'll look down at me with her head on one side and say, 'You so like Ellie!' and her eyes shine to overflowing. When I ask who Ellie is, she says she's my Auntie Ellie who is gone to Canada. And she looks so far away and sad that I don't like to ask how I come to have a new Auntie Ellie, or why she's to gone to Canada, or where Canada is. It's strange enough having a new grandmother all of a sudden.

We stop on the common at Southsea and my lady grandmother sends the cabbie to buy me an ice-cream cornet. He says I should step outside so as not to drip on his seats but my lady grandmother says no, I am not a messy child. I wonder how she knows that. She pulls a white lawn handkerchief from her bag, all crisply pressed and with lace in one corner, and spreads it on my lap. She says it will catch any drips and save my best frock. That makes me even more nervous for fear of marking her clean handkerchief. I take the greatest care, licking and turning, licking and turning, then sucking the hillock of ice smooth with my lips, nibbling the soggy edge of the cornet, pushing the last of the mound down inside the cone with my tongue and all the time making sure there's no leaky little hole at the bottom. The coldness numbs my tongue and my mouth and my teeth turn to velvet as the satiny taste slips down my throat.

While I am busy my lady grandmother turns back her veil, peels off her gloves and uses them to fan herself. So when I'm finished with my cornet I get a proper look at her for the first time. She isn't like any grown-up I have seen, except something about her nose and mouth reminds me of Dadser. I move my arm close to hers and I see that they match. I didn't know anyone as elegant as her could have skin like mine that doesn't wash quite clean. She sees me looking at our two arms and she puts her hand over mine and squeezes it ever so lightly. But I didn't imagine it. I wish she would come and stay in our house and read me bedtime stories and walk down the street to school with me so all the other children would see me with my lady grandmother who has arms the same colour as mine.

So I am sad when we get back to our house and my lady grandmother says she must be going to catch her train. She gives me a bag of cookies to share with my sisters. I haven't heard of cookies before. She says they are her special cinnamon cookies. When I put my nose in the bag I see biscuits and discover they account for some of the not-quite-sweet, not-quite-peppery smell. Whenever I sniff vanilla or cinnamon after that I'll remember my lady grandmother. For it's also the perfume that floats off her when she moves.

I ask my lady grandmother where she's going to on the train and she says to Plymouth, where she lives with my Auntie Ada. I am so amazed to discover yet another new aunt that it quite puts out of my mind all the questions that come to me later. Mum comes out to the carriage and scolds me for asking too many questions anyway.

My lady grandmother tells Mum she is sorry for her trouble and I wonder what trouble that can be and hope it isn't me. Mum goes back indoors when the carriage pulls away but I stand at the gate waving until it turns the corner, just in case my lady grandmother is watching, although I know she isn't. I want to take the bag of cookies into the cupboard under the stairs, but I know Nora will find me and tell Mum, so I put them on the table in the scullery and we all have one for tea.

Nora and Edna will call them biscuits and, when I put them right, they giggle and kick each other under the table. Then Nora pulls a straight face and decides to humour me to show how grown up she is. 'They're very nice cookies aren't they, Marge?' she says. But Edna tells our cousin Maude, who's two years older than me, and Maude and Edna taunt me with that word for weeks afterwards. Have I had my *cookies*? Shall we bake some *cookies*? How Marge loves *cookies*! Marge is in love with *cookies*! When I tell Maude she doesn't even know what a cookie is and smack her in the face, she runs screaming to her mother. I'm not allowed to play there for the rest of the holiday, which is fine by me. Mum sends me to bed without supper but I can tell she isn't really cross. She thinks Maude's a spoilt ninny. I heard her say so once to Auntie Rose.

There's one cookie over after our tea that day and Mum says I can have it with my milk at bedtime. Edna says that isn't fair because I've been for the ride in the carriage and had an ice-cream, but Mum tells her to hold her tongue and there has to be some compensation. Which I don't understand and nor does Edna, I can tell. She sticks out her tongue at me behind Mum's back and tries to hold on to it, which makes her choke, so that serves her right.

I keep that paper cookie bag until I've sniffed up all the smell. Weeks later, Mum finds it in my school bag and throws it away.

3

Neither of them noticed to begin with. Kate exhausted and euphoric, happy to hold a perfect baby, skin to slippery skin, a little girl as expected, who was already latching on to the breast. Daniel shaking with relief, overwhelmed by being present at the birth – all so different from Jack's arrival which had been fraught with complications. Neither of them noticed that the midwife fetched a colleague for an extra examination of the baby and a whispered exchange.

They simply hugged each other and Kate said, 'Flora? Do you think she's a Flora?' It was the name they both favoured. Daniel stroked Kate's damp hair and said, 'If you think so, then so do I.'

Kate had the first inkling when she leaned over the crib, once she was settled in the ward. It was something to do with the contrast between her daughter's tiny fingers and her own index finger as they curled around it. Not just that they were so tiny. Or maybe it was something to do with her tightly curled hair. The whole gestalt of this baby was so different from Jack. But then she was a girl.

Kate lay back on the pillows, her body sinking into deep rest after the work of labour. It was strenuous and painful, certainly, but nothing like the terror of Jack's birth. She had been lucky with the midwife and felt so thoroughly supported by Daniel. She wished he was still here with her, but he wouldn't be long. He was getting himself a coffee, making phone calls, checking Jack was okay with her friend, Morag. Her mother was on her way. Kate had nothing to worry about.

When the student midwife came to do the routine blood pressure and temperature checks Kate asked, 'She's not jaundiced is she?' The girl looked into the crib and back at Kate. She flushed across translucent skin that coloured easily. 'I don't think so, but I'll check.' She walked away to the nursing station and Kate saw her talk to Ruth, the blonde midwife who had delivered Flora. They both looked in her direction and moved out of sight, into the office behind the desk.

Another mother walked past Kate's bed with her baby. A rosy pink face rested on the woman's shoulder. She stopped and asked Kate how she was. Something in her face changed when she looked into the crib. 'She's beautiful,' the woman said. Kate shifted up on one elbow and smiled down at Flora. There was nothing pink and rosy about her, but she was certainly beautiful. And she was only two hours old, still glowing with the dark effort of birth.

Kate sunk into sleep and when she woke Daniel was there, bending over the crib and frowning.

'Hallo, darling. Beautiful, isn't she?'

He nodded but didn't smile. 'This is *our* baby, isn't it?' He was looking into the crib with narrowed eyes.

Kate sat up and looked down at Flora who was beginning to stir and snuffle. 'Certainly is.'

It was as if all the cells in her body reached out to her. So that was what people meant by bonding. An instant sensation of familiarity. It hadn't been at all like that with Jack. She'd been frightened of him. Frightened of a tiny baby. She started to tell Daniel, trying to describe what she was feeling.

'It's so different. From Jack, I mean. She feels like part of me. It's like a glow, such a relief.'

They'd had a bad time back then. The difficult birth, Jack's feeding problems, the broken nights and where that had eventually led. Don't even think of it, she told herself. That's not happening again.

'I know what people mean now, when they talk about bonding. It's so...well...joyful, I suppose. Oh, Daniel!'

Daniel took her hand but he wasn't really listening. 'That's not what's worrying me. You're sure nobody could have swapped her while you were asleep?'

'Don't be silly. That's her. I know. I've been looking at her, I feel so close. I was trying to tell you...'

'But don't you think she looks very – very dark? And this hair?'

It had always been a joke in the family, long before hair-straighteners came in, that Kate's dark hair looked as if it had been ironed. And although Daniel's blonde hair flopped untidily, there was not a kink in it. Kate was exceptionally pale-skinned and Daniel had sandy freckles and burned in the sun. By contrast, Flora's emerging complexion had the warmth of milky coffee.

'Well, she's certainly nothing like Jack, I'll give you that.'

The midwife called Ruth appeared and drew the curtains round the bed. She told Daniel gently and firmly that of course it was their baby and showed him the ankle-band. They'd watched it being put on in the delivery room. Daniel only nodded and frowned. Kate sensed a shift in him, but before she could say anything Ruth told them their friend was in the lobby with Jack.

Daniel leapt to his feet, too eager to be gone. 'Morag will be needing to get to work. I'll go and see to Jack.'

'You'll bring him in, won't you? You know you can.'

'Hmm. Your mother won't be long. She's stuck in traffic, but she'll be coming straight here.'

Kate grabbed his arm. 'She's all right, isn't she? Flora, I mean.' She wanted his reassurance, to connect with him before he went.

Daniel looked back into the crib. 'Mmm.' He seemed to hesitate, looked at Kate and looked away. 'I just don't understand,' he said slowly and was gone.

Ten minutes later he was back.

'Where's Jack? Doesn't he want to see Flora? It's okay, you know. He's allowed.'

'Thought it best not. Vanessa arrived. She's taking him home.'

'Mum's what? Taking him home?' Kate felt tears rising. More than anything at that moment she wanted to see her mother.

Daniel just shrugged.

Kate sunk back on the pillows, baffled. Jack must have wanted to see his baby sister. He'd feel left out, just what they wanted to avoid. She took a deep breath, tried again. 'I've got his present here, all ready.' She waved at the wrapped package on the locker. 'And Mum? Didn't she…?'

Daniel shrugged again. He had his hands in his pockets and his shoulders were hunched as if to support his head. 'Best to sort it out between ourselves before other people get involved.'

'Sort what out? And what d'you mean? Other people? She's my Mum. I wanted to see her.'

'We need to talk about this. I just don't understand how… I mean, how come we have a baby who looks like this? As I say, we need to talk.'

'Talk about what?'

'Well, her colour, of course. The baby. How come…?'

'Oh, Daniel. She's so beautiful, she's our…' Her words faded as Daniel turned abruptly away.

He paced to the end of the bed and swivelled on his heel. 'I mean, we need to get our act together, know what the story is. That sort of thing.'

It was his usual very deliberate way of speaking, each word clear and distinct, but there was a sheen on his forehead, and the way his eyes would not focus was making her feel panicky. 'Please, Daniel, sit down.'

But he didn't seem to hear her, barely looked at her and ignored Flora when she started to cry. Kate had to raise her voice. 'Won't you pick her up? Daniel, please! Pass her to me, will you?'

And he did, reluctantly, gingerly as if he didn't want to touch her, let alone cuddle her up.

'What's the matter with you?'

'Matter with me? Matter with the baby, you mean!'

'Daniel! What's possibly the matter with her?'

'She's the wrong colour! Haven't you been listening to anything I've said?'

'The wrong colour? Don't be silly.' Kate snuggled Flora to her, nuzzled her head with her nose, snuffing up her musky newborn smell. 'She's not fair like Jack, but she's fine, she's my flower.'

He gave an exasperated snort. 'I give up.' He paced to the end of the bed and back and his voice was different, almost crisp.

If her hands had been free she'd have covered her ears. As it was, the soft focus of her mind slid off his shiny words like rain off a waxy leaf. She couldn't, wouldn't gain a purchase.

'Obviously this isn't the time and the place. When you get home, blah-de-blah.'

She had a weird sick feeling in her tummy that was nothing to do with the after-pangs of labour.

'We need to blah-de-blah. Sit down and talk it all through…things you need to tell me. Straighten this out…'

Her attention zoned in and out, almost as if she lost consciousness and came to again. And still the voice went on. His gaze flitted from ceiling to floor, avoiding her, the bundle in her arms.

Then he was gone. She relaxed into the simplicity of feeding Flora, comforted by the pull of her tiny gums, glad to shrink her attention into the close focus of their shared world. Somewhere in her consciousness she knew her baby held a puzzle, but she wasn't yet ready to start solving it.

4

Kate was still feeding Flora when Ruth slipped in between the curtains. She put a thermometer into Kate's mouth and sat down quietly, gesturing she didn't want to interrupt. Kate watched Ruth shuffling through her notes. She had trusted her clear gaze from the moment she walked into the delivery room. It was nice the midwives didn't wear uniforms any more. Ruth was dressed much as Kate herself might dress, in cut-off jeans and a skinny top.

When she'd recorded the temperature Ruth spoke in a low voice. 'We've noticed you are expressing concerns about your baby, asking questions…'

Kate held her breath.

'And there is some tension between you and your husband?'

Kate looked at her sharply.

'I don't want to interfere, but it's part of our job to notice these things. We try to be sensitive to when it's best to say nothing and when parents may need some support. I just thought it might be time to have a bit of a chat.'

'My husband was… I have begun to wonder…where her colouring comes from.'

'Mmm?'

'You see, I've no idea. I suppose… Daniel must think…' Tears welled in Kate's eyes. 'He's so strange… I can't begin to say…'

Flora had stopped feeding and was fussing, about to cry. Ruth held out her hands. 'Let's change her nappy and I'll show you something.'

She spread a towel on the bed, sprung Flora's spindly legs from the babygro and removed the nappy. She rolled her over gently. 'See these marks? It looks a bit like a bruise – which is one reason it goes on the notes from day one. You don't want any allegations of child abuse.'

Kate gasped. 'How...? They don't think...?'

'Don't worry. It isn't bruising. But it can be mistaken for it – it's been known to happen to some perfectly innocent parents. No, this is a natural mark. For some reason it's known as the Mongolian Spot. Nearly all black babies have it, and mixed race babies of African and Asian descent, usually somewhere in this region of the body.'

'Mixed race?'

'Yes. I'm very familiar with these.' Ruth smiled and cooed at Flora, fastening a fresh nappy on her as she spoke. 'My husband's black and we have three children. They all had it when they were born, it fades as they get older. It seems the mark appears wherever there is an African or Asian ethnic background.'

Kate stared at Flora, frowning. She imagined Ruth and her cosy little family. That's all very well for you, she thought. But it doesn't give me a clue. African? Asian? Where could that be coming from?

Ruth looked up from fastening Flora's poppers. 'Maybe that isn't much help to you.'

Kate could hardly take in what Ruth had been saying in such matter-of-fact tones. She found it hard to form thoughts, let alone words. 'But how?' was all she could manage.

Ruth shrugged and gave Kate a questioning look.

'There isn't anyone. How could...?'

'I can't answer that question for you.'

Kate absorbed her level gaze. 'I know what you're thinking.'

'I'm not thinking anything.' Ruth let a silence fall as she rocked Flora gently on her shoulder.

'So is Daniel thinking...?' Kate couldn't continue.

Ruth nodded slowly.

'I didn't, you know. I really didn't.'

'I believe you. An affair, you mean? I *suppose* he could be thinking that. People can jump to conclusions sometimes. You don't have to have had an affair for this to happen. It can be a throwback, a rogue gene if you like, from an ancestor you never knew. It's rare, but it happens.'

Kate felt a surge of relief and hope she hardly dared trust. 'Will you speak to Daniel? He can be... He's someone who... Well, he can get a bee in his bonnet sometimes. He might believe it more, hear it better. Coming from you.'

'Sure. I'm on duty all day. And don't be too hard on your husband. You know how men are. He's probably feeling pretty frightened and jealous. I'll keep a look out for him.'

But Daniel didn't return. Kate called home, glad for once of the mobile phone which she rarely used.

But it was Vanessa who answered. 'No, he's not here darling. How are you feeling? I've been so...'

'What did he say?'

'Well, actually he's not been back to say anything. He's probably wetting the baby's head at work or something.' Vanessa sounded unnaturally bright. 'Anyway, how are you? Tell me...'

'Mum, why didn't you come in? I was expecting...'

'Daniel wouldn't let me. I thought there was something he wasn't telling me. But I didn't want to insist – make a scene in front of Jack. I've been so worried about you.'

'I'm fine, Mum.' Kate's voice cracked as she said it. 'Yes, and the baby. How's Jack doing? It was such a shame he couldn't...'

'Why wouldn't Daniel let me in?'

'It's just... He thinks she's the wrong colour. It's really strange... The midwife...' She wiped her nose with the back of her hand and took a deep breath.

'Oh, she'll be jaundiced. That often happens. You might have to stay in overnight, but...'

Kate could hear the relief in Vanessa's voice and didn't have the energy or the courage to contradict her. 'You didn't say how Jack is?'

'He's just fine. We're building a Lego hospital with nee-nahs and everything.'

Kate gulped.

'You all right, darling? I know. Bound to be feeling all emotional. When will they let you know when you can come home? I can't wait...'

'Maybe later today. It all depends. Mum, she's waking up. I have to go.'

'Big hugs, darling. Try and get a little sleep when she's settled. Can't wait to see you.'

Kate snapped her phone off and sobbed into her nightie until Ruth appeared with tissues and drew the curtains.

'Here, get this down you.' She passed Kate a tumbler of cold water and watched while she drank it down. 'Now sleep.' She whisked a pillow away, gently stroked Kate's hair and glanced at Flora. 'While you've got the chance.'

Kate felt so alone. No Daniel, no Mum, and her friend Morag at work. She tried to sleep but she was haunted by the image of Daniel talking at her. That glazed look, the distance between them. One minute sharing such joy, the next poles apart. He'd gone spinning off into an unreachable place, leaving her in a void where words kept rattling her awake. His words: *the wrong colour*. Ruth's words: *mixed race*. They weasled into her brain and repeated, over and over. She peered through the crib at her sleeping daughter and reached out to touch a finger to her cheek. So warm, so beautiful, so much part of herself. How could there be anything wrong with her? She turned over and let the warm wave of sleep suck her into its depths.

Kate texted Daniel as soon as she was told she could go home. She dressed Flora and hurried to pack up the contents of her locker. But he kept her waiting for hours. At least Ruth was around when he finally arrived, and she took him aside for a chat.

In the car Kate tried to have a discussion. 'Interesting what Ruth said about ancestry, that it can go back a surprisingly long way?'

'Hmm. Seems a bit of a long shot. I am yet to be convinced, statistically speaking. It appeared to me that the good woman was merely giving us a way out. A means of saving face.'

Part of Kate was genuinely puzzled at this remark, part of her was in despair because here was confirmation, if she needed any, that Daniel was thinking the unthinkable, that he didn't trust her. She couldn't bring herself to acknowledge it. Not yet. All she could say was 'Why? Why would we need to save face?'

'You tell me,' replied Daniel and they continued the drive in silence.

Home was not the sanctuary Kate still expected it to be. Daniel stalked off leaving her to follow him into the hall with Flora. Typical Daniel. Walking away from anything he didn't understand.

But then Jack rushed over to cling to her leg and Vanessa appeared, arms outstretched to hug her and the bundle that was Flora. Kate watched her mother's face as she smiled down at Flora and saw something clear as if a fog had begun to lift. Vanessa looked up and their eyes met, both asking a question, both suddenly brimming over. Then Vanessa shifted gaze and mood, taking charge of the bundle so that Kate could give her attention to Jack.

Kate stroked Jack's hair and squatted down to cuddle him. She wished Daniel and her mother and their questions would vanish. She just wanted to be with her children, show Flora to Jack, give him the present from his baby sister.

Home was not a sanctuary in another way. Alone in her bedroom, Kate laid Flora in the crib beside the bed and gazed down at her. All of a sudden she looked, well, *foreign*. Kate found the hairs on her arms standing on end. In the context of home, surrounded by familiar objects, aware of the blonde heads of her family downstairs, Flora's colouring stood out. The bubble of mother and newborn, which had protected them in hospital, had evaporated, replaced by the context of home and family where reality must be faced. Sure, she had noticed the skin colour in the hospital. Ruth had explained it. But it had seemed no more important than the fact that Flora was a girl. Now the implications crowded in on her. It dawned on Kate that she'd been avoiding the issue every bit as much as Daniel.

She bent over the crib and stroked Flora's cheek. 'My little love, fancy that you were growing in my tummy and I never knew. How did you manage to get in there?'

As she felt the flutter of breath on her finger, wonder and surprise gave way to something like indignation. How come nobody had warned her? No scan had told her what to expect. If she'd been having twins she'd have had time to prepare. Of course it was ridiculous to feel like that. But somehow it seemed so unfair, such a surprise, out of the blue. Her eyes pricked and as she turned away she was aware of Vanessa standing in the doorway watching her.

For a moment they stared at each other. Then Vanessa stepped forward and Kate ran into her arms. 'How did it happen Mum? What's going on?'

'So *that's* what it was all about – what's been going on all day.'

Kate nodded damply into Vanessa's shoulder.

'And it isn't just that she's dark-haired, is it? I'm not making it up?'

'No, you're not.'

'I mean, do you have any idea…?' Vanessa stepped back to look up at Kate.

'No, I don't. I haven't a clue.' Kate saw a nanosecond of doubt pass behind her mother's eyes. 'You don't believe me! You're as bad as Daniel.'

'Of course I believe you. But I did just wonder for a moment. I mean, there was a time… You did sleep around quite a bit…'

'I was a student, for godssakes! And, for the record, I didn't actually "sleep" with half of them. Though everyone thought I did. So, no, I didn't find myself a black guy.'

'Okay, so that's ruled out. Oh, Katie, don't look so hurt. I couldn't help it crossing my mind. I wouldn't be human… And I wouldn't blame you either, what with all Daniel's shenanigans. But I do believe you. I really do.'

'I know. I'm just being over-sensitive.' Kate sighed, sank down on the bed and told Vanessa what Ruth had said about race and ancestry.

'So it's all down to family, then. Where to start? You never did tell me much about Daniel's father.'

'Not much to tell. He absconded – that's Roz's word – when Daniel was three. Went to America apparently, but hasn't been seen since. A couple of letters and a cheque for fifty pounds was all his mother ever got.'

'Hmm. Any photographs?'

'Daniel's got one. And he isn't black.'

'That would be too easy.'

'Oh Mum, it's so weird. I was looking at her, just then. I suddenly felt as if I'd stolen her. As if her real mother must be frantically looking for her.'

Vanessa hugged her. 'There isn't any question…?'

'Not at all. Ankle band. We saw it put on. And anyway I felt such a close bond. It was just… Coming home, noticing… It was only for a moment.' Kate bent and stroked Flora's cheek. 'Hey, Mum, something's occurring to me. What about Nan? I mean…'

'Oh, but she's…'

'Spanish? So she says. You don't think…?'

'The crinkly hair, you're thinking?'

'And Nan making things up. You told me once – her motto – *Never tell the truth if a lie will do*. I just think you might ask her. Or have a word with Gramps, if you don't fancy asking her direct.'

Vanessa made a face at the thought of such a confrontation and they both laughed, relaxing a little at last.

'Of course. I'm going over there next week. I'll see if I can find a moment.' Vanessa ran her fingers through her hair, tugging at the roots.

Why do I not believe her? That gesture, thought Kate. She really doesn't want to.

'By the way, Lisa texted me, wants to come over of course. What shall I say?'

And now she's changing the subject. 'Put her off. Much as I love her…' The last thing Kate wanted just now was a dose of her sister's incisive comments.

Vanessa had cooked them a meal. She carried Flora downstairs. 'Come on. I ate earlier with Jack. I'll serve it up and leave you two in peace.' And she disappeared upstairs again with Jack to give him his bath and read bedtime stories.

Peace. The word echoed off the walls.

Kate imagined Daniel would drop his odd behaviour and turn back into the Daniel she loved, but he was still distant. She faced him across the kitchen table inhaling the sickly scent of some pink lilies in a vase on top of the fridge. They ate in silence, Kate picking at mashed potato, sipping water.

'Who brought the lilies?'

'Your mother.' Daniel answered abruptly and refilled his glass with white wine.

The smell of the lilies was mingling with the steam from her plate. It made her want to vomit.

'Bit overpowering.'

Daniel ignored her, focused on his food.

Kate wished Vanessa would come back downstairs. 'Jack liked his digger.'

'Good.'

Kate took a deep breath, gagged on the lily perfume. Maybe she'd go up and join the bedtime ritual. She must get away from the smell. But then again, she and Daniel really needed to talk. 'Perhaps you could move the lilies? Take them in the sitting room?'

Daniel exploded. 'We have this mega issue to deal with. At last some peace and privacy. And all you can talk about is the effing flowers!'

There was a silence, then Daniel gulped at his wine and scraped back his chair. He grabbed the vase and marched it out of the room at arm's length. When he came back Kate found she was holding her breath.

'Thank you.' Kate pushed at the salmon fillet with her fork. 'Why are you being like this? So distant? So – hostile?'

'Me? It's you that's not saying anything. Sitting there like the sphinx while I flounder around.'

'Daniel, I don't mean to be like that. I'm confused. I'm baffled by Flora's colour. But do you have to be on the attack?' Tears dripped off the end of Kate's nose onto the plate. She couldn't do this. She just wanted to curl up in her own bed. 'When we need to be helping each other?'

'Do I have to spell it out?'

Something snapped inside Kate. 'Can't you bring yourself to say it yourself? If you mean, did I go fuck a black man, then no. I fucking well did not!'

'There's no need to be crude.' Daniel pushed his plate away, refilled his glass.

'But it's what you think, isn't it?'

'What else was I meant to think? How could she be mine? I look in the crib and there's this alien...'

Kate looked down at Flora peacefully sleeping in the little seat beside her and opened her mouth to protest. Then she remembered her own reaction, minutes ago, in the bedroom. 'She's going to take a bit of getting used to, but...'

'Then I thought...' Daniel groaned and dropped his head into his hands. He sunk forward onto the table, shoulders shaking with sobs. Kate watched him for a moment or two, then put out a hand and stroked his hair, calmed by the familiar silky feel of it.

He looked up at her. 'It's what I was *afraid* of. So afraid. I was so scared it made me angry.'

'There was no...'

'So fucking jealous. You've no idea what jealousy can do to you.'

Kate knew quite a lot about what jealousy could do, but now was not the moment to pick another quarrel. 'But I didn't. I didn't do it. Look at me Daniel. I promise you. I didn't.'

He nodded and took her hand in his. 'I wouldn't be human if the possibility had not entered my mind.'

'That's what Mum said.'

'Did she now?' A look of relief cleared Daniel's frown. 'An unlikely ally.'

'But there are no sides! Daniel, please! How many more times...'

'Kate, I just couldn't bear the thought of anyone, anyone else, touching you. I can't imagine how I would survive without you.'

She squeezed his hand. At last they seemed to be edging back towards some kind of togetherness.

'You see, with Jack, everyone could see from the start that I was his father. Now what are people going to think?'

So that's the crux of it, thought Kate. And by "people" he almost certainly meant his dear Mama.

'And contrary to what you might be thinking, the irony's not lost on me, that I should feel that way. Entertaining such suspicions, I mean, in the light of my past history in that department.'

So he does acknowledge it, thought Kate, even if he does have to be so pompous.

'It better be past history. Let's leave that be. Let's move on from all that.'

'Yes. But first I have to say there will probably be others who will cast aspersions – on your fidelity, I mean. You may well find...'

Kate cut him off, thinking that dear Mama might be top of that list too. 'We'll meet that when we come to it. As I was saying, we need to think about our families, like Ruth said. What about your father's origins, for instance?'

'There's no need to bring him into this.'

'Oh, come on! I'd have thought there was every need. Roz must have told you something about him.'

Daniel held up his hands. 'Okay, okay. I really don't know anything. Mama would never talk about him. I've not the remotest clue about who his parents were. But it's hardly likely that Mama... No, I don't think so.'

Kate raised an eyebrow and chewed her bottom lip. Sometimes she wondered if Daniel thought he was an immaculate conception. She made no comment.

'So, what about your side? No unloved cousins with a touch of the tarbrush, as my uncle would say?'

'You're right. Just what he would say! It's going to be interesting to see how he does react.' Not to mention Daniel's mother and her dreadful husband, Blake? Aloud she said, 'I wonder what Blake will say?'

Roz Ward had married Blake around the time Daniel left home and came south. Kate could only assume it was to fill the void left by her beloved son, to have someone to boss around. She even wondered if it was to make Daniel jealous.

Daniel exploded at the mention of his name. 'Him? If he can be prevailed upon to string two words together. A closet racist if ever I saw one. Probably a member of the National Front. Let's not even think about him. Anyway, it was your relatives I was asking about.'

'Well, I have been wondering about my Nan – Mum's mother.'

'Never struck me she looked particularly dark. What makes you say that?'

'Her hair for a start. Mum's not convinced either, I can tell. But I do wonder.'

5

2005

'It's Lisa!'

Kate heard the back door slam and ran to greet her sister. 'Glad you came.'

'Well, there was no chance of talking when I came by at the weekend. And the atmosphere was positively arctic.'

Kate made a face. 'It was a bit tense.'

'Ma says Danny boy's still being a bastard.'

Kate breathed in hard. That was Lisa for you, jumping in with both feet. But a vice-like hug made up for it.

'I bet that's not what Mum said.'

Lisa wrinkled her nose. 'Not exactly. But that's what she meant. Is that right?'

'Well, he says he believes me, that I didn't have an affair, but...'

'You didn't, did you?' Lisa bent to gather coloured chalks from round her feet and replaced them where they belonged on the ledge of Jack's blackboard and easel.

'Lees! You're as bad as...'

Lisa put a hand on Kate's shoulder. 'Calm down, sis. Just establishing the facts, that's all. Clearly not, then. Though I wouldn't blame you if you had. He's had it coming, after all.'

'That's not like you!' She still thought of Lisa as her good little sister. Always doing the right thing at the right time. Doing well at school. Having nice boyfriends.

Lisa shrugged. 'It must be hell. We know what Daniel can be like. But he'll come round, won't he?'

Kate raised an eyebrow. Trust Lisa to oversimplify. Daniel could come round all he liked, but it was already too late. Aloud she said, 'Maybe' and put the kettle on. Then she added more emphatically, 'But that's not the point.'

'Isn't it?' Lisa was cooing over the sleeping Flora.

Kate felt an absurd pang of jealousy that Lisa's attention had moved on. She loved people to make a fuss of Flora, but right now she wanted her sister all to herself. 'Coffee,' she said and was pleased when Lisa came to the table.

'Cool,' said Lisa, admiring the mini cafetière Kate had set before her. 'Why isn't it the point? I mean, it must take a bit of getting used to for him. And you can't go on living the Cold War forever.'

Kate poured water on her peppermint teabag. 'The point is, how can I forgive him even if he does "come round", as you put it? The point is that Daniel didn't trust me. We were really, really close during the birth, immediately afterwards. And even from that close, intimate place he couldn't believe in me. The first thing he thought to do was blame me for the colour of her skin.'

'Mmm.'

'You don't get it, do you?'

'Well, it's just that I thought you said just now that Danny *did* believe you. And that he was sorry and all that?'

'Yep. That's what he says, but it's not how he's behaving. And anyway I still feel betrayed, deep down. Because he didn't believe me straightaway. And it will never be the same again, after how hard and cold he was.'

Lisa pressed down the plunger on the cafetière. 'It seems kind of odd, Sis. That you're being so hard line now, after all the times you've let him off the hook and taken him back in the past.'

'You're not saying I should, are you?'

'Not at all. I just don't see why this is different.'

'It's different. Believe me, it's different.'

'I mean, what he did before seems a lot worse to me.'

'The affairs you mean? I see how you might think that. But he didn't do those *to me...*'

'Well, I don't know who else he did them to!'

'No, listen. He had the affairs because of something that was happening to him. This time there was only him and me. No other issue. And he chose not to trust me.'

'But there *was* another issue. He looked at his baby and thought, "This doesn't belong to me." Issue of identity? Male pride? You name it.'

'But it was an issue we *shared*. Only he didn't share it. He attacked me.'

'I can't say I really get it. But I'm certainly not about to make excuses for him.'

'I can't explain it any better. Maybe I don't really understand it myself. Half the time it's just a load of soupy feelings.'

Lisa opened her mouth, then shut it again.

'What? Go on. Say it.'

'But it's not so extraordinary is it? For him to think that?'

'Because I had a reputation for...?'

'No! No, you've got that all wrong. He'd think it because it's what *he'd* do. What he *has* done, for pity's sake. Maybe he thinks you were getting your own back. It would make him *feel* better. Give him the moral high ground for once.'

Kate grunted. 'I can see what you mean, but...'

'Anyway. It was just a thought. I don't know why I'm wasting breath on Danny boy. What's a lot more interesting – what about where Flora *did* come from? Any leads on that little mystery? You must have thought about it?'

'Thinking about it all the time. And, well, I did think about Nan. But nobody else – neither Mum or Daniel, that is – agree that it might be a possibility.'

'Nan? Why did I never think of her? Omigod! Of course. I mean she's not that dark-skinned, but the hair!'

'Exactly. Mum did say she'd mention it when she next visits. But somehow I don't think she'll get very far. I think she's scared of her.'

'Why don't you go to see her yourselves? Take Flora? I mean, what nicer thing than to take the new great-grandchild for her to see?'

'Hey! Great idea. Of course! And that way we see them side-by-side. Daniel can see for himself.'

'Good plan,' said Lisa, leaping up as Flora started to cry and rushing to pick her up and cuddle her. Typical. Never asking permission. It used to get up her nose, the assumption Lisa made that whatever she did was okay. Kate sighed and allowed herself to be grateful that she was taking Flora off to change her nappy, although she suspected this was an excuse to examine Flora more closely.

Her impression was confirmed when Lisa reappeared with Flora over her shoulder.

'You'll be having a DNA test, I suppose?'

'A DNA test?' Whatever next?

'Okay, okay. It's none of my business, you're thinking. Just that it would sort Danny out and get it all over with. And we'd all be happier for that.'

Did she really imagine it was that simple? 'Ridiculous!' was all Kate could think to say and then felt ridiculous herself, saying it and knowing what her sister would think of her. But deep down she knew it was Lisa who was ridiculous. As if that physical proof would make a jot of difference to what was going on between her and Daniel.

'Not ridiculous,' Lisa was saying. 'Just practical. It's very straightforward you know – you can get a kit off the internet.'

'People do it all the time, do they?' Kate intended to be heavily sarcastic but Lisa took her literally, explaining the reasons people might have for such a test.

Kate shook her head. 'I thought I'd made it clear. It's not the sort of thing that's going to be sorted scientifically.' She took Flora and was glad to be able to focus on feeding.

Lisa just shrugged and Kate turned away, looking down the garden to where snowdrops were showing white against the bark of the apple tree. She hoped Lisa would take the hint and leave.

But her sister prattled on about people at work and a party she was going to. Kate reminded herself that Lisa was a police trainee, wanted to work in forensics. Of course it was the first thing she would think of, a DNA test. And she was a very concrete thinker anyway.

Kate tried again. 'I don't want to be unreasonable. About the DNA thingy, I mean. Maybe it's everyday stuff to you, but it's not something I've even heard of. For ordinary people, I mean. Makes me feel like a criminal.'

'Oh, they're pretty commonplace. I just thought, a DNA test would break Daniel out of his stuck place. I understand how you feel about it, I really do, and of course I believe you, so does Ma. We all do. We trust you, Kate. But, personally, as far as Danny-boy is concerned, I don't believe you'll move on without it. You'll never get back to normal.'

Kate shook her head. What else was there to say?

'It was only an idea. But never mind.' Lisa put a hand on her arm. 'Anyway I must be going. Need to get some shopping before I start my shift. Can I get anything for you guys? Drop it in later?'

'No, we're fine. Morag did a big shop for me yesterday. She's been a star.'

The house was eerily silent after Lisa left, a coldness in which the words 'DNA test' echoed off the walls and set themselves irritatingly to the jingles on Radio Solent when Kate flicked the radio on.

She wondered whether the same idea would occur to Daniel. Maybe it already had. Now if Daniel were to suggest a DNA test, it would be the end, it really would. Kate had a view of his mind and its workings where there was currently a window of leftover jealousy urging him to distrust her. But deep down he knew better. The window was shrinking as he got used to the reality of Flora. It was only a matter of time before he closed it and returned to the full screen of their relationship. If he did that of his own accord, without a DNA test and without having yet another affair, there would be a lot of mending to do, but she'd be able to live with it. If he required outside proof to close the window, it would mean that the taint of jealousy had taken over, and that he was ruled by it. That, Kate believed, would be the end.

What Lisa said made sense. And her sister didn't know the half of it. Daniel's womanising was like an addiction, a sickness. He had to have his fix, then he came back grovelling. When she'd got pregnant again, he'd promised he wouldn't stray. He'd be a reformed character. All the usual stuff. But he'd stuck with it. Got the new job with a prestigious firm of estate agents in Southsea. No more first-time buyers scrabbling for a mortgage. Now he was dealing with period properties, on correspondingly higher commission. He'd even managed to find this house so that they'd have more room. Worked his socks off.

'I suppose,' said Kate out loud, 'he reckoned he invested a lot in you.' She looked down at Flora who was drifting into sleep. She herself had invested a lot in this new start, another reason why Daniel's reaction to Flora had been so devastating.

But now there were signs that Daniel was "coming round", as Lisa put it – more and more moments of relative normality, times when their eyes had met in appreciation of something quaint Jack said. On several occasions they'd both forgotten not to share a family joke and Kate noticed Daniel was less reluctant than before to do things for Flora. This morning, for instance.

Kate had woken to Flora crying in the crib beside her bed. Having fed her at practically every hour during the night, it was difficult to pull herself from sleep. She opened an eye and saw a determined Jack pulling Daniel towards the crib. Kate almost closed both eyes so she could see hazily through her lashes. Jack held his nose and pointed at Flora's bottom.

'Flora done a poo. Daddy, you better change her nappy.'

Daniel had obeyed and Kate watched carefully to see him handle Flora tenderly, cuddle her up and show her to Jack. 'You used to be as small as this,' he said to Jack who looked dubious but planted a kiss on Flora's eye.

'Let's take her downstairs while I find you some breakfast. Let Mummy sleep.'

Kate had held her breath, not wanting to break the spell.

Now she sat on in the kitchen remembering the scene, considering this 'coming round' that Daniel seemed to be doing. If he could accept Flora enough to make their day-to-day existence as a family more comfortable, then they would rub along somehow. Once, she wouldn't have been prepared to settle for that.

'Funny how things change,' she said to Flora as she poked her cheek to rouse her and start her sucking again. 'See what you two have done to me?'

She'd always wanted to be a mother. Part of finding a soulmate was always the search for the right father for her children, and her passion for being a mother turned out to be even more intense than her passion for Daniel. 'And he senses that, of course,' she told herself. 'Ho, hum. Poor old Daddy.' She got up to let the cat in, a slender grey tabby with fine tiger stripes who'd turned up on the doorstep just after they moved into the house. That had been the trouble with that first affair. Daniel no longer getting the attention he was used to.

The cat, Willow, was competing with Flora, weaving herself round Kate's legs and stretching her paws up to test whether there was room on her lap. Kate fetched the box of dry cat food and shook some into her bowl.

Hard to imagine now, how Daniel said he couldn't wait to be a father that first time when she was expecting Jack. He'd be a modern man, the best, most involved father there'd ever been. The reality had been rather different. Daniel had been more demanding than Jack. Like a kid with his nose out of joint. Attention-seeking, sulky. Finding comfort with another woman.

Somehow or other they'd come through that. Suddenly fallen in love all over again. How on earth that had happened on a sheeting wet day on the Isle of Wight she never knew, but she could still picture it.

They'd come off the ferry at Ryde, stomping along the soggy boardwalk to the prom. Daniel was pushing the buggy, and Jack's grizzling revved up as needles of rain peppered his little face. They stopped while Kate pulled down the plastic screen to keep him dry.

'I hate this thing. I always think he'll suffocate in there.'

'Stop fussing and let's get into that shelter. I need a smoke.'

Oh brilliant, thought Kate. What a great day out, shivering in a shelter with a load of pensioners in plastic macs while Daniel has a roll-up.

Then Daniel pointed to a neon sign flashing steamily in the window of a café.

'*The Fancy Plaice*,' he read. 'Someone really strained the brain, thinking that one up. How about a plate of the national dish? Tell you what, I'll treat you to a feast.' He grabbed the handles of the buggy and started to run.

They arrived in the doorway, out of breath and streaming with water. A brassy matron came over and helped them with the buggy, cooed over Jack and said, 'My what a handsome lad! No need to ask who your daddy is!' Canny woman, she was.

It was the first time Jack had experienced chips, and Kate relaxed all her healthy eating rules and let Daniel dip them in ketchup and give them to him to chew. It all made a terrible mess. She watched Daniel present Jack with a chip, blowing on it to cool it. His hair was plastered back and they look more alike than ever. And suddenly Daniel grinned across at her, saying 'I love you!' and leaned over to give her a greasy kiss. It felt as if everything would be all right after all. Not just the day out, but their family, their life together.

Could they do it again? Kate lifted the sleeping Flora onto her shoulder and she burped in a most satisfactory way. She rocked her gently and nuzzled against her warm head. 'All this stuff, about me and your Daddy, takes away from the real question, the interesting question,' she murmured into the baby smell of Flora's neck. 'Which is, where you did you blow in from, my little love? I wonder. To hell with a DNA test.'

6

1918–1922

I don't like thinking about the time when I started school.

Edna took me on my first day. She held my hand going in the gate, but then she had to go to a different place and I was scared. There were lots of boys all kicking and shoving. I don't like boys.

Miss Tompkins was horrible. She was wearing great clompy boots with toecaps like soldiers have. My Dadser showed me the ones he used to wear when he was in the Army before he got sick. Miss Tompkins came right up close. She was holding a ruler and she smelled horrible, like when the milk goes thick and Mum shakes it down the sink and lumps get stuck in the plughole.

She asked me my name and I said Marjorie. And she said, 'Marjorie what?' and I said I didn't know.

Some people sniggered at that and she asked me again. I was getting a bad feeling. I didn't know what she was going on about but I knew I had to say something. The bad feeling was like when Billy Chapman gets me in the alley and won't let me go by. I don't know why, but I said Marjorie Daw. It's what my Dadser used to sing when he rocked me on his knee.

Miss Tompkins told me not to be so cheeky. She started whipping the ruler into the palm of her other hand, quite softly so it hardly touched her skin.

Then she told me to hold out my hand and she whacked it with the ruler. Not at all softly.

I shrieked and put my hand under my arm and she told me to hold it out again. She said she'd do it again and, if I made a sound, she'd do it a third time. I ground my teeth together and pressed the nails into my other hand. Out came a tiny grunt but she didn't hear it.

At playtime Billy Chapman and two other boys I didn't know got me in a corner up against the railings. Ethel Price from down our street ran up with her brother and hissed 'Sambo!' at me, and they both ran away. Sambo? Nora had a book called *Little Black Sambo*, but it was about a black boy. I didn't see what it had to do with me.

Billy pushed his face into mine. He'd got green snot glued round his nose. 'My Ma says your Ma wen' wiv a nigger.'

'Nigger? Where she go wiv Nigger?'

They all made silly faces and Billy went red. I was too worried to be frightened.

Nigger is our cat and my best friend in all the world, after Edna of course. S'pose Billy and his gang followed Mum and kidnapped Nigger and tied a saucepan lid to his tail like they did to Pansy Best's tabby kitten in the summer? Poor Nigger! I just pushed past Billy and ran to the gate, but I couldn't get out. I shook the bars and they were all laughing at me and then the bell went and I had to sit all afternoon and worry about Nigger.

I didn't wait for Edna at the end of school. I ran all the way home and shouted for Mum.

'Where's Nigger? Is Nigger all right?'

Mum looked cross because she'd been washing all day and her hands were all red and raw. She couldn't understand me because I was catching my breath and crying and getting the hiccups all at the same time.

'Nigger? I dunno. Out the back I expect,' she said in the end.

I rushed outside and Mum yelled to mind the sheets. 'They're for Mrs Sanders, and you know how fussy she is.' I was pushing my way through them as they billowed round me like clouds. And there was Nigger asleep in the patch of sun under the hedge, where he usually was.

'What was all that about?' said Mum when I came back in. She wiped my face with her apron.

'I just *said*. Billy Chapman said you gone somewhere wiv Nigger. I was afraid you was taking him to Lucy because Auntie Rose said she needed a friend.'

Lucy is my cousin and she used to be a cripple and I had to push her cart and be nice to her even when she pinched my arm. Now I have to be nice to her because her Daddy is away at the war.

'Slowly now.' Mum had sat down and she pulled me onto her lap. 'Say that again. Billy Chapman said *what*? Tell me *exactly* what Billy Chapman said.'

There was something about her voice that made me think Billy Chapman might be going to get what-for for telling fibs. I thought carefully.

'He said, my Ma says your Ma wen' wiv Nigger. He di'n't say where. An' when I ask him they all laughed.'

I felt Mum go suddenly all stiff. 'Oh my. That Elsie Chapman. Who does she think she is? We all know *she* grew up in Blossom Alley.' Mum wasn't really talking to me any more.

I knew Blossa-malley was a dirty place you wouldn't want to go and I hoped Mum wasn't taking Nigger there. But she seemed to have forgotten all about Nigger. She went all quiet and gave me a humbug from the Sunday tin. I wondered why, but I ran away to eat it in the cupboard under the stairs because I heard Edna coming and I knew she'd be mad at me for not waiting for her.

I'm a big girl now. Mum lets me take the red glass jug out to get it filled up when the milk cart comes. Edna's gone up to the big school and I'm in Miss Needham's class. I used to be frightened of her because she looks fierce. But it's only her eyes going in opposite directions. She's a kind person and she always points when she wants you to answer in class so you know who she's looking at. If that was Miss Tompkins she would make you guess and put you in the corner when you got it wrong.

I'm feeling happy inside today because my grandmother, who is a lady in a carriage, came to see me on Saturday and she took me for a drive and gave me an ice-cream on the common at Southsea. She is my secret special person and I can still smell her spicy smell if I wrinkle my nose in exactly the right way.

Today is composition. I am good at composition. I like making up stories. We have special books instead of slates. The books have red covers and pages with lines and a red line for the margin, and we are allowed to use pen and ink. Ethel Price is ink monitor and she's filled up all our inkwells specially.

Miss Needham is writing the subject on the board. *Write about your grandparents.*

I smile. I can't wait to start writing. It feels as if she has chosen the subject just for me. I will write all about my lady grandmother and the carriage and I will be top of the class and Miss Needham will read mine out. Then I hear sniggers. There was one snigger just now when Miss Needham read out what she had written on the board. But now the sniggers are passing backwards and forwards in the row behind. I look round to see what's going on. They are pointing at me and I feel my inside getting red and hot.

Miss Needham has also heard the sniggers. 'Billy Chapman stand up. I think you should tell us all what the joke is.'

Billy goes red and looks at the floor.

'If Billy can't tell us, then you can, Ethel Price. No, you can stay standing, Billy Chapman.'

Ethel stands up and looks straight at me. 'We was thinking it was funny Miss, that Marge had her grandma come to see her Sa'urday. She come in a carriage an' all, Miss.'

I am burning now. How did they know? I am cross my lady grandmother was spied upon.

'Thank you, Ethel. I fail to see anything funny about that. You can both sit down now, but come to see me afterwards.' Miss Needham turns to me and smiles. 'Well, Marjorie. That *is* a coincidence. You will have plenty to write about.' She smiles at me again, and she looks just like the wolf in Red Riding Hood when he says, "All the better to eat you with". But she only says, 'I'm sure Marjorie will have some *very* interesting things to write about.'

All of a sudden I hate Miss Needham. I almost wish I was back in Miss Tompkins' class. Miserably I start to write. *My lady granmother came in a carriage.* But I can't go on. I don't want to share my secret because then she won't be special any more. People will laugh at me. I scratch out what I have written until the paper goes all knubbly.

44

Then I chew my pen. When it's nearly time to finish I write on the next line *I do not have any granparents.*

It's nearly true because before Saturday I didn't know of the existence of my lady grandmother. And now she has vanished as if she was never there. Maybe I imagined her.

I have to stay behind after school and write a hundred lines. *I must not spoil my composition book.* And I have to write a composition about my grandparents for homework. But what happens in the playground is much worse. Billy Chapman and his gang creep round after me hissing, 'Marge is a toffee-nose' and 'Marge's grandma is a witch' and 'Nigger, nigger'. And by now I know they are not talking about my cat.

Last term in Miss Tompkins' class we did Africa. She said Africans were savages who danced round with no clothes on. Billy Chapman asked if Africans were niggers and Miss Tompkins said yes. She said they ate missionaries who went to tell them about God. My Dadser said that was nonsense and they had better things to eat than stringy missionaries and he went in the garden to have a smoke. When he came back he said the Africans were very civilised people who knew plenty about God, in fact they have a lot more gods than we do. Dadser should know because he was in Africa in the Army in a place called Sierra Leone. He said the missionaries should mind their own darn business. He said something about Miss Tompkins too, but Mum interrupted so I didn't hear.

Today the game is not to come near me. I am untouchable. At least they're not pulling my hair or pushing me over. One time I got a big lump on my head from hitting the ground. Mum had to pick pieces of grit out with her tweezers. Another time I got impy tiger from that Betty Wilson because she kept rubbing her scabby arm against mine to see if the colour came off. They circle round at a distance, gradually creeping nearer. I don't care. I think of my lady grandmother and hear her smile and I turn round and face them and give them a look. They all freeze and it's like playing "Grandmother's Footsteps", except this isn't a game.

I feel a tweak like someone's pulling the bow of my pinny undone and at the same time something like a hand on my arm, except it's *inside* my arm. It's as if someone is leading me away except there's nobody there. There comes a voice in my head that says:

Don't look around
Hold up your head
Don't run away

It sounds like a song. And I know my lady grandmother is looking after me and keeping me safe. I walk right away from all of them. I don't even see them any more.

I have to take a note home from Miss Needham. Mum reads it and goes, 'Oh my!' and puts it under the teapot. She gives it to Dadser to read when he gets home. He comes over quiet and is off out the back again for a smoke. I stay under the stairs until he comes looking for me. He isn't cross. He takes me on his knee and says, 'I'll tell you a story.' And he tells me all about how he was born at sea off the Spanish coast. All about the waves and the wind and the creaking timbers.

'And that is how I came to be born in Gibraltar, because it was the first landfall of the ship. And that is where you have to be registered when you are born at sea.'

I can hear Mum tut-tutting at the sink in the scullery but Dadser just says, 'I'll bet nobody else in your class has a father born at sea. You write about that, little one, and you'll get a star.'

'But I have to write about my *gran*parents.' I'm all ready to cry again because I can just imagine Miss Needham with the voice like a snail trail: *but this is about your father, Marjorie.*

'Of course it's about your grandmother,' says Dadser. 'She was the one who gave birth to me on the ship. You look a lot like her, little maid. She had to be very brave, don't you think?'

So I call my composition 'My Brave Grandmother' and Miss Needham says, 'Very good Marjorie,' but she doesn't read it out and I can tell it is not what she wanted. She gives me a strange look that makes my insides feel like they do when I see Billy Chapman. Which is odd, because Miss Needham is a teacher and she could not look more different from Billy Chapman.

I've got a new baby sister. She's a whole week old and she's still alive. I'm so grown up now that I'm allowed to hold her. A long time ago I had a baby brother, but he died and I'm not allowed to talk about it.

Edward, he was called, except no one actually called him it. I don't really remember him. Even though I screw my eyes up really hard I can't see his face. I just know I had to stand on tippy-toe to see over the edge of the cot. I couldn't get my feet warm when I got back in bed and then I heard the noise. It was like Nigger yowling when he's going to be sick, so I went back to see, though he always gets put out at night. But the noise was coming from Mum, and when Dadser saw me and told me to go back to bed, his face was all wet.

Binnie grows up quickly. She must be two years old, when I come in from school one day and get such a fright. There's someone sitting in Dadser's chair by the fire. No sign of Mum or Binnie. I'm starting out the door to find Mum and tell her, when the lady – and she is a lady, I can tell – says my name. She unfolds herself – she's very tall – and steps towards me with such a lovely smile.

'Your Mama has gone to the shop with May,' she says. 'I'm your Auntie Ada. I stayed here because – well, I've been in London and my feet were simply killing me.'

I notice her shoes put neatly together by the fender. Lovely shoes. Soft leather with a buckle at the sides and little heels. But so tiny for such a tall person.

'They're very small,' I hear myself say, as if I suspect them of not being hers.

She laughs. 'That's because I've got small feet.' And she pokes one of them forward for me to see. Yes, it is small and the ankle rather swollen. She's got the same wriggly hair as mine, but not so bushy. It looks knitted and it's the colour of a dishcloth.

'Anyway, never mind my feet. A little bird told me you had a birthday last week.'

'Yes, I was nine, and I had a cake with nine candles and I did blow them all out and Dadser had to light one of them again so that Binnie could have a go, she made such a fuss. She's only little.' It all comes out in a rush.

Auntie Ada gropes in her bag and hands me a parcel. It's wrapped in tissue paper with cut-out roses stuck to it and it's tied with pink ribbon. Maybe I can save it all and use it for Mum's birthday next month. So I take a lot of care opening my present.

'This paper is too pretty to tear,' I say.

'I like making things like that. Silly things, but it's fun.'

I can't imagine Mum having time to cut roses out of a magazine. I think Auntie Ada must be what they call a lady of leisure. I don't suppose she's ever taken in washing.

I set the ribbon aside and fold back the paper and, oh my! What a sight! On top are five skeins of silk – a deep red, royal blue, gold, leaf green and dark brown. I finger them.

'For embroidery,' says Auntie Ada.

'I know.' I'm indignant that she thinks she has to tell me. 'Nora does embroidery.'

Underneath the silks is a fold of special needles and a book of transfers – all garlands and baskets of flowers.

'I wasn't sure about the fabric,' says Auntie Ada. 'So I just went for natural linen. It shows up the colours nicely. They're for tray cloths which are a good way to start.'

I pull out one piece of fabric. It's a fine weave and there are no rough edges.

'I hemmed them for you. It's so boring to have to do hemming when you want to get started on the colours. Is it all right?' She sounds anxious. 'Flo, your Mama, always said you were good with a needle. I thought you might…'

'I love it,' I say and jump across the room to give her a hug. She smells of soot from the train and faintly also of rose petals. 'Will you show me? Now? Before they get back?'

I think it would be grand to be doing a lazy daisy, just like Nora, when Mum and Binnie come in.

I fetch Mum's scissors and thread a needle with the red silk. Auntie Ada shows me how to make a loop and pin it down and to get the needle in the right position for the next loop. Then I do a petal and another one until we have five in a circle. I've just done my second golden French knot in the centre of the flower, when Binnie rushes in and stops dead, followed by Mum.

'My, oh my. You've got the poor woman working already. After the day she's had. Oh my, Ada. What an ordeal. I'll put the kettle on and get you something to eat. Marge, up you go and change. Those things will do again for school tomorrow.'

As I leave the room I hear Mum say, 'Now, tell me all about it. I've never been to an inquest.'

An ink west sounds peculiar, so I sit on the bottom step of the stairs to listen.

Auntie Ada gives a big sigh. 'Oh dear, poor Ernest. Always was the black sheep of the family. In all senses.'

'Oh, dear. So what came out?'

It seems he got in a fight outside a pub down by the docks. A group of lads nigger-baiting, as I understand it. They beat him up and left him in the gutter. Oh, to think it. My own brother.'

What a horrid word. "Nigger-baiting." I think of Miss Tompkins and shiver.

'So have they arrested those men?'

'No. The death certificate says "Natural causes". You see, he came round and got himself back to his lodgings by all accounts, but he died in the night. It was a heart attack. It seems so unfair, because it's perfectly plain why he had the heart attack.'

There's a pause.

'But then again, I expect he brought it on himself, knowing Ernie.'

'He couldn't help being coloured, getting attacked,' says Mum.

'But he could help going to the pub, getting drunk, asking for trouble.'

I can hear Mum murmuring away like she does, making sympathetic noises.

'He was always like that. You see, of all of us, he was the one with the darkest skin. It was hard for him. Just a moment. They gave me his things, his "effects", as they called them. There's this photograph, taken a few years back. But you can see what I mean.'

'Oh my,' says Mum.

'He broke Mother's heart. He took to the drink, you see. Dick hasn't told you about that? People would pick on him, call him names. And he'd settle it with his fists.'

'Drink is a terrible thing.'

'At least with that verdict, I don't have to tell Mother about the fight. She'd hate to think he went that way.'

Mum's tut-tutting, and they fall silent. I creep upstairs and change.

Then Dadser comes home and there's a great commotion. While he's hugging Auntie Ada, I have plenty of time to look at the photograph, which is still on the table. Ernest is very dark indeed. His head is almost square and he looks like a fighter. I'm glad I'll never have to meet him.

7

It was one of those mornings when Vanessa found it difficult to break free of sleep. She dreamt that she was getting up, showering and dressing which allowed her to sink back into a dark well of oblivion. An hour passed before she persuaded her waking body to follow the dream self through those rituals. As the fizz of hot water brought her skin and her mind to life, she considered the day ahead, visiting Kate and the children. Her stomach lurched as her heart lifted at the thought.

David had already left for work and there was a note on the kitchen table asking whether she'd be home for dinner. She had every intention of leaving Kate's before Daniel came home from work. Which was probably cowardly. She texted David 'Yes' as she munched on muesli and reflected on how boring breakfast had become. She added 'Tiger House?' to the text and hoped David would remember to pick up their favourite Indian takeaway on his way home. She'd be too tired to cook. In fact she felt tired at the mere thought of the day ahead. It wasn't so much the children, although, like all four-year-olds, Jack could be exhausting. All babies can have screaming days, but Flora seemed a contented baby. No, it was the prospect of hearing about Kate's distress and Daniel's bloody-mindedness that she dreaded. Or worse still, sensing that distress, trying to get Kate to talk about it, and failing. Oh hell, don't let her be in one of those moods.

Vanessa drove off into the murk of a February morning and merged with traffic on the M27 in heavy spray. The only relief in the gloom was the sapphire pulse of an ambulance heading west towards Southampton.

Kate had always been the quiet one. Sensitive, creative. Devoted to every furry creature she could lay her hands on. Then she'd started going her own way as a teenager. Not rebellious exactly, but quietly subversive. Refusing to conform, but never confrontational. She had a Gothic phase, but otherwise she wasn't interested in trends or fashion and she certainly hadn't made the best of her looks as Lisa had. Boys left her well alone. Until the last term of school. She and David, even Kate's friends, had watched open-mouthed as the quiet, doe-eyed Kate, hiding behind a curtain of ordinary brown hair, had turned overnight into a magnet for much older boys. And so it had continued into Art College. How she hadn't got pregnant earlier, Vanessa would never know.

She pulled into the outside lane to overtake two competing lorries, wishing she'd taken the back road. At least there wouldn't be all this blinding spray. Thank God she wasn't still doing this as a daily commute. She had dreaded retirement, but David's idea that she set up as a private language tutor had been an inspiration. It was a luxury to be working from home, free of the noisy corridors of school, the depressing staff room and the constant challenge of trying to inspire teenagers with a passion for language. Sometimes she'd worried about them as much as she'd once worried about Kate.

Often when she lay awake at two in the morning Vanessa blamed herself for letting Kate move in with Daniel back then, for not giving her more boundaries generally. She'd been so concerned not to be controlling, like her own mother, that she'd made the classic mistake of going to the other extreme. David said that trying to stop Kate would just have made it worse. How, exactly, could it have been worse? David rolled his eyes when she asked that question and of course she knew he was right. Kate had a roof over her head, she was provided for and she had a healthy child – two now.

And what about the mystery of this second one, this utterly adorable little girl? Vanessa flashed her full beam at an idiot racing past without lights. Why was it always the drivers of road-coloured cars who didn't use lights? At least her red Golf was visible. As to the question of Flora's origins, she hadn't been able to explore that with Mother. Thea was having one of her awkward days. Dad had been depressed enough as it was, and raising it would only have made matters worse. She'd looked closely at Mother and it really didn't seem that likely. Personally, she suspected that overwhelming mother of Daniel's of keeping some family skeleton firmly locked in a cupboard.

Vanessa found Kate in the garden clearing out the rabbit hutch with Jack. A misty rain was falling and Flora was lying back in her buggy under the apple tree.

'We all needed to get out of the house. And poor Flopsy was living in a hovel.'

'Look at all the poo, Grandma!' Jack pointed at the heap of droppings and dirty straw in a sagging cardboard box.

'Nearly done. Jack, you could take the box and tip it on the compost. Perhaps you could give him a hand, Mum?'

Vanessa lurched awkwardly down the garden with Jack, with a hand under the bottom of the box. She breathed in musty straw, wet grass and the smell of vegetable matter decomposing and felt refreshed after the tense drive.

Kate straightened up. 'Now all we need is a rabbit.'

Vanessa and Jack cornered the lolloping Flopsy between shed and fence and Jack cuddled her so tightly that she was happy to dive out of his arms back into her clean, dry hutch.

Kate put the kettle on while Vanessa dried the children off.

'We'll take a drink through and sit in comfort. Coffee for you?' said Kate. 'Hey, mind her head, Jakey!'

Jack was already dragging Flora along the floor on her blanket. Vanessa ran to the rescue and they negotiated the door sill into the living room, where Jack quickly turned his attention to lining up his collection of cars. Vanessa smiled down at Flora who was still gurgling with delight. Serene and totally oblivious of the disturbance she's causing, thought Vanessa.

'She seems as happy as Larry,' said Vanessa taking her mug from Kate.

'You mean, in spite of everything.' Kate gave that characteristic little twist of her mouth.

'That's not what I said, but yes, if I'm honest.'

'Life goes on. Easier now he's back to work.' Kate glanced across at Jack. 'Just us.'

'So, have you still not got any clues?'

'Only what I said to you. And you said you didn't get anywhere with Nan and Gramps?'

'Like I said on the phone. Nan was having one of her bad days. Not making sense at all. Being difficult with the carers. And Gramps was so depressed by it all. He's afraid the carers will refuse to come if she keeps on playing them up.'

'Never mind. We're going to go over there anyway as soon as we've got a weekend free. Take Flora to meet them.'

'Oh, I don't think that's such a good idea. I mean, you never know these days what she'll do.' Vanessa sighed. 'Gramps would love it, though. He just loves to see people.'

'Then we'll definitely go. I mean she can't eat her, can she? She's not the big bad wolf.'

'I hope not.' Vanessa laughed and noticed how uneasy it sounded.

Vanessa had to fend off Jack who flung himself upon her, shouting, 'All the better to eat you with', and made her lie down so that he could eat her up.

Kate chewed on her lip, watching them. 'That's enough, Jakey. You'll get indigestion if you eat any more. Poor Grandma. How about fetching your new library book to show her?'

'She's a bit tough, anyway,' said Jack and disappeared upstairs, making exaggerated chewing faces.

'Why don't you think it's Nan, Mum? You...'

'I just don't see it.' Vanessa felt as if some portcullis clanged in the deep recesses of her consciousness. Why must Kate pursue this? It just didn't make any sense to her.

'Okay, okay. There's no need to be like that.'

'Be like what?' Vanessa sipped her coffee and wished Jack would come back with his book.

'You seem to have a blind spot, that's all. What with you, and Daniel with his fixed idea... I'm beginning to feel I'm being ganged up on. It's not like you to side with Daniel.'

'I am not siding with Daniel! Whatever gave you that idea?'

'Well, he won't look at the obvious either.'

'He doesn't still think you had an affair, does he?'

'Not really. He says not. But the more you and he won't look at

Nan, the more I wonder what you are actually thinking, both of you.'

'Oh, for goodness sake... Ah, Jack! Shall we read it?'

'Saved by the Gruffalo,' muttered Kate and went out to the kitchen.

Vanessa ignored her and focused on reading with Jack. It was no use arguing. She knew what Kate was like once she had an idea in her head.

The day passed with talk of feeding and marmalade oranges; with playing hide and seek with Jack and pegging washing on the line when the rain stopped; with making soup and eating lunch. When Flora went down after her afternoon feed, Vanessa sent Kate to get some sleep and took Jack for a walk by the sea. There was time to do a basket of ironing before they both woke up.

Why couldn't Daniel iron his own shirts? Vanessa resisted the childish temptation to scorch a collar ever so slightly and reflected on Jack's announcement, while throwing pebbles into the waves, that Grandma Roz was coming at the weekend to see his baby sister.

'I hear Daniel's mother's coming down,' she said when Kate emerged.

Kate rolled her eyes. 'That *will* be fun. The grand inspection. I can't wait to see her reaction. I overheard Daniel on the phone, telling her that Flora was very dark, not a Ward, not like Jack. What else he's told her I've no idea.'

Vanessa hung the last shirt over the door. 'Well, she'll love her to bits, that's for sure.'

'With the emphasis on the bits. I might have to ask you over to make it bearable.'

'Oh, no you don't! Two grandmothers is a recipe for disaster. Tell me how it goes.'

Vanessa said no more. She knew Kate was in for a tricky weekend. Hopefully, Roz Ward would come up with something helpful about ancestry, but she didn't want to mention the subject again.

Exhausted after the weekend with Daniel's mother, Kate pushed the buggy back from delivering Jack to his nursery. It was Valentine's Day. Nothing had happened that morning. No card, no little parcel with ribbons, no flowers or breakfast in bed. That was unusual but, she had to admit, it was a relief. She had no energy for dealing with a charade of hearts and flowers. After that suffocating atmosphere it was good to be in the fresh air, crisp and cleansing with even some snow flurries, which had been exciting for Jack.

Daniel always used to go overboard on Valentine's, one year hiring a Harlequin costume, another borrowing a lute which he could even play quite decently. He read Shakespearean love sonnets with all the verbal flourishes acquired at the School of Drama he'd attended for six months in Hull. He referred to it as the 'RADA of the North', which had impressed Kate in the early days but now caused her to chew her lip to suppress a smile. It had taken years for his mother to stop referring to 'My son, who's in the theatre'.

Roz Ward idolised her son. He could do no wrong. When Kate first encountered Roz she thought it was wonderful that mother and son had such a close relationship and expressed it so freely. Roz had even refused to change her name when she remarried, so that it stayed the same as Daniel's. With her snowy hair scraped back in an old-fashioned bun, Roz seemed a generation older than Vanessa, although there was only a few years between them. She'd swept into the grotty caravan where she and Daniel were living at that time and had it gleaming and tidy within half an hour, stowing enough home-cooked food in the tiny fridge to feed them for a week. Then she'd looked down her bony nose at Kate and said, 'Now I need to get to know my Daniel's girl. Tell me all about yourself.' And Kate had fallen under the spell of her intense blue eyes.

When Lisa first saw Roz and Daniel together she'd responded by opening her mouth and putting two fingers down her throat. Typical Lisa. Jumping to conclusions after ten minutes. How crude. But how right she'd been. Daniel could run amok with an axe and Roz would find a way to justify it. Lisa had been spot on. What was particularly sickening was the way Daniel continued to lap up all the syrup that Roz spooned over him.

Kate stuck out her tongue to catch a snowflake and wondered whether she would love her children as blindly as Roz. She hoped not. Unconditional love was one thing, but unconditional shouldn't mean blind. Roz was so different from Vanessa. Her gushing makes Mum look cold, thought Kate. The thought of Vanessa gushing made her smile. On the other hand Vanessa could be closed-off. Look at the way she clammed up about Nan and her origins. Refused to discuss it. What was that all about? It was silly, but she'd felt abandoned over that. She couldn't talk about it with Daniel, and Mum turned out to be just as bad, so she'd rung her friend, Morag.

But Morag would only focus on Daniel. 'Never mind your mother. Get that Daniel sorted out. Men! They never move as fast as we do. He'll get there though. You see. In a few weeks it'll all be fine.'

Which all rather missed the point Kate had been trying to make. So she tried Lisa.

'I feel as though I'm going potty.'

'Don't be daft,' Lisa had said. 'You're the only sane one. Make no mistake. Mum's always had a dodgy relationship with Nan. Must be something to do with that. Like I said, the only way is to go and see Nan yourself.'

So Kate had phoned Mead End and, after much repetition and talking slowly through the whistle of Gramps' hearing aid, had succeeded in making a date to visit.

The snow that had fallen was already melting by the time Kate got home. It hardly ever laid so close to the sea. She parked the buggy in the narrow hall and set about clearing away anything that would remind her of Roz's visit.

Roz's attitude meant, of course, that if anything went wrong in Daniel's world, it had to be someone else's fault. Which had been the exhausting thing about the weekend. Roz started out drooling over Flora and smothering her with kisses at the same time as turning a steely eye on Kate and saying 'Where did she spring from?' She progressed to 'What do you have to tell us, young lady?' and finished up ignoring Flora, with the parting remark, 'I'm really not sure I can acknowledge her as my granddaughter.'

'Who cares?' Kate had said to her back as she left with Daniel for the station. But of course she did care.

'Bother her,' said Kate out loud as she stowed the best wine glasses in the back of the cupboard. The worst of it was that she and Daniel would be back to square one. Roz would have cancelled out any progress. She'd given him carte blanche to wallow in being the wronged husband.

To cheer herself up, Kate ran down the garden to pick a few snowdrops. As she snapped the slender stems an idea nudged into her mind. Not even anything as definite as an idea, a message maybe from a parallel life – that she might not always be with Daniel. Never acquiring the substance of words, it slipped into her consciousness and was gone again like a snowflake melting on contact. Unthinkable, literally. She shook her head, took the flowers indoors and slid them into the tiny green vase she'd had since she was a child. Now Flora wanted a feed and the next task was to change the sheets on the spare bed.

The back bedroom doubled as her studio. It would be an age before she had the energy for painting, let alone the time. But it made her feel better just being in this room. It reminded her of a phrase her mother and her sister had used more than once. *Get back to normal.* She knew what they meant, but it felt rather a flattening prospect. She preferred the idea of coming back to life. For her that would mean starting to paint again.

With Flora asleep in the crook of her arm she opened a portfolio and started flipping through it with her free hand. Life drawing from the autumn class. That skinny redhead with no boobs. Not very rewarding to paint and she'd never managed to get her arms in proportion. Then there was Derek, the black guy who filled in when the redhead was off sick. Now *that* was good work. She'd really captured him, there was a sense of character. Kate pulled them out and spread them on the table. There were more of them than she expected given the guy had only sat for the class a couple of times. She'd worked fast. Always did her best work that way.

Flora started to wail and needed changing. Stripping the bed would have to wait. As she pulled a clean nappy off the pile, a rainbow of glittering hearts cascaded onto the changing mat. Kate laughed out loud. 'Hearts and poo,' she said, scooping them up and trickling them along the mantelpiece. A lot more real than hearts and flowers. Maybe Daniel was getting a sense of humour at last.

The incident lifted Kate's spirits. She texted Daniel a thank-you and was interrupted by the doorbell. Morag had brought Jack home from nursery and asked how the weekend had gone.

'Don't ask,' said Kate, but added that Daniel was beginning to lighten up.

'Nothing like Valentine's.' Morag hugged her. 'Not that you'd know it with Andy. I'll be lucky if he makes me a cuppa. He'll no buy me a present. It's not in his wee Scottish soul.' She exaggerated her strong Scottish vowels to make Kate laugh. 'Must dash. See you soon.' Morag was a physiotherapist at the local surgery and always seemed to be in a rush.

Kate took Jack's splodgy picture and put it under a magnet on the fridge. She was soon absorbed, hearing about his morning, settling Flora and getting lunch for the two of them.

But Valentine's Day ended badly.

Daniel came home from work with a bunch of daffodils. He said he would cook dinner. Kate was amazed.

'Call me an old romantic,' he said, tying his striped apron in place. 'Old habits die hard.'

Garlic smells made her tummy rumble as she read to Jack in bed, and when Daniel called her to eat there was a candle on the table and the usual pile of junk mail, Dinky cars and house keys had been swept to one end.

Daniel pulled out her chair and stood before her, his hands folded on his stomach which was showing early signs of developing a paunch.

'I was reflecting upon what my dear Mama put you through this weekend. I felt for you, I really did.' He opened his hands theatrically to emphasise his point.

But you didn't say anything, thought Kate. You didn't try to stop her.

'It really was excessive. But you must learn not to take her so seriously. She exaggerates. About disowning Flora, for instance.'

Oh, come on, thought Kate. Why must you always make excuses for her? She started to protest, then noticed the earnestness in Daniel's eyes, the spaniel pleading.

'I thought you did very well.' He sat down abruptly, dropping the pose. 'You did manage to humour her. I'm very grateful.' He lifted his glass. 'To us. Please?'

She relented and raised her glass to his. 'To us.'

He'd cooked a creamy risotto – chestnut mushrooms mixed

in with some wild chanterelles gathered in the New Forest in the autumn.

'This is wonderful. That really worked, bottling all that wild fungus. It's kept the flavour amazingly well.' She'd been sceptical at the time.

Daniel nodded. 'Told you it was a good idea.'

He beamed like a child who'd won a gold star.

Halfway through the meal the phone rang. Kate picked it up to hear Roz thanking her stiffly for the weekend and asking to speak to "my son". Daniel was monosyllabic and then took the phone into the living room. She could hear him questioning her about something, but couldn't make out what.

When Daniel came back he was quiet. The mood of the meal was broken.

Kate put down her fork, the happy feeling draining out of her like water through sand. 'What was that all about? Or don't I ask?'

'Not sure what you'll think of this. She was suggesting we do a DNA test. It was Blake's idea.'

'I'm sure you know exactly what I think of it.' Kate spoke quietly.

'It's not about not trusting you. It's about having something to show the world. People like Mama and Blake.'

'What's he doing sticking his oar in?'

Surely Daniel would reject anything coming from Blake. But Daniel wasn't rejecting it.

'It's simple enough, apparently.'

'Can't you just trust me?' said Kate. 'Why can't you tell *that* to the so-called world?'

'Of course, of course. But it would give us the evidence. You saw how Mama was, for instance.'

'But it's not about them, don't you see? It's about us and whether we trust one another. Do we have to humour her for ever?'

'No doubt that Blake thinks he can score one over me. I'd put money on that.'

'Oh, Daniel!' Kate pushed back her chair and went up to bed.

8

1926

Since I went up into Miss Knight's year in the big school I haven't looked back. That's what Mum tells Auntie Rose. Says she's been the making of me. I like to think I have been the making of myself. But I do admit I probably couldn't have done it without Miss Knight. She's a proper teacher. She isn't a bully like Miss Tompkins and she isn't sneaky like Miss Needham. She says I could be a teacher but I think that would be a horrid thing to be. Fancy having someone like Billy Chapman in your class.

Mrs Plum is our art teacher. She swoops about in strange drapey clothes and clasps her head when you do things wrong. But she thinks I have a real artist's eye and my watercolours are the best she's seen in someone my age. Mrs Plum says I should go to Art College and I might get into the Royal Academy, and she's talked to Miss Knight about it. Mum doesn't know what to make of that. She's afraid it will turn my head, but she likes telling Auntie Rose about it. Dadser says Mrs Plum is just an Army officer's widow and how does she know? But I don't see that means she can't be an artist. *She* wasn't an Army officer.

My reports say I show "great promise" and have "real talent" and a "strong sense of responsibility". Miss Knight says I am very capable and she's always putting me in charge of things. So at school I'm always pretending to be grown up.

At home I pretend to be little so I can play with my baby sister. Her name is May and Binnie for short. She started school last year but I couldn't look after her because I was already up at the big school. She's actually very good at looking after herself. She has dark colouring like me, which is good because now there are two of us. But she is pretty and has silky-smooth, wavy hair. Not like mine, which sticks out like a bush and makes me look like a wild girl. She's good at playing make-believe because she always does what I tell her except when she forgets what she's supposed to say, like passwords and things. But Binnie makes such funny faces when she gets it wrong that I can't get cross with her. We play in the hole behind the hedge mostly, and in the outhouse or the cupboard under the stairs when it's wet. It's a relief not to have to go out in the street to find someone to play with. I don't have to worry about Billy Chapman any more. I know Binnie and I will always be best sisters.

I'm worried about Dadser's tattoo. I've always rather liked it. That curly letter A on his forearm, all twined about with little leaves and tendrils. It's dark and mysterious, kind of tough and pretty all at the same time. But when I was round at Lucy's house the other day, she said tattoos were common. Mum says Mrs Chapman is common, so it would be awful if anyone thought Dadser was common. I'm not sure whether it's Lucy putting on airs and graces like Auntie Rose, or whether she really knows.

Lucy isn't reliable like that. But she's a year older than me and she's just started work in the newspaper office where her grandpa works. What with that and going to the posh school because she was supposed to be delicate, she thinks she knows everything. She isn't an invalid any more although she walks with ever such a tiny limp. But everyone got in the habit of always being nice to her and now she's spoilt to pieces. That's what Mum says anyway, when she thinks I'm not listening.

But how am I going to find out whether it's common to have a tattoo? And, if it is, how will I stop Dadser from rolling up his sleeves and letting people see it?

My sister Nora is getting married and I am going to be bridesmaid as well as little May and my cousins, Lucy and Maude. Mum and Nora are making all the dresses and we are to have matching hats and silk stockings. Except for May who is not grown up enough. Dadser is giving Nora away, even though he isn't her real father.

I was shocked when I found that out. It means Nora and Edna are only my half-sisters, but, as Mum says, why should it make any difference? Only that I always thought our family was a circle, straightforward, like we sit round the table every evening, and now I find there's a corner in the middle of it. I just wish she'd thought to tell me sooner. In fact I wish she'd thought to tell me at all. It just kind of came out when we were all discussing the wedding arrangements one Sunday. Nora was so excited about it all, I couldn't make a fuss. And yet all of a sudden our family wasn't as I'd always thought it was. It was like when your tram breaks down and you have to get out in the cold and wait for the next one. You get home just the same, but it's upsetting.

Of course, it must have been terrible for Nora and Edna to lose their Dad like that so suddenly, even if he was a hero. What a story! I was surprised I hadn't heard all about it. I asked Pansy Best if she remembered, because she's older than Edna. She gave me a funny look and said,

'Oh, you mean the story about the runaway horse and him being trampled rescuing the lady in the carriage?'

And I said, yes and she said, 'Yes, I remember Mum and Dad talking about it. It was in the paper.' And she still had that funny look, but when I went on about it she only said, 'It was a long time ago and I was only little. I don't really remember.' And she went all grown up on me.

Which was odd because Pansy is always very nice to me even though she's so much older. She's got a job working for Corrall's, the coal people, and walking all over Portsmouth. I thought she would get dirty from the coal dust but she laughed because she only collects the money. All that walking would wear me out, but Pansy's got long legs and looks a bit like a horse so I expect she's good at it.

Edna was working at the bakery but she couldn't get on with all the heat and the dust. She'd come home all white from the flour and be wheezing all night. So she left there and went to the chocolate factory. She still has swollen ankles from standing all day but it's much nicer. I want to be a milliner like Nora and make hats, but not just for anybody. I want to make them for grand ladies. Except that's out of date. Since Miss Plum, I want to be a painter and have an exhibition in London.

Dadser said I went all quiet after the story about Nora and Edna's Dad. I suppose it did set me thinking about things. It explains, of course, why me and Binnie look so different from Nora and Edna. Them all pink and white, and us two looking grubby next to them. I look at them and look at Dadser and look at myself in the mirror and wonder why I haven't noticed it before. Nora and Edna are nothing like him or me. They've got lanky hair for a start, except Nora's had a Marcel wave ever since she started courting. I keep wanting to look at myself and then wishing I hadn't. When I look in Mum's dressing table mirror I get a feeling like I'm falling off the edge of a cliff. As if I'd see all sorts of things if I kept on looking. It's like I almost remember something, but I don't know what. It makes me feel as if I'm going mad, like Pansy Best's Auntie Vi who had to be put away in the loony bin. So I try not to go into Mum's bedroom.

It's even worse in Lucy's mirror. She's got one of those mirrors with little wings at each side that you can angle to see the back of your hair. She's so vain, she's always putting curlers in her hair and patting her fat nose with a powder puff from her new compact. She bought it with her first wage packet and Mum was shocked because she didn't give the money to Auntie Rose. Sometimes Lucy makes me sit there and tries to comb my hair out straight, which she never can of course. She says she wishes she had curly hair like mine, but I know she doesn't mean it. When I look in that mirror it makes me giddy with all those reflections of me going on forever.

Nora's going to be a lovely bride in an ordinary pale and pretty kind of way. She's better looking than any of her friends and better than being dark and ugly like me.

I needn't have worried about Dadser and his tattoo at Nora's wedding. Dadser isn't the sort of man who drinks a lot and starts rolling up his sleeves and dancing. If he drinks, he does it at home and it makes him go even quieter and sadder than when he started. It comes on slowly, that mood, like he's cloaked in blankets for a day or two. Then he'll disappear into the front room with a half bottle of whisky (the one with the little dogs on the label) and he'll get out the tiny silver cup which is kept in the corner cupboard, and we know not to disturb him.

Dadser only ever rolls up his sleeves if he's digging the vegetable patch or cleaning the limescale out the copper for Mum. No, it was me who let the side down at the wedding and I didn't even know it at the time. About two weeks later Edna came home with the photographs we'd ordered and we were all excited to see them. Even I thought I'd looked good on the day. I'd never worn a hat before and it suited me, I could tell.

But as soon as I look I'm mortified. I'm sitting on a chair at one side of the group and I've sat down with my skirt hitched under me so the front of it doesn't cover my knees. And my stocking tops are showing! The silk stockings that go all the way up were far too expensive for us, so we had the sort which only go to the knee, and there I am sitting so grandly with my ankles neatly crossed but with the thick lisle tops for all to see. And Maudie's sitting across from me with her knees all covered, and her blonde hair waving down over her shoulders and she's the only one in the picture who's smiling ever so slightly. I've never liked Maudie, but when I see that photograph I hate her. I want to scratch her dolly blue eyes out. Why didn't anyone tell me? Why didn't the photographer notice? I thought that was his job, and he was so particular about the ankles being crossed and how we held the flowers.

Everyone is making remarks about how lovely Nora looks and how smart Edwin's spats are. They're wondering what happened to Edwin's sister Madge's dress. It didn't fit her and she's pulled it together at the neckline with a pin. I'm glad for Edna. She's the other matron of honour, with the same dress as Madge. I was worried she would look plain beside Madge, but Edna's dress fits perfectly and she looks really nice. Binnie looks sweet in her frilly mob cap and Lucy is obviously pretending she's the bride. As for Donald, the only page, you can see what a bad temper he was in. His little fists are clenched and he's scowling at the camera. And no wonder. He looks a total idiot in that white satin suit with short trousers. If it wasn't for me and my stocking tops, he'd be the one letting the side down. He looks common. Except he's too young to count.

I wonder whether anyone's going to mention my legs. They must have noticed. Then Dadser says, 'Marge looks elegant in that hat. Is that the right word? Would I be right in saying she's very stylish?' He says it in that funny way he has when he knows he doesn't understand something, like the words girls use for fashion. Then he goes on, 'Pity young Maude doesn't know how to pull up her stockings. They're all wrinkly round her ankles.'

And so they are. I didn't notice because I was so upset about my knees.

Lucy comes round next day and the first thing she says is about my stocking tops. But I come right back at her with Maudie's wrinkles. She rushes to look again at the photograph and pretends to make "Poor Maudie" noises, but I can tell she's as pleased as punch. Because for all she makes out she's best friends with Maudie, she's really dead jealous of her. Mum says they'd come neck and neck in a competition for spoilt children. And she doesn't mind any more whether I'm listening or not.

It's funny without Nora. We all miss her, especially Edna. Then she comes to visit with Edwin. They come down on the train from London where they live in a flat in Shepherd's Bush to be near Edwin's work. The odd thing is, she feels like a stranger. Right up until the washing-up, when all us girls go out in the scullery and it's just like old times again.

Now Nora and Edwin have gone back to London and me and Dadser are sitting on the bench out the back. It's been really hot and Dadser has his sleeves rolled up because he's been cutting the hedge.

'Dadser, why would Lucy say it's common to have a tattoo?'

He laughs his deep belly laugh that you don't hear very often. Usually Dadser only smiles, even when someone says something really funny. He laughs quite a long time and then he's quiet.

'That Lucy,' he says eventually. 'What next? She's too posh for her own good. I blame those elocution lessons.'

Auntie Rose was most insistent her Lucy should "speak proper" and paid for her to go to lessons at the School of Speech and Drama. She claims it was the reason she got her office job, but we all know it was because Grandpa Day pulled strings. I want to speak nicely too. But not like Lucy. She sounds funny, as if she's got cotton wool in her cheeks, especially when she remembers in the middle of a sentence. I want to talk like the lady who came to school to give out the prizes.

She spoke like she'd never had to have silk stockings that only went halfway up, and as if she'd find it really inconvenient to drop an aitch. I'll talk properly when I leave school. Otherwise they'll laugh at me.

'Penny for them?' Dadser asks, still smiling to himself. 'What else did she want to know?'

'Lucy?' I'd forgotten about her. 'She doesn't know you've got a tattoo. At least I don't think she does.' Suppose Lucy *did* know and was trying to needle me. I push the thought out of my mind. 'But what does it stands for? The A I mean.'

He gets a far-away look when I say that and it sounds like he says somebody's name. A bit like Amanda, but a softer sound than that. 'Who did you say?'

He looks round at me as if he'd forgotten I was there. 'A for *Amor*, which means love in Spanish,' he says. He says 'Spanish' softly with a long 'aa' sound and a bit of a lisp.

He's talking very quietly, as if he's sad. He says it doesn't matter whether a tattoo is common. The point is, having a tattoo is very foolish and he had his made when he was a foolish young man. I can't imagine Dadser being young or foolish.

'Never be ashamed of who you are. Or the colour of your skin. Once upon a time I was ashamed and it lost me everything. You must never be afraid to be who you are.'

Dadser never *ever* mentions the colour of my skin. It's embarrassing, and what's it got to do with the tattoo? 'What did you lose, Dadser?'

As soon as I ask the question I know it was the wrong thing to say. His eyes shut down.

His voice changes, almost brisk. 'The future brought changes I couldn't foresee. I thought I knew everything.' He rubs his arm as if he would rub out the curly A, and slowly rolls down his sleeve and fastens the cuff. 'I wouldn't hurt your mother for the world, but there it is.'

I wonder how it can possibly hurt Mum that he's got A for the Spanish for love on his arm.

Dadser sighs and squeezes my hand. 'You'll not be that foolish, that's for sure.'

9

2005

Kate hadn't seen Thea for a long time. What with taking Jack to nursery and keeping Daniel happy, not to mention being pregnant and having a baby, there never seemed to be a day clear for such a visit. She saw immediately how her grandmother had changed. Mum had talked about it, but seeing was believing. Thea didn't quite focus when she was looking at Kate. Then, when she did, it was more of a glare than anything else. Kate found it a bit unnerving but Daniel didn't seem bothered. He chatted her up the same as any other woman, no matter that she was ninety-odd. It was a total habit with him. And Thea flirted with him like you wouldn't believe.

'I trust you are keeping well?' He almost bowed and Thea narrowed her eyes as if she wondered for a moment whether she was being mocked. 'You are looking your usual elegant self.'

At that she gave a sliver of a smile and touched her hand to her hair in its crooked snood.

'A most fetching style, if I may say so.'

Kate had to look away when Thea beamed, absurdly pleased. But then Daniel peered too closely and Thea frowned and snapped, 'You're not a hairdresser, are you?'

Gramps seemed in a bit of a fizz. He took Kate aside in the kitchen and told her that Thea had tried her hand at making a cake for tea.

'At least, she thought that's what she was doing. But she had the Kenwood running with nothing in the bowl and the beater not even fitted in properly. Even I could hear it clanking round. Have a look, would you? I think the beater's bent, but as you know I can't really see.'

'Yes, it is bent. But it's been like that forever. I remember now. It still works though, I think you'll find.'

Not that he was bothered about that. Gramps wasn't about to start baking. But he was obviously upset that Nan didn't know what she was doing.

'I can't think why she's suddenly being so difficult today.' He frowned and sucked at a cut on his finger.

'Ooh, Gramps! How did you do that?'

'Oh, that? That was another thing. She had to interfere when I was cutting the bread for the sandwiches. Said it was common to have bread that thick. I expect they are a bit on the hefty side. But it was the best I could do.'

Kate took in the doorstep sandwiches and hoped the red bits were tomato. 'They're fine! But you really should have a plaster on that.' She rummaged in her bag. 'In here somewhere. Always carry some, just in case.'

Ted shook his head. 'She went to look for one. But never came back. Expect she forgot what she'd gone for.'

'Couldn't you get sliced bread? Wouldn't it be easier?' Kate stretched the plaster round his finger.

'Oh, that feels better. Sliced bread, eh? That would be something. But we've always had this loaf. Better not rock the boat. You know what I mean.'

'How did you get that scratch? Looks like it could do with some Savlon.' Kate touched his face where a red mark curved from cheekbone to jaw.

Ted rubbed it and winced. 'Must have been pruning the roses,' he said. 'Now let's be getting the kettle on.'

But next he was saying how he couldn't leave Thea alone, couldn't get out in the garden, not even for a short time.

'Because you see, she'll be up out of her chair and up to heaven knows what. Like boiling the kettle with no water in it. One time I caught her trying to stoke the fire. She nearly fell into it with the log she was putting on. Oh dear, oh dear, what have we come to?'

He told Kate that he kept the cooker turned off at the main switch ever since he came in one day and found all the burners red-hot.

'Of course it's not always like that. She just has her bad days. It's good to have someone else here. The children will be a distraction.'

Every time Jack came near Thea stroked his hair. 'Just like his father, isn't he? A fine looking little boy. Lovely fair hair.'

At first Jack smirked, then he giggled and then he kept well out of reach.

'Not a bit like you, is he?' Kate could tell this was meant as some kind of dig. She never did think her grandmother liked her much. She always favoured Lisa.

When it came to showing her Flora, Ted persuaded Thea to sit on the sofa so Kate could sit alongside and help her.

She made a great fuss. 'Good Lord! Anyone would think I'm not capable of holding a baby! Whatever next?'

Kate gritted her teeth until they hurt and took Flora from Daniel. 'Here she is, your first great-granddaughter.'

'Another little baby.' said Thea. 'I suppose she's just like her father too.' Her tone implied that Flora would therefore be redundant.

Kate had wrapped Flora in a blanket to make her easier to hold and placed the bundle on Thea's lap, resting it on her arm. She never got as far as sitting down. With her free hand, Thea hooked a bony finger over the edge of the blanket and pulled it away from Flora's face to get a better look.

All at once a spasm seemed to go through her. She jerked the bundle up in the air with her knees and pushed away with her hands, squawking, 'Dirty little thing! Dirty thing!'

Kate screamed. An animal sound, which echoed off the shell-pink walls and yodelled back from the red glass jug displayed in the alcove. Later, remembering, she wished the jug had shattered, but now she was on the floor gathering Flora to her. Kate glared up at her grandmother, and for as long as it took to draw breath, her eyes locked onto Thea's. Terror had broken through to the surface of their usually defiant gaze. 'You evil old woman,' Kate hissed.

Somehow she got to her feet. She had to get out of the room. Blinded by anger and tears she collided with Gramps coming in with the tea trolley.

'She threw Flora on the floor!' For once Kate was too preoccupied to be gentle with him. She blurted the words, not in explanation, but expressing her outrage.

'Thea's fallen on the floor? Oh dear, oh dear.' Ted abandoned the trolley, hurrying to help Thea up. Kate let him go, not correcting his mistake, not pausing in her flight.

She put Flora on the kitchen table and unwrapped her. She was perfectly fine, startled rather than hurt. 'No thanks to your great-grandmother,' muttered Kate, burying her wet face in sweet baby smell.

Her grandmother had thrown her baby onto the floor.

Thank goodness she'd still been standing close and wearing her squashy sheepskin boots. They'd broken Flora's fall. Her feet were far too hot what with the central heating and the blazing fire. She'd only resisted taking off the boots because she had holes in her socks and Nan could be really rude about things like that.

She'd have hit Thea if she hadn't been too busy rescuing Flora.

Kate walked up and down rocking Flora and staring out at the dead wilderness of winter garden. If she ever needed confirmation that Nan held the key to Flora's origins this was it. The fright in her eyes. No wonder she went on so much about Jack's fair hair. No wonder she was so rude when she heard Kate was pregnant for the second time. 'What does she want another one for?' she'd said to Mum in a very loud voice to be sure that Kate would hear. She must have worried about a baby just like Flora being born.

Ted interrupted her thoughts. 'Now she wants biscuits!' He came through the door, talking to himself, grabbed the biscuit tin, then saw Kate at the window. 'That is to say, she was going on about "cookies". What on earth? Your Daniel said she must mean biscuits. Since when did she talk American?' He put a scornful emphasis on the middle syllable and shook his head in irritation.

Kate stared. Thea threw Flora on the floor and here was Ted rabbiting on about biscuits?

He paused in the doorway and turned back. 'And she hadn't had a fall at all. What did you...?'

'No. I said Nan threw Flora on the floor.' She spoke slowly, articulating clearly. Gramps should know, he really should. He should know what Thea was capable of.

71

'Now you're talking nonsense! Of course she wouldn't do that. Lost her grip, maybe. That happens. I expect…'

'No, Gramps. She…'

But Ted wasn't listening. 'You coming to have some tea? I don't know what's going on. But the tea's ready.'

Before going back into the room Kate stood in the doorway for a moment, watching. There was a whole charade about biscuits going on. Nan poked her nose into the tin that Ted held out to her and then knocked it out of his hands in temper. 'They don't smell right,' she said. 'No cinnamon.' They were custard creams, so that wasn't surprising. Jack made himself useful picking them up and eating as many as he could manage. Which was a relief. He didn't seem at all concerned. Daniel and Ted were pretending things weren't happening in quite the way they were, Daniel pouring tea, Ted passing plates. Nan kept saying 'Cookies, I wanted *cookies*.' Gramps tried to laugh it off but he was clearly upset. The man is a saint, thought Kate. I don't know how he puts up with her. Except I do know: he copes because he can't see the half of it, the faces she makes and so on, and he's pretty good at not hearing the other half.

She felt a sudden need to down a cup of hot strong tea to restore her equilibrium. She never normally drank regular tea, the caffeine made her twitchy. But today it was just what she needed. She slipped onto the sofa beside Daniel and helped herself from the silver teapot. Gramps pressed her to have a chunky jam sandwich but she didn't think she could swallow anything solid. She stared across at Nan. The snood was falling over one eye and her fingers plucked at the fabric of her slacks. Kate looked from the nails, which needed cutting, to the scratch on Ted's face. Thea's eyes had glazed over again but fear was still evident in their constant flickering. Kate sipped her tea and breathed away the impulse to hit her, feeling the hot liquid steadying her inch by inch as it went down.

But Thea looked up and registered her presence with a glare that curdled the tea. Next she was rocking herself up out of the chair and advancing across the hearthrug faster than Kate could believe, waving her skinny arms, making a Captain Hook with one hand.

'How dare you bring your bastard baby under my roof? You're a bad girl Kate, or whatever your silly name is.' Her eyes glittered and she pointed at Daniel. 'You don't know where she's been, do you? You should be more careful.'

She paused to wiped the angry spit from her mouth with a lace-edged handkerchief, looked suddenly at a loss and started to mutter on with less conviction about there always being a rotten apple in the barrel.

Kate sat paralysed. Tea splashed on Flora's blanket.

By this time Jack was whimpering and tugging at Daniel's hand.

Gramps got to his feet, started to steer Thea away, back to her chair.

But Ted's grip on her elbow galvanised Thea yet again and she pushed him off with a violent shrug, turning back to peer round him at Kate. 'Rotten apple! Yes, that's you. Oh dear, your poor mother.' Then she gave in and allowed herself to be propelled into to her chair where she leant back and seemed to fall asleep.

But not for long.

Kate thrust Flora into Daniel's arms and took a long stride to stand over Thea's chair. She bent down close so that Thea's eyes flew open. 'You horrible old woman! You throw Flora on the floor, you say wicked things! You pretend to be so perfect, but if there's a rotten apple, you are it. Oh yes! I never want to see you again.' She backed off sharply as Thea's talons clawed up at her face. 'Come on, we're going.' Her knees were shaking as she grabbed Jack's hand.

Ted made a helpless gesture at the abandoned tea things. 'What was all that about? It really doesn't do to upset her. Whatever is going on?'

'Oh Gramps, you must have heard!' Kate wiped away sudden hot tears. 'She called Flora a bastard for a start.'

Ted frowned and shook his head in disbelief. 'This is silly. You mustn't take…'

'Sorry, Gramps. I really think it's best if we go. I – I actually I can't stay any longer. Oh Gramps, I'm so sorry.' Kate gave him a hug and they left him looking totally baffled and deflated at the back door as they strapped the children into the car. Just as Kate was getting in, Thea appeared and pushed past him carrying a small tattered book with a coloured cover, one board hanging loose, threads escaping from the binding.

'You'd better have this,' she said thrusting it at Kate. 'To read to your bastard.'

Daniel revved the engine, Kate closed her door, waved at Gramps and looked down at the book as they drove away. The title swam up through her tears: *Little Black Sambo*.

10

I left school this summer and – would you believe it? – I'm at the Art College. I took the exam and I won a scholarship. I can hardly believe it myself.

I won three prizes, too. One for English and two for Art – drawing and watercolours, of course. The only bad thing was, Mum insisted I wear my bridesmaid's dress to the prize-giving. I knew everyone else was bound to be in school uniform. She said my school dress was too short to go up on the stage in. And as I'd be up and down from the stage several times it was out of the question. I knew it would look wrong and silly and as if I was showing off. And anyway it's a whole year out of date. I'm sure Dadser knew I was right but he wouldn't back me up, said he didn't know anything about dresses. He should know by now. I'm always right about things like that.

The prize-giving was terrible because of the dress. Even Mum knew I was right in the end, but she didn't say anything.

But I don't care, because I'm at Art College now and I can't wait to get there every day. I work at the bakery when I don't have classes and often have to run all the way from the tram stop to get there on time. It's up three flights of stairs and they laugh at me because I am always so out of breath. But it's friendly laughing. We're like a family, united in what we're there to do. Art. Everyone is absorbed and obsessed by it. There's Eric, who wears little round glasses and looks so serious but has a wicked sense of humour – he's really good at drawing, fine detail that looks like a photograph. And Celia, who sploshes paint all over the place – bold, vibrant colours like her personality. And Vi – she looks so old-fashioned and buttoned up, but she can paint a nude as if you could stroke the warm flesh. We all have different talents and there's appreciation and awe and envy – but no jealousy or spite or bitterness. No one notices my colour. Or no more than Eric's glasses or Celia's red hair. We laugh a lot and exclaim and explore and experiment. There's so much to learn. The time always goes so quickly and I can't wait to get back.

Something awful has happened. I've got to leave Art College. Dadser is ill and has had to stop work. And Mum says we can't afford for me to stay at college and not be earning proper money, what with the doctor's bills and Binnie being still at school. When she told me, it felt like the end of my life. I had a terrible row with her and she told me I was selfish and only thinking of myself and how was Dad going to get better if he was worrying about money all the time?

It all happened just after Christmas and Mum couldn't get word to the doctor because of all the snow. There was a blizzard that started on Christmas Day and went on all through Boxing Day. Of course Binnie thought it was wonderful, and to be honest, so did I. But it's made it much more difficult for Mum and it's difficult to keep Dadser warm. The atmosphere indoors has been so awful that I just wanted to stay building a snowman with Binnie and playing snowballs, but then her hands went numb and Mum scolded me for keeping her outside so long. I just can't do anything right.

So today I'm busy trying to make up for all that. There's something I have to do before I can properly close the door on all my dreams. It sounds a bit melodramatic, but that's what it feels like. Mum has written a letter to the college Principal, but that's not enough. I can't bear to say goodbye to my friends. The questions would be too difficult. They'd find out too much. But Mr Faulkner's different. I can trust him and I wouldn't want him to think I'd just given up.

I've timed it right and Mr Faulkner is alone, cleaning brushes at the sink. I breathe in the reek of turpentine and oil paint. Huge rectangles of sunlight fall over the floor and table. Pools of colour glow from unfinished canvases on easels around the room. Rose Lake, Cadmium Yellow, Ultramarine. Only Mr Faulkner in his customary grey smock and trousers is drab. He turns and greets me. 'Marjorie!'

I think how feeble and short-lived was my attempt at dignity in asking to be called by my full name. It really isn't much better than Marge and now it's all at an end anyway.

'We missed you.' He turns his eyes on me, that surprising cerulean blue in a gaunt face, and I know he means it.

The knowing silences me and I bite my lip.

'What can I do for you then? I was hoping you'd finish that today.' He nods towards my easel and I see someone has set my bold sea and skyscape on the frame ready for me.

I was so excited when I started it, working from a sketch of the harbour mouth. Mr Faulkner was less enthusiastic. He stopped the class. 'Right. From now on, no pencils.' And he marched round the room removing pencils from all the students. Then he came back to me. 'Cut out all that detail. The less you paint, the more you show. Don't confuse my eye.' I had to start again, sulky, abandoning boats and buildings, feeling lost without the accuracy of the drawing. He was right of course. Without all those lines the sea and sky took on a life of their own.

He looks such a dowdy man with his sandy hair and droopy moustache but he's been an inspiration. He'd say, 'Think! Why are they called WATERcolours?'

The first lesson I took with him was on watercolour painting. I shall never forget his introduction. 'You are creating a rainbow. Mix your colours as if in a raindrop. Let the colour shine through the water. Be thirsty.'

Now he notices my stillness and crosses the room.

Before he can get too near, I blurt, 'I've come to say goodbye and thank-you. I have to leave. My father is ill.'

He starts to protest, to question, to offer sympathy. I try to listen. But I know if I stay a moment longer I will throw myself on his shoulder and weep forever. I turn away so he can't see the tears already spilling over. 'I had to come and say. I couldn't just go…' and I make it out the door and down the stairs, aware he has followed me and is watching. I have reached the second flight when I hear his voice floating down the stairwell. 'I'm so, so sorry. Good luck, Marjorie.'

I run from the place. Out of the light, down, down, down the stone stairs onto the grey pavement, blundering my way onto a tram and back to the street where I belong. I nose my way into the dark hall with its scuffed brown paint and worn lino, edge sideways past Dadser's bike and get a sharp call from Mum in the scullery before I can scuttle upstairs.

I freeze because seeing Mr Faulkner isn't all I've been doing today.

Before I went to the art college I went to Milady's, the shop where Nora used to work as a milliner, and asked to speak to Mr Cooper. He looked me up and down and I could see he was thinking I didn't look much like Nora's sister. He sent me down the corridor to see the supervisor, Miss Wilmott. I remember she always had a soft spot for Nora. She gave me some very easy sewing to do and told me to come back tomorrow with my mother and to bring references. I've as good as got the job as apprentice in the cutting room, subject to the contract being signed.

When I hear Mum call from the scullery all of a sudden it doesn't seem such a good idea I've been so independent and gone to see Mr Cooper on my own. I haven't said anything at home about going for a job at Milady's. I know she wants me to work at the bakery. It's better money. Even so I think she'll be pleased about the apprentice-ship. I'm wrong.

'How much will you be paid?' is all she says.

When I tell her she snaps, 'How many of Dr Perkins' bills is that going to pay?' And it isn't a question.

'You've got a nerve,' she goes on. 'Fixing it up without a word or a by-your-leave. What were you thinking of?'

I was thinking of me of course. Getting a job that wouldn't drive me mad with boredom. Giving myself some small compensation for not being able to continue at Art College. I go hot inside and look at the floor. I can see where this is going. She'll call me selfish again. I take a deep breath. 'Mum, it's a job with a future. The bakery's just a dead end.'

'Ballard's pay good money when we need it. What's the use of money in the future you might never get?'

'But Mum, it's a skill, a career. At least it's something. I'd go daft staying at Ballard's.'

'Well, now we're getting to it. I might have known. Ballard's isn't good enough for you. You always were the selfish one.'

She gives me a look and takes her battered shopping bag off the back of the scullery door. 'Now, mind out. I've got to get on. Go and see if your father's awake, get him a cup of tea. But don't wake him up, mind.'

I creep upstairs heading for my bed in the back room. The last thing I want is to talk to anyone. But Dadser hears the stairs creak and calls out, pats the bed for me to sit down.

'Don't take too much notice of your mother. She's worried, that's all.' His voice is pale and foggy.

So he's heard the whole thing.

'I thought if I got an apprenticeship... Like Nora.'

'The one thing you have to remember in all this,' He pauses and wipes his face with his handkerchief. '...is the hard time your mother had when she was your age.'

I think he's finished and start to protest, but he holds up his hand. It seems to wear him out just to speak. The whites of his eyes are yellow from the malaria and he's sweating all the time. He's always had bouts of malaria. He got it from the mosquitoes in Sierra Leone when he was in the Army. But there seems to be something else wrong now and nobody will talk about it.

'Your mother had to grow up fast when she was only twelve. That's two years younger than you are now. When her mother died there was no one else to look after Rose and Sid. As far as I can gather, old man James – that was your grandfather – he didn't see why she'd want to do anything else but look after them all. He took it all for granted.' He stops and looks at me.

'No wonder she thinks I'm selfish.'

He's silent for a while, then takes a sip of water. 'You're not selfish. But you want to better yourself. I know. I've seen it in you all along. Nothing wrong in that. But it can be hard for the ones you leave behind.'

'I'd never...'

'Never say never. Learnt that one years ago. Now, did I hear your mother mention a cup of tea?'

When I come back with the tea he says, 'I know you took it hard, having to stop with your art. Spent my childhood reading books and writing poetry, just like you with your drawing. But then my father sat me down one day and told me now I had to get used to the real world. He was strict but he was fair, and he was trying to warn me, prepare me. I always knew I'd join the Army like my brothers. And the time had come. Fourteen I was, just like you. Didn't know what hit me.'

I help him to sit up to drink the tea, his back all bones and damp nightshirt.

'Of course I knew I couldn't go on mooching about writing poetry all my life, but it all seemed to happen so quickly.'

'I just thought she'd be pleased. But I suppose I'll have to give it up, the apprenticeship.'

He flips my pouting bottom lip with his index finger. 'She'll be pleased. In her own time.' He sips the tea. 'As for you, my little maid, you knew quite well she wouldn't be pleased. Otherwise you'd have come in shouting it out. Instead of skulking through the door and trying to slip upstairs.'

Dadser never misses a thing.

I stay sitting on Dadser's bed as he drifts off to sleep. The room has a dusty smell of medicine, sweat and tobacco. I try concentrating on the tang of turpentine lingering in my nostrils. The studio glows in my head like a cube of light. It's a beacon I will visit in my dreams. Me and Mr Faulkner, loosely wrapped together and drifting above the city, like the painting he showed us by Marc Chagall. I will float in through the skylight, down to my easel and I'll paint until dawn. And my paintings will hang in the Royal Academy and I'll be famous and I'll...

Dadser gives a little snore and brings me back to the room. I hate the lank curtains with their shiny pattern and the nets shutting out the light along with the busybody eyes across the street. I hate the wardrobe looming over me, top-heavy with piled-up brown paper parcels of things that will "come in handy". I hate the lace mat and the fancy glass dish on the dressing table where Mum drops hairpins and her Sunday brooch. I hate it that the drawers will only open halfway before they hit the end of the bed.

How will I ever have such a dream from the bed I share with

Binnie in this pokey house in a mean street? There are no ingredients here to stir into magic like that, no beauty and no grand suffering either. It's all too ordinary and I'm too ordinary too.

11

2005

Kate hardly slept all night after the drama of their visit to Mead End. She was outraged that her grandmother could behave as she had, horrified at the things she herself had said in the heat of the moment and intrigued by what it all meant.

Next morning at breakfast Daniel said she was making too much of it. 'Storm in an elegant Minton teacup. I don't for one moment believe she deliberately "threw Flora on the floor", as you put it. She has an impeccable sense of decorum. Added to which, she's frail. She had a twitch. All a regrettable accident and no harm done.'

'But you were there!' How come Daniel had managed to re-invent the whole occurrence overnight?

Kate wasn't surprised to find the phone ringing when she got back from taking Jack to nursery.

Vanessa pitched in straightaway. 'Whatever did you do yesterday to upset Gramps so much?'

'Me? Upset Gramps? Well, yes, he was upset, but not half as upset as I was.'

'Why? What happened? Apparently Nan's been impossible ever since.'

'Oh, Mum, it was awful. Nan gave one look at Flora and threw her on the floor.'

'Oh, come on darling. She wouldn't do a thing like that.'

'She did. It was lucky I was right there.'

'Gramps said Flora rolled off Nan's lap and that you were

82

ridiculously angry with her and very rude.'

Kate swallowed hard. 'That simply isn't how it happened. Gramps told you that, did he? Well, I'll have you know, he wasn't even in the room. Nan pushed her. She went up in the air. She could have been really hurt. And then afterwards Nan was vile. She called Flora a bastard, said we shouldn't have come. Of course I feel bad about some of the things I said, but I do think I was justified in being angry.'

'Oh, my God. No wonder Dad chose not to hear what was going on. Is Flora okay? Are you okay? And Jack? Was he upset?'

'Yes, fine now. She was startled. That's all really. Jack was upset but he made up for it, scoffing custard creams. And I think I was in shock all the way home.'

'And how was Daniel in all this?'

'Oh, he was supportive at the time, backed me up when I insisted on going. But very quiet on the way home. Now he's back-tracked and he won't talk about it. Not sure what that's all about.'

'Oh well, that's Daniel for you.' Vanessa was about to go to Mead End to smooth things over. 'Can I say that you apologise? Poor Dad's in such a state. He has such a hard time with her.'

'You can tell Gramps how sorry I am that the afternoon was spoilt, but I am not saying sorry to Nan.' Kate took a deep breath. 'Actually, Mum, I'm getting a bit pissed off that everyone's so bothered about them. Of course I sympathise with Gramps, but at the end of the day, he married her and it's his choice to care for her. No one would blame him if he put her in a home, and it's admirable that he doesn't. But, just for once, I'm saying, what about me and my feelings?'

'Of course we care about your feelings, and Flora, of course we do. But she wasn't hurt and, with Nan, it would just make such a difference if you could…'

'Nan owes *me* an apology and she knows it. Everyone's always making allowances. She's not that frail, you know.'

'But you have to allow for the dementia. It…'

'She's not that demented either, not all the time. She knew exactly what was going on. So, now do you believe me when I say it's Nan? The key to Flora's origins? It's Nan who's the mystery link.'

'Oh. I see. You think…? Well, I suppose…'

'Oh, come on, Mum. She was terrified, defensive. It was all so obvious.'

'Aren't you reading rather a lot into…? I really don't know. I really don't know what to think. I need to think that one over.'

Did Mum really mean she hadn't thought it over until now? Kate knew she'd never get an apology from Thea. It was not in her nature to admit she was wrong. And it didn't look like she was going to get any support from Vanessa. All her questions must go on hold.

Her relationship with Daniel felt as if it was on hold too. It was almost as if Daniel was waiting for her to apologise. But what for? She had done nothing. And she herself was waiting. For an apology? Not really. It made no sense for him to say sorry for not trusting her, for being himself, for being his mother's son. It would be like apologising for the weather. None of those things could be changed by an apology. They could not be changed at all.

This state of limbo between them ended one Saturday. Saturday used to be a happy morning – eggs for breakfast, a trip to the market, gardening. When Kate got downstairs the post had arrived and Daniel pushed an envelope towards her. She saw it was the result of the DNA test. She'd forgotten all about it. So he did do it after all.

'I don't need to see.'

'It's positive.'

Daniel seemed strangely deflated. Wasn't this what he wanted to hear?

'Aren't you pleased?'

'But of course.' He made that typical expansive gesture with his hands but at the same time gave her a strange look and stomped off to into the garden.

Kate turned away and dropped a slice of bread into the toaster. The DNA test wouldn't make a jot of difference of course. Why was Daniel such an idiot as to imagine it could? The test proved he was Flora's father, but it did nothing to heal the damage between them. Only they could begin to repair that rift. If they both wanted to.

She watched Daniel slam into the shed. He came out with a fork and started jabbing savagely at the soil in the vegetable patch, hard earth matted with weeds. He wasn't a natural gardener and at any other time she'd have been amused. This morning it made her angry.

'You'll break the blooming fork,' she shouted, knowing he couldn't hear.

This was ridiculous. They had to talk. Behave like two grown-ups. She made him a coffee and took it out.

He leaned towards her over the fork. 'I suppose you think you've got away with it?'

Stung, she withdrew the mug she was holding out. 'What are you talking about?'

'The test result.'

'There was never anything to get away with.'

'I've been thinking. I mean, a positive test result clearly means Flora is my daughter. But it doesn't, of course, rule out the possibility that you had an affair.'

The word hung in the air, blocking out the sun.

'Are you mad? When are you going to give up? I thought this was about Flora. That now you'd be satisfied.'

'What about you and the black guy?'

'What black guy?'

'The naked one. The Adonis in the pictures.'

Kate covered her mouth with her hand. 'You saw them!'

'Certainly did. I thought I'd sleep in there that night. You were in such a mood. But I didn't fancy sharing the room with him.' He stabbed the fork into the ground and stood with hands on hips. 'Well?'

He sounded so cocksure and he was so wrong she could do nothing but laugh silently behind her hand. He pulled it away roughly. 'Don't!'

'You cannot be serious! Derek? He's a *model*. I *drew* him.'

'So? Models are alive, aren't they? You've told me. You chat in the coffee break.'

'Sure. Chat. Not fuck. What are you on about?'

'Then why was he draped around the room? For you to drool over? To let me size up the opposition?'

Kate dropped into a squat, pulled at a dandelion and rubbed the milk on her finger, watching it stain the skin brown. She took a deep breath, attempting calm. 'I was trying to cheer myself up. Make some plans about work in some far-off non-existent future. I came across them and I got them out – because they happen to be good.' Something snapped inside her and she shouted the last words up into Daniel's face.

'Not because *he* was good?'

Kate gave him a long contemptuous look. 'Now you're just being cheap.'

She turned on her heel. Jack had arrived with a small fork to help with the digging and Flora was wailing in the kitchen.

It was evening before Kate confronted Daniel as he worked at his laptop on the kitchen table. 'Why do you want me to have had an affair?'

Daniel frowned. 'What a strange question. I really can't discuss that now. I have to get these figures ready…'

'Daniel, if you won't discuss it you may as well go pack your bags. I'm not prepared to live with this. I've put up with hell from you and your sainted mother, and now you've got your precious proof and you're still behaving like I'm some harlot.'

Daniel gave her a world-weary look. 'I think you're exaggerating.'

'Would it make you feel better or something? If I'd had an affair? Like I was no better than you are? The moral high ground?'

'That's below the belt. It's not worthy of you Kate. You know I've changed. I was just checking all possibilities. It seems I was wrong.'

'Is that all you can say?'

'What do you want me to say, Kate?'

'You've certainly changed. I know you did change – for the better, I mean. And it was really working before Flora was born. We were together again. You know that. But now. It's a different matter. I don't understand you anymore. You said you believed me, but you didn't really – not totally. So you did the test. And it was okay. And you still think I had an affair. What am I supposed to do? It's like you're determined to blame me when there's nothing anyone needs to be blamed for. I can't go on living with it, Daniel. I really can't. Like I said, you may as well pack your bags.'

A voice came from behind her. 'Why does Daddy have to pack his bags? Is he going on holiday? Can I go too?'

Kate stooped to wrap her arms round Jack who was shivering in the doorway in his Spiderman pyjamas. 'Not going on holiday, sweetie. Not until the summer. Mummy and Daddy were having a silly argument. Say goodnight to Daddy.'

'Will we go in the tent?'

'Expect so.'

'Will there be room for Flora too in the tent?'

'Of course there will.'

'What was you arguing about?'

Kate led him away upstairs. 'Like when Adam comes here to play and you have a fight and you tell him to go home. And then you're friends again. Come on, you'd better have a wee.'

When she came back down Daniel was sobbing with his head in his hands. She sighed and put an arm round his shoulders.

'I've been such a goddam fool. You won't really send me away, will you? I couldn't bear it, not to be with Jack.'

His voice had lost its resonance, like a cello without a back. He did that rather well. She was being manipulated, she knew it. She'd seen him play this role before, worming his way back into their relationship after an affair. But what could she do? Never mind Daniel's pain. Never mind her own despair at the thought of waking up to Daniel every morning. All that was wiped out by the picture of Jack's tense, white face at the door. Imagine the devastation Jack would feel.

'All that stuff this morning, I didn't really mean it. Even when I was saying it, I could hear myself, and I knew it wasn't true.' He reached up a hand, feeling for her hair, pulling her down. 'What I meant was, other people would think that. That you had an affair. That I'm the sort of guy whose...'

'Who cares what other people think?' As she said it and saw the look in Daniel's eyes, she knew that he did care.

'Who cares indeed! Can we be friends again?'

Part of her wanted to smack him round the head, another part was being knowingly seduced. Neither of these parts was of any use to her. Slowly she said, 'I don't know how we be friends again. But we need to be parents together. If we can't manage that, nothing's going to work. And I mean nothing.'

He grabbed her round the waist and buried his head in her stomach, still soft from the birth. Was it really only three, four weeks ago? She tried to stroke his head but the temptation to pull him away by the hair was too great. Poor Daniel, she thought, I suppose he's been going through hell too. In his own way.

He was suddenly standing, his breath hot in her ear. 'You're mine, little bird, mine, all mine. You can't send me away. We belong together. You know that. My sweet, my little bird.'

Kate arched away. Not now, surely not now. But his fingers were in her waistband. 'Get these down.' He pushed her onto the table.

Her back ached, the table juddered and creaked, and images floated under her eyelids like a surrealist painting. Just don't let Jack wake up again, she thought and then her mind floated off while her body did what her body always did. Afterwards she pulled up her jeans and her mind floated back. But its mental furniture seemed to have been rearranged. She kept bumping into things, losing her footing.

Daniel was busy opening a bottle of wine, back at home in his voice. 'I kept asking all these questions, you see. Why would she? How would she? Who? Where? My Kate. I was obsessed'

'What? What are you talking about?' She was reeling from what had just happened, and here was Daniel clattering on as if he were describing a tricky day at work.

'I was just trying to explain…'

Kate took the glass he put in her hand, put it on the table, choosing not to drink. She felt she needed a clear head.

'You see I kept trying to imagine who this lover of yours was. And then trying hard not to imagine him.'

Kate clutched her head in her hands. God, back to that again.

'I know, I know – there was no lover.'

'That's not what you said this morning.'

'Yes, well. That was…not entirely rational. Under duress, shall we say. I'm sorry I said it. As I said, I didn't really believe it. But I'm just trying to give you a flavour of what yours truly has been wrestling with.' Daniel paced to the window and looked out into the night, into his own reflection. He always liked to play to an audience.

'I even started wondering whether I was a closet racist. I know I'm a lot of things. But I trust that isn't one of them. But when I saw those pictures. All the fantasies about black men came flooding in. Would I have been as jealous of a white man, for instance? But that's impossible to know because a white lover would have gone undetected...'

'Please, Daniel, let's not... There's no point...'

'I even thought, if Flora'd had carroty hair, would I have gone and taken our friend Andy by the throat? Of course I would. But then, Andy's a friend, so that creates a different scenario altogether. So who can judge? It's been a nightmare.' Daniel groaned and turned back to face her.

Kate thought, a nightmare of your own making and sighed. 'Poor Daniel.'

Daniel returned to the wine bottle, refilled his glass and sat down, crossing his legs, leaning back. 'So, as you so rightly say, let us put all that behind us and look to the future. There is, of course still the question, how did it happen?'

Kate raised her eyebrows. 'I don't know how you can sit there and ask that question – after what went on at Mead End last weekend. I mean, what more do you want? Nan's reaction? It's still giving me nightmares.'

'Ah, yes. There is that, of course.' He sounded as if he were considering it for the first time.

Kate rubbed her eyes. 'I know you don't agree with me and there's no point in arguing. And we can't ask Nan – obviously. So I've just tried to forget about it.'

'Quite a possibility.'

'And if I'm wrong, then we're back to square one. I've thought about it plenty. Once you go back a generation or two there are just endless permutations and unknowns. Untold stories. Fascinating for a historian. But it's just dead people. We've got a living daughter to think about. What do you mean? Quite a possibility?'

'You may be right. About Thea. It seems very likely, come to think of it.'

'That's not what you said before.'

Daniel looked sheepish. 'I hadn't really considered it, to be honest. I had this *idée fixe*. Ever since I saw those pictures of the black guy I was just totally convinced it had to be him.' He spread his hands in that familiar gesture that both asked and assumed forgiveness. 'But yours truly has been proved wrong by the wonders of modern science.'

Kate shook her head. 'No comment.' She had the feeling of bursting through a door she'd been trying to open for some time and finding the room inside disappointingly empty.

'So how do we pursue our inquiries? Can we pursue them?'

'I don't see how. Anyway we're going to have a whole set of more important questions to deal with. Like already, what do we say to people who are wondering? Like Morag and Andy. I mean, Morag knows what I think, but in confidence. It's not like the public story. Which Jack will need when the kids at school want to know why his sister's a different colour. And when she's older and she gets asked how she came to be part of our family. Kids in the playground, teachers. Like how might it affect her sense of identity?'

'Whoa, steady on. You *have* been thinking about it.'

'You mean, you haven't?' She couldn't believe that these questions hadn't been in Daniel's mind too. And then again, maybe she could believe it.

'I told you. My mind's been running on one track.'

'Yeah, yeah.' Oh, for Pete's sake, let's move on.

'Except that I must say Thea did give me an insight into how people might react. Not violently, of course, but...'

At that moment Willow clattered through the cat-flap and wound herself around Kate's legs. Then she stalked over to Daniel and head-butted the bottom of his wine glass.

'Bloody cat!' He dabbed at dark splashes on his jeans.

Kate got up to open a tin of cat food and tossed him a damp cloth. My life is about tins of cat food and dishcloths, she thought. That is what is keeping us together.

Willow stretched up Kate's leg, purring loudly. And all the time we're wrestling with these big issues, racism, marriage, identity, trust. They get bandied around. Sometimes they just seem like empty words. But when you get to grips with them, they're stuff full of meaning. Enough to get lost in. Words that aren't safe to be let loose between two people. Stick with the cat food.

She put the dish on the floor, decided to drink her wine after all. 'What was that you were saying about people reacting?'

'Doesn't matter. Just that Thea gave me food for thought, that's all. But there aren't many like Thea around.'

'So you think discrimination is a thing of the past and we shouldn't worry about it?'

'An interesting word that. "Discrimination".' Daniel leant back and crossed his legs, getting into his groove. 'Meaning to appreciate the qualities of something, be discerning. Diversity. That's the in-word now, the management speak.'

Kate rolled her eyes. 'I don't think the kids in the playground have heard about diversity. Try the other meaning. You know how kids pick on the one who's different. Bullying, it's called.'

'Bloody minefield.' Daniel's eyes were glazing over. 'Anyway, there are plenty of mixed race families these days.'

'Not round here. Not many. But I did meet a girl at the drop-in clinic the other day, Charlotte, her name is. She's black, Jamaican. At least, her parents came from Jamaica. She was born here. Anyway her little boy's as fair as you, looked quite like Jack. They get on really well, him and Flora. She's coming round next week. Her husband's white...'

'So no mystery there.'

'No. Quite. Of course we had the whole charade of people thinking we'd swapped children. Funny the first time, but after that...'

'Nightmare.'

He's not really listening, thought Kate. 'She said she found it really weird down here. People staring at her all the time. They've just moved down from Camberwell. It's so multi-racial there no one bats an eyelid.'

'Maybe we should move.'

'Move? Well, I suppose we could. I'd miss the sea though.'

Daniel was smiling. 'I didn't mean it.'

'You really can't take this seriously, can you? The point is, Daniel, we need to be able to talk about it.' Talk about it without bloody patronising me and without bringing sex into it every other minute.

He was still smiling. 'Talking makes me hungry. I don't suppose there's a chance of a bite to eat?'

'Oh, for crying out loud,' said Kate.

12

1928

Then it's Monday and I'm walking down London Road to my first day at work. Dadser was right. Mum did relent in time to come with me to sign the indenture, although she left it to the last minute on Friday. On the way there she said, 'You know I don't want to hold you back, don't you.' As usual with Mum, it wasn't a question or an apology either. She added, 'You won't be able to keep much back for pocket money.' As if I didn't know. Her eyebrows shot up when she saw my name on the papers, but she didn't say anything. When I'd first met Mr Cooper and he asked me my name I suddenly couldn't bear to say Marjorie, so I said Dorothea. He misheard it of course, so I was down as Dorothy. My professional name.

So here I am with my good shoes and my dinnertime sandwich in a shopping bag. It's only about half a mile but it starts to drizzle. I know what will happen to my hair. There is nothing I can do. I can feel the creeping on my scalp as the mass of it, carefully flattened under Mum's silk scarf since I woke up, separates and wriggles into a mad frizz. Mum made me a special "bandeau" – that's what Lucy called it – to keep it under control. But I can feel it escaping in all directions. That was one thing about working at the bakery. We all had to put our hair in cloths tied up like puddings, so that was taken care of.

What with the shopping bag, the hair and the old flat shoes I don't feel as elegant as I'd hoped, embarking on this career in high fashion. I'm pleased with the suit, though. It's Edna's. Nora made it for her to wear to her friend's wedding and it's shorter on me so it looks better. Edna doesn't actually know I've borrowed it, but she won't mind and I don't think Mum noticed. They didn't seem to think I should wear a suit, but I want to make a good first impression. It's navy-blue and I spent all yesterday trying on blouses to wear underneath. In the end I decided on plain white.

I go in through the courtyard and past the dustbins to the back entrance. There's a long-nosed shiny car parked there with a silver 'B' on the end of the bonnet. I go up close so I can peer in at the leather seats and the silk tassels hanging at the windows. One day I will have a car like that.

'Well, child!' comes a sharp voice. I turn to face Miss Wilmott standing at the entrance. 'Are you coming to work or to loiter?'

'To work,' I stammer.

'You leave Mr Cooper's car well alone.'

What does she think I might do? I bite my tongue and give her a look, then scurry past her, hang my coat on one of the hooks in the corridor and get the shoes out. I hear her tutting as I try to push my feet into them without bending the backs.

She looks me up and down. 'So the new apprentice arrives in a suit.'

I feel the heat creep up my neck as I take in what Miss Wilmott is wearing: a navy suit and a white blouse. Somewhere inside me there is a secret smile. I'm just the apprentice. She thinks I'm a child. Just you wait, Miss Wilmott. Just you wait.

She looks at my hair and shakes her head. 'You should get yourself an umbrella. Now get up to the cutting room.'

There's a lot of giggling and exchange of glances when I walk in. At least I know why. All the other girls are wearing grey flannel skirts, pleated or gored with white or pastel blouses and an assortment of hand-knitted cardigans. A girl with mousey hair done in finger waves tells me to sit next to her. 'I'm the improver and I'm to show you what to do. My name's Gwen.' She holds out her hand. She has quiet blue eyes and freckles. I like her immediately.

The first weeks and months at *Milady's* are disappointing. I'm not allowed to do the things I know I will be good at. For instance, in the first few weeks I only get to make tea, wash up and sweep the floor. I ask you. I mean, I know that's the role of the apprentice. But can't they see when they're wasting talent? Don't they ever make an exception?

Next I graduate to tidying the shelves and cupboards where the fabrics are stored – all under the watchful eye of Miss Wilmott. Months pass before I'm set to binding wires for the hat frames. It must be the most boring job in all the world, but at least what I'm doing will become part of a hat.

In between times there is always work to be done in the trimming room. The girls are supposed to drop snippets that are too small to be useful onto the floor and keep the bigger pieces on the long table where they all work. But they often leave the tiny shreds on the table and a larger piece may snag on a sleeve and get swept onto the floor by mistake. They don't like it when I draw it to their attention. It's my job to keep the table clear and the floor swept, and all hell's let loose if I get it wrong and throw away a shape someone has been keeping for a trim.

Gwen takes me to watch the process of moulding the felt in the steam room. That's a horror because you can imagine what it does to my hair. But luckily I'm not the only one with a problem. I see several of the girls wear hairnets and scarves to preserve their hairstyles. It's amazing to see what can happen to a flat circle of felt when the steam is applied. You put the hood – that's what the raw felt is called – on the steaming block and, as it gets damp, you shape it by going back and forth, back and forth with this loop of thick, spiralled wire. I'm mesmerised. From watching Gladys, who's the firm's expert, I can see there's a real knack to it, and I can't wait to get my hands on a steamer. Gwen assures me it will be months, if not years, before I do.

One afternoon when all the girls have left and I'm doing my final sweep-up, Miss Wilmott comes in. When she starts talking she looks blotchy round the neck so I know she's nervous.

'Dorothy, I'm saying this for your own good. I know you are impatient, and indeed, it's good you are keen.' She clears her throat. 'But the longer you go round with your nose in the air, the longer you will be sweeping floors. You should feel lucky to have the job. Believe me, Dorothy, there are those who don't think you should be here at all.'

Oh, I believe her all right. I walk home fighting back tears. Nose in the air indeed! She's as bad as those girls round the trimming table. They whisper things when I'm in there. Things like 'Needs taking down a peg or two,' or 'Pity she never takes a bath,' or 'Better not let her touch the white silk.' They think I don't hear. I've heard it all before anyway.

When I get home Dadser's in his chair by the fire, trembling. One of his bad turns. I put more coal on, fill him a hot water bottle and make tea. The shaking starts to subside.

'What's up with my girl, then?'

I tell him everything, even the conversation I overheard when I was in the lavvy last week. One of the girls asking Gwen to go to lunch with her, telling her she didn't have to be friends with 'that darkie, that Dorothy'. I start to ask him why I look different, but it seems to make his shuddering worse, so I change the subject back to Miss Wilmott.

Dadser smiles his secret smile and starts on a story about his old sergeant major. How he'd shout and call Dadser 'an 'orrible li'le toad' and 'scum of the earth' and much worse things he couldn't tell me. I wonder if it's the fever talking, for all I can see it has to do with me and Miss Wilmott.

Then he says, 'They have to grind you down, little one. To make sure you can take it. Something you've got to accept. And the sooner you do, then the sooner they'll let you rise up again. Think of Miss Wilmott as the Sergeant Major.'

I giggle at that thought and he pats me on the knee. 'You talk to that Gwen about it. She sounds a sensible sort. Now leave me be. Tea's helped a treat. I'll get a bit of shut-eye before your mother gets back.'

When it's nice, Gwen and I take our sandwiches to Alexandra Park. We cut through to Gladys Avenue, only a ten-minute walk. Then there's ten minutes to sit on a bench under the chestnut tree before we have to go back. Miss Wilmott and the senior staff get an hour, but not us. It's worth it, though. We kick off our shoes to feel the cool grass. Bloater paste or bread and cheese taste so much better with a breeze round your legs and the seaweedy smell coming off the harbour.

It's the day after Miss Wilmott spoke to me and I've brought a tomato for Gwen. Dadser's done well with them this year and it's one of the first crop, small and sweet. 'Gwen, you know you don't have to be my friend?'

She stops with the green tomato top pinched between her fingers halfway to her nose. 'What's that all about? Has that daft girl Annie been on at you?'

'I overheard. What she said to you, you know, the other day.'

Gwen sniffs at the tomato top. 'It's almost the best bit.' She holds out the tomato. 'This i'nt a bribe is it?' Seeing my face, she adds, 'Only joking. You know what? I'm always surprised you want to be my friend. I'm just ordinary, not an exciting person at all. And you, well you're different.' Again she sees my face. 'No, no. Not in that way. You're like… Well, if we was cakes, I'd be a currant bun, and without that many currants either, and you'd be a Battenberg!'

It doesn't seem the moment to tell Gwen I don't like Battenberg cake because she's really proud of her comparison. And anyway I'm too busy being pleased with what's she's just said. Nobody's ever told me anything like it before. I don't know what to say. Then I think of the Saturday treat Auntie Rose used to buy for me and Lucy.

'Well, Gwen Cook, I think you're more like a Whipped Cream Walnut than a boring old currant bun.'

Gwen blushes through all her freckles. We bend over laughing and I feel warm inside and like we'll be friends forever.

For two days I've noticed Billy Chapman hanging about on the corner of Gladys Avenue on my way home from work.

He's good-looking in a flash kind of way. I've seen him on the corner on Saturday nights combing his hair and fooling about with a group of other lads. He obviously thinks he's the cat's pyjamas. Me and Gwen don't mix with those sort of boys. Her older brother Danny and his best mate took us both to the pictures once. We sat in the back row but neither of them tried anything. Danny held my hand on the way home but you could tell it was only because he thought it was expected. A boy from the next road kissed me after Harvest Supper at the church hall last year. He was very polite, and it was exciting when he put his arm round me, but Edna saw and took me home. She said

I was far too young, but I'm sixteen now and Mum says I've lost my puppy fat, which is her way of saying I don't look too bad. I think it's time I had a boyfriend, but Gwen's not that interested.

And I'm certainly not interested in Billy Chapman. Seeing him there on the corner is almost enough to make me want to go the long way round, but it's too wet. He catches up with me as I cross the road and make for home.

He's twitching and jerking all over the place. Then he says he wants to ask me something. He's got a friend wants to go out with me. Thinks I might bring a friend and we'd make a foursome at the pictures on Saturday. I feel like I've been punched. It's bad enough having him walk beside me giving me sly looks. It feels just like the playground all over again, like he's got me up against the brick wall by that smelly drain.

'Why would your friend want to do that, when he doesn't know me or anything?'

'Bin watchin' you, 'e 'as.'

I burn inside. 'Why?' is all I can think to say.

'Thinks yer 'ot. Y'know. Your sort.' He leers.

In a beat of my thumping heart I know what he's talking about. And I know I've got him. I don't know how. But that'll come later.

'Yeah,' I say, trying to sound casual, off-hand. 'I'll ask my friend. It's the new Buster Keaton, i'n't it? Yeah, we might want to see that.'

He gives a nasty bark of a laugh. 'Won't see much of that. 'Alf six, outside, then?' And he peels off.

So here we are, Gwen and me, waiting outside the Palace in Commercial Road. Gwen didn't know Billy at school as her family only moved here about a year ago for the work in the dockyard. But she knows the Chapman family all right. Everybody round here does. Mr Chapman's a drinker, an ox of a man with a wide leather belt holding in his beer belly, and fists that don't need boxing gloves. Elsie Chapman's always having to say she's walked into a door. You'd think she was blind as a bat. And he's always beaten his boys. Except now Billy's big enough to hit back.

As soon as I told Gwen about Billy, all the bullying at school, and how I planned to get my own back on him, she knew what to do.

Having brothers, she's got much more clue than me. I always thought they were loud, messy creatures but now I see the advantage. There's a lot of gossip and giggling goes on at work about men and how to handle them, but half the time I don't understand what they're on about and I won't ask and look a fool.

Gwen offered to do the business for me – after all she's getting Billy for a date, seems like, but I wouldn't have it. This is my chance to get even and I want to relish it. I did get a bit worried Billy would tell his mates or his Dad and set them on me. Gwen thought I was joking. She said no lad would ever tell a soul he'd been caught out by a girl. We've practised the technique in Gwen's bedroom and nearly wet ourselves laughing. We're not laughing now though and I'm really nervous, shaking in fact.

Then Billy makes it easy for us. He turns up on his own. Afterwards Gwen said she wasn't surprised. She reckoned there never was a friend. It was Billy all the time. Which makes the whole thing all the more satisfying.

'Friend couldn't make it,' says Billy. 'Di'n't want to let yer down.' He leers at me, ignoring Gwen.

We join the queue and I let Billy put his arm round my waist, lean into him. After a bit I can see he's getting steamed up. His trousers are bulging.

'Hey, Billy, it's an age before the doors open. What d'you say we go round the corner?'

His eyes pop.

'You'll keep our place in the queue, won't you Gwen?'

We turn up the side road beside the cinema and he pulls me into the first shop doorway.

'You darkies. I knew you was 'ot.' He's practically slavering.

He stinks of Brylcreem and Woodbines with an underlying acrid reek that frightens me. I think of Danny Cook's ferrets, but it's male body I'm breathing in, up close for the first time. He smells of brute strength and I'm terrified. This isn't Billy, the boy bully, and this is no playground game. I think of calling out for Gwen, but Billy would have his hand over my mouth as soon as I opened it. And what would little Gwen be able to do anyway? I've got to play my part for real. If I get it wrong, I've had it.

I let him get his hands inside my blouse and bend and wriggle as if I'm enjoying it, getting myself in a good position. I want to slap his pimply face, but it's all I can do to stay upright. My knees are like dead balloons and I think my heart's going to stop me breathing. Then a thick finger reaches my bust bodice. He's fumbling with the top button. I'm scared he'll pull it off and rip the fabric. Then what will Mum say? A nail scratches my skin and gives me the rush of fury I need. I put one hand on the wall to steady myself and carry on running my fingers through his horrible hair with the other, like it says in the ad. Then I bring up one knee sharply into his crotch. As I feel it connect he gives out a yowl like a tomcat and doubles over. I feel like throwing up all over him but I clutch my coat together and run back round the corner.

Gwen hugs me and spins me round in a victory dance, but my heart's not in it. We'd planned to go ahead and see the film but I can't face it. I just want to have a good wash and curl up in bed. I can see Gwen's disappointed, but she comes back on the tram with me just the same.

I can't get to sleep for ages. I lie there listening to Binnie breathing like a flower and feel as if I've visited another planet and left part of me behind. If Billy'd sprouted antlers it wouldn't have been more shocking. It isn't until Sunday morning that I wake up and feel a little glow of triumph bursting inside me and spreading. I've got even with Billy Chapman.

There's only a small amount of dress-making done at *Milady's*. A wedding dress for a special customer maybe, or an ensemble with matching hat for the bride's mother. Veils of course we do all the time. But I'm still not allowed anywhere near the delicate and expensive materials. I've been at *Milady's* nearly two years before I'm allowed to lay out the pattern for an underskirt. 'No cutting, mind, not until I've checked it.' There's not much scope for showing my skill but I can tell Miss Wilmott's impressed that I've laid the thin tissue absolutely straight and wasted the minimum of fabric.

'I can tell you've done that before.' She smiles at me for the first time. She really isn't too bad when you get to know her. Dadser was right. All that fierceness at the beginning was to let me know my

99

place. Gwen says she's always like that when people start. She lost her young man in the war, Gwen says. It's hard to imagine her with a sweetheart, she must be at least thirty. I'm glad I'm not old.

She lets me cut out the underskirt and after that I often get cutting jobs, progressing from underskirts and linings to the full dress and eventually to garments cut on the bias. Of course what I really want to do is to get started on the hats. Gwen says nobody gets to do that until the third year, not unless they've had experience somewhere else.

Then one day I have a lucky break. It doesn't feel like a lucky day when I get to work. Several of the girls are down with a sickness bug and so is Miss Pritchard, who can't exactly be called a girl any more. Miss Wilmott is in a terrible mood as there's a big wedding at the weekend, several other orders to get out and Mr Cooper pacing up and down the corridor.

She escapes into the cupboard where I'm working with Gwen and asks me to fetch her a glass of water.

'I can't think straight with him marching about all over the place.' She mops at her blotchy face and we make her sit down. We both know the signs. She's about to have one of her migraines.

She sips at the water and looks at Gwen. 'Gwen, you can work in Miss Pritchard's place. But I can't possibly go to Mrs Atkins feeling like I do. Oh dear, oh my.' She puts her head in her hands.

Gwen comes to the rescue. 'Here, I've got some aspirin. And why don't you send Dorothy to Mrs Atkins?'

Miss Wilmott won't look at me. 'Really, I don't think so. Oh, thank you, dear.' Then as she moves her head to take the pills she winces. 'Well, maybe. Do you think she could?'

Gwen nods. 'You know the way to Southsea, don't you Dorothy?' As if that's the only issue.

But it works. Dear, dear Gwen. An opportunity. It gets me out of the dreadful atmosphere at work and I have a chance to make my mark with a client. Whatever I do, I must not mess this up. I thank my lucky star it inspired me to put on a clean blouse and wear my best shoes to work today.

Mrs Atkins is a well-established client. She isn't a Lady and she's well-to-do rather than wealthy, but she's a Regular, which means she can be relied upon to order Spring, Summer and Winter hats. I've seen her when she's come into the shop to look at fabrics and to inspect the new designs. I've never spoken to her but I've fetched and carried bolts of silk for her to look at and she's always pleasant and chatty with everyone and says thank you. So there is absolutely no good reason for the nervousness I'm feeling.

13

Vanessa felt a shiver travel up her arms and across her shoulders as she looked at her find. A shiver of recognition she didn't understand. The child in the photograph was dressed in white, which emphasised her complexion. Dark hair sprung out round a plump face, the curls tight and dense, not the sort contrived with curl papers or tongs. Her eyes were luminous, dark as dates and their expression was not child-like. They threw out a challenge; they were proud, scornful. They said, I may be physically sitting here in this vulgar dress, but my spirit does not submit. You may tease me and call me names and try to bring me down to your level but you will never succeed. I may be only four years old but I know things you will never know. You have no idea.

It was the same look Vanessa had seen Thea fling at her carers when they came to take her from her fireside chair to prepare her for bed. This time the look said, I may be ninety-three and I may be losing my mind, but you will not patronise me. You may be kind, but you are just ordinary women. You may think I am old and stupid, and I may humour your jokes and sing along, but there are things you will never get out of me. Secrets I have held all my life. You really have no idea.

Apart from that stare, the child was a shock, a stranger. Vanessa hugged herself in spite of the heavy heat of the room and looked across at Lisa sitting cross-legged beside her Nan's writing desk. With her pale blonde hair scooped back into a scrunchie, her daughter looked more like fourteen than twenty-four years old.

The desk was deceptively elegant. Normally the roll top and

curved drawers were kept closed, giving the appearance of a silky smooth, tidy life. It suggested that a lady might draw up a chair and pen a letter on a single sheet of headed notepaper. She would not go so far as to dip a quill into the silver inkstand, nor would she use sealing wax. But these rituals would be hinted at as she selected an envelope from one neat pigeonhole and a stamp from another.

This illusion of order vanished as soon as the desk was opened. Each available cranny was stuffed with opened letters still in their envelopes, photographs, old birthday cards, used paper napkins, theatre programmes, newspaper cuttings and adverts for patent remedies. Every drawer was crammed with larger items – bundles of fabric, half-filled photograph albums, balls of string, lengths of tangled wool, garments that had never been mended and old teddy bears. Biscuit crumbs silted the corners of the drawers and clusters of boiled sweets oozing from their wrappers trapped questing fingers.

Lisa looked up from the pile she was sifting through. 'What are you looking at, Ma?'

Vanessa shrugged. 'Oh, just some old photos.' She shuffled the disturbing photograph to the back of the wallet. She knew she was resisting the message it was giving her. She didn't want to show Lisa. Not yet. Lisa would take over. Vanessa sensed a need for caution, though whom she was protecting she wasn't sure.

Lisa's voice homed in from across the room. 'Hey, this is the last drawer and I still haven't found it. Where do we look next?'

Vanessa gestured towards the chest of drawers on the opposite side of the room.

Part of her attention was monitoring the breaths that rasped at uneven intervals from the room next door. She inhaled guilt with the smell of dusty carpets, beige stockings and the web of brown net that covered her mother's unwashed hair. Soon she would be free of facing the dead geraniums in dried-out pots in the conservatory. Soon she would no longer come down to the sad smell of burnt toast and the soot scraped into the sink, nor would she have to listen to the clack of loose dentures at breakfast. Soon she wouldn't have to avert her eye from the flare of her mother's pleated skirt on the back of the door where it had hung for weeks since she last wore it. Soon she wouldn't have to sit beside the churn of the incongruous water-bed provided by the NHS, or focus on the blue and white cow on the window sill in order to stay in the room.

For her mother was dying and the doctor, eager to focus on practicalities, had prompted this search for the birth certificate. He said it would be helpful when registering the death. As if you had to prove a person was born before they could come full circle into death.

Her father would be shocked and bereft in spite of being relieved of his burden of care. It would be a wrench to leave the place. They should have left it years ago and made a new life together. Dad knew that. Mead End was a mongrel house. It sprawled between wide lawns, a once productive orchard and a farmyard of dilapidated barns. The tone was set by lofty Edwardian reception rooms which gave way to the cosier scale of the original Georgian farmhouse, while at the back, a maze of sculleries converted more than thirty years ago served as a kitchen which was neither attractive nor convenient. Downright ugly and awkward, thought Vanessa.

Once it had been a retreat deep in the Hampshire countryside, and at weekends the lane was still a favourite route for horse-riders and the odd pony and trap. But on weekdays it turned into a rat run for commuters heading for the urban sprawl of Portsmouth and its commercial satellites. Her father was deaf so the traffic didn't worry him, but Vanessa feared for his safety on that road. Lately however, Ted hadn't ventured beyond the drive. He didn't dare leave Thea alone for that long.

Vanessa found the photograph doubly disorientating. It was bad enough that for years now Thea had not been the mother she had known. Ever since the dementia set in, her personality had been skewed. The onset so gradual, so insidious that it was easy to mistake it for a worsening of Thea's faults. By the time the disease was diagnosed, it was too late. Vanessa had already taken this new experience of her mother and woven it together with all the negative episodes of the years: the manipulation and lies; the clash of values; the criticism and coldness. She'd made it into a picture of a mother she disliked.

It felt both daring and indecent to be searching through her mother's possessions while she was still in transition, still hanging on to life. Vanessa half expected her to loom in the doorway, to tear into them for poking about in her things. She was said to be unconscious.

But how did anyone know? What did that mean? Her eyes were closed and she gave no flicker of response to words or touch. But how could anyone know what she was aware of and at what level?

Vanessa made an effort of will. 'Tea?' She didn't want Lisa to notice her dreaming. 'I'll make Dad tea.' She slipped the wallet of photographs down the side of the sofa and wondered why she was being so furtive.

'Coffee for me.'

Vanessa left Lisa still sifting papers, systematic, thorough.

In the kitchen she stood by the kettle cradling the old silver teapot and rubbing the dent in its side which perfectly fitted her thumb. Now she was faced with yet another version of Mother which didn't seem to connect to any previous version. And alongside that came Kate's voice in her head, insisting that Thea was the key to Flora's origins.

She could hardly go on kidding herself now. The child in that photograph looked exactly as Flora would in a couple of years. Over the last eighteen months the issue of Flora's identity had fallen into the background. All the family were so used to her that they no longer noticed her difference. And after the fiasco of that visit to see Thea, Kate had eventually gone quiet on the subject. Vanessa had allowed herself to forget the whole thing, and she'd had more than enough to occupy her recently, helping Dad to cope with Mother's illness.

Vanessa stood, still cradling the teapot, transfixed by the dawning realisation.

Of course she must show the photograph to Lisa and tell Kate about it. She knew that. But she needed time to take in the reality slowly breaking on her consciousness. Time to face Kate.

'Are we having a cuppa, or not?' Lisa was there, switching the kettle back on and taking the teapot from her. 'What's going on, Ma? You've been out here ages. You all right?'

'It's all getting to me. This place,' she gestured to the peeling wallpaper and the cracked wall tiles round the sink. 'All the rubbish they've accumulated. The thought of clearing it all.' All of which was true.

'It's a treasure trove, an archive. If I was an historian, I'd be having orgasms.' Lisa poured water on to teabags and got out the cafetiere.

'Well, you can come and help clear it out if you're so keen. Still no sign of that envelope I suppose?'

Lisa shook her head and took Ted his mug of tea. She came back making a face. 'He won't leave her. She looks just awful. Poor old Gramps.'

Yes, poor Ted indeed. Vanessa thought her father deserved a medal for hanging in there with Thea. Coping with her moods and violence, keeping her out of care. Keeping them together. Fulfilling a promise that she would die at home. However shabby it was now, Thea loved the home she had created. Ted respected that. It was everything to her. Vanessa found it almost shocking to see them together. No matter what she threw at him, sometimes literally, Ted treated her gently, tenderly. The only explanation was that he loved her. Still. In spite of everything. It was humbling.

'It can't be long now, she hasn't eaten for days. She just won't let go.'

'Wasn't there some odd story about Nan being born? Something about her being left for dead?'

'Yes. Yes there was. The midwife beat her with a tea towel to bring her to life. So she always said. Why?'

'I was just thinking, reluctant to come in to the world and reluctant to leave.'

14

1930

It's a crisp spring day, the air sharp as acid drops when I step down from the tram. I can feel the conductor's eyes on me. I feel like thumbing my nose at the man and catch my eyes flickering sideways. That's Marge, always on the look-out for places to run to, like I was in the playground still. I tell myself he's looking at me because I look smart and I ought to be pleased. I tighten my grip on the hatbox and place my high heels carefully. I'm Dorothy now. I'm a working girl.

Blossom is beginning to show pink in some of the trees lining the road. It makes you want to walk down it. Not like our street. The trees are what make this road 'residential'. I used to think that was a silly word. Now I understand. This is where people reside, in grace and elegance. In our street they just live, eking out a mean existence. One day I'll reside in a street with trees.

Clifton Villa is the third on the left, as Miss Wilmott said, easily identifiable by the monkey-puzzle tree in the front garden. The house seems very grand. Only a short drive but with two gateways, an 'In' and an 'Out' with a row of evergreen bushes in between. There are three steps up to a pillared porch and a front door with a gleaming brass knocker and letterbox. As I tread on the first step I notice the door at the side of the house that says 'Tradesmen's Entrance' and have a moment of misgiving. But no, Miss Wilmott clearly said to go to the front door. I set down the hatbox and ring the bell, hearing it sound into the depths of the house. I smooth my gloves, check the angle of my own hat and pick up the box, ready to look down my nose at whatever snooty servant may appear. But it's a young maid who opens the door, looking as flustered as I feel.

I'm shown into the morning room and sit by the window on the edge of an upright chair. It's cold in the room but outside the sun's falling on a bank of daffodils. They're not fluttering and dancing, as there's no breeze. Only an occasional current of air nods their yellow heads. Lemon Yellow, and a touch of Cadmium mixed with Chinese White for the pheasant eye narcissi, that's what I'd use. A haze of green is beginning to colour the hedge at the bottom of the garden and the grass has already been cut into broad stripes like the shantung silk Lady Brickwood's just ordered for Ascot. Then Mrs Atkins appears on a path at the side of the lawn. She's almost running, clutching at her beads and a scarf that tries to float away. Not very dignified. A woolly white dog scampers after her. It's a bit like the one on Dadser's whisky bottle, a Highland terrier maybe. I only hope it won't run in and jump up and make ladders in my stockings.

I hear a door slam at the back of the house and voices. Then Mrs Atkins appears, smoothing her hair into place.

'I'm so sorry to be late. Good morning, Miss erm..?'

'Dorothy.' The heaviness of that name. It's better than Marjorie but it's not right, especially not in this house.

'Good morning Dorothy. I forgot the time. Whisky, that's my little Westie, he ran off into the shrubbery and started digging and I had such a job to get him out of there.'

'I brought the hats, Madam. Mr Cooper sends his apologies, but Miss Pritchard is unwell.'

'Of course! Oh dear, my hair's been dragged through a hedge backwards.' She looks in the mirror over the fireplace and laughs. 'Well, a rhododendron actually. Goodness, it's freezing in here. Why don't you come up to the bedroom? Then I can do my hair and we can try the hats against my costumes.'

I follow Mrs Atkins across the hall, click-clicking on the quarry tiles. Mrs Atkins is wearing soft pumps that make no sound. As we start up the stairs a door opens on the left.

'Lily, my dear, where are you going?' The voice is gentle but with a dark edge like bitter chocolate.

I look round and see a man hardly taller than me with smooth features and a head as sleek as an otter. Mrs Atkins is explaining about the hats.

'My dear, I think it more appropriate for you to use the morning room. Send Rosie to fetch your dresses.'

'But it's so chilly in there. The sun will be in our bedroom.'

'Then have Rosie light the fire.'

Mrs Atkins shrugs and sighs, and the voice is about to withdraw behind the door again when his gaze shifts from his wife to me and our eyes lock. I step back and steady myself on the banister. It's almost as if I'd been hit. Mr Atkins bows his head, a little movement like an obeisance, a gesture somewhere between homage and impatience, a need to break away. Only seconds pass before he's gone and I'm following Mrs Atkins once again, back into the morning room.

I hardly notice Rosie coming and going, bringing coats and dresses, coaxing the fire into a blaze. The look Mr Atkins gave me was shocking. Did I imagine it? If so, then why am I shaking? Mrs Atkins seems to have missed the whole thing, thank goodness. She said something about Mr Atkins liking to observe the conventions. Not quite the impression I got. I busy myself opening the hatbox, taking the hats out of their tissue paper, putting my pincushion ready on the table.

Mrs Atkins likes the first hat as it is. The dove grey felt matches her dress and coat exactly and the soft lilac ribbon used to trim it lightens the whole outfit and brings out her grey eyes. Her eyes and a clear skin are her best features. But the summer straw, a wide-brimmed affair in an adventurous shade of green is not a success. I mean, whatever was she thinking of?

'It was supposed to look spring-like.' Mrs Atkins tips it this way and that in the mirror. 'I was so fed up with all the winter drabness when I chose it. Now I'm not so sure.'

I chew my lip in order to keep quiet. It's the lemon trim that's spoiling the effect. It reminds me of a school hat. It might just suit someone half Mrs Atkins' age with dark colouring. But not me. I wouldn't be seen dead in it.

'I was thinking daffodils.' Mrs Atkins turns to me. 'What do you think, Dorothy?'

It looks terrible. That's what I think. Mrs Atkins is no beauty.

She's got energy and charm but no sophistication. She isn't naturally elegant and doesn't have the height to carry off a hat like that. Somehow it emphasises her rather large nose.

I can't say any of those things. I turn away in case my thoughts are showing on my face and look out the window for inspiration. There's the lawn. I remember Lady Brickwood's shantung and in an instant I can see how a swathe of it would transform that hat into something sophisticated and original.

'You can be brutally honest, Dorothy. It doesn't suit me does it?'

'I think it's the trim, Madam.'

Mrs Atkins takes off her scarf and drapes it round the crown. The scarf is brown with a red line running through it. Without thinking, I shake my head fiercely.

'No? No, you're right. What should it be?'

'I'm only the apprentice, Madam, but...'

'Go on.'

'Well, Madam, I know what you mean about the daffodils. They're so fresh and light. But if you're putting the straw with the cream coat, then you have the lightness already. Look at the lawn. See the stripes? If you trimmed it with a darker green... I just think that would suit your skin tones better.'

It all comes out in a rush and I'm horrified that Mrs Atkins' response is to ring the bell. She must be summoning the maid to show me out.

'Rosie, fetch my green silk scarf, will you?' She turns to me. 'I can't quite picture it. Clive's always saying I lack imagination.'

When the scarf arrives Mrs Atkins flings it over the brim as if she's bored with the whole business. It hangs down looking ridiculous. I step forward. I'm not going to let the silly woman sabotage my idea. 'May I?'

Mrs Atkins hands over the hat and scarf and sinks into an armchair. 'I hate all this. I'm not built to be elegant.'

I'm glad my mouth is full of pins so I can't reply. The scarf isn't quite the right colour but it's an improvement. I wonder if I'll be able to get my hands on a few cuttings from Lady Brickwood's dress. When I've finished the pale lemon is quite hidden behind a broad band of dark green with a suggestion of a bow or a flower ruched up at one side. I place it on Mrs Atkins head and invite her to look in the mirror.

'Dorothy, that's amazing! It's like a different hat!' She slips on the ivory coat and surveys herself again. 'It's just the effect I was after. You really do have an eye, don't you?'

I know I've got an eye. I've always known. But Mrs Atkins is the first person to recognise it. It's intoxicating to be standing in this elegant little room with the warmth of the fire on my legs and Mrs Atkins' eyes shining with excitement at the hat that I, Dorothy, have just created.

'Thank you Madam.'

'We're going to get along so well, Dorothy. You'll have to design all my hats in future! And do stop calling me Madam. Call me Mrs Atkins, at least.'

I can't help smiling. 'I'll have to take it back to Miss Wilmott, Madam...'

'Mrs Atkins.'

'Mrs Atkins, and Miss Pritchard will re-trim it. Like I said, I'm only the apprentice.' I'm already worried about how I'll approach Miss Wilmott.

'You'd better leave it just like that then, so the Pritchard woman understands what to do. I've never been that impressed with her. And tell her what you said about the green needing to be a little deeper.'

'Yes, Ma – Mrs Atkins. You won't be needing the scarf then?' My opinion of her goes up when she says that about Miss Pritchard. She's been at *Milady's* forever. She's really old-fashioned and she's got a scrawny turkey neck that gets all red when she's flustered, which is most of the time.

'Never mind the scarf. You can bring it back with the hat.'

'I doubt it will be me bringing it next time. Like I said, it was only because Miss Pritchard is off sick.'

'Well, you must have some coffee and biscuits before you go.'

'Oh no, Mrs Atkins. I'm afraid I'm expected back. It's very kind, but I must be off.' I almost giggle to think of what Miss Wilmott would say if she got to hear I stayed to have coffee and biscuits.

On the tram back to North End I imagine what it must be like to be Mrs Lily Atkins and to live in such a grand house with Mr Atkins and his conventions.

*

Miss Wilmott is not impressed when I tell her about the visit. I've taken a liberty to use Mrs Atkins' scarf in that way. And what did I think I was doing, presuming to create a trim? That's for Miss Pritchard to design. As to trying to dictate the colour, it all depends on what is in the stockroom. The mention of Lady Brickwood's cuttings threatens to give Miss Wilmott a turn. What can I be thinking of?

'Dorothy, you seem to forget you are the apprentice. That's the last time I send you on an errand. Now, get that floor swept and make Mr Cooper his morning coffee.'

I haven't swept a floor since my first year, so I think of the blossom trees and the daffodils to stop myself from crying.

When Gwen raises inquiring eyebrows I shake my head and set about trying to forget the whole incident. I can just hear Mum saying, see what happens when you try to get above yourself.

So when I'm summoned to Mr Cooper's office a few days later I'm not expecting to find Mrs Atkins there.

'Dorothy, Mrs Atkins asked that I send for you. It is not my habit to involve apprentices with the clientèle, but she has been most insistent.'

From what I can gather Miss Pritchard re-trimmed the hat and delivered it when Mrs Atkins was out. On her return she unpacked the hat and tried it on, but was far from pleased with the result.

'Mr Cooper, Dorothy here did such a clever thing. She only did it with pins but she transformed that hat before my very eyes.' Mrs Atkins waves the silk scarf I used to make the trim. 'I insisted she brought it back here just as it was so that Miss Pritchard would understand. And what happens?' She picks the hat out of the box beside her and holds it up dramatically. 'This!'

My hand flies to my mouth. I can't help it, and Mrs Atkins notices and purses her lips.

Miss Pritchard has used pea-green velvet. Goodness knows where she found it. And on the brim she has pinned a ready-made flower of green silk, which looks just like a cabbage.

Mr Cooper frowns as he looks from the hat to me and down to the floor. I've never seen him when he wasn't in control of the situation.

'I do apologise, Mrs Atkins. As I said earlier, you can convey

112

your wishes to Miss Pritchard yourself. I will send for her. There is really no need to involve young Dorothy here. She really did step out of line somewhat...'

'Rubbish. She did a very good job. I have no idea what to tell your Miss Pritchard. But I know Dorothy knows what to do. I want her to do it.'

Mr Cooper paces to the window and back. 'Madam, that really would be most irregular.'

Mrs Atkins waves the hat in his face. 'You cannot tell me you are happy that a hat like this came out of your workshop?'

She pauses for effect and Mr Cooper hooks his thumbs into his waistcoat pockets and rocks back on his heels. I can't believe what I'm seeing.

'I'm afraid, Mr Cooper, that unless Dorothy trims my hat and gets it to me by the weekend, I will be withdrawing my custom.' Mrs Atkins gathers her bag and gloves and sweeps out of the room, winking at me as she passes. I feel so embarrassed and confused and I hope Mr Cooper didn't see the wink.

There's a silence in the room. Mr Cooper paces back to the window, takes out his pocket watch, fingers the chain and replaces it. I feel really sorry for him.

'Dorothy, we have a difficult situation here.' He is still facing the window. 'I wonder what you are really made of.'

I'm shaking. 'I'm sorry, sir.'

'Dorothy.' Mr Cooper turns to face me. 'None of this is your fault. At least I don't think it is. I think you were doing your best. Am I right?'

I nod. Whatever I do I must not cry.

Mr Cooper swings back to the window. 'Who do you think should trim Mrs Atkins' hat?'

I know whatever I say next will define my future, just as I knew what to do with the hat in the morning room at Clifton Villa. I think carefully. I want to trim that hat more than anything else in the world, but I'm afraid it's a trap. Miss Pritchard will be upset and angry if the job is taken from her. On the other hand, Mrs Atkins will move her account if Miss Pritchard does it. I take a deep breath. 'I think I should do it, Mr Cooper.'

'And why do you think that?'

'Because it's more important not to upset Mrs Atkins than Miss Pritchard.'

Mr Cooper smiles for the first time. 'Right...'

Why can't I stop myself there? 'And because I will do it better.'

'Hah! You've got a nerve. Look, Dorothy, there is no doubt you have talent. Miss Wilmott showed me your effort with Mrs Atkins' hat after you came back the other day. But you have to learn to walk before you can run. And it's best not to make too many enemies. Trouble is, ambition tends to make you enemies. Have to live with that sometimes.' He's turned back to the window and seems to be talking to himself.

I wait, unsure of whether to say anything, afraid of ruining any chances I have.

Then he spins round, his mood changed. 'I'll tell you what I'll do. You can trim that hat, but in your own time. I've got to stay late tonight. I'll supervise you personally, which will be less awkward for Miss Wilmott. And I'll square it with her and with Miss Pritchard. But this is not to get around. It will not be known you did this. Is that clear?'

I nod. 'Yes, Mr Cooper.' I know exactly where to find cuttings of the green shantung because I cleared the cutting floor only a few hours ago.

'If you do a good job I will speak to Miss Wilmott in due course about progressing you a little faster. If, on the other hand, your work is not up to standard I will find another solution and the matter will be closed. Report to me here at six o'clock with all the necessary materials.'

15

2006

Vanessa lay awake, tense and chilled. The stiff blankets wouldn't keep out the draughts from the rattling windows. Mother and Dad hadn't done any house maintenance for years. But it wasn't just the cold keeping her awake. She felt like a coward, but there was more to it than that. The photograph was still in its hiding place in the sofa. It was calling to her. It was as if there was something going on between her and the child staring out. Something beyond the shock and the anger. Something very personal and intimate.

There was cowardice in there as well. No doubt about it. She was remembering the palpable tension between Kate and Daniel at that awful time when Flora was born. Kate nagging at her about Thea's origins, her own refusal to be drawn.

Sad that she and Kate had never been quite so close since then. She'd babysat for them often enough in the last few months but they hadn't had many days together. She'd been busy with her private students and there'd been constant trips to Mead End to support Ted with Thea. But apart from all that, there'd been an arm's length feel to the relationship. Kate was always saying 'I'm fine' when she didn't sound it, and there were a lot of silences and 'Oh, nothings' when they spoke on the phone.

Now that she was forced to think about it, she saw it was her fault. Kate must have felt let down, unable to explore that possibility with her. She winced when she thought of her reaction to the story of Kate's visit to Mead End with Flora. She'd wanted to believe that

Ted's version was the right one, that Kate had exaggerated. But since when was Kate one to embroider? She'd always been straightforward, transparent even. Unlike Lisa, Kate had never seemed capable of the diplomatic or strategic lie.

She longed to talk to David, to hear his reassuring voice. To hear her own thoughts, so she could know what they were and begin to straighten them out. But she couldn't ring him at three o'clock in the morning. David was a long-suffering husband, always there for her, ready to listen and give support, especially where Thea was concerned. But there were limits. She made do with refilling her hot water bottle from the bathroom tap, pressing her elbows against her sides to retain body warmth, one finger under the tap, listening to the creaking of pipes as the hot water crept towards her.

She remembered the night when Kate first brought Daniel home. A charmer with a flop of hair, mocking eyes and a bunch of anorexic roses. He'd puzzled her. His old-fashioned manners – be grateful he's got any, said David – didn't fit with his lifestyle, the filthy caravan. She'd heard about that from Lisa who'd been round there, and Lisa obviously hadn't taken to him. An unfinished English degree, as it turned out – he was always careful to say, I *read* English. No job. And not particularly interested in anything in spite of that carefully cultured drawl. Was he a fraud? Was he lazy? She'd wanted to provoke him and find out.

The best thing he'd ever done was scarper when he heard Kate was expecting the first time. If only he'd stayed away. Kate would have had less to manage as a single Mum. Kate was always so philosophical. Nothing seemed to ruffle her. The odd thing was that she was so entirely besotted with the man, thought Vanessa, screwing the top tightly into the water bottle. He must have something, she supposed. To give him his due he'd worked hard in estate agency. Mind you, it would come naturally to him, spinning a smooth line, gilding the property lily, conning prospective buyers into making an offer. But he'd turned into the family man, got them that lovely little terrace house with a good garden. Nice for the children to be by the sea, even if it was Southsea.

One way and another they'd weathered a lot those two. But how much had Kate really weathered it? Vanessa shook her head as she made her way back to the bedroom, avoiding the boards that creaked on the landing.

She tried not to look at the dead flies massed inside the secondary glazing, and stared into the dark garden. A half-moon shone through the branches of the copper beech onto waist-high weeds choking the herbaceous border below the window. Was she kidding herself that Kate was happy? Was she coping? She felt a wave of remorse that she wasn't able to answer the question. How could she have let such a distance grow between them? Once they'd been really close. That time in Cornwall, for instance.

It was Vanessa's half-term and she'd hired a cottage by the sea. Then David had to go to a conference and to Vanessa's surprise Kate had agreed to come in his place. All week they'd been like kids on an outing. And then on that last morning she'd broken the news.

Kate had snuggled up next to her and it was just like when Kate and Lisa were tiny and they came into bed when David got up to go to work. Then she'd given a great sigh, rolled off the bed and crossed to the window.

She was standing on one leg leaning out and rubbing one foot up and down her calf and Vanessa noticed the way Kate's nightie clung to the curve of her buttocks. It was so unlike the skinny little-girl bottom she used to rub dry and chase into bed what seemed like only last week. Womanly, she supposed it was. It had given her a pang. Kate was still too young to be womanly.

Kate broke into those foolish thoughts. 'I'm pregnant, Mum.'

Her little girl. That man. His baby. That dreadful caravan. Thoughts went tumbling.

Then Kate was sobbing and Vanessa was leaning in the window beside her, hugging her close.

Daniel had done a runner. Vanessa went hot with rage at that, but then felt her heart lift with relief. A little baby. A grandchild. Kate a mother. And Daniel off the scene. She'd get her Katie back.

Vanessa's heart hadn't lifted for long of course. The wretched Daniel was soon back and they'd had a nightmare after Jack was born, what with his affair. And then to have yet another drama the second time around... All things considered, Kate had had a pretty raw deal.

Vanessa looked up into the beech tree. 'It looks like Mother could have stopped all that,' she said out loud to the moon. 'She had it in her power. In fact, if she'd always been open about how she got to look like that little girl in the photo, there'd never have been any problem, no questions, no wondering.' She felt a surge of rage against Thea, and with it, a sense of guilty elation. There it was, a legitimate reason, a concrete justification for her angry and unforgiving feelings towards her mother.

Thea had been a demanding mother and she wasn't exactly a doting grandmother or great-grandmother either. She was never a family person, didn't enjoy having children around her. Too self-absorbed, Vanessa reflected, turning away from the window.

Ted was different, of course. He just revelled in being 'GG', showing Jack his naval sword. Letting him polish his medals for Remembrance Sunday last year.

Vanessa hugged her hottie, climbed back into bed among the pinging springs and fell asleep wondering how she could tell Kate of this latest development. Acknowledging her own part in it would be the hardest thing, admitting she'd been wrong, saying sorry.

She went downstairs early next morning. The radiators were ticking into warmth and low voices came from her mother's room where the night nurse was handing over to the carer.

She was surprised to find Lisa already busy with paper sorting. It gave her the final push she needed.

'I think we'd best abandon the search. We're obviously not going to find it.'

'But it's all got to be sorted, Ma. Rubbish chucked out. Less for you to do later.'

'You've done a great job. Just now I've got something to show you. But promise me first you won't rush me. I need time to know what needs to be done and when.'

'Oh God, am I that bad?' Lisa made a face. 'This sounds all very mysterious.'

'Promise?' Vanessa pulled the wallet from its hiding place.

'Promise.'

'I found this yesterday.' Vanessa laid the photo on the coffee table.

'Who is it?'

'It's on the back'

'Marge, March 1917,' Lisa read aloud. 'Marge?'

'Nan. She was Marge when she was little. All her family always called her that. She was Marjorie Doro*thea*, hence Thea. And she didn't like Marge. Who can blame her?'

Lisa was staring at the picture.

'Well?' Vanessa watched her daughter, waiting for the photograph to make its impact.

'You're saying this is Nan.' Lisa paused, studying it.

Vanessa nodded.

'Well, she… She looks just like Flora. Omigod.'

'Quite.'

'Ma, how can you be so…calm. I mean, Kate and Daniel… Kate always said…' Lisa dropped abruptly onto the sofa beside Vanessa.

'I've been up half the night thinking about Kate. I found it yesterday.'

'I *knew* there was something. No wonder you were so…not there. But, hey, we must phone. I'll text Kate…'

'That is exactly what I meant about don't rush me.' Vanessa spread her hands as if to flatten her feelings, slow down time. 'Look, I feel a total idiot over this. No, worse than that. Blind. Stubborn. I feel I've let them down. And I know Kate will think so. And I also feel hurt, angry, disorientated, you name it. With myself. With her, with Mother. Like I've lost my identity or never had it. I could kill Mother.' She glanced towards the door, hoping the carer wasn't overhearing. 'I'm in just such a stew right now that I don't think I can face Kate – or Daniel for that matter.' She stood up and crossed to the window. 'And anyway this is not something that can be done over the phone. Or in a flipping text.'

She'd silenced Lisa. That was unusual. Maybe it was a mistake to involve her. 'I'm sorry. I'm not being very mother-like. I just needed to tell someone.'

'Glad you did.' Lisa joined Vanessa and put an arm round her. 'I just don't see why you need to feel so bad. I mean, I always thought it *might* be her. The missing link, I mean. But that was just because of the hair. And because Kate so desperately needed there to be someone. When Daniel was being such a pig, making out that she'd had an affair.'

'Well, I lived with her all those years, growing up. And I didn't notice. I mean, I look at that picture and it doesn't seem like my mother.'

'Well she was only, what? Four years old? What do you expect?'

'I know, but usually you can see the adult in the child. Apart from the look she's giving the poor photographer, I can't see a likeness.' Vanessa trawled dust off the window ledge, contemplated her blackened fingertip and wiped it on her jeans.

'But that's it. That's Nan. I recognise that look. It's the original "if-looks-could-kill" look. When she disapproved, or you'd done something naughty. Me and Kate used to run a mile. But otherwise, I agree, there's no resemblance.

'What happened? Was I blind? Or did she change?' Vanessa walked back to the coffee table and glared down at the photograph.

'Like I said, I only really thought it because of the hair. And Kate wanted me to agree with her. But I'd never have thought Nan could have looked like this.'

'Mm. I never saw that photo before. She kept it hidden. She knew it would give her away.'

Lisa shook her head. 'You're imagining things. I mean, why would she? I think that's taking it too far.'

'Why would she? I can think of a thousand reasons.'

'So? Like what?'

'Well, for a start, looking like that, in those times. She must have been half-caste. I mean, I never met her father. "Half-caste", that was probably the polite description in those days. It showed when she was little.' Vanessa gestured at the photo, then took in Lisa's doubtful frown. 'We're talking nearly a century ago. You've no idea how prejudiced people would have been. Ignorant. Fearful.'

'But attitudes changed. As she grew up. Surely she'd have left all that behind.'

'Not Mother. Not if she had a bad time as a child. She left the identity behind all right. But she'd have carried the memories with her. It would have coloured her view of the world. She's never been one to change her opinions. I mean, if she takes against someone or something, it's for life. And she's always been very black-and-white – huh! There's ironic.'

Lisa still looked doubtful. 'It seems so unnecessary, to go on keeping it secret.'

'To you, maybe. But she's always been mistrustful. And she *liked* secrets, being mysterious.' Vanessa gave an impatient sigh. As she stared at the picture a whole new person was threatening to emerge, like a slowly developing negative. 'She used to drop hints. I see that now. Like she told me she was painfully shy as a teenager. Self-conscious, couldn't walk into a room. She never said why. Like she was playing a game – now you see it, now you don't. I just kick myself I never saw it.'

'I don't see how you could. You're being too hard on yourself.'

'That's not what Kate's going to think.'

'Rubbish. That's not at all what Kate will think. Why don't we get some breakfast, Ma?'

Vanessa agreed. She couldn't continue this conversation. Lisa had no idea how hard Kate had tried to discuss Thea's background, how stubbornly she'd resisted. The guilt made her feel sick. She refused cereal and dropped bread into the toaster, aware that although she did feel bad, she also agreed with Lisa. She was being hard on herself. She felt indignant, like a child who stamps her foot and says, 'It isn't fair.' She'd been a sleepwalker all her life, manipulated by the most powerful person in the world. A mother. She'd seen what Thea intended her to see. And even if Thea hadn't been so controlling, she probably wouldn't have noticed. How much does a child really "see" her mother? Mother is mother is mother. She buttered toast, watched a robin hopping about on the gravel and made the right noises to Thea's carer when she came to say she'd finished.

Hours later they were back in the sitting room. Vanessa began to think she would never be released from this duty. There was nothing to do and yet that nothing weighed on her and used every ounce of her energy. It was tough to be feeling more, rather than less, resentment towards her mother. She'd worked hard at generating some kind of warmth toward the skeletal woman in the bed, but now all progress in that direction had been replaced by anger. The doctor had just left. He was amazed Thea was still clinging on to life. It couldn't be long now. Meanwhile Vanessa was making a list of people to phone about the funeral.

'Who's Mrs Silking, Ma?' Lisa's voice reached her.

'Nan's mother.'

'No. I know what she looks like. That's her over on the mantel-piece.'

Vanessa barely nodded. 'Well, Nan's grandmother I suppose. Paternal, that is. She'd have been a Mrs Silking. Why?'

'There's a photo. Just found it tucked in the back of this album.'

'Oh yes.'

'She's a black lady, Ma.'

Vanessa stared. Lisa was beaming with the satisfaction of having made a find. She scuttled over and dumped the album in Vanessa's lap.

'Look! In the front it's got the usual shots of us kids in the garden with our heads cut off and so on, and at the back I caught sight of this. I was just about to put it back.'

Vanessa picked up the photograph. Another one she'd never seen before. On the back was written 'Mrs Silking, Plymouth or abroad' in her mother's handwriting.

She found herself gazing into a serene face. The woman was standing in sunlight, her shadow thrown against a low white building, and she was fingering the leaves of an exotic plant. Grey hair was gathered into the nape of her neck, Edwardian dress – a long dark skirt and quietly striped blouse with deep buttoned cuffs and a white lacy frill down the front. But it was her features that drew Vanessa's attention. Lisa's words repeated again and again in her head. 'She's a black lady, Ma.' And so she was. Mrs Silking, her great-grandmother, was a black woman. Vanessa had the sense of many nameless things becoming clear. Answers to questions she hadn't known to ask, wrinkles in the past being ironed out.

Her gaze slid off to the side to the studio portrait of her mother at four years old which still lay on the coffee table. Her Afro-Caribbean origins were perfectly clear.

Lisa turned the photograph over. 'It says "Plymouth or abroad". What's that about?'

'Hmm. Mother told me a story once. It's coming back to me.

About a grandmother coming to visit in a carriage. It must have been this woman because the other grandmother died young. She always said she was on her way to Plymouth.'

'Your grandmother? Or Nan's? I'm confused.'

'My great-grandmother. We've got five generations here, mothers, Nans, grandmothers. We're never going to know who we're talking about.'

Lisa waved the photograph. 'So the black Mrs Silking comes first.'

'Yes. She was the mother of Dick, who was my grandfather. I never knew him. He married my Nan, who was called Florence.'

'And Florence was the mother of *my* Nan, who's called Thea.' Lisa fetched the silver frame from the mantelpiece.

'Right. Except, as I told you, she used to be Marge.'

Lisa rolled her eyes and Vanessa smiled inwardly. Her daughter liked things to be orderly, clear-cut. She was lining up the photographs.

The older Mrs Silking on the left, followed by the framed picture of Florence with her bush of white hair taken in 1939 at Thea's wedding to Ted. Next came the four-year old Marge/Thea and, alongside that, Vanessa forty years ago in cap and gown collecting her degree in modern languages. Lisa finished off with the only up-to-date likeness, a snap of herself which Kate had taken the previous summer.

'So you say Nan remembered meeting this person, her grandmother?'

'Yes. She must have been quite small. She told the bit about the carriage, like that was pretty grand. And she was on the way to Plymouth.'

'Did she describe her? I mean, she must have noticed she was black.'

'No. I guess she noticed. Or maybe she was more impressed by the carriage. After all she was only little.'

'I wonder why Plymouth? And where was "abroad"?'

16

Of course I did a good job on Mrs Atkins' hat that evening. And after a decent interval I did get promotion and Miss Wilmott stopped treating me like the scum of the earth and even showed a little respect for my work. But what I learnt that day was about more than trimming hats.

That time in Mr Cooper's office gave me a lot of food for thought. I suppose I should have been flattered that Mrs Atkins winked at me. Like she was my friend or something. But, quite apart from being embarrassed to bits, it made me uneasy. It took me a while to work out why. It was partly that she was so different from how she'd been at home where she'd seemed so gentle and, well, scatty really. But the way she'd treated Mr Cooper! Then it dawned on me why that made me wary. If she was like that with Mr Cooper, then how might she behave to me, a mere apprentice, if the tables were turned? It reminded me all too clearly of what Mum's always said: 'It's them and us, and don't you forget it.' Mum always meant that to be a lesson to me to stay in my place. But it's only made me more determined to be one of them. It's the only way.

An awful lot's happened this year. Dadser lost his job with the council and there's no getting any work these days. Even the dockyard's laying people off. Everyone's been talking about something called the Wall Street crash. I have to admit I was relieved about Dadser's job. Not that I'd ever say so. But it was so embarrassing. One time when I was out with Gwen and we came round the corner, there was Dadser sweeping the road. He was pretending he hadn't seen me either, I could tell. Gwen was the only one who wasn't embarrassed. She just said, 'Good afternoon, Mr Silking,' and he raised his cap and I felt awful that I couldn't make myself stop and chat.

The other big event was the birth of Nora's baby. Not long after the business with Mrs Atkins' hat we got a letter from Nora saying she'd fallen, and we were all very excited. She came home for her lying in. In fact she stayed on after Christmas, she was that close. She had a little girl and called her Michelle. Lucy says it's a French name but it doesn't sound very French when Nora says it. She's a dear little thing and we all missed her when Nora went back home to London. But they all came down for Edwin's holiday in the summer. Michelle is sitting up already, and it's funny to see Nora being a mother and not bothering about what she looks like any more. She's so serious and she was worried we were spoiling Michelle too much. Nora seems really happy, contented. She's excited that they're getting one of the new houses being built out at Rayners Lane, but I still wouldn't want to live with Edwin. He's a kind gentle man and I know she loves him, but he's a person who likes to do the same thing at the same time, and it must be lonely looking after a baby on your own all day. It's another thing making me all the more determined to have a different sort of life.

The light is mellow as honey as I walk down Mrs Atkins' road for the second time. I turn my face to the sun filtering through the residential trees. The foliage is beginning to turn, with a splash of saffron here and there. I can feel a fluttering and loosening in the branches, a letting go of tired leaves.

I was summoned into Mr Cooper's office on Monday and given an invitation. Mr Cooper looked at me strangely as he handed me the note. 'You're to discuss the autumn fashions. Mind you don't make a fool of yourself.'

I was puzzled until I read it. I was actually invited to take tea and discuss autumn fashions, in that order. So what Mr Cooper meant was, don't get above yourself, don't let *Milady's* down. I had no intention of letting myself, or *Milady's*, down and every intention of getting above myself. I've worked a lot for Mrs Atkins in the last year and a half, but she's always come to the shop and the relationship has remained suitably formal.

Now I'm sitting in Mrs Atkins' drawing room for the first time with a delicate cup and saucer in my hand, inhaling the smoky aroma of China tea and feeling like a perfect lady. The drawing room is larger than the morning room, but the soft creams and pinks save it from being grand. Personally I'd furnish it more formally, but I approve of the chaise longue in the window upholstered in yellow silk and the scatter of matching cushions on the sofa. They bring some style to the room. I try to breathe calmly although inside my stomach is in spasm, wondering why I'm here taking tea. Mrs Atkins is different today, which is unsettling. Almost frivolous, laughing a lot.

"I sent out for Battenberg cake. I hope you like it.' She indicates the plate on the cake stand. 'It's my favourite and Clive doesn't like it.' In fact he doesn't *approve* of it.' She gives an uncharacteristic giggle. 'So, as he's away...'

I can't help smiling. It's a relief Mr Atkins is not at home, not about to walk through the door with his 'Lily, my dear' and his disquieting gaze.

'I never heard of anyone disapproving of a cake.'

'Exactly. I expect it's the colours – rather vulgar. Madeira is so much more genteel.' Mrs Atkins giggles again.

I'm careful not to laugh. I prefer Madeira to Battenberg but I don't say so. I also prefer Mrs Atkins when she's serious and focused on her wardrobe. 'Mr Cooper sent the latest designs...'

'Oh yes, we mustn't forget the hats.' She pauses and smiles across at me as she passes a salver of egg and cress sandwiches. 'Really I just wanted to have you to tea while...' She breaks off and blushes.

'While Mr Atkins is away?'

'Well, it *is* unusual to invite one's milliner to afternoon tea. And Clive has a more traditional approach.'

'Mr Cooper thought it was unusual. You should have seen his face. It was kind of you to invite me, Mrs Atkins.'

That crazy laugh again. Really, at her age. I wish she'd play her part as hostess with more decorum, a manner more suited to the delicately-flowered tea service and the elegant silver teapot.

As if she hears my thoughts, Mrs Atkins smoothes her skirt and there is the whisper of silk on silk. But then she says, 'Please call me Lily.'

'Well...'

'After all, I call you Dorothy, and it feels, well, rather one-sided.'

I summon my sense of professional identity. 'But that's different, because Dorothy is my working name.' It all comes out sounding haughtier than I intended.

'I had no idea!' Mrs Atkins looks flustered for a moment. 'May I know your real name?'

I hesitate, regretting my moment of pride. 'Marjorie Dorothea.' I rush on. 'You see Doro*thea* feels to me altogether different from *Doro*thy. And yet I don't like either. They are so heavy.' I feel the colour creeping up my neck into my face. I've gone too far and revealed my feelings, as well as exposing the vulgarity of my name in this elegant room.

'So Dorothea it is. I think it a pretty name and not at all "heavy", as you put it.'

I'm relieved Mrs Atkins has ignored the Marjorie part. And in spite of her giggly mood she isn't laughing at me either.

She's looking at me thoughtfully. 'Of course, you could shorten it.'

'Oh no, not Dot. I couldn't stand to be Dot.'

'No, you certainly aren't a Dot. That wasn't what I was thinking of. How about Thea? If you wanted something lighter?'

I can't believe Mrs Atkins is taking this much trouble over my name. I feel embarrassed and excited. 'Thea,' I mouth and then repeat it aloud. The two short syllables thrill me. They're so different from the clumsy Marge, which falls like a slab of fake butter. Thea is so slick after the plummy weight of Dorothea. Thea brings sophistication and a whole new identity which cancels out the past. I may have to be Dorothy for Mr Cooper, but for everyone else I'll be Thea. I'll never have to be ashamed of my name again.

Mrs Atkins is speaking, sounding concerned. 'You don't like it? I've offended you. That was the last thing...'

'Oh, but I love it. I'll be Thea from now on. It's the new me.'

'Oh, I'm so pleased. It really suits you and it sounds frightfully modern, don't you think? I think I will be quite jealous.'

'But Lily is such an elegant name.' It's the first time I've used Lily's name to her face and it feels daring. I'm probably getting above myself.

'Thank you, Thea. Yes, I do like it.' She pauses and then continues with an almost pleading tone in her voice. 'I do hope we can be friends.'

I try not to look startled.

'You see, one spends all one's time as a girl longing to find a husband and fantasising about the married state and what bliss it will be... And then, well, some years on, one can find oneself rather lonely. I was not born to this kind of life. So I thought we might have something in common.' Lily faltered and flushed.

'I don't think that's very likely.' Again I know I sound haughty. She's no better than Miss Needham, trying to winkle out things about my background.

'I worked as a governess before I married Clive, and I planned to become a teacher. I find it hard to be so, well, empty-minded, I suppose. I just wish I could be more creative.'

Maybe I'm being harsh on her. It never occurred to me she might be lonely or bored. This is something I can relate to and I see my way out. 'I was planning to be a painter. I had a place at the art college, but my parents didn't approve.' I have a pang of guilt about poor Mum and Dadser, but it doesn't feel like a lie. More a stretching of the truth. It works on Lily. She stops being curious and we talk about art and it suddenly doesn't seem so ridiculous we might become friends.

We have such fun trying on the sample hats I brought with me. She insists I try them on too and it's Lily this and Thea that. It feels just like the game I used to play with Binnie. Lady Sugar and Mrs Potato go shopping, entertain, go on holiday. I was Lady Sugar of course and the game was for Lady Sugar to say snooty things to put Mrs Potato in her place. It never really worked because Binnie could never say "Mrs Potato" or hear me say it without collapsing on the floor laughing. Thinking of all that must have made me forget where I am. All of a sudden I'm saying to Lily that I wish I could wear a hat all the time and of course she asks why.

'Then nobody would see my awful frizzy hair.' I never talk about it, never draw attention to it. Why now?

'Not awful at all,' says Lily. 'But if you don't like it, why don't you have it straightened out?'

My mouth falls open. I know it does. I never knew such a thing was possible.

'I tell you what. It'll be my present to you for all the work you do with my hats. It can be a "new you" present for Thea. I'll make the appointment myself.'

And before I know it she's written down the name and address of her hairdresser's and made me promise to put it on her account.

'I want to see it when you bring the hats I've ordered. I'll be offended if you don't.'

17

2006

'Why Plymouth? And where was "abroad"?'

Lisa's questions still echoed in Vanessa's mind as she traipsed through the rooms of Mead End: from sickroom to kitchen to sitting room, looking after Ted and frequently returning to the photographs of four-year-old Thea and the black Mrs Silking propped on her bedside table.

Lisa had persuaded her to get Kate and Daniel over without delay.

'Basically Mum, I can't not say something myself if we don't see them today or tomorrow. Don't worry, I'll manage the whole thing.'

Which wasn't quite the reassurance Vanessa needed. But Lisa said she would cook and had asked them over that evening 'to discuss something important'. Kate said it all depended on getting a babysitter. She didn't want to bring her children near the place. Which was no surprise, thought Vanessa, as she peered at the picture of Thea as a child.

Where did your grandmother's footsteps lead you, oh mother of mine? Nowhere you cared to follow. You chose instead to cover her tracks, kick over the traces and generally muddy the trail. Bad enough to be raised in the back end of Portsmouth, but let that be enough to keep dark. Let the scent go cold, there in a mean but respectable street. Don't follow the carriage on its way to Plymouth. Don't ask where 'abroad' might be.

What of the shame you felt at school when asked to write about grandparents and you alone had "none"? You told me the teacher set the subject deliberately. Why would she do that, I asked, all innocent. You would not say, would not go there. You took me only so far.

What if you'd told me back then why that teacher was targeting you? The only dusky, crinkle-haired one in a class of pasty-faced, rat-tailed, mouse-coloured children?

Vanessa remembered the house where Thea grew up. What a contrast to Mead End. A tiny mid-terrace at the wrong end of Portsmouth. Just two rooms and a scullery downstairs. The smell of motorcycle oil mixed with coal dust, gritty soap and wet dish-cloths. No bathroom, but the luxury of an inside toilet – which was unusual in that street. A narrow back garden barely big enough for a washing line and a few rows of vegetables. The front door straight onto the pavement.

Those visits stuck in her mind. Not exactly clandestine, but not talked about either. Catching the bus to the harbour, then the ferry and another bus. Mother's heels echoing as they passed the high brick wall of the laundry. Mother pointing out the grim Victorian building next door to it and making her promise *never* to reveal that this was where she went to school. I suppose she showed me because everyone wants to be known at some level, thought Vanessa. And we were close then. It was good to have a secret.

It was Edna's house by then, of course. They always sat in the back room with the coal fire. The fender had boxes at either end with padded lids covered in brown Rexine. Inside one were wriggly firelighters like concertinas, which Auntie Edna made by rolling and folding newspaper, her fingers moving too quickly to see the magic. In the other was kindling wood.

Edna was a lop-sided person, a bit skew-whiff, head at an angle with a sideways look from the light catching her dark framed glasses. That was how Vanessa remembered her, standing in the scullery doorway in her wrap-around flowered apron. She was not a sophisticated aunt. She liked knitting and cooking and reading *Woman's Weekly* magazine, which she gave Vanessa to look at. It was full of knitting patterns and doctors-and-nurses love stories. But best of all was a strip cartoon about a robin. It always ended with a moral, for example:

This is a Watchbird watching a liar,
And this is a Watchbird watching you!

That made her look at robins with new respect. For a treat she'd get to play with the little man on string who bounced up and down between two sticks. Normally he lived in the drawer with the crinoline tea cosy. Edna knitted those cosies in two contrasting colours with left-over wool. Mother had a green and yellow one for years, probably still somewhere in a drawer in the kitchen.

Edna was always at the sink, at the cooker or pouring tea, always laughing in spite of the fact she was married to Uncle Len, who worked in the dockyard. Mother laughed a lot when she was with Edna. They laughed until they cried.

Yes, Mother was always another person there. She relaxed, dropped her guard. They were so close, Thea and Edna. And yet they looked so different. You'd never think they were sisters. But of course they weren't. Only half-sisters. Something Mother, come to think of it, tended to skate over. If you were a fly on the wall, the outsider looking in, you'd think Edna and Mother came from different planets.

On the way home it always seemed to be winter, dark by four o'clock. They'd stay too long and hit the rush hour from Portsmouth Dockyard. Hordes of shadowy men in belted raincoats pushing and scooting their bicycles down the gangway to the ferry and stacking them in the bow. How did they ever find their own bike again? Mother refused to sit in the fuggy cabin next to a dockyard matey. She'd stalk off to the slatted benches in the stern. Vanessa would snuggle into the fur of Mother's coat. The smell of wet fur. And deeper in, traces of Mother's perfume. She could get lost in that.

Who had her mother really been? So many people. As Thea slipped away from life, Vanessa found herself obsessed with those identities. She would escape upstairs from the sickroom, sit on the edge of her bed and conjure them. At the time, of course, they were all just her mother and she had to keep on her toes.

You are sitting by the fire in your grey flannel skirt and the grey jumper Auntie Edna knitted for you with the Fair Isle across the chest and the tops of the sleeves. A band of jewel colours. Red, yellow, emerald green.

Red yellow, emerald green. Interlocking shapes. Traffic lights of my life.

I know everything will be all right when you're wearing that jumper. The green light says go. I can climb up and kneel on your lap and snuff up the smell at the back of your neck where the zip fastens the jumper, the smell that is essentially you. It's a smell of hair and grease and cooking. It's the smell of safety.

It goes with your nose being big and shiny and your hair frizzing out and you telling me stories and not caring about tidying up and having bread and butter and condensed milk out of the tin. I help you with the dusting. We read books, play with the doll's house and listen to the wireless: *Listen with Mother* with Daphne Oxenford – "Are you sitting comfortably? Then I'll begin"; *Mrs Dale's Diary* – "I'm worried about Jim"; *Children's Hour* with Uncle Mac. You make rissoles for picnics on Portsdown Hill where we have to climb over a stile, and we have tea parties – just the two of us and the dolls, under the rose arch in the garden. You are not at all dangerous and the world is a safe and happy place.

This version of you will paint a ceiling at two in the morning or weed flower borders all day with nothing to eat. It is the you that pulls me down behind the sofa to hide when there's a knock at the front door.

This you vanishes when people come or when you go out. She is not the same person who wears the emerald green taffeta dress.

That was the "Wallis Simpson" version of Thea. One day, not that long ago, Vanessa had been wicked enough to pay Thea the compliment that she was always as groomed and elegant as Wallis Simpson. She knew Thea would be pleased in one way and furious in another, because the infamous Mrs Simpson was, of course, on her personal hit list of people she would have liked to exterminate with a withering look or a venomous comment. It was seventy years since the abdication. But Thea's grudges never lost their passion. She was a dangerous woman, Wallis: the wicked witch, American bitch, filthy rich. She seduced the King away from his duty.

Your Wallis days seduced me certainly.

Hair smooth, make-up. The Dolly Mixture smell of Pond's Vanishing Cream followed by lots of pale compressed powder from the compact with the raised gold crown on the lid. Earrings that clip on and hurt so you rub your ear lobes when you pull them off. Another smell, Chanel No. 5, the same perfume that's buried in the fur coat. The "pretty" eyes you make when you try on a hat or look in the hall mirror before going out or answering the door. And, of course, the emerald green taffeta dress with the printed pattern that makes it look as if it's overlaid with black lace. Heart-shaped neckline, nipped in waist and full skirt swirling above those black suede slingbacks with the peep toe. Never was Wallis more glamorous. A pretty mother kissing me goodnight.

And then there was the other photograph beside Vanessa's bed, Mrs Silking senior. The two women were so different, her mother and her great-grandmother. They both had dignity, but there the similarity ended. Her mother had always stood on hers, but the dignity of the black Mrs Silking was part of her being. It flowed from her. She looked tranquil, as if life had brought her contentment as well as pain. Here was a woman who'd made decisions she was able to live with. Which was not true of Thea.

The "look" made so much sense now. How much had it cost her mother over a lifetime to keep her secret? What price the holding of that look for the best part of a century? Not merely the look, of course, but the whole stance. The approach to all comers that said, I am better than you. For make no mistake, this was no easy self-confidence. This was not the relaxed sense of an identity at peace with itself. It was a taut line, a high-tension wire, tightened, loosened and constantly readjusted over the years. It must have required rigorous attention, antennae consistently alert to the dangers of intimacy, the risk of exposure.

Only her child could truly be trusted. It must have been so tempting to make little revelations to the innocent Vanessa. But the child would grow into a treacherous adult. Would she remember? Surely not. But just in case... *Never tell... You do not know... You did not see...* Promises had to be exacted. Vanessa sighed, remembering.

What conversations we could have had! What speculations and explorations. How might we have laughed and cried together? But this was not to be. It was your choice.

Later, of course, there were no proper choices. Dementia set in. It was difficult to pinpoint when it started. In retrospect, incidents that had been inexplicable at the time made sense. There had been that spate of phone calls in the early Eighties, for instance. Ted had been working abroad, leaving Thea alone in that big house. Her mother's friends kept ringing Vanessa with concerns about Thea's state of mind. They said Thea had phoned them, incoherent, after a few drinks maybe? Would Vanessa pop over and check her out? Would it be a good idea to have a word with the GP?

What happened when you lost your mind? Vanessa had heard it described as a dimmer switch fading the personality, but with Mother it wasn't like that at all. If anything it was like a light switching on. An infra-red light that showed up all the things that had been kept in the dark. An exaggeration of all her faults.

She would kick off like a cornered animal. Lashing out with verbal abuse, spitting, clawing, biting. Vanessa guessed that, at some level, Thea knew she had lost control of the carefully contrived façade, the image she had created and maintained all her adult life. A well-groomed hostess who'd become incontinent and smelly. But that was the least of it. Worst of all, Thea had lost control of her hair. It was looking more and more like her own mother's bush of white wire wool. And her skin by contrast seemed darker. It was like looking at the negative of a photograph.

So it was small wonder in the weeks and months before the end, when she could still be taken to a pub for lunch and behave badly, that she insisted on wearing that snood. A piece of pleated fabric, elasticated, which she would put on herself, crookedly, and often back to front. If only she'd worn the red hat Lisa gave her for her ninetieth. That would have been stylish, but somehow she distrusted it. She'd look at it sideways and shake her head, as if it wasn't a "proper" hat. Not a hat a milliner would make. She'd mutter about 'keeping it under her hat' but wouldn't put it on. And what was this milliner keeping under her hat? Her hair of course. That crazy, giveaway mass of greying frizz. Perversely Thea would reach for the snood instead of the hat. She imagined it flattened and smoothed her hair to its former elegance. It actually made her look like a batty old woman.

Of course she was an old woman. At ninety-three that was unequivocal. But Vanessa never thought of her that way. Not as an old woman. And she wasn't entirely batty. Of course she had dementia. That was clear. She talked to Jesus and her mother, but that didn't make her mad. She began scrambling memories in stories she had related a hundred times and now muddled up. She imagined her trusted cleaner or the carers were stealing from her, thought the very worst about people. But there were other strange and complicated delusions, which showed paranoia and a loss of knowing where she was and who was who. Like the *Coronation Street* fantasy about the hospital staff being actors in a soap opera. Hitting the doctor. That had all happened after her first fall, when she broke her hip. Vanessa wanted to put it down to the effects of the anaesthetic, but as time wore on, she had to drop that theory.

But for all of that, Mother managed to maintain a meta-awareness, a sliver of alertness like a security camera that monitored what was afoot. For instance, the violence and abuse she showed towards Vanessa. It wasn't just the physical lashing out, inflicting bruises and scratches, but the nasty things she said. Accusing her of spying on Ted, being a wicked daughter, an evil person. Vanessa told herself it was the dementia speaking and reflected that maybe all the wicked stepmothers of folklore had dementia. But Mother never behaved that way if anyone else was present. David once came into the room quietly behind Thea so that she didn't know he was there. He was shocked by what he witnessed.

Thea tried to cling to shreds of housekeeping and cooking. When Vanessa prepared a meal Thea would pad around behind her, her hand hovering, her eyes tracking Vanessa's every move. Vanessa was so strongly reminded of Thea's supervision of her as a teenager that it was all she could do not to scream at her to go away. It was easy to understand how elder abuse happened.

Then there was the business with the crossword. Having Vanessa there to read out the clues gave Ted a rare opportunity to tackle the cryptic puzzle.

One evening when Thea was snoring in her chair, she said to Ted, 'Shall we have another go at the crossword, Dad?'

Ted nodded.

'Seven letters beginning with S.'

Ted pursed his lips. 'F or S?'

'My bonnie lies over the ocean,' came a quavering drone from Thea.

'S for sugar.'

'Bring back, bring back...' The song, if it could be called that, was gaining volume, drowning out Vanessa's reading of the clue.

'What was that?'

'Oh bring back my bonnie to me.' Thea reached a crescendo worthy of the Wailing Wall. She beckoned urgently to Ted and shot a venomous look towards Vanessa.

Ted crossed to her side of the fireplace, bent over her, solicitous, enquiring. 'Would you like your feet up? A cup of tea?'

Thea moved things about on the table beside her, jerking about, her mouth set tight, eyes flicking sideways. She realigned a napkin, a biro, a magazine. 'No!' she almost yelled.

Vanessa tried to concentrate on the crossword, her head hot with rage where logic should be. She could find no compassion, just wanted to shout, 'Shut up you selfish cow! Give him a break. Just give him five minutes doing what he enjoys.'

Every night after that, if the crossword was mentioned, Thea staged a similar jealous charade.

Vanessa now had a context for understanding Thea's racism. She shuddered to remember how Mother used to behave whenever the issue of race came up. Indian and Anglo-Indian naval officers and their wives were socially acceptable: 'So cultured, you know. An ancient civilisation.' But "coloured people", by which she meant people of African descent, were simply "natives" and were best left to dance around their primitive fires.

'The poor Queen, having to watch cannibals jumping about,' had been her reaction to a televised display of tribal dancing put on for a royal visit to Africa. Thea could hardly watch it.

Oh Mother, thought Vanessa. You did protest too much.

They were here at last. The waiting was over. It was only Daniel's third visit to Mead End and he was stiff and clearly uncomfortable. Kate was edgy, remembering their last disastrous visit. The news of their West Indian ancestor, waiting to be told, got in the way of all conversation, paralysing Vanessa's attention. She had imagined she would rush up to Kate and hug her and tell her all about it. But she found she couldn't do it.

Instead Lisa took control, sitting her sister and Daniel at the kitchen table, pouring wine. Lulling them into a false sense of security, Vanessa thought later. Which was unfair on Lisa. It was just that she liked a drama. One minute Kate and Daniel were relaxing in the way parents do when free of their children, ready to mellow into the wine and the evening, and the next minute they'd sprung apart. Lisa held the photographs loosely between the fingers of both hands, letting them drop to knock on the table, sliding her fingers down, lifting them, dropping them again. Oh, for goodness sake, get on with it, thought Vanessa. She was about to intervene when Kate obliged with a sigh. 'What have you got there, Sis?'

'Mum and I made a discovery. We found these.' She waved the pictures. 'One is a photograph of our great-great-grandmother.'

Kate reached for the photo but Lisa held it close.

'You'll notice she's black. My guess would be West Indian.' She handed over the picture. 'We thought you ought to know.'

Daniel's fingers tightened on his glass at the word 'black' and he exploded into 'Good God!' and 'What the hell?'

Vanessa watched Kate ignore him and gaze at the photograph.

'So, Nan's grandmother.'

'Yes,' said Lisa.

'Well.' With that one quiet word Kate looked up and slid Vanessa a look that said, *you see?*

Vanessa swallowed an urge to protest, absorbed the look.

'I know. It's extraordinary isn't it?' Lisa was looking across to Vanessa, passing her the baton.

'Lisa and I still haven't got our heads round it.'

Daniel was talking at her. 'Well, Vanessa, I must say, it's pretty goddamn odd. For you to be totally unaware of such a thing.' He seemed to be enjoying the discomfort that could be felt around the table. The toad.

He leaned in towards Kate to peer at the picture and Vanessa noticed how Kate moved slightly to avoid his hand on her shoulder. She was smiling, but not at Daniel or at any of them. Kate was smiling at the image of the woman as if they were sharing a secret.

Lisa continued, 'And this one's a photo of Nan as a little kid.' She swivelled the picture of the four-year old Thea. 'Would you believe she could ever have looked like that?'

Daniel gave the picture a long look. 'Well, no, actually Lisa. If it had been that obvious, we wouldn't have had a problem. Would we?' He poured himself more wine and left the room.

Kate grabbed the second photograph. 'As I thought. This could be Flora. In a couple of years.'

Vanessa rubbed her eyes. 'Should you see what Daniel's up to?'

'Oh, never mind him. He'll get over it. Here's our mystery solved at last and all he can do is go off in a huff.' Kate tapped the photo. 'I mean, as you know, I always thought there was something with Nan. But even I never thought it was that obvious.'

Vanessa kept her surprise to herself. This was a very different Kate. Once she'd have rushed after Daniel to placate and soothe and make everything right again. It made her realise, once more, how little she knew of Kate's life. She sighed and rubbed her eyes again.

'You all right, Mum?'

'Oh, I'm fine. Just…'

'I bet you're tired after all this.'

Too right, I'm tired, thought Vanessa. Families. And then Ted shambled in, looking for his hearing aid batteries.

'Ah, wine,' he said. 'Might I have a little red?'

'It's your wine, Gramps,' said Lisa and fetched another glass. 'You may as well sit down, food won't be long.' She motioned to Kate to put the photos away and started straining off saucepans.

Vanessa went to find the batteries, last seen on top of the bureau. A cold draught and a waft of smoke drew her attention. Daniel was standing in the conservatory with the door open. What a nerve. Kate didn't let him smoke at home, not even in the garden.

At her approach he stubbed the cigarette out in a plant pot. 'Apologies from all positions.' He made a little 'hands-up' gesture of surrender. 'But you will understand I was feeling a little tense.'

Vanessa could only nod.

'You realise this family secret of yours,' and he turned those mocking eyes on her, 'could have shattered our marriage. Kate got it into her head that I thought she'd been unfaithful.'

My God he looked smug. Vanessa resisted the temptation to wipe the look off his face. 'Kate got it into her head? I rather thought...'

'Preposterous of course. She became totally paranoid. Even thought Mama was getting at her. I ask you.'

'You ask me? I think you've got an almighty nerve to blame Kate. And if you ask me, I think it's far more likely your own behaviour in that department put your marriage at risk.'

'Ah, mea culpa, mea culpa. But that is all long in the past. Adapting to fatherhood and all that. Suffice it to say I am a reformed character.'

Pompous prat, thought Vanessa. Why do I have to listen to this?

'Fortunately we have both had the strength to come through it.'

'Well, I'm glad. For the children. They need you both.' Vanessa knew that was true, although she'd love to think they only needed Kate.

'And this news is welcome. It must be surprising for you.'

'Yes,' said Vanessa shortly. She turned on her heel. Patronising creep. She was annoyed to notice her hand shaking as she picked up the packet of batteries.

18

Lily's hairdresser, or her "salon" as she calls it, is in Osborne Road. I ride on one of the new buses which makes a change from the dirty old tram. *Maison LaRoche.* The moment I step inside the door I wish I hadn't come. I feel like a freak and the sight of me confirms it – reflected in the thousand mirrors lining the walls. Everything that isn't glass is gleaming chrome or eau-de-Nil. I'm a naughty little devil who's wandered into heaven by mistake. But before I can back out of the door I am gathered up by a waif-like angel wearing a helmet of the finest, pale blonde hair and delivered to the chrome reception desk. Here presides a magnificent lady who has red hair swept up in a chignon and long fingernails to match. I'm caught in the cloud of her perfume before I reach the counter.

She snarls in my direction, 'I'm afraid we have no vacancies at present.' I almost expect smoke to puff from her nostrils. 'Our clientèle would not want…' She trails away.

What *is* she talking about? Oh, the mortification as it dawns on me. She thinks I've come for a job. And I'm not even good enough for that. I'm about to turn tail and rush from the place when I think of Lily's eyes watching me. I take a deep breath, and lift my head, looking Dragon Lady in the eye. 'I have an appointment. It was arranged by Mrs Atkins.'

Dragon Lady transforms. Her lips relax from her teeth into a radiant smile. I give my name and am wafted onto an eau-de-Nil leather sofa where I do my best to cross my legs elegantly and look as if I always spend my afternoon off in such surroundings. All sorts of fragrances float past my nose, mostly delicate, but there's an underlying harsh tone that reminds me of drain cleaner. The mirrors have leaded ribboning in a geometric design with stylised leaves where the ribbons intersect at the corners. I wish I had a sketchbook with me.

Hipless men and elegant girls come and go through double mirror doors at the back of the waiting area, and I glimpse rows of smaller mirrors each with a one-legged chrome chair looking like a cocktail glass. I'm watching one of the men in particular. He's wearing lavender trousers and a matching waistcoat and a grey silk shirt. I'm noticing the fine self-stripe of the shirt when I realise he has glided to my side. Next thing I know I have three hipless men standing round me as I sit in my eau-de-Nil upholstered cocktail glass which swivels disconcertingly in their hands so I feel like a swizzle stick. One is Grey Shirt, one has an Italian look with slicked back hair and the third is an older gentleman wearing black pinstripe trousers and spats whom the other two address as "Monsieur". I think he must be the owner of the salon. They all comb and tweak and pull out the kinks of my hair, something I normally hate. But to be the centre of such sophisticated and professional attention feels wonderful. After the consultation Grey Shirt, whose name is Pierre, brings sketches and photographs and gives me advice. It seems ridiculous that I can look like any of the models, but I point my finger to make the choice he guides me to, and am swept away to the basins to have my hair washed. What bliss. My hair swept backwards into a basin specially shaped to support your neck, fluffy towels, firm hands massaging my scalp and no drips down my collar. All so different from the rough-and-ready treatment you got at *Marion's* in London Road where Nora used to go and sometimes took me. Since Nora left home, Mum's put a stop to that and she's been cutting my hair herself.

Pierre combs and snips, combs and snips, swaying his non-existent hips this way and that, pursing his lips and standing back, only to pounce back at my head just when I think he is finished. He spreads evil-smelling paste all over my hair and stretches it over huge rollers, ties the whole thing down with a net and a cloth and has me led away to a dryer at the far end of the salon. At *Marion's*, the dryers are pink and cosy. These are high-domed chrome monsters which purr seductively, and one of the waif-like girls brings me magazines and coffee. I feel like a queen.

But that is nothing to what happens when my hair is dry and Pierre has combed it out and styled it. He makes a great play of what a great surprise it will be and hangs a towel over the mirror. It all feels rather ominous. When he is done he whisks the towel away and I actually look round to see where I have gone, to see the person whom the mirror is reflecting back. Because it certainly isn't me. The mirror must be angled away from me. Pierre is bent over with laughter, his hand to his mouth. He even flourishes a lavender handkerchief and dabs at his eyes. It is me in the glass. He wields a hand mirror so I can see the back of my sleekly helmeted head. My hair, that rampant bramble patch, is as smooth and glossy as the castanets Dadser keeps in the kitchen drawer.

Antonio, the Italian, is summoned. He coos 'Bellissima, bellissima' and disappears to return with Monsieur. Pierre helps me to my feet, removes the protective cape, flicks a soft brush round my collar and presents me to Monsieur who kisses my hand. Pierre has me pirouette in front of them all. I was never so embarrassed or so proud. Monsieur murmurs that Madame Atkins will be proud of her *protégée*. And it is Lily I am thinking of as I walk out into the sunshine, fully fledged as Thea.

I can't go home. They won't understand. I haven't even told them what I was going to do. More than anything I want to show myself to Lily. I want to thank her for her present. And I'm afraid I will never look quite like this again, unless I sleep sitting up with a silk scarf on my head. The magic of Pierre and Monsieur will evaporate and I want her to see it while it is still fresh. The day is overcast but there is no wind and no sign of rain. Lily's house isn't far away and I set off to walk there.

It never occurs to me that she won't be in, ready to receive me in her drawing room. But Rosie answers the door and informs me Madam is out. I give her my name, emphasising the 'Thea' in case she has remembered me as Dorothy. She puts out her hand and looks disappointed I don't have such a thing as a calling card to give her. As I turn to leave I catch a movement in the back of the hall and a voice calls out, 'Who is it, Rosie?' and before I know it Mr Atkins stands before me. He stares down at me and I wish I hadn't already started down the steps. I feel at such a disadvantage.

I find my voice at last. 'I'm Mrs Atkins' milliner.'

'I know that. I'd know those eyes anywhere.'

His words throw me right back into the confusion of our first encounter.

'We haven't been formally introduced. Clive Atkins.'

I step up onto a level with him and shake his extended hand which is firm and dry. 'Thea Silking.' I love the ring of it.

'Why don't you come in and wait. I am sure Mrs Atkins will not be long.'

Terror fills me at the thought of being in the house with him. Will he sit and make conversation or leave me in the chilly morning room feeling foolish on the edge of a chair?

'No, it really is no matter. It was only a trivial question and I found myself in the neighbourhood.'

He smiles with one side of his mouth. He knows I'm lying. 'It would be no trouble.'

'Thank you, but I must be getting home. It's later than I thought.'

I escape down the steps and onto the pavement without looking back, sensing his eyes on me. As I walk away I hear the front door click shut.

I have made a fool of myself. In front of Mr Atkins and, more importantly, in the eyes of Lily when she hears of my unscheduled visit. What was I thinking of? Lily might call me her friend, but I know it's not the same as being Gwen's friend. Gwen and I drop in on each other all the time and we do things like washing up in each other's houses. That word Monsieur used comes into my mind. *Protégée*. It felt special when he said it but now I feel embarrassed. It makes me feel like a hobby Lily has taken up to avoid feeling bored. Like last year it was needlepoint and this year it's Thea.

Who is Thea anyway? Is she a hairstyle or is she real? If she's just a hairstyle then she won't last long. I certainly will never be able to afford another visit to *Maison LaRoche*. Dragon Lady's words echo in my head. *Our clientèle would not want*. What? To be touched by a coloured person? I shudder. Then I catch sight of my reflection in the window of the tram. Thea *is* real. I *will* be that person. And the first step is to take her home with me. I must get that over with.

As I turn into our street I can see Dadser walking slowly towards me. I wave but he doesn't wave back. He's on his way to the shop to get his tobacco. Since his last illness he doesn't go out much and he looks as if he's sleepwalking. When I get closer I wave again. He's staring at me. Then he raises a hand. But I know he didn't recognise me at first. He doesn't know what to say. Nor do I.

Then he smiles. 'Well, well. Marge goes out and a lady comes home.'

I offer to fetch his baccy for him but he shakes his head. 'You better get in home and show your mother.' He has a look that says, I'd love to see the look on her face, but on second thoughts I'd rather not be there.

Mum's in the scullery peeling potatoes and Edna's rolling out pastry. Edna drops the rolling pin and goes, 'Oh my!' and gets flour in her hair and all over her face from clutching her head. Mum looks up once and carries on peeling. I go out to the lavvy, and when I come back Mum's finished the potatoes and Edna's made a pot of tea. Nothing happens in our house without tea.

Mum dries her hands, eyeing me. 'You'd better sit down and tell us all about it, young lady.'

'Remember Mrs Atkins? The one who told Mr Cooper how good I was?' I told them all about that but I haven't mentioned Lily since, other than to describe some of her hats.

I tell them about going to Lily's house, except I call her Mrs Atkins, and I explain about being called Thea. It sounds very silly in our living room with the clock ticking on the mantelpiece and Mum's knitting bag spilling onto the floor next to her chair. Then I tell her about Lily's present and the salon, except I call it a hairdresser's and don't mention Pierre or Monsieur. Mum would find it odd that I had my hair done by a man. She's only ever heard about *Marion's* from me and Nora, and Marion is just Mrs Williams from round the corner.

When I've finished she shakes her head. 'I don't like it. I don't like it one little bit.'

'Oh, Mum.' I put my hand to my hair. 'Why not?'

'It's not the hair. It's a bit modern, but it's what you girls like.

And I can see why you've done it. No, it's this Mrs Atkins worries me.'

'But Mum, she's my friend. She told me to call her Lily.'

'Did she now? And is she the sort of friend you'll be inviting round for tea on Sunday?'

I can't answer. I actually think Mum would like Lily, but I can't imagine Lily in this room crammed round the table with me and my sisters, Mum in her overall and Dadser looking on from his chair in the corner. I curl up inside to think of Lily knowing where I live, walking down my street.

'Well, that tells me everything,' Mum says when I say nothing. 'You stick to making her hats and don't go taking any more so-called presents.'

'What d'you mean, "so-called"?'

'I'm sure she means well. But you don't want to be beholden to folk like that. There's always strings attached.'

I know it's no use arguing with Mum when she gets on that tack. And anyway I don't want to think about it because I know she's telling me what I'm already afraid of. *Protégée.* She's probably never heard of the word but she knows what it means all right.

'And as to this Thea malarkey, don't imagine I'll be calling you anything but Marge.'

Just then Dadser comes in with Binnie. Mum's just about to get Dadser involved in ticking me off when Binnie shrieks, 'It's Lady Sugar! Are you going to be snooty *all* the time now? Poor Mrs Potato!'

And when she's finished collapsing with giggles she climbs all over me touching my hair and sniffing it and saying how she wants to have hers done the same. Edna comes in from the scullery, and Dadser puts on his posh voice and walks up and down with me on his arm and before long even Mum has to laugh. Sometimes I just bless that little sister of mine.

There's a postscript to this whole episode. Dadser and me are home on our own one evening a few days later. Dadser suddenly looks very serious and lays his pipe on one side.

'We've not been very good, your mother and I, at explaining about my family, where you come from. Why you look as you do.

Wanting to straighten your hair and so on. We tried to explain it when you were little. But you were too young to understand. Then we kind of forgot.'

He looks sheepish and picks up his pipe again, starts to fill it, tamping it down with his fingertip. I start to protest and he holds up a hand.

'And I know you've had a few attempts since then and we've avoided it. There was a falling out and it was painful, but that's another story. No excuse, either. Well, truth was, we, I, didn't know how to put it. We kept putting it off. So here I am, trying to make up for that. You've not had an easy ride. Folks round here don't understand.'

I feel hot inside and I wonder if that is all he is going to say. Part of me hopes it is. It's all very uncomfortable and he's not finding it easy. But it's about time somebody said things out loud.

'Don't understand what?' I know perfectly well it's about the colour of my skin, but I want to hear him say it.

'You remember your grandmother? You probably don't. You were very small when she came.'

I nod, smelling cinnamon, getting that warm feeling all over again.

'Oh, you do. Well, she was from the West Indies.' He strikes a match and sucks the flame down into the bowl of the pipe until the tobacco glows. 'Well, your grandmother, my mother… She came from Barbados. And she wasn't a settler, you understand. She was coloured. And *her* mother,' he pauses, sucking at the pipe. 'A slave, she was, on a sugar plantation.'

I stare at him, taking this in. My great-grandmother was a slave. A nigger.

'I'm sure you know, the slaves were taken across from Africa to work for the white settlers, work the plantations.'

Africa. Pictures of dancing natives, stories of cannibals eating missionaries race through my mind.

'The slaves lived a pretty dreadful life. It depended on the plantation of course, but the white man generally treated slaves like animals.' He shakes his head and draws on his pipe. 'So what my mother achieved in her life was remarkable, given that background.

147

I remember, you see. Growing up in Gibraltar. She was a force to be reckoned with. Quite something.'

He fiddles with the pipe. I'm holding my breath, waiting to hear more.

He sighs then, as if the next bit's going to be difficult. 'My mother's father was German, the son of the plantation owner, you understand. They would go with the young servant girls, it was their right. That was the sort of thing that went on in them days. Even after Abolition. Not a thing you'd want to talk about nowadays, of course – neither that nor having a German in the family. But he was a good man in his way, by all accounts. Set up home with my grandmother as housekeeper, but they lived like a family, which was unusual. He loved her, or so my mother said. That was in Bermuda, which is how she met my father. He was posted there, in the Army. Big Gunnery place, Bermuda. Keeping an eye on the Yanks.'

Dadser turns to look at me, holding his pipe on his knee. 'So you see, Marge, that's the story. That's where you get the colour of your skin and your eyes and your hair. From your grandmother, and her mother. And don't you ever, for one moment, believe the evil things some ignorant folk say about coloured people. Because they ain't true. Not at all. I should know, after all the time I spent in Sierra Leone. Another story.' He looks at my questioning face and shakes his head.

'My mother used to tell us children how her mother said she could take her pick of what she called herself. West Indian or German. But she was always proud of being West Indian.'

'I'd choose to be Spanish,' I say without thinking. 'Because of where you were born, in that ship at sea off the Spanish coast.'

'A very proud people, the Spanish.' He smiles and shakes his head. 'Your grandmother would understand your not liking to be called Marge. She liked to be called by her full name, Henrietta. Letters used to come from Bermuda starting, "Dear Hattie". She'd tut-tut and say, "I left Hattie in Bermuda." She used to say that women must be sure of their dignity, because they held no power. I can't think where she got that idea.'

'I wish she was still alive.'

Dadser looks up. 'Oh, but she is.'

'Where? Why...?'

Dadser shakes his head. 'Plymouth. That's where they live. As I said, there was a falling out. Sad really. When last I heard she was thinking of going abroad.' He sighs. 'A step too far.'

So many questions pop up in my head like hands in a classroom, but when I see Dadser's face they all shrink back down again.

It all turns out to be an awful anti-climax. Nothing interesting happens after my new hairdo. Lily enthused about it, but I got the impression she'd forgotten about it, lost interest. And now of course you wouldn't know I'd ever had it. I can't afford to go back and it would have to be done at least once a month to really make a difference. I even asked Mrs Williams at *Marion's* but she just gave me an odd look, obviously offended when I described how they'd done my hair at *Maison LaRoche*, even though I didn't say where I'd been. She simply doesn't have the right equipment.

There may be no trace left of that momentous day in my hair, but it certainly left its mark inside my head. The encounter with Mr Atkins, for instance. I see his eyes all the time. When I go to bed at night, when I'm on my own in a room, when I go to the lavvy. Whenever there's nobody about to hold my attention. I haven't told anyone about it, not even Gwen. It's as if I carry something exciting and precious around with me. Something that would be taken from me if anyone else knew. The odd thing is, I don't think Mr Atkins is at all handsome. And he's rather short for a girl as tall as me. But something happens inside me when he looks at me and I can't decide whether to be thrilled or frightened. It's enough that I both want it to happen again and dread it. Which is why, on Saturday afternoons, I sometimes catch the tram to Southsea and walk past the end of Lily's road, then hurry away again in case either of them comes out and sees me.

The other thing that stays with me is my grandmother's story. I think about her a lot. I want to be like her. Brave, strong, dignified. But I do think she got one thing wrong, and that was choosing to be West Indian. I choose to be Spanish because Spanish is exotic and interesting, but mostly because Spanish is white. I choose to be white. I can't alter my skin – and believe me, I've tried. Lemon juice, bleach. Scrubbing away when I've been alone in the house. It doesn't work, just stings and hurts. But I can dress and behave like a white person. I am one really. I *feel* like one, no different from Nora or Edna, except better looking. I can learn the manners and speak correctly and then maybe nobody will even notice my beastly skin. I've made up my mind. It's my new resolution.

We're very poor and Mum's been taking in washing again. Resolutions like mine don't count for much, and the only things getting white in our household are other people's sheets. It's Christmas but it won't be the same. Nora isn't coming as she says they have to go to Edwin's parents with Michelle. We can't afford a proper Christmas dinner and we're all going to Grandma Day's. And that means Lucy will be all lah-di-dah with her nose in the air and being made a great fuss of because Grandma Day is Lucy's grandmother. She says we can adopt her and call her Grandma too, as we haven't got our own grandmother, but she doesn't spoil us like she spoils Lucy. Mum says the worst of it is we will have to take gifts for Grandma and Grandpa Day. Every evening we sit around making Christmas presents. Edna is knitting socks for all the men in the family and a dress for Michelle. I am embroidering handkerchiefs and Mum will launder them so they look as good as new when wrapped up in tissue paper. Binnie is making lavender sachets, and every time she finishes one she's allowed to add to the paper chain she's making to hang in the front room.

Christmas day really isn't as bad as I expected. Grandma Day gives us such a welcome and we have mulled wine round the fire. Of course I was upset not to have a new dress this year, especially as I'd overheard Auntie Rose was giving Lucy one for her Christmas present. Hemlines have dropped, and Mum said there was enough material left over to add a frill to my old frock. She has no idea. That would be so obvious, and anyway it would be all the wrong shape for the latest styles. It's only family, so I wear the old dress as it is. Sure enough, Lucy has a new one and as soon as I see her in it I feel better. It's a pinky shade of lavender which doesn't suit her at all, and the bias cut is too tight over her hips and doesn't have the slinky effect it's meant to have. When Lucy goes to fetch more glasses, Dadser whispers in my ear, 'The colour of Lucy's dress, is that what they call mauve?' He has a funny way of saying "mauve" as if it rhymed with "Maude" and I get the giggles.

It happens again in the evening. We are having a sing-song round the piano and Lucy likes to do a turn. She thinks she's a contralto but she always sounds as if she's singing down a rolled up newspaper, like when we used to play in the dark and pretend to be ghosts. She's chosen "I Passed by your Window" as her party piece and she's just getting into her stride when Dadser mutters, 'I hope she passes pretty quickly.' Auntie gives him a look and clacks her teeth, although she couldn't possibly have heard what he said. I look to see if Mum has noticed, and her shoulders are shaking and she's looking hard at the carpet.

19

2006

Thea was dead. The night nurse had woken Vanessa in the early hours and she'd got Ted up in time for him to hold Thea's hand as she finally let go of life.

Now Vanessa was trying to write a fitting tribute for her mother. She didn't want to lie, but she couldn't be entirely honest. Somewhere there were words to be found which would do justice to Thea, while concealing the confusion and negativity Vanessa was feeling. David suggested she might pass the task to Kate or Lisa. But Ted had asked her to do it. Plus, she owed it to her mother ever since the last tribute she'd written. That had been for Mother's cousin Lucy, and Mother had got into quite a state.

Those two had been pretty much brought up together, being only a year apart, and Lucy was the last remaining member of her family. So Vanessa wasn't surprised Mother was upset. But there turned out to be more to it than that.

It was the evening after Lucy's funeral. Thea was tight and upright, thin as a cut-out in her puffy armchair. Vanessa remembered how David had to catch her as she walked towards the chapel of rest that morning. She was almost toppled by a gust of wind, frail as a leaf, tough as old boots.

She sat there against the backdrop of her collected elegance: white porcelain, clear crystal and gracious ladies in gilt frames arranged against shell pink walls. Two white swans glided across the silk surface of an inlaid mahogany chest.

Vanessa knew which gilt mouldings were mended with pastry dough, which pictures were "real" and which were torn from a Sunday colour supplement. She knew where it all came from. She could still smell the aroma of rotting fish that once hung on certain pieces. Together they used to unearth treasures from a dilapidated back street warehouse frequented by stray cats. The Steptoe-style owner fed them off enamel plates randomly placed on Sheraton tables and Chippendale chairs. In those days Mother had an unerring eye for a rare piece – a long-case clock, greyed by rain from a hole in the tin roof, now gleamed and ticked steadily in the far corner of this room. Victorian chairs Thea reupholstered and polished back to life, figurines whose vivid colours she coaxed from beneath layers of grime and bird droppings. But these stories were not to be told, not here, not in her drawing room. These pieces were not bargains, they were heirlooms, they were Vanessa's inheritance.

The silence had been broken by Thea speaking. 'I was so ashamed!'

Vanessa questioned her, attentive, curious.

She was describing the time when she left school, breaking her own taboo, telling stories of her girlhood. The presentation by the Watch Committee for being the best prefect at school. The school Vanessa had been taught never to mention.

'Mum made me wear my bridesmaid's dress for the ceremony. I wanted to wear my school uniform. It wasn't right. So out of place. I looked awful. As if the wedding wasn't bad enough. That fiasco with the photos.'

'Whose wedding was it?'

'Your Auntie Nora's.' Thea said it dismissively, as if it were completely irrelevant. Then she clammed up and wouldn't answer any more questions.

After an interval she started up again as if what she had to say wouldn't be contained in her head. 'Mum didn't understand. I could never make them understand.'

She changed the subject. Or so Vanessa thought, talking about the tribute Vanessa had written for Lucy, full of words like "feisty" and "warm" and "special". Thea said, 'It was good, and you read it so well, nice and clear, so people could hear at the back.' Her mouth set into a thin line. What was that about? Was Thea jealous? Jealous of Lucy, three times widowed, living in a bungalow and whom she considered more than a little common? It made no sense.

Vanessa's attention wandered to the cherub on her left supporting a lampshade of palest peach shantung. She remembered the careful binding of the wire frames of the shades, the stretching of the fabric, Mother's mouth puckered with pins and concentration. The even pleating, smooth lining and immaculate professional finish. 'A darn sight better than the ones in that snooty shop!' she would say. 'You can see their stitches! And the prices, you wouldn't believe!' Now she didn't see that the material had rotted and split with the heat of half a century's light bulbs.

Thea was off again, talking about her scholarship to Art College. Telling how she'd run up three flights of stairs to get to the studio, to get painting. Her whole face lit up and one hand demonstrated how she flew up those stairs, a gnarled claw cast in the part of her youthful energy.

'It was very light, the studio, right up there at the top. It looked out over the harbour.'

It was hard to imagine, that running up the stairs. And Vanessa thought of the house at the wrong end of town where she grew up, the dark hall, the narrow stairs. Art College. Mother's first dream of escape. Odd, she'd said nothing when Kate went to college, took no interest in her granddaughter's talent. Yet it must be where Kate got it. Certainly not from herself or David.

Suddenly Vanessa heard, 'I was horrible!' The words hung in the air between them as one hand tightened over a lace-edged handkerchief. 'Horrible to Mum. A real bitch.' Mother had to spit to get that word past her teeth. 'I had to go to work, you see.' She was silent again, eyeing Vanessa sideways. 'I took the job at the milliner's.'

Vanessa nodded, in shock.

'Wouldn't go to work at the bakery. The smell, the hours. But it paid twice as much. Mum needed the money. I was mean, so mean to her. And she let me, she let me go to *Milady's*.'

Her fists dabbed at tears, wiped that awesome nose. Vanessa held her then, clumsy, and thinking about how you can crush a sparrow in the palm of your hand.

Then Thea said, 'They liked that reading. Lots of people want copies.'

Again that shift of focus. Or was it? Was it a glimpse of how unworthy Thea felt underneath the bravado? Vanessa thought of composing a tribute for Thea to give her while she was still alive. But she'd never done it. Now she must make up for that. She started to write.

There followed a week of making impossible choices. Choices that seemed banal in the face of Thea's secret and its impact. What did it matter what music Vanessa chose to be played in the chapel or what the coffin was made of, when it was no longer possible to get answers to her questions? She found herself breaking off in mid-task to rummage in yet another drawer, although she had no idea what she was looking for. Washing-up water went cold while she marched into her mother's old room addressing the empty bed, imagining conversations that were not to be.

David had come, to "Support you with the practicalities". Dear David. He always knew what must be done. He insisted on taking her to register the death. "It won't be what you think".

He was right. She'd thought it was just a piece of paperwork, but being the one to register the death seemed to make her responsible for Thea being dead. She came away shaking.

When David returned to work, he had to unhook her hands from his shoulders.

At night her bedroom seemed haunted by malevolent spirits. As if all the veiled threats and manipulative ploys, her mother's stock-in-trade, had slipped into the shadows to roost. All the migraines with their message of "Now look what you've done" thickened the air until she choked with rage and terror. Thea was still punishing her for being herself. Thea had never been herself. It was not a permissible state.

Ted meanwhile would stand and glare at an ornamental plate or teapot or drop into a chair and stare at the ceiling. Then he'd cross his legs and start lining up the toe of the upper foot with the glazing bars on the window. How often she'd watched him do that, suppressing emotions, whatever they were, into the rectangular confines of a pane of glass. At mealtimes she tried to get him to talk. But he just stared at her blankly, shook his head and pushed food about his plate.

She reminded him he could get out into the garden now. For a moment he looked almost angry, but soon he was out there in his saggy green gardening cardigan, coaxing the ancient motor mower into life. He carefully placed white cardboard boxes at either end of the lawn to give his failing eyes something visible to aim for and moved up and down the lawn like an automaton, carving it into respectable stripes for Thea's wake. She hadn't seen him looking so contented in months.

She'd often hear him in the night padding about, going down to the kitchen. One night she followed him, made hot chocolate, put it on the kitchen table. She sat down with hers. But Ted took his mug and set off upstairs. She followed, exasperated, pausing at the foot of the stairs with her mouth open to speak. She watched Ted's legs climbing. Cracked leather slippers, blue-veined ankles sticking out of pyjama stripes, and the old rayon dressing gown. That maroon robe was ancient, covered in a design of mustard and black triangles and circles.

He'd worn it as the Wizard of Oz one Christmas when Kate and Lisa were small. Kate grabbed it and trailed around in it all afternoon, waving a wooden spoon as her magic wand. Lisa shadowed her, trying to jump on her "cloak" as it dragged along the floor and Thea told her off because it would tear. Lisa had turned her grinning face up to Thea's angry one, all blue eyes and blonde curls. 'There's a good girl!' Thea said, triumphant. Whereupon Lisa had continued as before. After that it was war between them, Thea determined to have control, unable to leave well alone.

The dressing gown had survived. Vanessa watched it flapping round Ted's bony legs as they disappeared up the stairs, and knew he could not continue in the house alone.

Now they were all back from the crematorium and Vanessa saw an opportunity to talk to Kate, who was standing apart from the other guests looking out at the rainswept rose beds. They'd hardly spoken since the evening of the photographs.

Kate half turned from the window at her approach. 'Hello, Mum.' She didn't smile and Vanessa could see the muscle at the side of her jaw clenching as if she were chewing more words and swallowing them.

'Thank God that's over.'

'Awful wasn't it? People liked what you said about Nan. They've been saying to me what an extraordinary woman my grandmother was. Extraordinary is right.'

Vanessa nodded. 'That's a very useful word. Especially today.'

Kate took her elbow and steered her to the far end of the room, away from the groups of guests. She could feel Kate's tension vibrating into her own arm.

'I always knew it was her. And yet I was still surprised by those pictures. And you would never talk about it.'

'I'm sorry Kate. I feel awful about that and I still don't really understand why. The whole thing made me feel ill, scared. I just couldn't make myself.'

'She was a bit of a witch, wasn't she? That feeling, I can understand that, remembering how I felt that day with Flora. In this very room. Scary.' Kate looked across at the chair where Thea used to sit and shuddered.

Vanessa nodded. 'I see now why she was like that. She must have thought the game was up. After all those years. She must have been terrified.'

'Yes, but it's no excuse for what she did. And don't tell me it was the illness. She knew exactly what she was doing.' Kate paused and rubbed her eyes. 'What I've been trying to figure out is how come no one ever noticed? She did an amazing job. She pulled it off. You have to admire her for that, in spite of everything. And what about Gramps? Lisa said he hasn't seen the photos.'

'Gramps may have known. But I somehow doubt it. I haven't talked to him about it yet. He's got enough on his plate. And he wouldn't be able to see the photos anyway. But if she wanted to keep it quiet – and she obviously did – then he'd have done what he was told. As for me – she was just my mother. I guess I didn't really see her in any objective way. Your mother is your mother.'

'Yes,' said Kate.

The two of them fell silent, watching rain-drenched daffodils, a blackbird yanking a worm out of the grass.

Vanessa felt the heavy weight of that "Yes". 'I hope we can be close like we used to be? Forgive me for not seeing, refusing to talk about it?'

'Don't talk about forgiveness!' Kate spun round to face her, hair flaring out like a skirt round her narrow face. People nearby turned at the pitch of her voice and she dropped a tone.

Vanessa frowned. This wasn't like Kate. She'd obviously touched a very raw nerve.

'This has stirred everything up again. Okay, it answers some of the questions, but it raises a whole lot more. Imagine what it's like, meeting new people and you can see them looking at Flora and me, looking at Jack and Daniel, and wondering. And I'm supposed to be tolerant, say nothing, be nice. And then there are the people who've been working hard at forgiving me. Like Roz and Blake. Forgiving me for something I never did.' Kate turned slowly to go and spoke quietly now. 'I mean, what is forgiveness anyway? Heaven knows I've had enough practice with Daniel, but I still don't know. And will this make it any easier for Daniel to accept Flora? And will I be able to "forgive" him if it doesn't? As for Thea, my sainted grandmother, forget it!' Over her shoulder she added, 'No, I can't say I have much interest in forgiveness any more.' She walked away, threading her way through the knots of guests.

Vanessa stayed by the window watching the rain, taking in this speech, fearing for her Katie, for Jack and Flora.

Vanessa was back home at last, the funeral behind her. With Ted insisting on some time on his own – "Just a day or two on my own. Get my bearings" – there was a lull before the house-clearing must begin.

Now she waited for David to go to bed. She wanted to do this herself and not have questions to answer if it all came to nothing. In the little room they used as an office she turned on the computer. "Steam-driven", Lisa called it. Feeling furtive, she pulled a scrap of paper from her jeans pocket and typed in the address of the first website listed. Lisa had phoned that morning adamant it was possible to do all sorts of family research without going out of the house. 'You've got the time, Mum. Why don't you have a poke around?'

Tentatively Vanessa entered the name "Silking" in the search box and clicked on the button. She didn't have much to go on. Just that name, the link with Gibraltar and the features of the lady in the photograph. She wasn't even sure of her grandfather's first name, although it might be Richard. Her cousin Michelle said he was known as Dick. The screen went blank and then filled slowly with a host of people with the same family name. All those long dead strangers revealing themselves to her. They were listed with their relationship to the head of the household, place of residence, place of birth. Before she could start a systematic scan, the word "Gibraltar" seemed to vibrate on the screen a few lines down, grabbing her attention. A quick skip and she spotted it again, further down the page.

She selected the first "Gibraltar" entry to view the image and found herself holding her breath. The house was quiet. She could hear David snoring softly in the room above her. She'd been doubtful at first, but now to her amazement she seemed to be on the trail of her grandfather's family.

Data began to appear on the screen. She seemed to be viewing an actual page of the 1901 census, a form completed in a bold cursive hand, very regular. Painfully slowly it jolted down, line by reluctant line. When it was finished, realising it was all far too small to read, she pressed on the icon of a magnifying glass and waited again for it to load, this time taking even longer.

For goodness' sake! She'd be up all night. She began to see the point of the faster internet system Lisa said was in the pipeline. But by now she was hooked. Something stronger than curiosity kept her there. Almost a longing. A need, to know her roots, to understand why Thea had clung on so determinedly to this secret.

Eventually she could scroll down gradually. Unfamiliar hand-writing, an old-fashioned script she found hard to read. Abbreviations. Slashes and words apparently struck through or marked, making them even more difficult to decipher. What did the marks mean? There was nothing here she recognised. She could pick out an Albert, a William, a Sarah. Aah! So a capital "S" looked more like a "J". She moved on down the page and reached the bottom. Ready to give up, she scanned up again and found them: four "Silking" entries almost at the bottom. She felt the hair lift on her arms. Then she had to return to the top of the form to check the column headings.

William, aged sixty, was head of the household, and his wife's name was Henrietta. She was fifty-six. Which meant she must have been born in 1845. There were also two daughters – Ada, twenty-five, and Eleanor, seventeen. No mention of a Richard or any other son. Could this be them? William was listed as a brewer's agent. The address was on the High Street in Sheerness. Sheerness? She clicked across to the right-hand side of the form where place of birth was listed. William in "Somerset, Bath", the daughters both in Gibraltar and Henrietta in Bermuda. Nearly everybody else in the street was born in "Kent, Sheerness", so Gibraltar and Bermuda stood out as unusual.

There she was. The lady in the photograph. The Gibraltar connection confirmed it. In the final column, as if to reinforce the identification she found the words "W. Ind". Vanessa paged back up wondering why Henrietta was the only person to have an entry in this column. She expected to see it headed "Ethnic origin" or something similar. Her skin crawled when she saw the label:

"(1) Deaf and Dumb (2) Blind (3) Lunatic (4) Imbecile, feeble-minded".

It appeared that being West Indian was classed as a considerable disability. Vanessa wondered whether Henrietta found it so in Edwardian Sheerness. She fetched the road atlas from the bookshelves in the hall to check where Sheerness actually was, discovering it on the Isle of Sheppey sticking out into the Thames estuary. She shivered at the thought of the north-easterlies whipping across the flats of East Anglia to hit that exposed shoreline. She had no idea what the place was like, but it looked a pretty bleak location.

And what about Ada and Eleanor? So her grandfather had two sisters. She'd always been given to understand he was an only child. A nagging doubt materialised. Why wasn't he listed? Was this the right family? She reminded herself the census was a snapshot of one night in 1901. Whoever happened to be present at that address on March 31st. He'd probably left home anyway.

She printed the page, returned to the first screen and continued to scroll down, moving onto the next screenful of names. Another Gibraltar birthplace. Someone called Frederick Francis. A click on him took her to a different kind of list. No addresses, just a list of names, each one listed as a soldier and, at the top, a reference to an institution. It was the census return from the barracks at Shoeburyness. Frederick Francis Silking was listed as a corporal with the Royal Garrison Artillery, aged twenty-nine. Not Richard, but Frederick could be shortened to Dick she supposed. And born in Gibraltar. Surely it had to be him. The age was roughly right as far as she knew. And of course, he was too old to have been living at home. So many things to check on. Where was she going to begin?

'Henrietta', she said aloud and picked up the framed photo on the table beside her. 'So you're called Henrietta.' It was a surprise and also, she had to admit, a disappointment. It seemed such a buttoned-up kind of name and very English. 'I can't say it doesn't suit you, because I don't know you, but it's about the last name I'd have guessed. You look a lot wiser than a Henrietta.'

She looked from Henrietta to the map. What a shock it must have been. She'd have grown up in the West Indies, then spent however many years in Gibraltar in a Mediterranean climate. Long enough at any rate to have three children. And after that to fetch up in Sheerness. Vanessa felt a rush of sympathy. The poor woman must have frozen to the spot.

The room was dark and cold, lit only by the blueish glow from the screen. Vanessa shivered. The heating had long gone off. Now, of course, she wished David was awake. She wanted someone to tell. In the morning she could phone Kate.

20

1931

I think I'll be a fish out of water, at the same time as knowing I will be in my element. It means this Christmas is going to be much more exciting than last Christmas. And not just because we can afford a chicken this year.

I kept the party invitation secret at work. It came near Christmas when lots of the girls got cards from their special clients, some with ten-shilling notes tucked inside. So I made out it was just a card. I could tell Gwen was sorry for me that I obviously didn't have a ten-shilling note. But I thought the invitation was much more precious. I can just imagine what Mum would have thought about that.

I've said as little as possible about it at home. I told Mum I'd been asked to help out (which is true) and she didn't comment. I couldn't resist showing Dadser the invitation. It's so beautiful. Gold round the edge and you can feel the raised up letters of the "At Home" when you run your finger over it. So Dadser knows I'm not just helping. He just said 'Go and enjoy it. Make new friends, but don't forget where you're from.'

The Atkins only got home from the Med (that's what Lily calls it) in November and she relied on me to catch her up on current fashion. She's been in Malta most of the year because Mr Atkins' ship was in the Mediterranean. She seems almost like a stranger. Our conversation was all about hats and Lily seemed subdued, almost sad. So the news of the party was a surprise.

'A Christmas *soirée*', Lily said. 'It's just a cocktail party really, but Clive likes to do something special at Christmas.'

Of course, the first thing I thought was, what shall I wear? Nothing I've got is suitable and certainly nothing in Edna's wardrobe either. I'll have to make something. Which means money for material and making it at Lucy's house so Mum won't know. She'd say I could wear a clean white blouse for helping, but I'm not dressing like a waitress.

I'm surprised how helpful Lucy is when I mention it. She says Auntie Rose has a spare length of dress fabric under her bed and she'll get round her somehow. We'll have to pretend it's a surprise for Christmas. I don't care what Lucy says when she shows me – it's ruby red silk, quite heavy so it will drape and hang well. Auntie got it for Lucy but it wasn't bright enough for her. That's so Lucy. She's right of course. When she held it up to her face all her colour drained away. But it suits me just fine. I don't want to draw attention but I do want to look sophisticated.

We cut it out the Sunday before the party and Lucy wants to pin it *and* tack it together, like she learnt in school. But I say there isn't time and just run it up on the pins, which turns out to be tricky because the silk is slippery and I can't get the tension right on Auntie's machine. It's difficult to keep the two layers of fabric from stretching unevenly. I have to send Lucy off to make tea because she keeps standing over me making helpful suggestions. In the end I manage it, and I still say it's quicker than tacking the pieces together.

When I try it on Lucy says I'd better change at her house and stay overnight after the party. I know what she means. Mum would never let me go out looking how I'm going to look. I can hardly bear to think about it, I'm so excited. Lucy offers to lend me a necklace but I say I'll just wear Mum's gold chain she gave me. Lucy's stuff is flash and cheap. There's still a lot of finishing to do on the dress but there'll be plenty of time to do that after work on Saturday afternoon.

Come Saturday, when I get round there, Lucy is in bed with a cold. She comes down to help me because Auntie's in the shop. But she's all thumbs as usual and I'm getting frantic as she's sneezing and dripping all over the place and I'm afraid she'll mark the silk. I'd like to get on with it by myself but even I can see I'll never finish it on my own. Then Auntie comes in and she's mad at Lucy for getting up and mad at me for letting her. She says she'll catch her death and sends her packing. She takes Lucy up a hot lemon drink with her usual fuss. Auntie makes a great palaver over all the things Mum doesn't, and doesn't turn a hair at the things Mum thinks are important. When she's done fussing over her darling little Lucy, which she pronounces Luc*ee*, making her sound like a pet mouse, she comes to see what I'm doing.

'So what's this party all about?' The thing about Auntie is there's nothing she likes better than a secret or a mystery or a juicy bit of gossip, so she's obviously curious.

'I'm just helping out. It's a client of Mr Cooper's.'

'Helping out, is it?' She looks at the dress which is laid out on the table so I can get the hem straight. 'I see.' And she gives me an old-fashioned look.

'That's if I ever get there in time.' I'm close to tears. 'I'm supposed to be there in an hour to put the canapés together.'

Auntie goes to the cupboard in the corner and clinks a bottle out from the back. I hear the cork squeak and the tinkle of it as she pours into a glass. I know this ritual well. But now she comes over and hands me the glass.

'Here, just a little of my parsnip. Do you good. Can't have you getting all upset now.' She takes the needle from me and carries on with the hem. 'What else is to do?'

'I didn't have time to put the zip in, so I've got to put some fasteners down the back.'

'Oh, my. You'll miss the tram for sure. Best I sew you in.'

That is exactly what I hoped she'd say. What's more, she'll be a lot quicker and neater than Lucy, so I can see my luck has turned.

When I arrive, I can see Rosie the maid, is flustered. She shows me into the morning room, but she doesn't know whether to take my coat. I tell her I've come to help before the party but she looks me up and down, goes pink and hurries out of the room muttering something about asking Madam. I hear her going upstairs. A few minutes later she comes and tells me Madam will be down presently. She still doesn't take my coat. It's cold in here anyway. I check my hair in the mirror, glad it's stayed flat under the silk scarf Auntie lent me.

After what seems an age Lily appears in a black dress with dia-mante earrings and necklace and brooch. I want to tell her she really shouldn't wear all three together, but think better of it. Black doesn't suit her. It makes her skin look grey and the way she's done her hair emphasises her nose. She calls Rosie to take my coat and takes me through to the kitchen. There are silver salvers laid out on the table covered in tiny squares of toast with dabs of cream cheese on them. My job is to cut stuffed olives in half and place each half on a square of toast. Lily is poking in a jar with a teaspoon and pushing little piles of black seeds onto her toast squares. She's getting seeds all over the silver salver. I finish my olives really quickly, so I take over from her and clean up the mess she's made while she rearranges pieces of toast that don't need rearranging. All the time I can see her giving sideways looks at my dress and I have to concentrate really hard not to squirm and wonder if she can see I'm sewn into it. All the time she chatters on about who is coming and how she hopes there's enough to eat.

Then I hear a door opening and footsteps which stop just outside the kitchen. *That* voice says, 'Lily, my dear?' and she rushes out, licking a cluster of the black seeds from the end of her finger. She shuts the door behind her.

Rosie comes through from the scullery, tying on a starched, frilly apron. She looks up at the clock and mutters that people will be arriving any minute. She grabs two of the salvers, and sighs in irritation as she has to put one down to open the door. She pulls the door to with her toe and I hear her say, 'Excuse me, Madam,' still with the sigh in her voice.

Now I can hear Lily. 'I really don't see why it's a problem.'

'The servants just don't know how to treat her, that's the problem.'

'Rosie, you mean. Really Clive. There's only Rosie. And Thea's much more use than I am.'

'Which underlines my point, my dear. You shouldn't be in the kitchen in the first place. Why did you not get in an extra girl as I told you?'

I can't help overhearing. I don't want to hear and yet I do. In any case it would be too pointed to shut the door now. I should have done it straight away. Then the doorbell rings. As the two of them hurry off I hear Mr Atkins say, 'And I hope you've worked out how you're going to introduce her.'

165

Just as I'm wondering what to do next, Lily puts her head round the door and says we must go through to the drawing room. I pick up a silver salver, but she says, no, no, to leave those for Rosie. I smirk to myself as I follow her down the passage, and notice her zip hasn't been put in straight and has a pucker just above the waist.

Lily introduces me to the first comers as "my friend, Thea" and I say, 'How do you do,' because Dadser has told me it's considered common to say "Pleased to meet you." He gave a little shrug as he said it, as if to say, "How silly and I don't hold with such nonsense". Which it is, but that's not the point. He knew I would think it was important.

Everyone starts arriving at once. Rosie can't cope with all the coats and Lily starts helping her. I don't need Mr Atkins to tell me that's not right, so I take over from Lily so she can welcome people in the drawing room. The coats are being laid on the sofa in the morning room. Rosie has lit the fire in there now and the lights on the Christmas tree have been turned on. Some of the women follow me in to pat their hair in the mirror or to poke at their perfectly reddened mouths with a lipstick. One of them squeezes past me to the Christmas tree and places a gaily wrapped parcel among those already there.

She sees me watching and smiles. 'For Lily's children,' she says and puts a finger to her lips.

'Lily's…? I didn't think…' I am confused and suddenly wondering. How could Lily have children and yet never mention them? How come I have never seen them?

The lady laughs. 'No, my dear. Not Lily's *own* children. Every year she has the little ones round from the Board School and gives them jelly and a present from the tree. Hardly anyone knows. That's Lily for you.' And she's off, swinging a sequinned bag on a gold chain, eager to claim her cocktail from Mr Atkins.

I stare at the fringe of parcels round the tree and wish Lily had lived near my school. Then I straighten the coats as Rosie comes in to bank up the fire and hurry back into the drawing room to get out of her way.

I watch Lily greeting people. She has a wonderful way of grasping people's hands and making them feel they are the only person in the room. She glows with welcoming warmth, quite unaware that by now her nose is shining and her hair out of place. She only cares about her guests and I see that makes for a very good party. People cluster round Lily. They make conversation with Mr Atkins as he circulates with the cocktail shaker, but he finds himself neglected much of the time and his eyes are often on me, I notice. He watches me sideways as he mixes the drinks, or his eyes slide in my direction over the shoulder of the lady he is talking to. He looks away quickly when I look up. At first I am worried, remembering the conversation outside the kitchen door. Will he send me away? Or tell me to stoke the fire? I think he won't because it might cause a scene with Lily, but I think he would like to. As the room gets warmer and the cocktails have their effect, he no longer looks away. Our eyes meet and I have a strange hot sensation in my tummy, which reminds me of the first time I met Mr Atkins. He doesn't speak to me all evening. He is a very odd man.

I only have one cocktail. Lily passes it to me as it's quite clear Mr Atkins isn't about to offer me one. Anyway, I don't like the taste. I decide to get a glass of water from the kitchen but on the way the Christmas tree catches my eye. I creep into the morning room which is in darkness except for the lights on the tree that wink in amongst the branches and make the coloured glass balls shine and glow. I sit on the edge of the chair by the fire and gaze at the tree. I think of the "tree" back home, a branch out of the overgrown hedge at the bottom of the garden stuck in a bucket Mum covered up with red crepe paper. Binnie's decorated it with twisted sweet papers (she's been saving barley sugar wrappers for weeks) and cut out paper snowflakes and bits of cotton wool. This tree is like another world, an enchanted place. I feel as if it is speaking to me at the same time as being wrapped in its silence. The spell is broken by a movement at the door. I don't know how long I've been sitting there. Lily has come to find me. 'I wondered where you had got to. No, don't get up. I just wanted to be sure you were all right.'

She stands beside me also looking at the tree. Without her smile she looks old and worn out. She says, 'Clive won't have it in the drawing room. He thinks it's rather vulgar.' Then she lightens her voice. 'And he won't let me put my angel on the top.' She lifts the lid of a footstool and pulls out a feathery thing. 'Look!'

She hands me a tatty creation with goose feather wings, which must once have been white but are now yellowed with age and stained brown with glue. I think Mr Atkins has a point.

'It used to belong to my mother. We always had it at the top when I was a child and I got away with it until this year.' She giggles. 'But I won't throw it away. I hide it in here.'

She tucks it back inside the footstool and points to the golden-haired fairy on the top of the tree. 'Now *that* is what I call vulgar, but he prefers it. Dear Clive.' She sighs, gazing down at the presents round the tree. 'He also thinks it ridiculous for a couple with no children to have a tree at Christmas.'

There is a catch in her voice and when I look up there are tears in her eyes. I feel like when you step off the pavement and the kerb is much deeper than you expected. She shakes her head. 'I must just go and powder my nose. Perhaps you would help people find their coats. They'll start leaving soon.' She switches on the light as she leaves and the room is ordinary again.

When I get home Auntie and Lucy are having cocoa by the embers of the fire. I tell them all about the guests, the dresses and the canapés, and how odd the cocktail tasted. Auntie tells me that the black seeds were caviar, which is the roe of a fish and a great luxury. No wonder they tasted so salty. That's one luxury I can do without. I don't mention the Christmas tree or Mr Atkins or Lily's children. Then Auntie snips me out of my dress and I climb into bed with Lucy who smells of the camphorated oil Auntie's rubbed on her chest.

21

2006

Vanessa stopped at the display of lilies, automatically selecting the right bunch for Thea with a few already open, lots of closed buds. Her hand stopped in the act of lifting the cellophane out of the bucket. She didn't need lilies today. Move on. Cherry tomatoes, Indian snack selection, tasty but not too spicy. Bin-bags, she'd need no end of them. Bottled water seemed a waste, but she really didn't trust the pipes.

She was on her way to Ted's to start the painful process of clearing the house. There'd always been a routine to visiting her parents, calling in at the supermarket to pick up something special for supper. Smoked salmon for Thea maybe. Nothing too heavy, it kept Ted awake. Not that any strategy would help him to sleep right now.

When she arrived Ted was in a hopeless muddle of clothes and papers, trying to reduce his life to a few suitcases and half a dozen cardboard boxes. He was moving in with his younger sister, and Aunt Peggy could only accommodate a few favourite items. He'd be fine there, Vanessa told herself. He and Peggy shared a love of gardening, cryptic crosswords and proper coffee. He'd know where he was with her. She called a spade a spade, as Ted put it. They had a similar sense of humour, she was an excellent cook and she wouldn't let him drink too much wine.

'Pity about the wine, but then again I don't want to become a drunken old bore. Old bore is quite bad enough.' He grinned. 'Don't worry, I'll be all right. We can reminisce about Mother and Father, cricket matches at Stinchcombe and cycling in Bavaria. She says she'll be glad to have someone to cook for. What she really means is, someone who can finish the crossword.'

He smelled clean but his clothes needed attention – food stains on his tie and moth holes in his jumper. Through all the difficult months of Mother's illness he'd dressed impeccably as if they were about to go out for drinks, even though she no longer noticed.

Vanessa watched him from a doorway. He moved a box from one side of the room to the other and placed a pair of shoe trees on top of it. He picked a clothes brush off the chest of drawers, put it back and sat heavily on the edge of his bed. 'I'm doing unnecessary things.'

He waved his arms at the gaps where the family had removed pieces of furniture and pictures and shook his head. Vanessa had taken a couple of chests, a favourite table and a desk, Michelle's family chose a table and some pictures, Kate had wanted nothing and Lisa would only accept the blue-and-white cow with the broken leg and a lustreware plate. 'Nan really loved them,' she said. Ted had been keen for them to take the things, but Vanessa understood how he felt: their absence changed the whole feel of the house.

Vanessa started on the wardrobe in Thea's bedroom. Stacks of shoe boxes containing nearly every pair of shoes Thea had ever owned. Court shoes, sandals and what Thea had called her "flatties". Most had cracked linings, broken straps or missing heels. Some were obviously uncomfortable and hardly worn. These went into a bag for the charity shop, the rest nearly filled a black sack. One pair made Vanessa's eyes prick as she opened the box. Mum's party heels. Much higher than the rest. Black suede in a classic Fifties style. She pushed her feet halfway into them and staggered across the room to the mirror. Like a seven-year-old in dressing-up clothes. Ridiculous to walk in, but irresistible. She put them aside to take home.

Ted shouted from the kitchen that he'd made coffee. He made good coffee, strong and aromatic, in a willow pattern jug, and poured it through a tea strainer. The smell of hope, thought Vanessa as she went downstairs.

'The cutlery,' said Ted.

Vanessa frowned.

'We must sort it out. Put it in the canteen.'

'The canteen?' Once upon a long time ago, Vanessa remembered, the cutlery was always returned to its heavy wooden box with inset brass handles. In recent years it had taken its chance, muddled up in the drawer with the stainless steel set.

'Oh, come on.' Ted wagged his head in irritation. 'It's in the hall.'

'But now?' Why this urgent need to restore order to knives and forks?

'Before the auctioneer comes.' Ted looked at her fiercely. 'I do know what I'm doing, you know. It just might not look like it.'

He'd already pulled out the cutlery drawer and was clattering forks and spoons on to the work surface.

Vanessa fetched the canteen and put a firm hand on his arm. 'You go and finish packing the suitcases. I'll sort this out.'

Ted pursed his lips doubtfully, but shambled off upstairs. Vanessa watched him go. Poor old Dad. For five years now he'd been gradually taking control as Thea's mind and grip on practicalities had slipped. At the same time her faults had flourished like weeds in a hothouse, smothering her qualities. He'd coped with it all with a patience that astounded Vanessa. When she was a child it was always: "Get a move on, it doesn't have to take all day," and "Why all the song and dance?" While motorists in front of him were forever doing "One mile a fortnight".

Vanessa weighed an ornate fork on her fingers and wondered again about the curly A engraved on the handle, which she used to think was a pair of scissors. It was years before she asked why that should be. A for Atkins, she was told. A mystery in itself. The canteen was a wedding present. Second-hand, she'd supposed. Half a lifetime later it occurred to her that, if the set were second-hand, it would be unusual to know what the A stood for. Vanessa wandered up to the bedroom.

'Dad, what about this engraving on the silver?'

'What are you talking about?'

'The A on the cutlery.'

'A for Atkins. I thought you knew all about that.'

'Atkins?'

'Well, not Tommy Atkins.' His voice cracked with impatience.

'But how did you know it was Atkins? Did you know the people?'

'He was your mother's first husband, dammit.'

'First husband?'

Ted looked up, his annoyance falling away. 'You did know, surely?'

'No.'

'They weren't married for long.' As if that made it easier. 'He died. Cancer, poor devil. Clive Atkins, his name was.'

'And she kept the canteen.' It was all Vanessa could think of to say.

'What was she supposed to do with it? Perfectly good stuff. Rather fine quality in fact. His folks had money. We didn't. There was a war on. You were glad of what you could get. Here, sit on this.'

Vanessa knelt on one of the suitcases while he heaved on the leather strap and coaxed the buckle to engage.

Back in the kitchen she tried to digest this new information. Moths had been at the baize inside the cabinet and crumbs from her childhood were gathered in the corners. She wanted to clean it savagely, but took care not to make holes. Slotting the cutlery into place was soothing. There were little labels that told you where to put everything and they were still intact. She used to enjoy this task as a child.

Over lunch at the local pub, Vanessa told Ted about nearly buying the lilies.

He nodded and smiled. 'It's the unexpected things that get you.' He stopped abruptly.

Vanessa was thinking of the crystal vase across from Thea's chair and how her mother would watch her putting the lilies in the water. Her clawed hands would jerk about in the air as if they were arranging the flowers, willing her to cut that stem, move the shorter blooms to the front. When it was finished she would relax and sigh. It was the only time she smiled.

'You'd better take the vase,' said Ted as if following her thoughts. 'That was hers too.'

Vanessa frowned. 'Well, of course it was...'

'Lily's.'

'Lilies. I know. It's all she ever wanted.'

'No. *Lily's*. It belonged to Lily Atkins. Clive's first wife. It was her vase.'

Vanessa's eyes and mouth fell open until Ted laughed. 'So *he* was married before!'

'Oh yes. For many years.'

'So not your dashing young beau?'

'He was old enough to be her father.'

'Why on earth...?' Her beautiful mother.

Ted shrugged. 'Made her feel safe. Or so I presume.'

'Did she love him?' She'd chosen comfort food, but the conversation was putting her right off her sausage and mash.

'Who knows? What is love, and all that?' Ted looked into his beer, tipping the glass from side to side.

'Oh, Dad.' Vanessa took a deep breath. 'And then you came along and she must have been pretty relieved she was free and well out of that one. It was you who was the dashing young beau.'

Ted grinned. 'But of course.'

'But she hung on to the vase. It was her prize possession. What *was* going on? Didn't you mind?'

Ted leaned back, pushing his plate away. 'Just things. It was no big deal, as they say.'

'But second-hand things. Third-hand actually.'

He lifted his hands in a gesture of letting go. 'Just things.' He got up to pay the bill.

As they walked to the car Ted said, 'Actually not just "things". Fine things, beautiful things. In her eyes. Hadn't had many of those in her life.'

Back at the house, Vanessa returned to Thea's bedroom. Her energy of the morning had drained away, leeched into adjusting her picture of "Mother" yet again. She turned her attention to the chest of drawers Thea had used as a bedside table. On the top was a pile of telephone directories and Yellow Pages dating back to the Seventies, a lamp with a burnt silk shade which was once pink, the *Rubiyat of Omar Khayam*, and a blue tumbler with a hard water mark a third of the way down. The first drawer contained a collection of headscarves and handkerchiefs overlaid with all the tidyings from the top surface that had taken place over the years: before a dinner party; when the room was due to be cleaned. She could just imagine Mother sweeping inelegant clutter out of sight: boxes of Anadin, tins of Strepsils, boiled sweets in a sticky bag, spare and outdated reading glasses, rose catalogues and recipes torn out of magazines. As the contents of the drawer slid towards an open bin bag a small book with its cover half off caught Vanessa's eye.

A prayer book. She read the inscription inside the broken cover: *To Frederick from Almira, in remembrance of Gibraltar, September 29th 1893. "Love one another".*

Frederick. As in that census record. This must be Thea's soldier father, known in the family as Dick. So, her grandfather's prayer book. But who was Almira? 1894. He'd have been a young man, twenty-ish if she remembered correctly. Might even have been for his twenty-first birthday. An odd present from a sweetheart in this day and age, but that was another time, another place. *Love one another.* A commonplace text or a hidden personal message? Who would ever know? It was an incongruous exhortation to find among the debris of Thea's life. Startling almost. It reminded her of Ted's loving devotion to Thea in her last weeks, which so starkly contrasted with her response to him. Vanessa detached the hardened remains of a rubber band from the flyleaf and put the little book aside to take home with the peep-toe shoes.

The middle drawer was full of jumpers with underwear stuffed round the sides, not all of it clean. Cellophane bags of stockings were crammed into the corners. She salvaged a couple of decent acrylic tops for the charity shop but the rest was either stained or moth-eaten. The bottom drawer seemed to be full of Gor Ray pleated skirts in dreadful checks. Mail order mistakes, Vanessa guessed. There was only one she remembered Thea wearing. They could all go to the charity shop. Underneath was a collection of handbags, only one fit to join the fearsome skirts.

The last item in the drawer was a large plastic carrier bag. Good God! Full of her old dolls. She started pulling them out, intrigued to find she could still name each one. Sally still wearing the taffeta wedding dress Aunt Peggy sewed for her. Red-faced June with an arm missing. Daphne winking one cornflower blue eye. Judith muffled in the crocheted outfit Mother made, complete with matching knickers. Heather looking serene in spite of having no legs. She was the one with the disconcerting lift-up lid on top of her head. As a child she'd shivered to look down past the backs of Heather's eyes to the array of elastic bands and hooks holding her arms and legs in place.

The last was a rag doll lying face down. She was made of white cloth, an albino. Vanessa remembered she was christened Lily – her mother's idea because of her extreme pallor. Lily. She turned her over and gasped. Her features had been scribbled over with a biro and a darning needle was sticking out of her thin chest. Love one another, thought Vanessa. She dropped the doll face down when Ted appeared in the doorway.

'This is her,' he said, holding something out. 'That's Lily.'

Vanessa recognised the miniature in a leather case that had always hung on the wall next to her mother's chair. The fold-out wings were padded and covered in cream silk, now shredded with age. An oval miniature hung on the middle panel on faded velvet. A young woman in pensive pose and frilled collar and cuffs leaned, chin on hand, and gazed into the top right of the studio to reveal her profile. Vanessa exclaimed in surprise. 'I always thought she picked this up in an antique shop on one of her sprees. I never thought it *was* anyone.'

'Oh, it was someone all right. A someone to be reckoned with.'

'So Lily used to watch over her. All through the years. What *was* going on Dad? This is really weird, you have to admit.'

'Well, I suppose it was a bit strange. I just got used to her, you know. You see Lily knew how things were done. She came of a good family. That's what I gathered anyway, from things your mother used to say. And Clive, well, I got the impression that, shall we say, he liked things done properly.'

'Didn't Mother measure up?'

'Well, think about it. She was very young, inexperienced in running a house. He was probably a bit set in his ways.'

'You mean he was always nagging Mother and saying, Lily did this, Lily did that?'

'Who knows? But something like that. I'm only speculating you understand. Your mother never said in so many…'

'I don't suppose she had to.'

'Well, no.' He smiled fondly into the half distance.

Vanessa took the picture to the window, looking at it with fresh eyes.

Ted shambled over to join her. 'I expect that was done for Clive to take to sea. He was in the Navy. Purser, I believe. Travelling photo-frame.'

'I suppose so. Funny, she looks quite a gentle soul. Not a bit like a tyrant.'

'Oh, I don't believe for a moment she was a tyrant. She was merely the source of the tyranny. She was quite innocent. After all, she was dead.'

'So she was.' Vanessa glanced down into the bag where she'd dropped the rag doll.

'What's all that?'

'Just turning out Mother's chest of drawers. Would you believe she kept all my old dolls?'

'I would believe anything, my dear. Now, don't be long. The auctioneer will be here soon. Pleasant chap, deuced awful job. I'll put the kettle on.'

The auctioneer was quite excited about the canteen and asked about the date.

'It was a wedding present, 1930s,' Vanessa said, skating over the few years represented by the fastidious Clive.

'Hmm.' The gentleman appeared doubtful. 'Much earlier than that, I'd say. 1910 to 1915. Something like that.'

'Oh well, I guess it was second-hand.' Vanessa avoided Ted's eye.

After the man had gone, she remarked that Clive's family were not as generous as they seemed.

'On the contrary. You see, the canteen wasn't their wedding present to your mother and Clive. It was for his first marriage, to Lily. Sound chap, that auctioneer. Knew what he was talking about.'

Vanessa felt as if something broke inside her. 'For Chrissakes Dad, what next? Didn't you ever put your foot down? What about *your* life? Didn't you ever feel...?'

He stopped her by putting his hands up in front of his face, palms out, batting her words away. Vanessa put her arm round him. 'Sorry Dad. I just can't get my head round all this.'

'It's no good getting on your high horse. It's all water under the bridge now.' He sighed and lowered himself into his favourite armchair with the worn chintz cover.

'It's just so bizarre.'

Ted gave a dismissive laugh. 'I never even thought about it. It's only three things after all. Amongst all this. In all those years.' He waved his hand at the shelves of what he called "knick-knacks" surrounding them.

'Well, it's been a bit of a shock I suppose.'

He beckoned her over and she squatted by his chair, wobbling as he put a hand on her shoulder. 'She was a very special woman, your mother. Don't let us be forgetting that. She might have come at a price, but she was worth it. My word, she was.'

22

1932

Dear Mum, Dadser & Edna
It is HOT here. I wish you could see the beach by our house. The
sea is so blue. I have a tiny room looking over the gardens. We
have a verandah looking out to sea.
Miss you all, see you soon.

It's the first postcard I have ever written because it's the first time I've
ever been on a proper holiday. I don't count going to stay with Aunt
Kenchington in the New Forest when I was little. And we all went
then, so there was no one left at home to send a postcard to, anyway.

It's difficult to believe I'm really here. The letter from Lily came
completely out of the blue. After that Christmas when I went to the
Atkins' party, I didn't see Lily for ages. She didn't come into *Milady's*
and all I heard from the general gossip was that she wasn't well,
and later that her husband had been posted to a ship and that, once
again, she might be going to join him abroad somewhere, which
would mean having summer hats made in winter, like before. 'It's all
right for some,' said Gwen. I felt quite hurt that she hadn't contacted
me after making out I was her friend. All I could guess was that
Mr Atkins had put her off.

So imagine my surprise when a letter came for me, care of *Milady's*. Lily wrote she was travelling abroad to join Clive while his ship
was in Gibraltar. He thought the Mediterranean climate would do

her good, and had told her she needed a companion for the journey. Would I be willing to come with her?

Me? Go abroad? I was almost too excited to speak when I took the letter home. Of course, Mum poured cold water immediately. What about my job? It was all very well gadding off to be a lady's maid, but when I came back I would have lost my job. When I said I'd be a companion, not a lady's maid, she just went, 'Hurrumph,' and repeated the bit about the job. Of course Lily had thought of all that, bless her. It turned out she had come to an agreement with Mr Cooper. Mum muttered, 'I'll believe that when I see it,' but I heard her say to Dadser that I must be very well thought of for Mr Cooper to even consider it.

Then, of course, I was sewing for weeks and going on about being the only one in the family to go abroad. Dadser said Gibraltar wasn't really abroad, just England with palm trees. Mum said Dadser had been abroad plenty and all it did for him was to give him malaria. That shut me up because Dadser kept being off sick all this time and I did feel a bit guilty, being so excited when Mum was worried all the time about him and money. But I could tell by the way she told Auntie Rose that she was pleased I was getting the opportunity and not Lucy. I knew Auntie noticed that, too, because she clacked her teeth in the way she has when she's annoyed, as if she'd like to bite someone.

The journey was the biggest excitement. First the ferry and then the sleeper train from Paris. Me, in gay Paree! Not that it was very gay on a station platform. Going to bed on a train! With a compartment all to ourselves! And waking in the night to hear men shouting things in French I didn't understand and then drifting off to sleep again with the rhythm of the wheels on the tracks, knowing it was a *French* rhythm. Lily taught me how to say *Gare de Lyon* and that was what the wheels were saying, all through the night. It was so exotic. We had to change in Madrid which was a bit frightening. There were so many people rushing about speaking Spanish very fast that I was afraid we would lose our luggage or get on the wrong train. But now Lily took over. She'd been dreadfully seasick on the channel crossing (which I was not, to my pride and relief) and she seemed wiped out on the train. She spoke what she called "schoolgirl" Spanish, but it was good enough to organise a porter and get us to the right platform with no difficulty. Which all goes to show why a good education is essential.

Mr Atkins, or Lieutenant Atkins, as I now have to call him, arrived at the house to settle Lily in. I had already unpacked all her clothes and put them away as best I could in the tiny cupboard. He kept apologising to Lily because the house is so small. It's the beach house belonging to a friend of a friend, and the only place he could find. To me it is wonderful. To be right on the sand with the water lapping! It might be small, but there are two servants to cook and clean and serve us.

After unpacking we relaxed with Lieutenant Atkins on the verandah, which is like a downstairs balcony running right across the house with a table and easy chairs and a basket-weave chair on a swing. It looks out over the bay. Here in Gibraltar he is quite different from the Mr Atkins of England. I suppose he is very proud and pleased to have been promoted and to be an officer. He's witty and keeps laughing and smiling in my direction, at the same time as being most solicitous of Lily, fixing her cushions and a footstool and even fanning her in a jokey kind of way. There are none of those odd looks, so I quite look forward to his visits, which is not what I expected.

I have been paddling in the sea and I love it, because here the water is warm and the sand soft. Nothing like the pebbles of Portsmouth. I've lain in the sun and pinched myself. I am really here, Marge Silking, alias Thea, lying on a beach in Gibraltar with Mrs Clive Atkins, alias Lily, my *friend*. Before dinner Clive takes orders for cocktails and goes to mix them. Lily and Clive have been talking about love.

'There are things women know about love.' Lily lies back in her deckchair, lacing her fingers behind her head. 'They know for a start that most of what passes for love is not love at all. It is need and greed and lust. It is selfishness and jealousy. It is fear and loneliness.'

I draw circles in the sand with a pebble and wonder about the feeling I have for Lieutenant Atkins. What category does that fall into? It feels more like a disturbance than anything else. 'So what about real love?' I ask.

Lily burrows her feet into the sand, obliterating my circles. 'Real love doesn't look like love at all. Real love is wanting someone else's happiness and fulfilment. Mostly we're only after our own. Even when we pretend the opposite.' She lifts her head and looks at me longer than is comfortable. I have to drop my eyes. 'Real love, I suppose, is letting go.'

'Surely only a saint is capable of that,' comes Clive's voice as he returns with the cocktails.

I can't look at him as I take mine.

'A saint, or someone with nothing to lose,' Lily replies.

'And letting go – that sounds very cool. Lacking in passion.'

'It depends what you mean by passion. You can care intensely and still let go. If you really see the other person for who they are.'

I'm keeping quiet. It feels like a dangerous conversation. I don't understand it and I don't know where it's going.

Clive says, 'Quite the little philosopher, we are this evening, my dear. Here's to love.' He raises his glass.

Lily looks annoyed but I'm relieved. We sip our cocktails in the glow of the evening sun, looking out towards Africa. As we eat, the darkness gathers around us and a half moon dapples on the blackness beyond the beach.

When Clive leaves to go back on duty, Lily gives that little giggle I've come to associate with Clive's absence. Gone is the philosophical mood. She holds out her hand, pulling me down the steps and running over the sand. Her dress is a pale ghost leading me beyond the circle of light from the lantern on the verandah. When we reach the rocks she strips off her dress and her underwear, tells me to do the same and pulls me, laughing, towards the lapping sea. Oh, the sensuous pleasure of it! Nothing coming between me and the velvety water. I've already told Lily I can't swim, and now she takes my body and spreads me backwards like a tablecloth on the surface of the water. Miraculously, I float. I open my eyes and look at the stars, rocking to the rhythm of Lily swimming round me and think it is a wonder Lily is my friend.

Then the rocking stops. There are no ripples from her arms slicing through the water. No breaths and exclamations. Lily has gone. I'm alone in the ocean, nothing between me and the dark mass of Africa. I panic and splutter upright, salt in my nose, feeling a fool.

The water is only a few feet deep and I push through it, thankful for firm sand under my feet.

Where is she? Is she hiding? Of course it's a game. But I feel a sudden dread that Lily has abandoned me. Why did I trust her? I could have drowned. Suppose Clive should come looking for Lily? He might find me here naked and alone, him with his smiling eyes. I feel myself blushing in the darkness. But no. Clive returned to his ship after dinner and he's on duty until the morning. I remind myself that this is the reason I am here on this holiday. I must always be aware of steering a fine line between the roles of friend and companion, a word that makes me shudder. Tonight I have drifted effortlessly into the reaches of friendship but maybe it's an illusion, a bubble blown between the sand and the stars. I shiver and look round for my clothes. I'm sure I left them on that rock ledge. Then I hear a strange snorting noise and creep round the jutting rock. There is Lily, covering her mouth with her hand, the moonlight catching the gold cross she always wears.

'Thea, don't look so scared!' Lily throws her arms around me, rubbing my back while our breasts dance against each other. 'You're so cold, darling!' She holds out my clothes. 'Sorry, darling. I thought it would be a laugh.' She makes a pout at her failed joke.

I shrug, pulling on my dress over damp skin. 'I suppose you just took flight.' The sarcastic edge in my voice shocks me. I didn't realise how angry I felt, that it was possible to feel anger towards Lily. If Lily notices she doesn't show it. She is still full of her joke.

We have moved to the newly opened Rock Hotel. It is so smart and grand and the very latest thing in architecture. I have never seen anything like it. Lily's room has a balcony with the same view we had from the house but from very high up. All of a sudden Africa seems close enough to touch. There is a breeze up here but I miss the water lapping and, although there is a swimming pool in the hotel garden, I wouldn't be brave enough to go in it. It's full of a noisy crowd diving in, with glamorous girls sipping drinks on the sides.

We had to move out of the house because the people wanted it back. I'll be going home alone at the end of the week. Lily says I'll be fine. Of course I will. The plan was that we went home together, but

Lily is to stay on. She's to move into a quarter Lieutenant Atkins has found for her in Castle Road. Lily says it will become available at the weekend. I couldn't stay as it only has one bedroom, and in any case I have my job to think of. Lily says she is used to this place now and will manage fine without me. She says it to reassure me, but I know she has made some new friends and I think she is bored with me.

We sit on the terrace every evening looking at Africa and sipping martinis and Lily says she gets bored with that too. I don't know how she could say it. I could never get bored. There are so many people to look at, different fashions, ways to drape a scarf or to hold a cigarette holder. What I'd like more than anything in the world is one of those long cigarette holders with a matching cigarette case. So elegant. I don't even smoke but I'm sure I could learn. What Lily wants is her own apartment to make homely. She's crazy, but she's a dear.

One thing is worrying me. Dadser asked me to "look someone up", as he put it. And I haven't done anything about it. It means walking in to town and Lily can't manage that. She can't cope with the heat. For me, that is one of the best things. Being warm when it's freezing cold in England. Lily likes to wander in the Alameda Gardens under the shade of those great trees. I like the Elephant trees best but I'd rather soak up the sun. I haven't said anything about Dadser's errand, in case the person he wants me to look up isn't the sort of person the Atkins would want to know. I'll walk down to Main Street while Lily's having her nap tomorrow afternoon.

I tend to forget Dadser used to live here. Born at sea off this very coast, growing up here with my grandmother, going to school and everything with his brothers and sisters until he joined the Army. He must have known everybody in the old days. Now I'm here, I wish I'd questioned him more about the place. I was so wrapped up in Lily and Mr Atkins, it didn't occur to me.

It's crowded in town and I must say there are more coloured people to the square inch than I've ever seen before. All colours from pale sand and yellow ochre, through burnt sienna and warm sepia to polished skins as black as the kitchen stove. Nobody takes any notice of me. I ought to be pleased, but I find it disturbing. Is it because I blend in with all these colours? I don't want to blend. I'm not one of them. I'm a white person. Of course, there are plenty of other white people here too, so maybe that's why I'm not noticeable.

Dadser asked me to go to a shop called *Spoleto's* in Main Street. I find it with no trouble as it has a black-and-gold sign saying *Luigi Spoleto, Tobacconist*. I clutch the page of Dadser's notebook on which he has written, "Consuela, a friend of my mother, Henrietta Silking". I step over the threshold and inhale the smell of Dadser's pipe mixed with other, spicier aromas. It is dark inside after the sunlight of the street and it takes me a while to see the young woman watching me from behind the counter. She asks how she can help. When I say I have come to see Consuela, she says that is her name but she does not know me. I laugh and explain how old Consuela must be to have been a friend of my grandmother.

'You must talk of my great-aunt. I am named after her. Sadly she passed away last year.' She speaks in that soft lispy way that reminds me of Dadser when he says "Spanish". It's annoying when he does it, because I know there are lots of things he's not telling me. But in Consuela the accent is attractive.

I say I am sorry about her great-aunt and she says she will fetch her mother.

A tall thin woman appears with dark hair stretched into a bun at her neck. She has a deeply lined face and streaks of white in her hair but she is still very striking. She must have been beautiful when she was young. When I explain I am Dick Silking's daughter she beams and her eyes fill with tears. She opens her arms as if to embrace me, and then steps back as if she remembers, just in time, that I am a stranger. She talks of her aunt with great affection and then asks after my grandmother.

'They were very good friends. My aunt missed Mrs Silking very much when she left Gibraltar. I remember her well. Always smiling, and always, when we were small, she brought cookies for us children.'

A whiff of cinnamon among the tobacco scents seems to tease my nose for an instant. It is strange that this woman in a foreign country knows my grandmother better than I do. Now she is enquiring after her and I tell her she too passed away, remembering too late that Dadser said she was still alive. I can hardly correct myself, and anyway that must be a couple of years ago. I don't want to admit that I didn't really know her – my lady grandmother who seemed to vanish into the dust of a hot day. Here, in this dark little shop, she is more real to me than she has ever been.

We talk some more about Aunt Consuela but I am feeling confused and want to get away. When the gentle lady offers tea, I say I must get back to my friend who is unwell. I thank her and shake her hand and she kisses me lightly on both cheeks. As I step outside, I realise she is still beside me.

'Tell your father I think of him very often.' She speaks softly and her eyes are brimming again. 'Tell him he is in Almira's prayers.' She touches my arm and is gone.

As I walk back along Main Street I feel strangely sad. I have only met Consuela's niece for a few minutes and yet I don't want to leave her. I have touched on a mystery. Why should Dadser be in her prayers? Why did she follow me and speak as if it were a secret?

When I get back to the hotel Lily is having afternoon tea in the lounge. For once I am relieved to sit in that dim interior with the rattan fans whirring gently above us. The heat of the day and the meeting have made me feel quite faint. Lily is so normal and English and it is reassuring to eat cucumber sandwiches. I even feel homesick and take a cream horn from the cake trolley to stave off the pangs.

When I close my eyes that night I cannot get rid of the image of Almira, her beaming smile and brimming tears.

23

2006

Vanessa dreaded returning to finish the house-clearing job. The creaking of boards and pipes, scampering of rats and tapping of branches conjured presences which made the nights impossible. David found her a Bed and Breakfast to stay in. At least the process of clearing would be faster now Ted had departed. He had tried so hard to monitor what went where, but eventually he'd simply given up. 'It's too much, too much. Always too much,' he'd said one evening, head in hands. Vanessa had driven him to Aunt Peggy's the next day.

'You did what she wanted, Dad,' she reassured him as they drove away and his eyes filled. 'You kept her at home.'

'It was the least I could do.'

'Not the least. It was huge, Dad. You know how hard it was.'

'No, not the least.' There was a sudden energy in his voice and he spoke precisely. 'It was the *only* thing I could do. The only possible thing. The house meant so much. It was her life's work.' He set his jaw on those last words and nodded to himself.

Vanessa considered the truth of this. This house had taken root in Thea's soul, or she had taken root in the house. Either way, the two of them had been inextricable.

At first it was a wonderfully symbiotic and growthful relationship. She remembered Thea's spirit flourishing and expanding into her domain. She would walk the rooms with pride, following the sun round during the day: early morning tea at sunrise in the east-facing bedroom; breakfast coffee on the terrace; a bowl of soup for a late lunch in the warm bay of the drawing room and an evening glass of wine as the last rays slanted on to the kitchen table.

Her imagination had soared as she painted walls and ceilings in colour schemes celebrating the unique character of the house, with its mixture of architecture and styles thrown together over the years. She cut fabric and draped curtains and hangings. Auction rooms were scoured for just the right piece, a bleached pine corner cupboard and jewel-like plate for a dark corner, rich rosewood against formal striped wallpaper. Thea and the house glowed in the light of her creativity.

It was a triumph, especially considering where she had come from. You had to admire it. From that little kid in North End to much-courted and sought-after hostess, entertaining in the setting she had created. Ted was right. The house was her life's work. Vanessa had never thought of it that way before. And Thea had never had any training or a role model for the life she chose for herself. Except for Lily of course. Lily had provided a foundation which Thea had built on. Anything you can do, I can do better. She was more beautiful than Lily, had more flair and style, at least on the slender evidence of that photograph. Vanessa could see how hasty she'd been in judging the apparent obsession with Lily.

When the house was finished Thea basked a while in its beauty, but then her energy declined. Something went out inside her.

Vanessa started to notice when Thea made changes, that they were now in poor taste. Furniture that didn't fit. Crude reproductions instead of restored antiques. Colours that clashed. An overstuffed element crept in. Mead End became a suffocating place to be.

Occasionally the old magic had flickered to life again like the last blaze of a dying fire. When the lamps were lit and Ted poured a glass of sherry. Or in early summer, when the lawn was mown in stripes, pink and gold roses romped over collapsing arches and creeper covered the rotting window frames.

But deterioration set in. Repairs were no longer made. The outside began to invade unchecked. Damp, tendrils and branches, insects, rats and mice crept in where the fabric was slipping and loosening. Ted, his eyesight failing, literally did not see the dilapidation. With Thea, her eyes still magpie-sharp, the not-seeing was another thing entirely. It was her failing mind that would not see, or no longer made sense of what she saw. An early sign of the dementia, Vanessa realised in hindsight.

Now that Vanessa no longer had to consider Ted's sensibilities, she ordered the largest available skip. The wheelie bins had long become irrelevant and before long the skip had been emptied three times. All drawers and cupboards were bare. The auction house took away the valuable items, including the canteen of cutlery. A book specialist slaved for two days transporting endless shelves of paperbacks and hardbacks to his shop. All those books Ted had saved to read in retirement and which he now couldn't see. There were enough volumes of value that there was no charge for the service.

Vanessa struck a similar deal with a firm of house clearers recommended by the auctioneer. With them a container arrived, considerably bigger than many houses. The telephone wires had to be tied up to allow it to pass, with millimetres to spare, between the house and the barn. It filled the farmyard and the two men filled it. One thin and wiry, strong as steel, the other like an ox with a body odour to match. They didn't just fling the stuff in, as Vanessa expected. They packed it as carefully as a suitcase. At the same time they loaded anything saleable into their truck and drove it away each night. It took the best part of a week.

Kate came over with the children one sunny day. 'I just want to say goodbye to the place,' she said on the phone. They had a picnic in the overgrown rose garden and Flora toddled in and out of the collapsing arches playing hide-and-seek with Jack.

'I'm surprised at you, feeling so sad. After what happened. I thought you'd be glad to be shot of the place.'

'End of an era,' said Kate.

'Certainly is. And what a relief that is.'

'It must be.'

'Is that awful? You know how hard I found Mother. Even before she was ill. And Dad, well he was hanging on by his fingernails. He's devastated now, but it's got to be a relief for him too, when he recovers a bit.'

'They had something special though, didn't they? And the garden

– happy memories of when me and Lisa were kids. It reminds me of the other side of Nan. Oh, she could always be touchy, but she could be funny, fun even. If Gramps got her going.'

'How do you mean? Gramps getting her going?'

'Well, it was like he could – unlock her, somehow. I mean, it was never any good asking Nan if we could do something. Like have a picnic in the garden. We used to ask Gramps to get on to her – that always worked.'

Vanessa nodded. It was strange to have her daughter telling her things she didn't know about her own mother.

'I've thought a lot about what happened with Flora,' Kate went on. 'I feel ashamed at how I behaved. I know that's with hindsight, but even so. Maybe not so much ashamed as sad – that it was the last time I saw her. I suppose I just wanted to make my peace. Now that I understand what was going on for her.'

'Wish I could do the same.' Vanessa looked across at Kate remembering her outburst of a few months ago. 'You've come a long way since the funeral – "forgiveness", and all that.'

'I was in a bit of a state then. An emotional time – and Daniel wasn't helping. Everything's calmed down now. Things have fallen into place.' Kate eyed her mother. 'And before you start wondering and don't like to ask, we're getting on fine, me and Daniel.'

Big rain drops splashed on the left-over food and thunder rumbled in the distance. Flora shrieked with delight and the children danced about in the downpour as she helped Kate pack up. When they'd gone she went inside to make tea for the men. One weak, no sugar, one strong, two sugars. She felt deflated and lonely.

At last Mead End was a shell. The walls were branded with the imprint of pictures, the outlines of furniture. Without the glint of porcelain and glass to distract the eye, the cobwebs and damp stains were prominent. Vanessa stood on the sacred ground of Thea's drawing room and yelled. The sound echoed round the corners, out into the hall and up the stairwell, meeting nothing but empty space. The house had been set free.

She felt a new lightness as she locked the door for the last time and delivered the key to the estate agents.

*

Vanessa had taken trays and trays of bedding plants away from Mead End. A woman had turned up one morning in May, just after Ted left.

'They have them every year,' she said and her eyes filled with tears when she heard Thea had died. How did Thea *do* that to people? Vanessa hadn't had the heart to turn the woman away.

Now, nearly a month later, the plants were potbound and struggling. Pansies, splodgy begonias (which she loathed), powder-blue ageratum and French marigolds which screeched beside Vanessa's favourite blue and purple campanula. David always said colours in nature couldn't clash, but she didn't agree. In any case, the prissy bedding plants were going to look out of place in a garden full of old roses and overgrown shrubs. But it was a beautiful June day and for once she would enjoy getting outside and digging her fingers in the earth to rescue those that had survived. It would be a challenge to make them look a bit wild.

As she dug and cleared space, memories surfaced of Mother gardening. Thea had only ever relaxed and been truly "herself", whatever that meant, with her immediate family, when decorating the house or in the garden. A series of images ran through Vanessa's mind: Thea in a cream cotton dress with a bold design of orange nasturtiums, kneeling on the grass, busy with a trowel and filling a cardboard box with weeds; Thea wearing the same dress and a battered straw hat, collapsed on the seat against the garage wall, soaking up the sun; Thea with her hair blown into a frizz, digging in the vegetable patch or planting out wallflowers; Thea up a ladder with a paintbrush, wearing a shower cap spattered with magnolia emulsion paint. The everyday Thea was quite, quite different. And even this everyday Thea had two faces: the glamorous, charming hostess who was adored by all her friends; and the critical, judgemental, nit-picking wife and mother. It was this Thea who had dominated Vanessa's childhood. And flattened her.

Vanessa sat back on her heels and reached for a box of ageratum. Flattened. That was the word. Always Mother had flattened her. Not in an obvious, bulldozerish kind of way. She was much more subtle. If they argued – and could you even call it arguing when one person was a small child with no power whatsoever? If they argued, Mother would eventually shrug and give that sideways look which was like the poison in Snow White's apple. 'Have it your own way', she would say. 'Do what you like.' And for a moment Vanessa would feel triumphant, elated, just as Snow White must have felt on sight of the shiny red apple. But in the instant she sank her teeth into that moment, she knew how Mother would make her pay, as she had in the tussle over her "fat dress".

It's after breakfast and we're going upstairs to get dressed. I'm doing one stair at a time and it's slow because my legs aren't really long enough, so you're hauling me up to hurry things along.

'We're going to Auntie Edna's today.'

Auntie Edna is my favourite auntie so I go, 'Auntetna! Auntetna!' Then I stop, because something funny is happening in my bottom tummy. I'm watching your face and there's something about your glittery eyes that doesn't look good.

'You can wear your new dress.' You've gone ahead into my bedroom.

I don't say anything because the rest of me is catching up with that bad feeling in my tummy.

'Auntie Edna's looking forward to seeing it now I've finished it.'

'Horrid fat dress,' I mutter so you can't hear. I go hot all over in case you heard.

'What did you say?' You're opening the wardrobe to get the dress out.

'Nuffing.'

'Auntie Edna gave you the material. You loved it. Remember?'

'Pretty blue.' I remember when Auntetna opened the bag from *Bulpitt's*, the drapers. The material was covered with tiny pink and yellow and white daisies. I couldn't wait for them to turn into a dress.

'Yes, it's a lovely blue. Brings out your eyes. Here we are.' You sit down on my bed with the dress.

I grunt and pick up my teddy.

'Come here.'

'Won't wear fat dress,' I mutter into my dressing gown which is hanging in the wardrobe for the summer.

'I beg your pardon? I can't hear if you put your face in the cupboard.'

I say nothing. You're not meant to hear. That's the whole point of putting my face in the cupboard. Plus it's dark and it smells of lavender in those little bags Granny gives you. Plus I can't see your glittery eyes.

'It doesn't make you look fat. It's nice and cool.'

I say nothing. You were meant to hear really. But without me actually saying it to you.

'See the pretty smocking. You chose the colours. Remember?'

I fall for it and go and look. Of course I remember. But right now I feel so hot from my tummy right up into my throat that I think I might be sick.

'Here we go. Arms up!'

I hold my arms down by my sides.

'Come on, my love.' You only ever call me that when it's really important. You take an arm and pull it upward.

I twist away. 'No!'

'Auntie Edna will be very sad not to see it.'

I'm back in the wardrobe and I spot the dress with the shiny black belt. 'Want to wear this one.'

'Oh, the one Auntie Lucy gave you. No, don't pull it.' Your mouth has gone all hard.

'This one. Want this one.'

'It's a bit too old for you.' You give the dress the look that turns you into a witch.

I touch the dress again to make sure it's still there.

'Oh, now look what you've done.'

It's just come off the hanger, that's all. But you steam across the room as if the dress was ruined and put it back.

'Now don't be silly. Here we go. Arms up or we'll be late!'

I wriggle under your arm and out onto the landing.

'Come here! Come here at once!'

I wonder if I dare not go to you. I'm leaning on the banister rail watching you from under my fringe, ready to run if you start to get up.

'Now you're just spoiling everything. Spoiling the day for everyone. Auntie Edna will be waiting, looking forward to seeing you in your new dress.'

It's too much. The lovely material, the pretty smocking, the picture of her stitching away under the lamp, the sight of myself in the mirror wearing the finished dress. I let out the hot feeling in a great bellow.

'Just come and get dressed.' You sigh like you do when I won't eat my dinner.

I want to and I don't want to. I shan't, I can't, I won't. I bellow again.

'Oh, wear what you like then. Just don't say I didn't tell you.' You get up off the bed, stalk off into your bedroom and start slamming drawers and doors open and shut.

I edge back into my bedroom. My bottom tummy feels like it's full of frogspawn like Eddy next door had in a jar. I finger the pink fabric of the dress with the shiny belt. I can actually wear it now. You said so. But I know that's only true in the same way that I didn't mean you to hear what I said was true.

I fiddle with my vest and look from the pink dress to the blue dress laid neatly on the bed. If I wear it, you will be happy and Auntetna will be happy and it's only me that won't be. If I don't wear it, I'll be happy for ten seconds and you'll be mad and you'll say something to Auntetna who will be upset and that will make you even madder and it will all be my fault and it will go on for days.

'Are you dressed yet? We have to go in ten minutes or we'll miss the bus.'

I slide over to the bed and dive into the blue dress, pull it over my head. As I turn round you come into the room.

'Aaah! There's a good girl. Didn't I tell you how pretty you'd look?' You lead me to the mirror in your room.

I see ugly. Fat red face. Fat dress billowing out from the smocking. Fat legs sticking out. I feel like a slug.

'Let me do it up. Turn round. There you are. Now dry your eyes. Here, blow. There's a good girl. All better.'

I say nothing, just turn away from the horrible mirror.

'Come on. No pouting.' You flip my bottom lip which makes me want to bite your finger really hard.

'What a face! The wind might change and you'll be stuck with it.'

You brush my hair more gently than usual, which makes me want to bite your hand. Today I want the tangles to really hurt.

Vanessa tore at thick fibres threatening to strangle a pansy plug, fanned out the roots inside and pressed the plant into the earth. It was all too vivid. She'd been a wimp, Mother's creation. Before she started on the house.

After university her main concern had been to put distance between herself and Mother. She'd escaped to Spain on a language course near Cordoba and met David, who was researching the harmonious co-existence of Islam and Christianity in the city. She'd fallen in love, only to discover that he'd just taken a post as junior history lecturer at Southampton University. So Vanessa had returned to home territory, but this time with her boundaries carefully set. Thea, of course, had been appalled at David's lowly status – she could still hear her indignant protest, "Not even Oxford or Cambridge!" – and never forgave him, even when he became a professor at fifty.

As a child she'd been Mother's doll. She could see that now. Wound up and set going, or switched off when it suited. Thea had made her clothes and dressed her up. Curled her hair and put her to bed on the hard little bundles of knotted rag, as if her scalp was as insensible as the ceramic lid on that doll, Heather. She shoved marigolds into a huge clump under a yellow rose. The poor things were probably too close together, but at least they made an impact. God, how that used to hurt. She used to work at each group of stretched hairs to loosen them and ease the pain in the roots before she could go to sleep. Ironic, really, that Thea had put so much effort into curling Vanessa's hair when she'd been so obsessed with straightening her own.

Vanessa shook her head, scraped soil from her trowel and stood back to see the effects of her work. The ageratum was a bit fluffy but it was fine with the campanula. And the pansies were great tumbling down that bank. The begonias were really more than she could stand, and she flung them onto the compost heap with unnecessary force.

David appeared at the back door and walked down the path to join her. 'Looks good.'

'They don't look too much like Thea's flowers, do they?'

'What *do* you mean?' He hugged her shoulders. 'Silly old thing. Of course they don't.'

There was something cleansing about getting wet and muddy

in the garden. It gave Vanessa a fresh perspective on the pile of evidence collecting on the desk beside her computer. There was a family history jigsaw to be completed and she could already see how some of the pieces fitted together. The wedding photo, for instance, in the pile of family papers sent by her cousin. It was a portrait of Thea, puzzling when she first saw it because the gown and headdress didn't match the pictures of her parents' wedding.

It must be of Thea marrying for the first time. She'd found the record easily enough, but it was not enough. November 1935. Her mother only twenty-two, her bridegroom more than twice her age. Vanessa needed to give the event some context. She tried looking for the groom's first marriage, starting in 1920. It was painstaking work. The screen would eventually offer a set of quarters to be searched, January-February-March and so on, for each year.

David came in and stood behind her as July-August-September 1922 was juddering into view. This was a likely year and summer a popular time for weddings so she scrolled down eagerly.

'Sorry, darling. But if I lose track of where I am I have to go back up to the top. You can see how long it takes.'

'Looks a tedious business, but it's amazing it's on there at all when you think about it.'

'I suppose.' Vanessa peered at a splodgy column. 'At least these are typed. The earlier ones are hand written of course.'

'Do you really need...?'

'Yes, I do. I need to *know* it, see it in black and white. It's not enough to be told.'

David had to say goodbye twice.

She had a stiff neck by the time she'd finished the Twenties, but found nothing. Maybe they married abroad. Maybe Lily was all a myth.

She turned to the pile of books she'd salvaged from Mead End. On top was a cloth-bound book with *Album* printed on the cover amongst elaborate scroll-work. It had gilt-edged pages but inside it seemed as if the cover might be home-made, as the cloth was folded onto the marbled end-papers and tightly laced into place with brown string.

On the last page was a contribution signed *Clive* and dated March 1911.

MY OPINION OF A GIRL
A girl a curious animal is:
A bundle of emotions;
Full of frolic, craft and "fizz";
A mixture of all notions.

How times had changed. It was an autograph book: pastel pages full of rhymes and riddles, exquisite miniature watercolours, pen and ink drawings and paintings on silk, signed by Winifreds, Violets and Flossies and others with more formal initials, possibly male. All those outdated Victorian conceits carefully copied out.

Vanessa had an impression of a popular girl who had grown into a young woman with a thriving social life. The centre spread of the album was filled with white wedding cards, the sort to send out with a piece of cake to friends who couldn't attend the reception. The cards were garlanded and embossed with silver flowers, bows and ivy. Often the bride's maiden name was crossed through with a genteel arrow. It was all very fussy.

As she turned the page a plain, flat rectangle fluttered to the ground, released from its blob of dried-out glue. As Vanessa picked it up the name transfixed with an arrow caught her eye. *Lily Osborne.* Another Lily. But below that name stood *Mr and Mrs Clive Atkins.* The date was September 1915. Vanessa turned quickly to the front of the volume.

The first peach-coloured page was inscribed *Lily Osborne* with carefully scroll-laden letters and the date, "25th September 1903". There was both a home and a school address in Southsea.

So that's who Lily was. She flipped forward again to the last page. Yes. Clive was the signature on the coy little rhyme. Their wedding date fitted exactly with what the auctioneer had said about the canteen of cutlery. Of course. What an idiot to have forgotten that vital clue.

24

1932

It's Lily's birthday and I'm invited to join her for a picnic in their garden. Rosie shows me out to the lawn and there is Lily sitting on the seat in the sun with her eyes closed. I am surprised she seems to be alone and wonder where the rest of the party is. As I cross the grass she opens her eyes and smiles and I think she looks sad for a birthday girl.

She pats the seat beside her and says how good it is to see me, that it's been too long. I say nothing to that. We haven't seen each other since I left her in Gibraltar and I know she's been back for a month at least. She sent a note to work saying she had "a few things to sort out". It's not how a friend would behave.

I hand her a card I painted myself and a little tissue paper parcel. In Gibraltar she admired a bow in the shape of a rose I had pinned on my afternoon dress. Just the thing for her birthday. I've made her one in ivory crêpe-de-chine which will suit a number of her dresses. She holds my gift in her lap for a moment and is about to say something when there's a whoop from behind the hedge and a crowd of people rush into the garden. I feel cross that she seems to forget all about my present in the activity that follows. The group are all wearing tennis whites and have been playing on the local courts. I'm introduced to Lily's brother, Fred Osborne, who is known as Ozzy, and to Claire, Angus and Charlie, short for Charlotte. I catch Claire and Charlie exchanging looks which I try to ignore.

'And, of course, you know Clive,' says Lily. And Clive nods and barely looks at me. His eyes are different today, as if he were wearing an ordinary pair, just like anyone else's. My stomach doesn't lurch and it's a disappointment and a relief all at the same time.

I gather that Claire and Angus are engaged to be married and that Charlie is a friend of Claire's and that they are all chums of Ozzy's. Chums. So people do actually use that word. Will I be a chum? I wonder. Claire is pretty, with a heart-shaped face framed by curly brown hair and looks far too good for the rather stolid Angus. I imagine Claire playing genteel tennis and letting Angus win. Charlie is tall and slender with cropped blonde hair and fantastic legs. I bet she's got a killer service and wipes the floor with everybody.

Clive disappears into the house while the others gather round Lily. He comes back with a gramophone. He sets it on the end of the seat and begins winding it up. Rosie appears with what looks like a photograph album but which is clearly very heavy. It's full of records, each one in its own cardboard sleeve. There's some classics but mostly they're recordings of popular songs and dance music, all the big bands, the well-known names. I am entranced just looking at the labels.

Lily comes to look through the records with me and keeps exclaiming over her favourites.

'This one, darling.' She turns to Clive, who puts the record on the turntable and lowers the needle.

'Oh, everyone's vanished!' She sounds almost as if she might cry and I'm shocked at this new, uncertain Lily. Only Claire and Charlie have disappeared, but Lily looks crestfallen and Ozzy steps forward to dance with her as if humouring a child out of a tantrum. Clive and Angus head for the house leaving me to look through the record album, wishing I hadn't come, wishing I was anywhere else in the world.

But before long Clive and Angus return with a trestle table which they set up under the apple tree and cover with a white cloth. Rosie hurries back and forth with lemonade, sandwiches and cakes, and the girls reappear having changed into floaty floral dresses, followed by Clive with a tray of glasses and Angus with a bottle of champagne. The cork pops and sails off into the shrubbery, we all clink glasses and toast Lily, and it is a party after all.

My memory of that afternoon swims into a haze of colours and smells. The fizz of alcohol in my nose, the peppery tang of lupins past their best in the herbaceous border, the purple and pink of Claire's dress merging with the purple and pink of the lupins. And the music. It seems to be floating down from the tree branches and jumping through the grass. I dance with Ozzy, who is funny and jokey and tells me I must be bored with these old numbers. He thinks I'll be dancing to the latest crazes in London and thinks I'm teasing him back when I say I've never been to London. Angus is stiff and formal and clearly doesn't like dancing. I'm glad when we're interrupted by Rosie bringing the birthday cake in a blaze of candles. We all sing "Happy Birthday" and Lily cuts the cake into slices and passes it round, seeming to be her usual self again. Then she and Charlie start dancing the Charleston and soon we're all doing it, all over the lawn, giggling and breathless.

Dancing is something I've never done. Nora is the only one in the family who is a dancer. She and Edna used to have lessons when they were little. I know because we came across their ballet shoes when we had a turn-out once. Little pumps in softest pink leather with long tapes to criss-cross round your legs. Nora laced them onto Binnie but she screamed, 'Take them off of me, take them off of me,' insisting she couldn't breathe with them on. So Nora put them on her hands and demonstrated first position, second position and so on. I thought it looked very boring. That was all in what they used to call the "good old days", when Mum was married to Nora and Edna's father and they had a shop and were well off. They had a pony and trap and went for picnics in the country and had parties in the winter.

'Trays of cakes were brought in from the baker's,' Nora would say, her eyes shining with the picture in her head. 'I liked the ones with pink icing and hundreds and thousands.'

Edna liked the square ones with angelica and they argued over which were nicest. Sometimes Mum joined in and told the story of Mrs Pink sitting in the jelly. 'I only put it down on the chair for a moment while I picked up a napkin. But that was the moment when Mrs Pink chose to sit down. And she was wearing a velvet dress. It was never the same. Oh dear, oh dear.' And Mum would shake in silent laughter until she had to mop her eyes. It's a funny thing, but Mum never makes a sound when she laughs.

Nora has always played all the latest tunes on the piano and would save up for the sheet music. So she was thrilled to discover Edwin liked to go dancing. He took her to the Palais on one of their first dates and they never looked back after that. But me? I haven't a clue, and I would really be struggling now if it were not for the champagne and the fun in the air.

I can hardly believe I'm enjoying myself so much doing something I can't do. But the music seems to get into my feet and legs and I feel as if I'm doing what I can see the others doing.

But now the music suddenly stops and it's as if someone has been spinning me round and round and suddenly lets go, leaving me to whirl towards the shrubbery just like a champagne cork. Something stops me before I land and the next thing I know Ozzy is sitting me down and bringing me a long glass of lemonade.

'My, you were flying,' he says as the lupins and the girls' dresses gradually calm down and come back into focus. 'You'll feel better if you drink that.'

I'm just about to say I feel wonderful when I realise I don't any more and am grateful for the cool tartness of the lemonade and the solid taste of the meat paste sandwiches he brings me. The mood of the party has changed and we sit around talking and sipping lemonade until Clive puts another record on the gramophone and holds out a hand to Lily.

All the others start clapping and Ozzy leans over to me and says, 'You must see this. Their favourite foxtrot.'

I haven't really noticed Clive much until now, not since I saw his eyes were changed. Now I can see he is an outstanding dancer. He and Lily swoop about the grass as if it were a polished floor. It's a tune I know from hearing Nora play it at Christmas, "You're Driving Me Crazy". We all fooled about to it in the front room but it feels quite different in the sultry warmth of the late afternoon. After we've all watched Lily and Clive as if they were a cabaret, Angus and Claire join in and Ozzy stands up and holds out a hand to me.

'I could never do that,' I say, drawing back.

But he insists and I find myself doing my best to follow his lead and getting in a hopeless muddle. At least I know it's not because I'm tipsy. I feel steadier now. When the record finishes Ozzy calls Clive over.

'We need your help here. Thea would like to learn to foxtrot. It's a little beyond my clumsy skills to teach her.' Ozzy makes an elaborate gesture of passing my hand to Clive and I think I might fall at his feet and die on the spot. Anything not to endure this. Everyone is watching and Clive avoids taking my hand and is trying not to look at me.

I find my voice at last and say, no, I really don't think I'm any good at dancing, I have no sense of rhythm. 'No one,' I say, exaggerating wildly, 'has ever been able to teach me to dance.' Apart from this being untrue (I don't recall anyone ever trying), it is the wrong thing to say.

'I see,' says Clive. He presses his palms together and looks at me over his fingertips. 'In that case, this is a challenge I cannot resist.' He turns to face the others. 'What do you say, Lily, my dear? Should I take on this challenge? Will anyone have a wager with me?'

Lily laughs and nods and Ozzy fishes out a sixpence and throws it in the air. It lands on the table and he slaps it flat. Clive places his coin alongside. 'Right then, let's have some music and no watching! You talk amongst yourselves and then I think we should break open another bottle of bubbly. Ozzy, you know where it is. Lily isn't twenty-one every day.'

'Not every day, but every year!' Ozzy kisses his sister and winds up the gramophone.

I think I am going to be humiliated, but Clive is serious. He walks through the basic steps and has me do them alongside him, over and over again. Claire tries to join in but he ignores her.

'Do it until you don't have to think about it,' he says. And then, 'Who says you've no sense of rhythm? You're doing fine. After all, it's bound to be in the blood.'

Claire titters at that and they exchange glances. I could hit Claire but I pretend not to notice.

When Ozzy opens the champagne he fetches us both a glass. I sip and remind myself to take it slowly. I don't want to get woozy again. Clive knocks his back. He shouts to Ozzy to rewind the gramophone and set the record playing again. 'Right, now let's put it all together.' He steps forward and bows and as he takes me in his arms I realise his eyes are back. They have just looked right through me.

'All you have to do is follow me and follow the music.'

Follow me and follow the music. Follow me and follow the music. You're driving me crazy, what did I do? You're driving me crazy and follow the music. Follow me, you're driving me crazy.

The laughter and voices of the others fades into the leaves of the trees, their dresses a haze in the background. Clive is strong and sure and his confidence seems to travel through his guiding arms into my legs and feet. I miss a step and he carries me past it and on to the next, we flow and turn, pause and swoop as if we were joined together. In fact we are joined. I can feel his energy against my body and his thighs against my thighs. I hardly know I am touching the ground. There is a vibration in my ear and, just as I realise it's Clive humming along with the melody, he breaks into the vocal. '*You're driving me crazy*' burns into my skin. My ear is on fire, his breath is hot and damp on my cheek. The record stops abruptly and there is a burst of applause.

Clive bows to me elaborately and strides to the table, sweeping up the two coins. 'I believe honour is satisfied,' he says, filling his glass and raising it to the group and to me. There is a burst of chatter and I feel once again as if I shouldn't be here, suddenly cold and naked now the music has stopped. The sun has left the garden and, as I rub my arms, Lily shivers and asks Clive to fetch her a wrap. But the spell is broken. Claire exclaims about the time and then everyone is saying they must leave. The girls go indoors to fetch their tennis things, Angus and Ozzy clear the table and fold it away and Clive takes in the gramophone. I follow with the album of records and hesitate in the hall, unsure of where to put it.

A voice floats down from the landing. 'I don't know, Lily always has her pets, and this one's a sweetie, but...'

Claire cuts across Charlie. 'She may be sweet, but a darkie! I mean I know Lily loves to break the rules, but... And seeing her with Clive – right in front of poor Lily...'

'I even wonder if Lily didn't set it up – for Clive's titillation, don'tcha know.'

'That's ridiculous! She'd never do that – but he's certainly smitten. The lure of the exotic. You can see why the foxtrot is considered so risqué! He was all over her.'

I go hot and cold, drop the album on the hall table and rush back out to the garden. I must fetch my bag, say goodbye to Lily. I can't wait to be gone but Lily pulls me down beside her.

'I haven't opened your present,' she says and retrieves it from the grass.

She tears it open, not bothering to save the paper. 'Oh, you clever thing! Just what I wanted! You remembered.' She flings her arms round me and kisses me. She doesn't notice I'm shaking.

Clive calls from the house for her to come in before she gets chilled. I start to get up, thanking Lily for the party, trying to say something normal about the shop, winter hats.

But she stops me with a hand on my arm. 'There is something I have to say.'

I try to swallow but my mouth is too dry. She has watched me dancing with Clive, seen what Charlie and Claire have seen. She is about to tell me to stay away from her husband.

'There won't be any hats this season.'

She's taking her custom away from *Milady's* and all because of me and it isn't my fault at all.

'I have to have an operation. I have known for some time things were not right. A lump. I went to the doctor when I got back from Gibraltar. Nothing to worry about he says, but best to take it away.' Her voice is bright and brittle and her eyes are wet.

I stare. 'Take it away? The lump?' I wonder where it is, what it is. I don't understand.

She nods and puts her hand across her chest. 'My breast. Take it away, take it – off. Just to be sure.' Her eyes overflow down her thin cheeks and I pass her my handkerchief, put my arms around her and let her head rest on my shoulder.

'Oh, Lily.' It's all I can think of to say as I picture her breasts so innocently dancing in the moonlight on the beach in Gibraltar.

25

2006

Kate took the leather case Vanessa was holding out to her.

'This is what I wanted to show you,' said Vanessa.

Kate pressed the spring in the top and the front hinged open in two halves, forming a stand for the miniature hanging inside. 'Who is she?'

'Lily,' said Vanessa as if announcing the Queen of Sheba. 'You remember I told you about her on the phone? The first wife of Thea's first husband, Clive?'

'Oh yes.' Kate set the frame on the table. She'd asked Vanessa to baby-sit and suggested she bring the results of her research. It was Henrietta she was interested in.

'And then there's this.' Vanessa placed a tatty volume on the table. 'The dealer who cleared Dad's books picked it out. Thought it was a bit of family history I might want to keep. I only took it because I didn't want to offend him. Didn't realise what it was, whose it was. Until I found this.' Again, Vanessa sounded triumphant.

Kate watched as her mother turned to the middle, a double page filled with wedding cards. 'Look at the one that fell out!' She held out a card with the name *Lily Osborne*.

'And look!' She pointed dramatically to the inscription on the front page of the album.

So what, thought Kate and tried not to yawn. 'So it was Lily's. You have been doing your detective work.'

'And here – at the back!' Vanessa showed her the last page where a verse was written in immaculate copper-plate script.

Kate obliged by reading the verse. It made her cringe.

'You see? It's from Clive.'

'Yes, yes. I see.' But where was the great-grandmother in all this?

Vanessa leafed through the book showing her paintings, cartoons, riddles. Some were skilled, others crudely drawn.

'It's all so fussy,' was all Kate could think to comment.

'But accomplished, and a glimpse into Lily's world.'

'I don't see the fascination. Lily looks pretty ordinary to me. Now Henrietta. What about...?'

'Mother was obsessed with Lily, though she never spoke about her...'

'You don't think you're reading too much into all that?'

'No, I don't actually. You see, I think Lily was her role model. Quite significant therefore.'

'Hmm. I see,' said Kate not really seeing and wondering if they'd get on to Henrietta before she and Daniel had to leave.

'I've been trying to understand. Maybe I've caught the obsession. But you're right. I've been side-tracked from Henrietta. It's all been part of seeing another side of Mother.'

Daniel came downstairs at that point with Jack, who burst in to see Grandma and they left Vanessa reading him bedtime stories.

The evening – dinner with Daniel's colleagues – was as Kate expected. Daniel had too much to drink and flirted with one of the wives, which caused a tense moment with her husband. It was midnight before Kate could get him home.

Vanessa had laid out a whole lot of papers on the kitchen table.

'You were asking about Henrietta. There's stuff here from the archives in Kew and some bits my cousin Michelle sent.'

'Ah,' said Daniel, steadying himself on the table and peering at the documents. 'I anticipate a family history session. I will love you and leave you, as they say. Thank you, Vanessa, for liberating us for the evening. A most pleasant evening, I have to say, although I fear I am not in good odour.'

Kate watched him go and rolled her eyes. 'This calls for some wine. I missed out tonight, my turn to drive. And he had enough for both of us.' She uncorked a bottle. 'I assume the children were okay? No problems?'

'Not a thing. Jack wangled a good few books, but what the hell? His reading's coming on.'

Kate kicked off her shoes and settled at the table.

'The archives at Kew are amazing, you know! It's a wonderful environment to work in and the staff, they're so helpful. It all works like clockwork.'

Vanessa was rabbiting on. Really jumpy. What was all that about? Kate picked up the nearest sheet of paper. This was more like it. This was interesting. Vanessa had begun to chart Henrietta's life: marriage to William Silking in Bermuda, kids in Gibraltar, move to Kent. There was the Army record of the marriage and the baptisms of the children.

'Wow, she had six kids!'

Vanessa passed her an outsize photocopy. 'This is William's joining up paper. 'Imagine. I held the paper he actually signed when he went in the Army – at *half past two o'clock on the seventeenth day of October*. It's funny, but having the time brings it alive somehow, takes you right into the room with him holding the pen.'

Kate read it and tried to imagine her great-great-grandfather signing his life away over a hundred and fifty years ago. Vanessa was right. That time of day conjured a dark panelled room, a desk, the squeak of a pen.

'Good for William. Here's to Henrietta. Henrietta and William.' She raised her glass.

'And then there's this letter from Ada, writing from Plymouth. Their eldest daughter.' Vanessa pointed to Ada in the list of children. 'She's signed it from Ada and Bert.'

'Where did you get this?' Kate took the letter and read it.

'Michelle had it. It's about her mother, Auntie Nora, getting married. It doesn't even say anything much. Beats me why anyone kept it since 1926, but I'm glad they did.'

'So it's a link in the chain. And Ada was Henrietta's daughter. Wasn't it Plymouth that was written on the back of the original photograph of Henrietta? Wow! We've got an actual address now.' Kate loved the idea of the detective work, following each tiny clue.

Vanessa had collected all the photos into an album. Thea as

a child, some with her younger sister and a few as a moody teen-ager. They both smiled over a family snap where Thea's scowl almost merged with the hedge at the back of the group. In all the photographs Thea was noticeably darker than any other family member.

Then, suddenly, a wedding portrait. It was recognisably Thea, but an ugly-duckling-into-swan transformation had taken place. The bush of hair was sleek, the complexion only mellow. It was now her beauty, not her skin colour that was arresting.

'You see it wasn't just me being blind. Was it? I mean, she must have done something, surely? To alter her appearance?'

Kate studied the picture. She could feel Vanessa's anxiety idling beside her.

Vanessa cleared her throat. 'I mean, I suppose you must blame me for not noticing. And it was partly what I said before. When a person is your mother, you accept what she is. You don't analyse it and say, her skin is darker than mine. She's just Mother and you assume she's the same as everyone else's mother.'

'Mum, you've got it all wrong. I do *not* blame you. Not at all. There's no point in blaming anyone.'

Vanessa sighed. 'I guess I still blame myself. But something my cousin Michelle said helped. About Dick, Thea's father.'

'Henrietta's son, right?'

'Yes. My grandfather. And Michelle's step-grandfather. They moved in with her family during the war, when Portsmouth was bombed. So she knew them really well. She said, we never thought of Grandpa as coloured. We just thought he was suntanned.'

'Even in winter, in England?'

'Well, that's what she said too. A tan like that, in Rayners Lane in 1941. Like they thought a tan *lasted* – for life! She suddenly saw how silly that was. But at the time it didn't occur to her. That's my whole point.'

Kate nodded and laughed. She flipped the pages of the album back and forth, comparing the photographs.

Vanessa leaned back in her chair to let Willow jump onto her lap. 'I've been thinking about it a lot. About Nan, I mean. She was also a manipulator, an actress. She made you see what she wanted you to see.'

'Hmm. Makes you think, doesn't it?' Kate peered at Thea through

Vanessa's magnifying glass. 'What a lot of power mothers have. Frightening.'

'She was a total control freak. But at least now I see why. She thought her life depended on it.' Vanessa unhooked Willow's claws from the fabric of her trousers. 'But in a way you have to admire her. The more I find out, the less anger I feel. If only it hadn't affected you and Daniel so badly.'

'Ah, well. Daniel. But that's another story.'

'Might you tell it?'

Kate shrugged and poured herself more wine. 'I suppose so. If you won't say, I told you so.'

'Would I?'

'Probably not in fact. But you never wanted me to marry him.'

'Is it that bad?'

Kate made a face. 'I nearly chucked him out at one stage. But that was just after Flora was born, ages ago. He's been better since then. But...'

'Compromise?'

'I don't see it as much of a compromise that he can give me hell for an affair I didn't have, while it's okay for him to have a woman on the side whenever he fancies.'

'What?' Willow jumped from Vanessa's lap with an indignant mew. 'I thought you said he'd been better?'

Kate watched the little cat begin to wash, back turned. What was she doing, telling on Daniel like this?

'He has been better. Not so many women. Better when he's home too, with the kids, helping out.'

'I thought it was just the one affair. No?'

'No. I've lost count. Kept it quiet. For obvious reasons. I've taught myself not to think about it.'

'But that's awful, darling. Katie, Katie. I don't know what to say. What will you do?'

'Do? Nothing. There are the children... I've come to terms. I cope. Though it's not like I thought it would be. Like it used to be.'

'It must hurt.'

'Of course it does if I think... That's why...' Tears brimmed over. 'Please don't...'

Vanessa had her arms round her now. That familiar smell of childhood, warm and safe.

'I don't know how you can stay with him.'

Vanessa sat down again and they were both silent. Kate tipped her wine from side to side.

'It's being a mother that's important. That's what I always wanted, and that's what I've got. Maybe I asked for it in a sort of way.'

'That's rubbish. Don't ever, ever talk like it's your fault...'

'No, I don't really think that. But focusing on the mother bit, it's how I cope. I'm lucky. It would drive some people mad, like Morag for instance. She's always worked and she says she could never stay at home. But I'm content – and I've got my painting, of course.'

'I couldn't do it. Well, I didn't, as you know. You're a brilliant mother. You know that don't you? Much better than I was.'

'I enjoy it. And that's daft. You were the best – where d'you think I learnt it from?'

Vanessa shook her head and picked up the photograph of Henrietta. 'Certainly not from me. I wonder what sort of mother she was.'

Kate examined the photograph. 'Tough, but fair. She looks a pretty strong character. Quite egocentric. She'd have liked to queen it with all her family round her, but equally, she'd knit them all socks and be the best cook in the regiment. And she'd defend them to the death whatever they got up to.'

They both laughed.

Kate shook her head. 'What you can read into a picture. Seriously though, she wouldn't have let anyone walk all over her.'

Vanessa nodded. 'I think you've probably got her to a tee. Which makes it all the more frustrating we know so little about her. I've come to a grinding halt. There's only so much you can do on the Internet. Have to get out and about.'

'Well, I bet Dad can't wait to spend a weekend in Sheerness!'

'He's already refused. Said he'd go to Plymouth, but Sheerness was a step too far.'

'Tell you what, we could all go – you, me and Lisa. How about that? Girls' day out?'

'Why not? If Lisa could get time off. It would have to be in the week, to see the librarian.' Vanessa ran her hands through her hair. 'Of course Gibraltar's the key place. I couldn't get any joy from the archivist there. Doesn't answer his emails. People say you have to go there, which seems crazy. But then I'd love to see where she lived. It's more appealing than Sheerness, but I'm not sure your father will be keen on that either.'

Kate was piecing together fragments, on the kitchen table and in her mind. Shards of crazed porcelain were spread around her, parts of Nan's plate she'd brought from Mead End. Daniel had been playing ball in the kitchen – forbidden – with Jack, and had failed to save one of Jack's wilder shots. The mental jigsaw related to Saturday's conversation with Vanessa and her own strange encounter with Henrietta the night before.

She mused on why Mum had got so caught up with this Lily. So Thea had a picture of her husband's first wife beside her chair for years. Put that way it sounded odd. Like me having a snap of Daniel's mistress on my mobile, thought Kate and made a face at the thought. But Lily was probably a friend. Thea probably knew her first. Widowers often marry friends of their wives. Friend, role model even. There was no need to make it into an obsession.

Shit! A triangle of blue she'd positioned so carefully stuck to her finger as she took it away. She tried again with tweezers.

And all that stuff about the possessions. Mum really was being a bit gothic about that. Objects just became part of a household. You didn't think about where the cutlery came from every time you had a meal. She searched the table for a missing fragment of blue and white.

Mum had been very shocked about Daniel. Indignant, on her side in a big way. It was reassuring. Sometimes she thought she was unreasonable to mind as much as she did. Mum made it feel absolutely okay to mind. She'd even said, don't know how you stay with him. She squeezed more glue from the tube. Don't go there, don't even think of it.

Poking some small pieces into place with a cocktail stick, she wondered what Henrietta's marriage had been like, tried to imagine how it was for her to come all that way across the sea to bring up her family. Why did she do it? Was it love? Or security? Or a sense of adventure? When she looked at the photograph those eyes seemed to smile at her, as if Henrietta wanted to tell her, was glad to be noticed again.

Kate fingered the plate. She was pleased she could just feel the joins. They gave it a new texture, like the early signs of wrinkles on a face.

She was back with *that* face. She was sure it was Henrietta's. She'd been falling asleep the night before, descending fast into a sink of darkness, when an interrupt buzzed across the inside of her forehead, a sensation of it being ripped in half like a sheet of paper. And there was the face. Right close up. She was looking into dark eyes which seemed to widen, just slightly, into a smile although the lips didn't move. She'd watched and waited. She wasn't asleep and dreaming, but this was no waking state either. The eyes were making a connection, drawing her steadily, smoothly into another place, another time.

Then she'd fallen deeply asleep, woken early, colonised by dreams. Only half awake, she'd painted fast, page after page: a black woman and brown child framed by gnarled trees, dense growth of grasses and shrubs, orange and red flowers tingling among the greens; clocks in rows; a street of houses, tall and narrow; a flight of stairs where a carving of a Black Madonna stood in a niche; a young girl leaning on a bridge, staring out to sea.

Two hours must have passed when Daniel had appeared carrying Flora, Jack trailing behind.

'You'll have to give them breakfast, I've got to be off.'

Kate held out a hand to Flora, passed her a brush and a sheet of newspaper and carried on painting. 'Mummy won't be long.'

Daniel peered at the canvas. 'Not your usual style.'

'Painting my dreams. It's Henrietta.' And when Daniel frowned, 'My great-great-grandmother.'

Daniel groaned. 'Don't forget to give the kids some breakfast.'

A shout had come from Jack, already downstairs, 'I can make breakfast my own. I'm a big boy.'

Kate called back, 'Jakey, bring up some bread for Flora, will you, please?' She'd kept painting until there were no more images queuing to flow down her arm onto the page.

Now she sat back and stretched, held the plate at arm's length. It wasn't an expert restoration job but it served her purpose. It was her special plate again. What it all meant, the vision of the face and the dreams she'd painted, she had no idea, but for the whole of that day she hadn't been able to get Henrietta and the idea of the family history quest out of her mind. She squeezed her eyes shut and rubbed away the tension of focusing.

She fetched the phone and pressed the speed dial number for Vanessa. The answerphone clicked in.

'It's Kate. I've been thinking. Mum, why don't we go to Gibraltar together?'

26

1933

I'm caught in Clive's gaze as he lounges against the doorframe, a lean diagonal across the entrance to the kitchen. I look from him to the leftovers of Lily's funeral tea: triangles of white sandwiches still stacked on the plates, sugared sponge cakes with their cut wedges, Clarice Cliff cups elbowing their way across the table like dancers eager to tango. Everything's in triangles. The sunlight shafting in the window to lay a lozenge of light on the floor tiles, the cartoon highlights in the bubbles of soap on the plates I've just washed, even his shirt front and the planes of his face, with his cheeks hollow from exhaustion and grief. Our triangle of love and jealousy. That's my fantasy anyway. Imagination running away with you as usual, Mum would say.

I can hardly bear to look down the garden. It reminds me of that awful last birthday of Lily's. Clive tried to recreate the happy party of the year before. The same apple tree and lawn, the table laid with a white cloth, the fading lupins, candles, champagne. The records revolving on the turntable, but Lily not dancing. She was a grey hunched figure, sitting on the bench doing her best to smile but clearly struggling with her pain. I was haunted by the conversation I'd overheard and could barely look at Charlie and Claire, while they gave more attention to Rosie than to me. When it started to rain we were all relieved. We stopped pretending and went inside, and Lily went to lie down. I washed up that day, too, because Rosie had gone home. It's November now and the trees are bare out there. It's just like that poem Dadser's always quoting when he gets depressed in winter.

No shade, no shine, no butterflies, no bees,
No this, no that, no something!
November.

Except my poem has to end, No Lily. Which isn't the same I know. Dadser would say, it doesn't work as a poem. It's just how I feel.

As to Clive. I don't care any more. At this moment I wish he'd go away. He's annoying me, standing there. It feels like a game. How dare he play games with me on this day of all days? Then I look round and he's gone.

Rosie appears, red-faced and flustered and shoos me away from the sink. 'You in your nice frock, and not even a pinny. I'll finish this.'

I find my coat and I'm just putting it on and wondering whether I should just slip out when Clive appears. 'Go up to my study. I'll be up shortly. Second on the left at the top of the stairs.' He goes back into the drawing room where a few guests are still lingering.

So this is Clive's room. I can't help smirking to myself. It could be the original brown study. I wonder if the effect is deliberate. Would Clive's sense of humour run to that? Or maybe he just thinks it's clever rather than funny. That's more like Clive.

There is every shade of sludge, from the parquet floor with its square of chocolate carpet to the mud-coloured armchair and the array of fawn books on dark-oak stained shelves. I doubt the clean logs in the grate are ever set ablaze. Flames would be too disturbing to the cool beige of Clive's thoughts, his tidy reckoning of the household finances, his orderly planning. Lily said Clive "broke out" when he furnished this room. Funny expression to use. She must have meant the contemporary style, the art deco bookshelves and fireplace. It's out of tune with the rest of the house, which is full of Lily's antiques and period pieces. 'Such a masculine room,' Lily said, with such pride that I looked forward to seeing it. Now I'm disappointed. Self-conscious is the word I'd use.

I hear voices in the hall, the mournful rise and fall of condolence. Clive's voice cutting into their lingering tones. I can't hear what's being said but I can guess. It's been the same thing all afternoon. Then footsteps on the stairs and Clive is in the room. He goes to the desk and stands with his back to me.

'Thea, I wanted to see you. I wanted to say...' He tails off and leans forward holding the edges of the desk. 'I can't cope...'

I force myself to speak. 'I know how you feel. I can't cope without Lily. It must be worse for you, much worse.'

'Oh yes. I can't cope without Lily. But that's not what I meant. I can't cope with you.' He gives a little groan and straightens up. 'Come here.'

I cross the room and stand beside him. I want to put an arm round him but I dare not.

'Comfort me.' His voice is faint and hoarse.

I stretch an arm round his shoulders and the moment I touch him he turns into me and rests his head next to mine. I smell him as I did before, dancing at the garden party, a spicy perfume, sweat. I stroke his head as if it were a small animal. His breathing changes. It's all sharp and gaspy and I think he's sobbing, when he lifts his head and pulls me into him and kisses me hard on the mouth. He keeps on kissing me, pushing his tongue past my teeth and I can feel his part hard against me down there. For a second I am horribly reminded of Billy Chapman. Then he's clawing at my dress and I know this has to stop. Does he have no shame? To be kissing me on the day of Lily's funeral? But there is another reason. Somewhere deep inside me I know if I give in to Clive now, I will never see him again.

I push him away and step back. 'No. I can't. Today of all days.'

'I can't get you out of my head. I've been wanting to do that for so long.' He groans. 'That Charlie, she once described you as exotic. I'd change one letter. Erotic. I don't know how I contained myself in Brittany.'

Ah, Brittany. I'm shaking as I leave the house, my lips smarting and my head full of memories of that strange visit in September. It all started off so well. The excitement of the new Morris Tourer, all red and shiny, which Clive unveiled on Lily's birthday, the only light moment on that grim day. Watching it being lifted by crane on the dock at Dover. The three of us holding our breath as it swung, high above our heads, and was lowered onto the deck of the ferry. When we landed in Calais it was warm and sunny, that mellow September light, and we bowled along with the hood down, singing and laughing and forgetting, just for a while, Lily's illness. I sat in the back with the extra luggage on the seat beside me and couldn't believe how wonderful motoring could be. Me, on holiday in France. At the hotel I looked after Lily while Clive unstrapped the suitcases and carried them in. We had tea on the terrace before we went to our rooms because, already, Lily needed to sit down.

After that she hardly moved from her room. She'd lie on the sofa or on a chaise longue on the balcony in the sun. Every afternoon I would walk with Clive. Through the hotel gardens and onto the sands. It would have seemed the most natural thing in the world to hold hands, but we never did. Lily was always there, between us, because we loved and cared about her, not because she might be watching from the balcony. We'd come back and have tea under the hornbeams and wave to Lily if she appeared after her nap. Then we'd go up and have cocktails with her in their room. In the mornings I read to her or we looked through magazines and she taught me French words. Lily was just the same as she'd always been with me. Clive supervised her doses of morphine and most of the time it was keeping the pain under control. It was all very innocent and relaxed. Until Charlie turned up.

She was staying with "chums" at a villa further down the coast. A tennis party, so jolly. A group of them had motored over for the day and dropped Charlie off to see Lily while they went shopping in Deauville. Charlie spent the morning closeted with Lily, and came walking with me and Clive in the afternoon, always taking care, it seemed, to position herself between us. Lily said she was too tired for cocktails, so Clive went up to be with her, leaving me with Charlie while she waited for her friends to pick her up. I remember it so clearly. Charlie was drinking gin and tonic. She drained her glass.

'You know he loves her very much?' She was trying to sound casual.

'Of course. I've always known that.'

Charlie was giving me a searching look and fishing the lemon slice out of her glass. I bit my dry tongue, trying not to pucker my lips as she sucked it thoughtfully, looking away from me out of the window.

Eventually she spoke again. 'Just so long as you know that.'

What was going on here? I managed a response. 'You only have to see them together.'

'Quite.' I thought she'd finished, but then she added, 'Which would not of course prevent him from being *in love* with you.' She made that emphasis sound so scornful.

I looked up sharply.

Charlie gave a short laugh. 'It's what you think, isn't it? Oh, come on, Thea. You know it. How could he not fall for you, when all's said and done. Just look at you. The lure of the exotic.'

Lily's pet darkie, that's what she was thinking. I was tempted to tell her I'd overheard her and Claire that time. Glad I decided against it. I just told her Clive liked to be friendly.

'Friendly! I've got eyes in my head...'

'We have never...'

'Of course you will say that. Maybe it's true. But what you two get up to with your eyes is positively indecent. Lily may be ill but she can still see.'

She crossed her long shapely legs and leant back in the chair. 'I like you, Thea. Don't take offence. Just don't have any expectations, that's all.'

'I don't know what you mean. I don't know what "expectations" you're talking about. Lily invited me...'

'Oh, certainly. We know all about that.' Charlie fitted a Turkish cigarette into her holder, lit it and inhaled. She exhaled slowly and deliberately. 'Just be aware Lily has good friends and we'll carry on looking out for her after she's gone. We wouldn't let her memory be dishonoured by her widower behaving inappropriately, being indiscreet with a mistress.' She gathered her bag and swept out to the driveway where a sleek black motor car had just pulled in.

Behaving inappropriately. Being indiscreet. As he was just now in his study, I reflect, as I round the corner into Commercial Road. The memory makes me gasp, a strange little grunt that takes me by surprise. I cringe at the thought of Charlie. Supposing she'd seen us? But I did the right thing. I pushed him away. I am *not* that sort of girl, whatever Charlie may think. It's a wonder she or Claire didn't see me off the premises. But they were too busy treating me like a maid. Ozzy was all right, he talked to me. He's always treated me like a friend and he still does.

I've been so wrapped up in these thoughts and the shock of it all that I've walked all the way to North End without noticing. There's something that draws me like a magnet to Clive. It goes off inside me like fireworks. And yet there are times when I'm not sure I even like him. He's just shown himself up and it's dawning on me how naïve I've been. I'm beginning to understand what Charlie was getting at. I'm not going to give Clive another thought.

Everybody's out and I've just finished blacking the grate when there's a knock at the door.

They've all gone Christmas shopping but I haven't got the heart. I've got no energy since Lily died. My whole sense of direction for my life has been taken away. Even Binnie can't cheer me up, and Mum and Edna don't understand. She was my friend. I keep telling them. I heard Mum saying to Dadser she understood only too well, I'd lost my "benefactor". He told her to go easy on me. So Mum didn't push me to go shopping with them. Just gave me a list of chores.

So here I am with blacking all over my hands and on my apron and someone at the door. It's probably the parcel we're expecting from Nora. I don't even stop to wash my hands. And who should be standing there but Mr Atkins. Clive, I should say. He looks so sombre and severe that I don't recognise him until he lifts his hat.

Eventually he says, 'Aren't you going to invite me in?'

And I show him into the front room because – well, because the back room's full of stove blacking and dirty newspaper. But also because I've never been able to imagine Clive in our house. Only Lily, who never came. And so, if he's coming in, he has to be put into the most formal and unused room. I offer him tea, but he declines and bows stiffly and says he has come to deliver a small legacy from Lily.

He takes a dark red leather box from his pocket and an envelope addressed to me. How did she know my address?

'Lily was meticulous in making her will. I did encourage that. She was sometimes a little disorganised in her life, but it is best to leave things in order.'

I wipe my hands on my apron and take the box and put the envelope on the table.

'I would like you to open it,' he says.

So I do. Inside on black velvet is a beautiful cameo brooch. The moment I see it I know it is a good one. I don't know how I know, except Auntie has a cameo which is larger and coarser and which she says is valuable. This one is much finer, more delicately carved and with subtle colouring.

When I look up Clive is smiling for the first time.

'Hold it up to the light,' he says and I do, marvelling at the soft translucence.

'I bought it for Lily in Sicily. It is a fine piece. As soon as I saw it, it reminded me of Lily. The long neck, the sweep of the hair, the ivory skin. Unblemished. She was a wonderful woman. A wonderful wife. A perfect English rose.' He pauses. 'Wouldn't you agree?'

I feel strange and hot inside as I listen to him. He is like a man in a play, word perfect with not a quaver of emotion in his voice, and I have just missed my cue.

'Yes,' I say. 'Yes, of course. She was a wonderful woman. A good friend.' Not only have I missed my cue, I don't even know which play I'm in.

'And it is a special mark of her affection for you that she wanted you to have this. She knew how much I cared for it.'

When he has gone I sit on the edge of the sofa and stare at the cameo. It is indeed a fine piece. But not at all like Lily, whose nose was large even if her complexion was clear. The phrase "the perfect English rose" repeats in my head and I understand the message Clive, that is, Mr Atkins, came to deliver. It doesn't matter whether or not Lily was an English rose. The point is that I am not.

I clear up in the back room and wash my hands. Then I take the letter upstairs and sit on my bed to read it.

My dear Thea

It is strange to think I will be dead when you read this. It is not a state I have managed to imagine. I hope it is like the peaceful time when the pain lifts and I drift into sleep. But then again I'd like to be more alert when I get to heaven – if that is where I am going.

I could not think what to leave you that would truly reflect our friendship. I chose this because I think you will value it and because Clive will like to see you wearing it.

Please know it is given with much love and gratitude.
Your affectionate friend,
Lily

"Clive will like to see you wearing it". This seems extremely unlikely to me. Either that he will see me wearing it, or that he would like it if he did. What did Lily imagine? That I would continue to visit their house for *soirées* and garden parties?

My thoughts are interrupted by the return of the shoppers. Binnie shouts to find out where I am. When I go down Mum is sitting in her chair and easing her feet out of her shoes with little groans, while Edna is putting on the kettle.

Binnie laughs when she sees me. 'Mrs Potato has a very smutty nose!'

My hand flies to my face and comes away black. I say nothing of greeting Mr Atkins in this state. I expect he thought it was all very appropriate.

27

2006

The plane banked, Kate woke to a sharp nudge in the ribs, and followed Vanessa's pointing finger. They'd emerged from the cloud and, as she looked down the wing, she caught her breath. There she was, the Rock: unexpectedly massive, and definitely female, an ocean-going vessel, tethered to Spain and making steam before casting off. Kate felt her skin prickle all over and the hairs on her arms lift. Strange.

A moist heat came to meet them as they descended the gangway. Kate turned to Vanessa to comment but instead was transfixed by the cliff face rearing abruptly skywards, dwarfing the aircraft and the terminal building.

'I've been here before.' The words blurted out and once again her hair stood on end as tears ran down her face. She felt overwhelmed, as if that great mass might fall and flatten them. And still the white vapour smoked off the summit. A warning of imminent eruption? Or a safety valve? Ridiculous thoughts about a bit of mist, feeding her unease, the shock of arriving in this place.

The Rock, the beach, the coastline, it was all so elemental and the low-level development around the airport had a temporary air about it. It couldn't have changed much since Henrietta's time. She looked back towards the mainland beyond the border control at La Linea. No wonder the Spanish hate Gibraltar, she thought. It was so in-your-face, showing two fingers to Spain, this British fortress at the bottom of a Spanish beach.

Vanessa was handing her a tissue, steering her to follow the straggle of travellers to the terminal building, passport control and the queue for a taxi.

They checked in to the Rock Hotel and stepped back fifty odd years into 1930s architecture and old-fashioned colonial luxury. At any other time Kate would have found the formality of the staff chilling, but now she accepted the distance it created, which left her undisturbed with her own thoughts. Their room had two enormous double beds, a wall of built-in mahogany wardrobes and a stately ceiling fan of brass and rattan. Vanessa was preoccupied: unpacking and exclaiming at finding a right place for everything. Then she settled at the phone to make appointments. 'Must organise tomorrow, maximise the time we're here.'

Kate had different ideas about how to maximise the time. She poured a finger of complementary Scotch from a cut glass decanter, stepped from the cool room onto the balcony and caught her breath at the heat: Africa sending a furnace blast across the water.

The strange sensation of déjà-vu had left her wondering what to expect. It was as if Henrietta had been greeting her, plucking at her arm, wanting to show her things. But now everything was normal. New and different, yes. But normal. She sipped the whisky and gasped as the fire of it caught her throat, matching the heat on her skin.

Those had to be the lights of Tangiers she could see. The Rif Mountains loomed so close to the left of the view that she almost reached out a finger to touch them. The town was far below, heavily built up to the water's edge, while Spain lay to the north with its coast curving round to Algeciras opposite her in the west. She wondered how it had been for Henrietta to end up so close to the continent of her ethnic origins for so much of her life. Did she even think of herself as African? One thing was certain, wherever she lived in Gibraltar, she had to be aware of Africa. It was impossible to ignore.

The location of the hotel, halfway up the Rock, afforded insulation against the noisy traffic and pollution of the town. A place for rich people, cut off from reality, thought Kate. She wasn't going to find Henrietta here. But it gave her a view of a strange and beautiful place where already she sensed contradictions and a strong local culture such as islands often have, a personality almost.

She fetched her mobile and phoned Morag, who would be giving the children tea before Daniel fetched them after work. She spoke to Jack and told him about the plane and the African mountains. Morag repeated her offer of keeping them for the night.

'Of course they can sleep over if they want to. Maybe tomorrow? Fix it with Daniel. I'm off duty, remember?'

She felt euphoric with the freedom, the view and the whisky, which tasted as strong and hot as Africa.

Dinner was a strained affair, presided over by unsmiling and slow-moving Moroccan waiters serving a menu from the Seventies.

Vanessa rattled on about the curator of the museum and the city archivist. 'They were so affable on the phone. Both of them, really charming. Eager to meet us. No trouble fixing appointments. Though they were both totally unreachable from home. Simply wouldn't reply to anything.'

'Another contradiction,' said Kate but Vanessa only nodded vaguely and started listing off the enquiries she wanted to cover, questions to ask. Kate told herself that this was why they had come, to look for records. She tried to be interested but, now she was here, the purpose of the visit seemed to have shifted. She couldn't have explained to Vanessa how or why that was, so she said nothing. She was impatient with being shut into this self-sufficient world. The sight of the Rock on arrival had been so powerful, as if Henrietta were at her elbow. But, not surprisingly, in the marbled foyer of the hotel with its haughty receptionists, her presence had evaporated and was staying away.

In the morning they took a route through the Alameda Gardens.

'She would have come here, she would have brought the children,' said Vanessa, pointing her camera in all directions. 'Imagine what a relief to come in to the shade with all this space.'

Kate agreed and tried to imagine. Shady park with elephant trees, stranger than the animal, with those smooth grey trunks. *She would have come here*, click of Vanessa's camera. A red telephone box, bizarrely out of place among tropical plants; a monument with some soldier on a column, this bit more like a municipal park in any English town; children playing on little guns as if they were hobby horses; *Imagine her with her kids. My grandfather would have clambered on there, just like that little boy.* Click, click. Mum was absolutely right. It was interesting to imagine. But she couldn't feel it.

The walk into town along Main Street was long and hot. Kate felt herself expanding into the warmth, but Vanessa constantly sought out any available shade.

'Pouf! It's like a sauna. But she'd have walked down here lots of times I guess.'

Kate gave a short laugh. 'But not coming from the Rock Hotel, I think. And, of course, she'd have been used to heat.'

Vanessa stopped abruptly opposite an imposing building announcing itself as Wesley House, the Methodist Church. 'Hey! We should go in there. They were Wesleyans. We know that from the Army records, the baptisms. All signed by a Wesleyan minister.'

'If it's open,' said Kate, preferring to keep on walking.

The church was very much open, complete with the Temperance Coffee Bar on the first floor.

'For the soldier's wives, you know,' said the gingham woman who greeted them as if welcoming them to a WI meeting in rural England. 'Keeps them on the straight and narrow. Someone to chat to, somewhere to come with their problems.'

She was immediately engaged with Vanessa's search and to their amazement was able to produce a ledger, one of many, where all baptisms had been recorded.

While Vanessa exclaimed over pages of copperplate handwriting, Kate used the toilet on the half-landing and wondered if Henrietta had sat in the same little room, but on a wooden seat over a flowered toilet bowl pulling a Victorian chain. Vanessa emerged from the coffee bar triumphant, with a bundle of photocopies of all the Silking baptisms that had taken place in Gibraltar.

'Wow, Mum. That's fantastic,' managed Kate.

'Well, I'm glad you're showing a little enthusiasm at last. I was beginning to wonder.'

'Sorry, Mum. It's just, well, not what I was expecting. It's a weird place, don't you think?'

'Good idea, if you ask me. A bit like social services, but more acceptable. I bet Henrietta was a prime mover in this place. It's been a temperance café since it was built, so in her day too. As a sergeant's wife she'd have been just the person to run it. Counselling the soldiers' wives who got beaten up when their husbands were in drink.'

'I suppose so.' This was a possible aspect of her ancestor Kate hadn't considered and hoped she wasn't as patronising as her successor. 'Actually, I didn't mean the church. I meant the whole town.'

'It feels horribly familiar to me. It's like the UK was when I was growing up. Dirty, tacky. Nobody much ate out and, if you did, it was pretty vile. Hangover from rationing still. But you're right. It *is* weird. It feels run down, like a time warp, and yet the town's obviously thriving at the same time. Strange combination.'

They walked on past tall houses with elegant shutters, an official-looking residence flanked by brass cannons next door to a seedy-looking pub, and on into the shopping area where modern chains co-existed alongside traditional businesses with hand-painted signs in green and gold and red: "Established 1870, Luigi Spoleto, tobacconist"; "Sanguinetti, furniture restorer and funeral director".

'Can't you just imagine old William coming down here for his baccy? Or a cigar perhaps to celebrate a special occasion? The birth of a son perhaps, like my grandfather. Or the first daughter, maybe, when Ada was born.'

'More likely Henrietta was celebrating the daughter – an ally at last after three boys! At least one who wouldn't follow William into the Army. She probably had a nice cup of tea in the Temperance Café.'

The museum curator was enthusiastic and escorted them to see a vast model of the Rock which took up a whole room. It had been completed in 1858, the year before the family had arrived.

'What luck! This was exactly how it was in her day!' Vanessa peered at streets of individual buildings and exclaimed over the shadows of the trees in the Alameda Gardens.

While Vanessa took photographs, Kate wandered back to the foyer to admire the one-horse taxi carriage, a lightweight four-wheeler with springs, shafts and wheel hubs painted bright blue, and a fringed yellow canopy with cream silk curtains tied back at each corner. The seats were upholstered in red leather with buttoned backs. A fine example, the blurb assured her, of the public transport available in

Henrietta's day. She reached across the rope cordon and fingered the brass-bound wooden mudguard and thought how precarious it looked, how unsuited to the rough, steep streets. Just that light touch made the whole thing sway.

At the Garrison Library they were told they would find no reference to William.

'Oh! He wasn't an orfficer?' The librarian was clearly shocked. 'Then he won't get a mention, I'm afraid,' she said, turning her back with a rattle of gold bangles.

The archivist was of the same opinion, but was more sympathetic and presented them with a print-out of a military census taken in 1871, just weeks before Vanessa's grandfather was born.

However, a search of the huge, leather-bound copies of the *Gibraltar Chronicle* stored on the archive shelves confirmed that news of the military rarely appeared and news of non-officers, never. They read reports of the weather in London (skating on the Thames) and accounts of social occasions on the Rock. Kate got side-tracked by the reporting of current fashions.

'Hey, this comment's worthy of Jane Austen! "Some things were not so much to our liking – good lace may be spoiled by being worn over a particoloured ground. We shall never accustom ourselves to the fashionable stragglingly long brown gloves – and we like sleeves of a certain length."'

'Imagine the bitching and snobbery behind all that lot.'

Kate nodded. 'It must have been the *Hello!* magazine of its day.' She imagined the ladies pouncing on the paper to see whether their toilette had been praised or criticised, or worse still, ignored. But then she stopped and told herself, Henrietta would have had no part in all this. Imagine the horror of the ladies if the sergeant's black wife had turned up at their ball? Unless, of course she was washing up or sweeping the floor.

Kate obediently scanned the volumes she was given, eyes heavy with the dust of history. It wasn't that she wasn't interested. She wanted to find stuff too, but it simply wasn't getting her excited. All the time she was nagged by a sense of disappointment and a feeling that she should be doing something else.

Yes, she could imagine. She could place Henrietta in various locations around the town. She agreed with Vanessa about how it would have been, what she would have done. But so what? Those images were framed in her mind like pictures in a museum, scenes at a distance in which she, Kate, played no part. They convinced her that her experience of Henrietta in her mental "videos" was different and special. But, here in the town where she had lived so long and achieved so much, Henrietta had so far deserted her. She certainly wasn't going to be hanging out in the National Archives.

Eventually Vanessa sighed with frustration. 'I'm hungry. Let's call it a day.' But as she flipped the pages to close the volume she was scanning, she gave a little shriek, 'Got him!' The tension in her index finger threatened to deface the column in question – a whole paragraph about William's leaving party. 'Read this!'

The passage reported in detail that William had been honoured beyond all expectation of a non-officer, with a smoker and concert attended by seventy people.

Even the archivist was impressed when Vanessa danced down the corridor to tell him.

'A smoker! He must have been extraordinary – his expertise, and his personality maybe – to achieve such a send-off. And to get it reported.' He explained that a smoker was a men-only event and agreed to make an exception and photocopy the page.

At last Kate felt a frisson. 'After all that we've been told about people who weren't officers! From what I've seen, even an officer had to be a hard-riding, hunting type to get in these pages. Unless your wife wore interesting ballgowns.'

William had made his mark in this extraordinary Rock society in spite of having a black wife. Or might he have owed part of his success to the fact that Henrietta, too, was exceptional?

To celebrate, Vanessa insisted on going to lunch and spotted a likely-looking restaurant with window boxes and sunshades where they could sit outside. It was a mistake. The terrace overlooked one of the busiest traffic intersections in town. Tyres squealed, trucks revved into low gear, and mopeds knifed through this cacophony at the pitch of a dentist's drill.

Back at the hotel, Kate reflected that she hated Gibraltar at the level of the raucous, dirty streets, but that it was easy to love it from the balcony. Which felt like a betrayal of Henrietta, whose only sanctuary would have been the Alameda gardens and the Temperance Café.

They were leaving next day but not until the afternoon. Kate was restless for a second night, waking in the early hours with an uneasy feeling of a task left undone. The thought, *She must have something she wants you to know about*, repeated itself in her head. The only place of known significance that they had not visited was the Moorish Castle. Vanessa had said there was really no point. But the place nagged at Kate's consciousness until morning. She spoke to Vanessa at breakfast.

'There's something I need to do. I really don't think I can leave until I've done it.'

Vanessa nodded.

'The Moorish Castle. I know you don't want to go...'

'I'll come with you. There's a bus from the hotel. The view should be spectacular.'

Damn. She'd been sure Vanessa wouldn't want to come.

Catching a bus was not straightforward. Apparently they'd missed the one that ran past the hotel, but could catch another further down the road. When no bus appeared they set off on foot. After a sweaty, uphill mile it came – but sailed past, half empty, in spite of their waving and leaping into the road. They rounded a bend and saw it waiting a few yards further on, apparently at a designated stop. As they drew level, it pulled away abruptly and left them gasping.

'He's playing games with us.' As the bus paused in traffic, she sprinted after it, battering the sides of the bus with her hands and causing passengers to look round in alarm.

'Bastard!' she shrieked at the driver.

'Kate!' Vanessa caught up with her and tried to pull her away. But she was caught in the stares of the passengers. Wild-eyed, scared, angry. One of them was shouting something back at them. Something snapped and fizzed inside Kate's head.

*

Wide, staring eyes, glaring eyes, frightened eyes. A mouth gaping, bared teeth, tongue darting, lips moving. The driver looking over his shoulder, dismissive, scornful, waving an impatient arm. A whipping through the air and she was jumping back to miss the lash aimed at her. What was happening? She sank down onto the pavement with a heavy feeling in her body that was strange and at the same time familiar. She put a hand to the gnawing in the small of her back.

All she could see were the eyes, although her own were closed. And the smell. A stench of sewage and rotting matter was making her gorge rise. Shouts and whispers surrounded her, a glimpse of something ragged, a skinny leg running away.

Then there was an arm round her shoulders shaking her, and water was splashing into her face. Kate looked up and was faintly surprised to see Vanessa looking worried, waving her Evian bottle on an empty street.

'Here, come into the shade, there's a bench through here.' She led her into an archway between buildings, the entrance to a courtyard shared by several apartment blocks.

'You stay there. Here, drink some water. I'll get us a taxi.' She thrust the bottle in Kate's hand and vanished.

Kate leant forward with her head in her hands and looked up as a boy ran in from the street carrying a water melon. Skinny brown limbs, olive eyes. He darted her a look, and the fizz came again behind her eyes.

There was the smell of drains again, the reek of poverty. Weeds grew between paving stones and in the cracks of plaster on the walls. Grey washing flapped limply on lines criss-crossing the courtyard and women yelled from window to window across the open space.

Her melon! He'd stolen the melon that she'd just lugged all the way up from the market and she shouted out and tried to move to go after him. He was looking back at her and stumbled, dropping the melon in the rank water running in a channel through the cobbles. She shouted at him again. A ragged old woman appeared from the courtyard, her face wrinkled like the bark of an ancient tree. She scooped up the melon and cuffed the boy all in one gesture, then shook her fist and disappeared.

'Come on,' Vanessa was saying. 'I've got a taxi to stop. He won't go to the hotel and he won't wait long.'

Kate looked into the courtyard where a woman in a red apron was rounding up some children. She glanced without curiosity at the mad tourist woman resting on the bench and disappeared in a volley of Spanish.

In the taxi Vanessa raised inquiring eyebrows.

'Don't ask,' said Kate. 'I just don't know,' and was relieved Vanessa didn't pursue it.

The driver took them to the Moorish Castle where he had a fare to pick up, but promised to return for them.

'I'll believe that when I see it,' said Vanessa.

The view from the Castle was magnificent, but it was a military building, a fortress, built at the top of several steep, rocky acres. It was unlikely that Henrietta had ever set foot in it, though William would certainly have been at home there. The married quarters had been hard against the lower walls, nearer to the town and as much as a quarter of a mile below. That part of the enclosure was now inaccessible from the land around the tower. The scale of the place was far greater than either of them had realised.

The environment around the castle had been made pleasant for visitors with a pond and a shaded seat. A gnarled olive tree grew at the corner of a herb garden.

'Henrietta might have planted that,' said Vanessa.

Kate sat in the garden pinching leaves of rosemary and thyme, sniffing up their strength and pungency and trying not to think about what had just happened to her. She gazed at the olive tree and agreed that the ground would have been cultivated for fresh vegetables in Henrietta's day. In a perfectly ordinary act of imagination, she pictured Henrietta and her children digging and weeding and harvesting their crop.

Vanessa felt obliged to climb the tower. While other tourists snapped the harbour and the Rif Mountains, she took photographs of the piles of rubble visible in the bottom corner of the estate, reporting back that she had seen "where Henrietta lived". Kate failed to enthuse about the images of ruins displayed on the camera.

'Seriously, Kate, that heap could be what's left of her house. Or the house she lived in – with several other families, I guess.'

'What makes you think that?'

'The curator. Don't you remember? When he showed us the Moorish Castle on the model, he particularly pointed out the family quarters. Bottom corner of the site, nearest to the town. That's exactly where these ruins are.'

'If you say so, Mum. I do remember he said lots of families lived down there somewhere.'

'Can't have been much fun. No privacy, pretty basic.'

'Could you be pregnant?' Vanessa said in the taxi when it did reappear to collect them.

Kate laughed. 'No!' But as she said it, something snapped in her brain and said, Oh yes. And jigsaw pieces seemed to be falling through her mind like pebbles. She held on to her head. That's what she had glimpsed. Henrietta heavily pregnant, climbing up from the market in town, trying to hail a taxi carriage which wouldn't stop for her.

'I think you must have sunstroke.' Vanessa's voice betrayed an edge of impatience.

'Maybe,' said Kate, grateful not to have to explain, wanting to stay with her own thoughts.

'So what was going on up there?' said Vanessa when Kate joined her on the hotel terrace. 'Sit down and have a drink. I've got one. I feel much better.'

Kate frowned and lowered herself into the chair opposite. On the wisteria-shaded terrace of the hotel with its rattan chairs and potted palms, the sweat and dust of the day seemed a world away. So did Henrietta. Kate shuddered at the glimpse she had been given of Henrietta's world. She was sure that's what it was. The heat, the struggle, dirt and disease. Being black. Being near the bottom of the pile among rich white people.

A waiter appeared at her elbow and, feeling a traitor to her ancestor, Kate gave in to the luxury of ordering a vodka and orange with ice. The smooth cold orange sheathing the spirit spread good humour into her veins. Vanessa raised her glass and smiled. 'I'm glad you're better. It wasn't sunstroke, was it?'

'I guess it's time I told you about Henrietta. It all started when you gave me that photograph.'

Kate described how she'd "dream-painted" the pictures. 'It started with seeing her face – like a kind of video – as I was falling asleep. Then I woke up early and I just had to get up and paint. It was like a command. And it was like my brush was driven. Nothing like I've ever painted before. Different style, different subjects. It was like a tap turned on and I had to keep painting until it turned off. And then everything was perfectly normal again.'

'Wow! How strange.'

'It was like I became part of another world. A world she wanted recognised. Exotic flowers, strange icons. I'll show you next time you come over.'

'Sounds like you were almost channelling her. Isn't that what they call it?'

'Yes, I think so. I didn't know the first thing about paranormal happenings but I had a look on the Web. The thing was, it didn't feel the slightest bit weird when it was happening. The only explanation I found that made sense to me was tuning in to another frequency – like a station on the radio. It's there all the time, but suddenly you pick up the wavelength. That's exactly what it felt like.'

'And it was the same sort of thing today?'

'No. Yes. Same and different.'

'Like looking behind a curtain?'

'The veil between the worlds? No, that wasn't quite it. Today it was almost like I *was* her. Just for a few minutes. I'd been to market, had heavy bags. Tried to stop a taxi – I guess like the one we saw in the museum. And they wouldn't let me on. Like us with the bus. I suppose that all triggered it. And the driver aimed his whip at me. And I felt pregnant. I didn't realise that until you asked the question. Then it all made sense. And I'd got this special melon. Again, seeing the boy with his melon must have set me off. In Henrietta's world, he'd stolen my melon, so I yelled.'

'I'm glad I came with you. God knows what might have happened to you.' Vanessa shook her head. 'Does she worry you? Frighten you? Henrietta, I mean?'

'Not at all. I don't think she's a troublesome spirit. No, I kind of trust her, if that makes sense. I think she just wants recognition, kind of introducing herself, now that we know she exists. It's good to talk about it and make sense of it.'

'I knew there was something going on, but I could never have guessed what.' Vanessa rooted in her bag and pulled out a booklet. 'Just remembered. I got this at the museum. It's about cholera outbreaks here – in Henrietta's time. I wonder if that's what it was about. People get scared in times like that. Maybe they were scared that Henrietta might give them the disease.'

'Could be. Or maybe she looked too poor, or too black, or too pregnant. Maybe they were afraid she'd drop the baby! Poor woman.'

'Yes, poor woman. Not easy times, whatever it was. And now, if we're going to catch our flight, we must get a move on.'

On the plane Kate reclined her seat and shut her eyes. In a few short hours she would once more be a full-time mother of a five- and a two-year-old. She wondered how it was to be mother to six children, like Henrietta. She'd have liked to talk to her about that. How much was different for her? How much would they have had in common? On take-off they'd looked down at the receding Rock and it had looked quite ordinary. Henrietta was letting her go without further dramas. As she drifted into sleep she was met by those eyes, swimming up to meet her, smiling in quiet acknowledgement.

28

1934

Nora's Michelle was lovely as a baby. She's still a dear. But having her to stay and having her to live here are two different things. They say the best thing about grandchildren is that you can give them back. The same goes for nieces, but we can't give her back and everything has to fit round Michelle.

As for the new baby? Poor Nora. He's a pathetic little thing. More like a mouse-baby, and not that much bigger. And crying and fussing all the time. Can't feed properly, can't sleep properly. Can't breathe properly, either. He's got asthma, poor little mite, and can't be left for fear of him not breathing. I feel sorry for him, I really do, but I feel more sorry for Nora. It was clear she was never going to cope. So when Mum said, leave Michelle here, she'd have been daft to refuse. But Nora was so upset leaving her. You cannot imagine. Michelle's going to have a better time with Mum and Edna than watching Nora cope with the baby all the time. It puts me right off having children.

Anyway, it's all done me a good turn. When Nora came to have the baby I went to stay with Auntie in Battenberg Avenue. It was the obvious thing, to make room for Nora and Michelle. Edna and Nora were always really close as sisters and anyway Edna's wonderful with children. She'll make a lovely mother one day. It was only going to be for a few weeks, until the baby was born and doing well enough for them all to go home to Rayners Lane. But when Philip was such a sickly creature and then Michelle stayed on, Auntie said, why not move in permanently? It was company for Lucy.

It's very different living here. The house is bigger of course and they have a proper bathroom. There's a side passage and a verandah at the back, so you can dry washing out of the rain. What Mum would give for one of those. But that's not what I mean. Life is much frillier here. A bit too frilly, if I'm honest. I like things to be nice and it's good they think serviettes and things like that are important. Things Mum gets impatient about. But it all comes out rather fussy. Uncle Jim is very fussy too, in a different way. He likes his meal on the table when he comes in from work at the tramway and Auntie flaps round him like a mother hen. What about me and Lucy? We've done a hard day's work, too.

Lucy is lazy. After tea she always sits with Uncle Jim and tells him about her day while he has a pipe. He's always made a great fuss of her ever since he came home from the war when she was a little girl. Lucy used to boast about that because Dadser didn't fight in that war, but Dadser says Jim didn't do any fighting and had a jammy time in India looking after boxes. But my cousin Maudie told me that Uncle Jim has to make it up to Lucy because he couldn't bear to look at her before he went away to war, what with her not being able to walk and being in that cart. All of which means I have to do the washing-up. Auntie says Lucy's bad leg aches after being at work all day. Maybe. She does still walk a bit hoppity, but it only seems to ache when there's washing-up to be done.

But never mind. It all takes my mind off Lily and Clive not being there in their different ways. Clive wrote me a letter, well a note really, sometime last month. He said he was going to sea and would be away all year. Auntie had her eagle eyes on it, of course.

'Who's that from? An admirer? Wonderful, dear. Wonderful.'

She winkled it out of me. Instead of disapproving, like Mum when a neighbour told her Mr Atkins had been to see me and she saw the cameo, Auntie seemed to think it was very exciting. Auntie understands about bettering yourself. But I don't like it when she says, you'll be happier here, meaning the nicer house, the better road. I hate it when she makes herself out to be posh compared with Mum. After all, it's only got her to the other side of London Road. I plan to improve on that.

Auntie thinks Clive is a good prospect. 'Why would he write to tell you what he's doing?'

I've wondered that myself, but Auntie doesn't wait to hear. 'Because he intends to come for you when he gets back. There has to be a decent interval. That's very proper.'

'It's not just proper. He loved Lily. And so did I.' Auntie doesn't understand how I feel about Lily. 'I really miss her.'

Auntie takes no notice. She's chewing at her front teeth, thinking. 'House in Southsea, motor car. Naval officer. There you have a rich widower with a career. A good catch, my girl. No harm if he is a bit older than you. I always say, "Don't marry for money, but marry where money is." That's my maxim.'

I can see she reckons that if I don't want him, he might be a good catch for Lucy. I bet she makes Lucy a new dress just before Clive is due home.

Meanwhile she's busy making sure I have a better twenty-first birthday party than I would have at home. Auntie and Lucy are doing a lot of whispering in the kitchen and staying up after I've gone to bed. In the end it means more sponge trifle and doilies and silver keys on pink ribbons than I've ever seen. Clive would think it vulgar, I'm sure. But they mean well and I do enjoy it all the same. Mum and Dadser and Edna and Binnie come over with Michelle, and I'm allowed to invite Gwen from work. I know Mum thinks Auntie's wasted a lot of money on "fripperies" but I can tell she's pleased they've made a fuss of me and she hasn't had to do any of it. She gets pretty tired, having Michelle all day while Edna's at work.

I've been getting on well at *Milady's*. Miss Pritchard retired and there was quite a reshuffle. Now I'm one of the chief milliners and have some status at last. Most people were very good when Lily died, although some had to go muttering about pride going before a fall. I really don't know what they were talking about.

I like having more money and the independence of living with Auntie. I do miss Lily, but I know where I am. What I need before too long is a husband. Meanwhile, I'm enjoying myself. I'm not going to sit around waiting for Clive. I'm not too sure about him, anyway. I can see what Auntie means, but I never did know where I was with him. That look he gave me in his study after I stepped away from him. It's like a haunting. There was something I can't explain, almost dangerous, about it. I shall refuse him, and not just the first time like Auntie says. I shall keep on refusing him.

Lucy goes on dates with young men from the newspaper. Clerks mainly, a reporter once. It never lasts long. She says it's because they always see her sitting down in the typing pool. They don't see her wonky walk until they take her out. It might be that, but I think it's more because she makes herself up like a vamp and then behaves like a child. I went on a foursome with her one time and she did a little pout every time she didn't get what she wanted. I think she thought it was alluring but it wasn't. At home she laughs it off and says variety is the spice of life, and I have to admire her spirit.

Clive did come back. He did ask me to marry him. I stuck to my resolution and said no. Auntie said that was the right thing to do. But she doesn't like it when I say I still mean it.

He's taken me out a few times, but he's never kissed me again like he did in his brown study. He'll just hold my hand and stare at me with *that* look. Sometimes he'll be shaking. Now he's gone on leave. He said he needed to see his father. I was surprised, as he spent Christmas with his family and it's only the end of January. I was disappointed he didn't invite me to go with him. Auntie must have thought the same.

'You be careful you don't lose him. There's such a thing as too cool.'

'I told you, Auntie. I don't want to marry the man.'

She gave me a look and clacked her teeth. 'I just hope he hasn't got a girl up there in Sheffield.'

It's weeks before I see him. He's obviously off on quite a jaunt because he sends me a postcard from Gretna Green. That gets Auntie going I can tell you. I don't know what to think, but it's an improvement on the card he sent on his way across London – a picture of a chimps' tea party. What's that supposed to mean? And what's a grown man doing visiting the zoo? At least the blacksmith's shop has a romantic message. I've put them both in my special box. No one ever sent me postcards before.

I'm even beginning to think silly things like absence makes the heart grow fonder, when he turns up one Saturday afternoon driving a brand new shiny black Lanchester motor car. Evidently his father is in the motor trade. We drive out into the country and I've never felt so grand. Over tea and cakes in Petersfield he shows me a newspaper cutting from the *Yorkshire Star* or some such paper, which he gets out of his wallet and unfolds as if it's a royal proclamation. It's a write-up of how Sir Arthur Atkins had been awarded a knighthood for his services to the town of Sheffield during his reign as Lord Mayor. Sir Arthur and Lady Atkins were to attend a reception in their honour in the Town Hall. When I look up Clive is grinning at me.

'This isn't your father?'

'What do you think? I told you I had to see him.'

'To congratulate him! How exciting. And is that why he gave you the car?'

'*Sir Arthur* was feeling very generous. I told him I was planning to get married.'

'But Clive…'

'Not another word about it. Now, another slice of Madeira?'

I don't like the way Clive seems to be making assumptions. How dare he? He even shows Auntie the newspaper cutting, as if he thinks it will stand him in good stead. And of course Auntie has to tell Mum.

Next time I see Mum she's muttering about *All that glisters is not gold* and says she supposes I fancy myself as a Lady one day. Of course it has crossed my mind, though I say no, of course not. Sir Clive and Lady Atkins. Even Lily wasn't a Lady. Mum gives me a look and says that Auntie told her it didn't work like that and I'd only ever be plain missus. But what does she know? I can tell Mum doesn't quite trust Auntie on this subject. She probably clacked her teeth when she said it and was thinking of Lucy. I can hardly ask Clive.

Mum and Dadser are dead against any idea of me marrying Clive, even if the idea is only in Auntie's head. Dadser takes me in the front room one Sunday.

'This man is old enough to be your father. I want to give you away, not throw you away. I want to give you happily to a man who will appreciate you.'

'He does appreciate me.' For some reason I leap to Clive's defence.

'Clive is more than twice your age. He has no children, which maybe is just as well. But he may be too old to think of having them now. What sort of marriage would that be?'

I don't say it would be just the sort of marriage I want. 'I wouldn't mind about that.'

I know Clive doesn't want children. When he goes on about getting married, which he often does, he's always clear about that.

Dadser is speaking again. 'You might not mind now. But you will mind. Why don't you come back home and think about it? As you know, Michelle's going back to Nora in the summer. You can have your old room back. Your mother would like that.'

I know Mum would like that. To have me back and keep an eye on me. To get me away from Auntie's influence. Looking around the familiar room, I feel almost tempted. It would all be so much easier to let go of making difficult decisions. I could concentrate on work and start going out with Danny Cook. He's much the better looking of Gwen's brothers and she's always telling me he likes me, but is too shy to ask. I'd only have to give her the word.

Then Clive does something unforgivable. He raises the matter of children again. He seems almost obsessed with it. He says we don't want to take any risks and that he's telling me so I can take care of it, fix myself up. That's mystifying. I must remember to ask Gwen what he means. But the point is, whatever he means, he's making assumptions again. As if, once that's sorted out, we can go ahead and get married. What a nerve. How dare he talk about such personal things when we aren't even engaged. And not likely to be. I saw Danny yesterday. He's got such a lovely smile. Shame he works in the Dockyard.

29

2006

It was a wet weekend when the phone call came. For once Daniel was involved in an activity with Jack, finishing a model aeroplane, holding the whole thing steady while Jack bit his tongue in concentration as he stroked glutinous silver paint on the wings with a tiny brush.

Flora had fallen asleep on the sofa and Kate was enjoying watching the scene as she finished the ironing without interruptions. A normal, peaceful Sunday afternoon.

'That'll do. Any more and it'll start to run.' Daniel stretched and sat back to admire their efforts. 'You've done a good job there. You're a good little painter.'

Jack grinned with pride and waved the brush around.

'Go clean the brush like I showed you. We need to let that dry before we put the markings on. How about a cup of tea?' The phone warbled, and Daniel picked it off the wall bracket with one hand as he stretched for the kettle with the other.

Kate looked up to see Daniel buckle at the knees, slumping back on to the chair like a puppet with broken strings. He dropped the phone, sending it spinning on its back across the table. Jack screeched, 'Daddy!' and caught it just before it crashed into his precious aeroplane.

'Who is it? What?' Kate grabbed the phone from Jack, but the line was dead. She had to dial 1471 to find Blake at the other end. Roz had fallen off a stepladder while painting the kitchen ceiling.

'You know, the bit where we had the old boiler taken out.'

Kate did know. Only too well. On their last visit Roz had gone on about how Blake wouldn't get the job finished off. 'Hit her head on the Aga and knocked herself out. By the time the ambulance got her to hospital she was – well, dead. Never regained consciousness,' said Blake, sounding like a voice from the dead himself.

Blake hung up again before Kate had found any coherent response. Daniel was staring ahead, his eyes glazed over.

'Daniel, Daniel!' She took him by the shoulders and shook him, gently at first and then more vigorously, but he remained stiff and motionless. 'Daniel, look at me.'

He turned his head but didn't focus. Shock. It would be shock. She found a bottle of whisky at the back of a cupboard and poured some into a tumbler. She had to hold it to his mouth, press it onto his lips before he drank. He coughed, drew breath, spluttered, then took the glass and gulped it down.

'Mama,' he said and looked at her wildly. 'Mama had a fall.'

'Yes, Daniel. Roz is...'

'Mama's in hospital. In hospital. Blake said. In the hospital.'

'Yes, Daniel, but... Roz was...'

'I must go to her. Mama needs me. She is in the hospital.'

'Daniel, you need to know... I don't know what Blake said to you.' Of course she knew what Blake must have said. What else could he have said? 'Daniel, you won't find Roz in the hospital. Roz is dead.' She managed to get it out at last.

'Don't say wicked things. I must go to her.'

'Daniel, of course...'

Daniel got to his feet and put his hand over her mouth pushing her back against the wall. She pulled it away and held off both his hands. 'Of *course* we will go, Daniel. But you need to know the truth, that you won't find Roz...'

Daniel broke free and ran from the room. She listened to his footsteps thud on the stairs, getting slower and fainter as he reached the top. She realised that Jack was wedged beside her, still clutching his paintbrush.

'What's wrong with Daddy?'

'Jakey, we've just had some very sad news. Grandma Roz had a bad accident and she died, Jack. She's gone to heaven. You remember, like Flopsy Bunny?'

Jack nodded and went to the window to look down the garden. 'Will we bury Grandma Roz under the apple tree?'

'No, darling. She'll be buried where she lives, in Hull. We'll have to go there to help Grandpa Blake. Here, give me that brush before it drips everywhere.'

Jack made a face and surrendered the paintbrush. He peered at his model aeroplane. 'Is it dry yet, Mummy?'

'Not yet. We'd better put it up on the shelf, so Flora can't reach it when she wakes up.' Her mind raced as she lifted the model to a place of safety. 'Can you be a very big boy and help Mummy get ready to pack?'

'Mummy, does it mean that Grandma Roz won't come and make biscuits with me any more?'

'That's right, Jakey. You won't see Grandma Roz any more. That's going to be very hard, isn't it? For you, for all of us, and specially for Daddy.'

'Why specially for Daddy?'

'Because she was his Mummy.'

'I'd better go and look after Daddy, bet'n't I?' Jack dug his knuckles into his eyes and set off after Daniel.

Kate started throwing things into a suitcase. 'Ready for the morning.'

'Morning? No! No! We must leave straightaway or we might not be in time'.

Eventually Kate took the line of least resistance and agreed to drive through the night. At least the children would sleep and there'd be less traffic.

They crunched onto the driveway of the house in Hull at seven in the morning. Blake took an eternity to answer the door and Jack had to pee behind the pampas grass in the front garden.

Daniel, who had fallen asleep on the motorway, woke in a fury. 'Why have you come here? We need to be at the hospital!'

Kate said nothing and pulled bags out of the boot.

She'd always found it a depressing house, a 1930s double-fronted covered in beige pebbledash and set in its own garden in a road with suburban trees. Kate noted a fresh pile of weeds at the side of the path and could picture her mother-in-law on her knees in her gardening apron "Just doing a quick tidy" while the Sunday roast sizzled in the oven. All so predictable. But yesterday it hadn't been predictable. As she wielded her trowel she'd have been thinking about getting that kitchen ceiling sorted in the afternoon while Blake had his nap. And not knowing.

Blake stared at them blankly. He might just as well have said, who the hell are you? He seemed to have slept on the sofa in his clothes. There was an empty bottle of Scotch on the living room table. Kate took in the paint roller, which was still on the kitchen floor where it had fallen, and understood why Blake refused to go anywhere near the kitchen.

Daniel, far from joining Blake in grief, refused to be in the same room with him. He stormed in and out unpacking the car and then charged back out of the front door, saying 'I'm off to the hospital.'

But he found his way blocked by a neighbour on her way in, a voluminous blonde in a billowing dress of green and purple roses. Kate hung back as he allowed himself to be pressed against her ample and leathery cleavage. Evidently he'd known Doris since childhood, and Kate was grateful when she quickly took the hint about Daniel's plans to visit the hospital and swept him off to her house with the comforting words, 'I'll make us a pot of tea and you can come to yourself, my love.'

As she found bread and eggs for the makings of breakfast for the children, Kate sincerely hoped he would be persuaded to come to himself. Blake responded to strong coffee and was visibly cheered to find that Daniel had been taken off by "that old bat next door". Together they made a list, and she sat him down with the phone while she scrubbed paint off the kitchen floor and cleared away the signs of the accident.

It gave her the shivers. There was so much evidence of Roz around the kitchen – the apple pie on the side with two slices out of it, the fat she'd poured off the joint set to cool in a pudding basin, a fresh loaf in the bread bin, home-made, of course – that it was hard not to imagine that she would walk in at any moment. All those familiar tasks that Roz had completed, not knowing she was doing them for the last time.

When she'd first heard the news, Kate had felt relief that there would be no more difficult visits from Roz, then guilt that she should harbour such feelings. But now she too was feeling the shock and an unexpected sense of loss. Her mother-in-law had had such energy and enthusiasm for life. What a waste that she was gone. Her absence created a vacuum in the house. Daniel and Blake wandered about avoiding each other, like actors in a play with no director.

'Blake is unbelievable,' Kate said as she and Daniel went to bed on the first night. 'D'you know? He accused us of eating him out of house and home.'

'He's a mean bastard, all right. He should never have let Mama up that ladder. Too much of a skinflint to have someone in.'

Try stopping her, thought Kate. 'I'll go to the supermarket tomorrow. Apart from anything, it'll be something to do, get the kids out the house.'

She had an alarming conversation with Jack in the check-out queue.

'Mummy, what's a gogglywog?'

'A gogglywog? I don't think I know. Why?'

'Just a thing that Grandpa Blake said to Flora. That's what he called her.'

'He what? He called her a golliwog?' The old bastard, thought Kate. So that's what goes on when we're out of earshot.

'That's what I said. A gogglywog. Mummy, why d'you look like that? Is it a naughty word? Oughtn't he should to have said it?'

'Well, in a way. A golliwog's an old-fashioned toy like they had in the olden days.'

'Why did he call Flora a toy?'

'I expect he thought her hair was curly like a golliwog.'

'So why was that bad, Mummy?'

Get yourself out of that one, thought Kate, I'm not ready for this. 'Well, you wouldn't like it, for instance, if someone called you a – let's think. I know. Supposing someone called you a Barbie doll?'

'Yuk!' squawked Jack and rushed down the nearest aisle being an aeroplane to get all thoughts of Barbie dolls out of his hair.

Kate rolled her eyes at the woman behind her who'd been pretending not to listen.

She smiled at Flora, who was in the trolley seat trying to open a packet of biscuits. 'Old attitudes die hard.' She sighed, as if she could say much more but decided not to.

The priest came next morning, eager to let Daniel know exactly what Roz would have wanted, which turned out to be the whole Roman Catholic ritual. The open coffin at the wake, the full mass, the interment. Kate dreaded it.

Roz looked more peaceful in death than in life. And she looked more like a horse than ever, thought Kate. Something about the high brow, long nose and the mouth carefully closed over her prominent teeth, reminding Kate of a mannerism she'd had. A pulling down of the upper lip over those teeth, mostly when she'd said something slippery – an insincere or flattering comment. It was a relief to be able to look at her face without the piercing blue eyes.

And what about this custom of the vigil? It sounded mawkish, but in the event Kate found it the most natural thing to do. The rarely used dining room was warmed by the candles and by the serene presence of the dead woman. That was the thing about Roz. She'd never been able to put her finger on it before now. Roz always looked serene, but, in life, she never was.

Kate's other concern was that Daniel would go to pieces when he saw Roz or do something melodramatic like trying to get into the coffin with her. But the priest met Daniel on the threshold of the room, clasped his hand and closed the door behind them. She could hear the priest's voice talking, then intoning a prayer. A soothing, comforting sound. She could understand when Daniel came out looking calm and in control, said goodbye to the Father and invited the other guests to pay their respects.

Later he insisted she went to bed. 'I want to be alone with her. I'll probably sleep in the chair, she won't mind. The Father said that was fine. As long as she isn't alone.'

Blake had already gone up, saying he didn't hold with "all that mumbo jumbo she believed in". He'd kept a low profile all evening, not wanting to speak to the priest, barely greeting the neighbours. At least, thought Kate as she cleaned her teeth, we can get clear of Blake tomorrow. Daniel will be a different person once we get away from here, and he'll be better when he's gone through the ritual of the funeral.

But first she had to endure Blake alone over toast and tea at breakfast, while Daniel caught up on sleep after his vigil. Blake had shaved and seemed to have perked up at the prospect of the funeral later that morning.

'Get the whole thing over,' he said, stirring sugar into his mug. He eyed her and then continued. 'You'll be doing well out of all this. You might as well know. I get the house, of course, but she had a small fortune in stocks and shares and so on. Daniel gets most of that, as I understand it.'

Kate stared. 'I had no idea.' It had never occurred to her that Roz had money.

'I'd prefer it if you didn't tell him while you're here. Don't want any discussion of that sort. I might say something I'd regret. He'll hear from the solicitor soon enough.'

'All right. But anyway, Daniel's too distraught to be thinking about...'

'You'd be surprised! How money changes a man's mood. And that one. Well, I don't mind telling you. He took advantage. She, she worshipped him really, spoilt him rotten. That's how I saw it, any road. But 'twas none of my business.' He stopped abruptly, swallowed hard. 'We never got on. Couldn't bear to see his mother with another man. And she always missed her precious boy. Held it against me.' He paused, wiped his mouth with a grubby handkerchief and shook his head. 'It wasn't me drove him away, you know. Twaddle, that were, though he liked people to think it. No. That was girl trouble.'

Kate didn't want to hear all this. He spoke as if Daniel were an outsider, not her husband. As if she wouldn't care. Or as if she weren't there.

'With all due respect, I don't think he deserves a penny of it. Not that I want it. My life's a simple one. And I'll not contest it.'

Evidently exhausted by this speech, Blake gathered up his newspaper and took it into the front room. Kate didn't know what to say, so said nothing. She wondered what Blake considered a small fortune.

It was well after midnight when they got home. They all fell into bed without unpacking.

'Kate, I don't know what I'm going to do without her.' Daniel's voice cracked and he looked away, hitting the bedhead with his fist so that the vibration jarred her body. 'She wasn't supposed to die.'

'Somehow you'll manage. We'll get through it.'

Daniel buried his head in the pillow. 'It changes everything.'

But when Kate asked what he meant by that, he shook his head and promptly fell asleep.

30

1935

The lace is beautiful. I can't believe my luck. It will be the most elegant and sumptuous wedding dress I have ever seen. For the first time ever I feel nervous about making the first cut.

Auntie said I couldn't make my own dress but I knew I'd make it better than she would. She must have known that too and gave in. She's being very good and she and Lucy are going to help with tacking and so on. The lace came from Grandma Day. She died in the spring and we found it under her bed. Auntie said immediately it would make a lovely wedding dress and looked at Lucy. But Lucy turned up her nose and said she wanted to get married in satin. So there it was, waiting for me.

That wasn't why I changed my mind and accepted next time Clive asked me. Of course not.

I gave him the cold shoulder after that conversation about children. But then I couldn't get him out of my head. The man does something to me and eventually I have decided it must be love. And he did take the hint. He's never mentioned children again. He's been so kind and we've been having such fun driving off to places in the Lanchester. And it was all very romantic when he proposed. Candles, a table overlooking the harbour, the little red box appearing by my place before dessert. So exciting! This beautiful sapphire ring. Sapphire and real diamonds. The girls at work all crowded round to admire it. I can't stop turning it to catch the light. It's set in platinum, which impressed Auntie no end. My wedding ring's going to be platinum too.

Gwen's getting married this autumn. Even Billy Chapman got married at Easter. But that was because he had to, which was no surprise to anyone. It's funny. I almost miss Billy. Not really of course, but I never had any more trouble with him. He avoided me for ages, then he'd pass the time of day. Respectful. He even offered me a ciggy in the bus queue once. I didn't take it of course. It's a pity about Billy, him being so common. He's got style, which is more than you can say for Danny Cook, and he's taller than Clive. But no prospects. And where am I going to meet someone with prospects? I don't want people muttering about me like they do about Lucy, that she'll soon be "on the shelf".

Mum and Dadser aren't at all happy, of course. But I am determined. I have made up my mind. It is my chance to escape. And I'm going to get married from Auntie's house, not from this old street with all the neighbours gawping. Whether they like it or not.

Dadser's got an extra sadness of his own, on top of me marrying Clive. Last month, an envelope with a black border and a Plymouth postmark arrived on our doormat. Dadser knew immediately, of course, and went into the front room to open it. His mother, my lady grandmother, had died. It's no great surprise, as she was ninety years old. Dadser went on about missing the funeral, not being able to pay his last respects. He was cross that his sister, Ada, hadn't written sooner. But what with the wedding at the beginning of November, there's enough to do. I know Mum's relieved. It's an expense we can do without. Dadser will still be wearing an armband when he gives me away, but otherwise, it won't affect anything. At first, I was upset that my lady grandmother wouldn't be looking after me anymore. But, on second thoughts, she can still do that from Heaven, which will be a lot more convenient, in the circumstances. The last thing I want is a grandmother with skin the colour of hers turning up at my very white wedding. Even so, I'm sad that I won't ever see her again.

Gwen and I are helping each other with the preparations. She's marrying a policeman. He's such a big man, but so gentle. I can't imagine him arresting anyone. Gwen's going to be my matron of honour and Binnie and Michelle will be bridesmaids. Gwen's also putting me right on several points about married life. As I thought, she does know what Clive meant for a start. She agrees that I must get myself fitted up. It sounds horrible. We're in the cutting room at dinner break and everyone else has gone out. I decide to be brave and ask her something else that has been bothering me.

'I know what you do and everything. Of course. But I don't see quite how it works. That *thing*, you know, hangs down. Doesn't it? So how does it, you know?'

By this time Gwen has got the giggles. She can hardly talk, so she takes the scribble pad we use for sketching details of hat trims and starts to draw. Eventually she says, 'When it's – you know – it doesn't hang down any more.' And she hands me the pad. I've hardly got time to look at it when I hear footsteps, so I tear it off and screw it into my hand as Miss Wilmott walks in.

'I hope you're not wasting paper. What have you got there?'

I make a straight face. 'Just a design Gwen was showing me. It won't work.'

Miss Wilmott holds out her hand. She takes the paper, spreads out the crumples and frowns. Then the red starts to creep up her neck. She rips it across and hands back the pieces. 'Not something that would find favour with our ladies,' she says and leaves the room. Gwen and I don't know what to do with ourselves. But for me a mystery has been solved.

The light is different. Entirely different. I've heard it talked of, that changed quality of light in St Ives, but I never believed it. Now I see the clarity with my own eyes. It's as if the colours are washed through with light.

And the sea is so unlike the Solent: the open Atlantic, brilliant, enticing, with nothing between us and America.

I want to paint. But I've no materials with me. It's so long since I've even thought about painting. I'm not sure Clive even knows I used to paint, and it is my honeymoon after all. I shouldn't want to give attention to anything other than Clive. He'd be hurt if he knew how I crave to be alone with a set of paints at the water's edge. He's lavishing attention on me: loving gestures, lingering looks, presents.

In the dawn he begins to caress me, and I let him do what he wants while I keep watching the slate-hung house on the far side of the bay surfacing out of the darkness. As Clive's hands and body move against my body under the covers, it steadies me to fix my eyes on the white-painted window frames and to imagine inhabiting those rooms.

There was no house to hold me in Lyme Regis, where we stayed for the first night. Only the surge of the sea stretching into the darkness. Nothing could have prepared me for the wildness that took hold of my restrained and methodical husband once he took off his clothes and climbed into bed. It was like a possession. Frightening, but quickly over. I suppose I saw the shadow of it on the day of Lily's funeral. That darkness in his eyes when I stepped away from him up there in his brown study. It speaks to some dark place inside me that I don't want to find out about.

Here in St Ives I'm less frightened, and I can't be sure if this is because I know what to expect or because the watchful eyes of the house are comforting.

I was disappointed we didn't go to Paris. Somehow I thought Clive would take me there. Of course, I didn't say so. I decide to ask why he chose St Ives and was it because he knew I was a painter? Clive looks shocked and says, no, it's because he's never been here. By which I understand he never brought Lily here.

Early on he made it clear we are not to talk about Lily. He says he doesn't want me to think of him as Lily's widower, and he doesn't want to think of me as a second wife. I think that's really lovely. But sometimes I would like to speak of her, not because she was his wife, but because she was my friend. I referred to her once. I said something like, 'Lily used to love that song.'

And his eyes went dark and he said, 'Don't! I don't like to hear her name on your lips.' He was moody all day.

I'm shivering, partly with cold, but it's really quite warm in the room. A moment ago I pulled up the blankets but Clive tweaked them away, playful. 'I want to see you.' He spread my legs, told me to stretch out my arms, so now I'm lying like a star.

I'm trembling all over. I can't help curling over onto my side. Clive's undressing at the long mirror. As he turns he flicks the tie he's just removed so the end of it stings my right buttock. 'No! I told you. I want to see you. Like this.' He grabs my ankles, jerking me back into the splayed formation. Then he pads around the bed, still undressing, running his tongue along his teeth, wetting his lips. His gaze feels heavy but it doesn't warm me. I can feel the hair rising on my arms and, if I squint down my nose I can see my nipples bobbing like corks.

We've been home a week now. Home. Well, that's a strange word. I really expected he'd have dismissed the tenants from Clifton Villa, and set it up as a surprise when we got back from honeymoon. He set up a surprise all right. A flat on London Road. Of all places. It's just round the back of *Milady's*. I kept asking about Clifton Villa. I should have known better. I mean, it was like talking about Lily. In the end he lost his temper and admitted the truth. He didn't own Clifton Villa. Never had. It was rented. Well, of course, I made a point of admiring the flat, appreciating his thoughtfulness in finding somewhere so close to my home. But I made it clear I didn't need to be near my family when we found permanent accommodation. It never occurred to me the flat was anything but a temporary measure. My big mistake.

When I started house-hunting he revealed another layer of lies. Lily's parents rented Clifton Villa for them. He could never afford such a house. Not then. Not now.

Well, that was a mystery. I thought he was well off. But I didn't dare ask any more questions. He felt humiliated. And it was my fault. He was courteous but withdrawn by day. He continued to teach me his routines. For instance, he showed me where to put the heavy silver cutlery in the correct slots in the baize-lined canteen. It was like a game. I loved polishing the forks and spoons with the curly A engraved on the handles, which reminded me of Dadser's tattoo. One day, when I was in a hurry, I put the knives and forks we always use into a drawer instead. All ready for the next meal. He found them there and stormed about saying, 'What is the meaning of this?' I wanted to laugh and wished I was back in the scullery with Mum and Edna. I knew then it wasn't a game. I understood there'd be penalties, but I'd no idea what they might be.

Now, as I lie on the bed in this shabby bedroom and he prowls around me, I feel like a woman of the street he's brought here for his pleasure. This is what *I'm* fit for. But for Lily, it was Clifton Villa.

There is nothing I can do. It happens to me while I concentrate on not making a sound. If I cry out, he will smack me.

When he's finished, he kisses my forehead and slips my nightdress over my head before pulling up the bedclothes and falling asleep.

It's spring and we're invited to visit Clive's cousin Eric in Devon. A treat for my birthday, Clive says. I never guess for a moment what a surprise I'm in for. Eric introduces his wife and it's Charlie. Clive knew, of course. His idea of a joke, no doubt. To be fair, I suppose he never knew what a hard time Charlie gave me in Brittany.

She eyes me and says, 'We meet again.' Then she leans forward and pecks my cheek and whispers, 'And in very different circumstances.'

'Indeed,' I say with all the dignity I can muster.

Later in the kitchen she says, 'Who'd have thought it? Never thought he'd *marry* you.'

Who'd have thought it, indeed! That Charlie would end up married to a chinless wonder like Eric, a clergyman at that? And me actually married to Clive, respectable at last? She tells me she liked me that time in Brittany when she gave me that talking to, and funnily enough I think she means it. Once all that's out of the way, we get on really well.

The next day there's another surprise. We're to go for a day at the races in Newton Abbot, which seems an unlikely activity for a clergyman. But it's all down to Charlie, who's well-connected and knows the Lord Lieutenant of Devon. She's got us special tickets for the VIP enclosure, with access to the Paddock and everything. I hope I'll know what to do.

We're lucky with the weather. It's cold but at least it isn't raining, so my shoes won't get ruined. Charlie's made sure we have a sumptuous picnic and "plenty of booze to keep us warm". We have to wear special badges to give us access to the places only VIPs can go. It feels very grand, although I am worried that the pin will hatch the fabric of my coat. Clive takes over when the racing starts and goes off with Eric to place bets. It isn't until he comes back that I get a look at the race card. I see there's a horse called Edna May in the two-thirty and get very excited and say to Clive that I must put some money on it. He gets all pompous and says it would be 'Most unwise, Thea, my dear.' He says one should only place bets after studying form and won't hear any more about it. I wait until he's watching another race and go off and place the bet myself. It's so loud down by the bookies' stands and they're pretty surprised to see a lady there, especially a lady with a badge. Some of the men make way for me and I hold my own. Sometimes it comes in useful to have been brought up in the back end of Portsmouth.

Of course, Edna May wins and Clive's horse comes in second to last. I'm so beside myself with excitement that I don't notice what a disaster that is. Charlie's as excited as I am and most impressed that I've been to place a bet all by myself. She insists on coming with me to claim my winnings and brushes aside Eric's offer to escort us. Clive is standing back, saying nothing.

I put half a crown on to win. It seemed a small fortune to me, but I know it won't seem much to Charlie. Apparently I put it on at thirty-three to one, whatever that means. Charlie tries to explain but I'm too busy counting the notes. I've never had so much money all at one go.

Charlie pours a drink to toast my success and has to persuade Clive to take a glass. He won't look at me on the way home. I'm disappointed he's made no reference to my win and in our bedroom I try to get him to talk about it.

'What a bit of luck,' I say. 'I can't wait to see Edna and May's faces.'

He looks up sharply. 'You won't be needing any housekeeping money next week.'

I'm outraged. 'But that's my special money! It's a surprise present for Edna and May. Well, I might keep a little bit back for myself. I could have my hair done. You'd like that.'

Evidently he would not like that. He gives me a cold look and stalks out of the room.

He's moody and silent all the way back to Portsmouth next day. And when he leaves for work on Monday there's no ten shilling note with a little pile of coins on the kitchen table. Seventeen and sixpence. The first time he gave me the housekeeping he told me he'd worked it out exactly and I should be able to manage. I know he hasn't forgotten. Clive doesn't make mistakes like that.

I refuse to be bullied. As soon as I've done the housework I go round home and tell Mum the whole story. I don't say anything about Clive, of course. I leave the money for Edna and May with her, two whole pounds each. I won't be there to see their faces but I daren't be late home, or wait for the weekend. For all I know Clive might pinch the money out of my handbag. Mum won't take anything for herself so I call in at the Post Office and put a bit in my savings account. Clive doesn't know about that.

In the end I've only got twelve and sixpence left to buy food so it's going to be a bit of a struggle, but nothing to what Mum's had to cope with over the years. At least growing up poor has taught me plenty of recipes for eking out and making do. But Clive doesn't like it one little bit when we're eating bread and dripping by the end of the week.

I know I'm in for some of his bedroom games that night and, sure enough, he gets me spread-eagled on the bed, but his mood isn't at all playful.

He brings my comb and starts teasing out my hair and spreading it on the pillow. 'Struwwelpeter,' he murmurs. He's not caring about the tangles and it hurts. I see in my mind a picture in a book Lucy once had of a boy with crazy hair and long, long nails. And I wish I had those nails. I'd scratch them down his smooth cheeks and scrape them down his back. I close my eyes for fear he might see my thoughts and when I open them he's climbing on to me. My arms move automatically to embrace him, but he grabs my wrists and forces them back. My nipples are hard with anticipation but when his teeth move onto them I can't stop my arms coming to the rescue. I cry out, 'Gently, gently.'

'I'm not feeling gentle.' Clive gets off the bed and goes to the wardrobe, returning with a handful of his ties. 'I can see Thea needs tying up,' he says in a flat voice.

Softly he wraps my wrists, so I wonder, is it a game after all? But then he ties them roughly, tightly to the bed struts so the metal binds on the bone. When I say, 'You're hurting me!' he ignores me. I writhe to be so exposed, so helpless, and cry out in pain.

'If you don't move it won't hurt.'

'Why are you doing this? Why do want to hurt me?'

'I told you there would be penalties to be paid.'

'But I haven't done anything.'

'If Thea insists on speaking she will have to be gagged.' He pounces down with his mouth on mine, pressing hard, hard, hard, so I gasp and his tongue invades me. I want to bite it but I dare not. Then I have air again. 'And I don't want to have to gag you. Complete quiet. You understand?'

All the while until now he has been wearing his robe. The dark green silk Lily gave him. When he slips it off I sees he is bigger than he's ever been. It excites me in spite of myself. As soon as his head dips down I lunge forward and sink my teeth in his ear. His howl and the taste of his blood release a rage in me. I'm bucking like the bronco they talk about, and the dark place inside me rips open. For a moment it's flooded with light. But not for long. I feel as if I've joined him in a shameful place. I deserve the pain that follows.

When I wake in the morning and remember, I'm frightened. But Clive is already in the bathroom. I run to make his coffee and toast, put out butter and marmalade. I can't believe it when he appears as usual, says good morning, pecks my cheek and eats his breakfast while finishing yesterday's crossword as he always does. We follow the ritual of his departure for work and I take special care that his meal is on the table when he comes home.

I obey the rules and follow the routines. I slip up and get punished. Some of it I enjoy, but that makes me feel dirty. That is how we live. The 'other' Clive only appears at weekends or when I transgress, as he calls it. Often I don't know what I've done. Sometimes I wonder why I'm putting up with it. There are so many reasons. One, if I were to run away I'd have to go back home and I couldn't face that. I'd be that half-caste who tried to make good. I can just hear the wagging tongues: *He had to throw her out. They're not the same, you know.* Two, one day Clive will inherit and we'll have a fine house and I will be a Lady. Three, I'm addicted. I never have enough of the good days when his eyes go through me and he grabs me and has me there and then, up against the sink or the back door, or wherever we happen to be. All the same, there are times I want to kill him. I really do. He always ties me up when we go to bed on Saturday, for instance. Next day we go to Sunday dinner with Mum and Dadser, and I look at him sitting there eating their food and I feel ashamed.

Edna is getting married in the summer. She's marrying Len Nextdoor. That's not his real name, of course, but it's how we've always talked about him, like he was a fixture of the house. Which is why we were all so surprised when Edna started walking out with him and very quickly got engaged. They've known each other for years, of course, and been friends, and no one noticed when they started being more than friends. Edna isn't a noticeable person. I look at Len and think he is a very ordinary and predictable man and will suit Edna very well. At this point I quite envy her. Then I remember how wrong you can be about men and I hope he doesn't turn out to be as dark a horse as Clive, or as boring as he looks.

31

2007

Kate experienced an exaggerated sense of setting off into the unknown as the car moved through a duvet of whiteness. Thank God she wasn't driving, it was totally disorienting. Occasionally the fog thinned enough to reveal a pale disc of a sun but mostly it was unremitting.

For once Lisa was sticking to the inside lane. 'Bloody idiots,' she said through gritted teeth as cars hurtled past.

Lisa had a new job with the Metropolitan police and Kate and Vanessa had stayed overnight at her new flat in Camberwell. They were on their way to the Isle of Sheppey.

Vanessa peered at a looming road sign. 'Here comes our exit.'

Kate watched the countdown signs drift by like marker buoys at sea. The tinka-linka of the indicator was the only sound inside the car. Then an intake of breath from all three of them as they turned. The veil of fog parted abruptly and sunshine illumined the way ahead.

'Wow! Good omen or what?' Vanessa relaxed back into her seat.

Lisa let one hand off the wheel and stretched the fingers. 'Phew! That's a relief. I was beginning to get a bit tense there.'

The temperature dropped steadily to one degree as they moved through an ashen landscape of heavily frosted vegetation with the occasional chill gleam of marsh water.

The two in the front were chatting but it was hard to hear in the back. Her head was woolly from a cold which made her feel as cut off from the world as the fog. Sinus pains were gripping her temples like a visor, and neuralgia had started shooting down from her ears into her gums. This winter, every time she'd picked up a cold from Jack it had ended like this, and drinking wine the night before hadn't helped. Her mind drifted back to what Vanessa had reported over dinner about her visit to Plymouth. Mum had been so excited about a chimney stack, and she and Lisa had done a lot of eye-rolling.

Mum and Dad had been on holiday in Devon and decided to visit the address on that old letter from Henrietta's daughter, Ada, just to see if the house was still standing.

'And guess what?' said Mum. 'The house only had a sale board on the gatepost.'

Not an opportunity Mum would pass up. Kate smiled to herself, thinking how embarrassed Dad must have been, going along with the cock and bull story Mum dreamed up about her daughter moving to the area. Mum had shown them all the photos she'd taken inside and out, and went on endlessly about the silky banister on the stairs that Henrietta would have swept down in rustling skirts.

Back home, Dad had applied his precise mind and interest in architecture to the chimney visible in a shot of the house from the back garden. She and Lisa had to peer closely to see that it exactly matched the chimney in the original picture of Henrietta discovered when Thea was dying. Good old Dad. Nobody else had even noticed it was there. So I guess that *is* pretty exciting, thought Kate. Mum stood pretty much where Henrietta had stood when that photo was taken.

Then there were the new cousins Mum had gone to meet next day. Found them through the phone book, apparently. Four generations of them had turned up to meet her and the old lady had been married to Henrietta's grandson, was it? Or great-grandson? Kate couldn't remember. Anyway, the old lady had a box of treasures that had belonged to Henrietta's daughter, Ada. In fact she remembered Ada. That was quite something. They'd been pretty interested in Henrietta because it answered their question, Mum said, about where the 'colour in the family' came from.

Colour in the family. Still such an emotive issue, and one that she still felt Daniel wasn't really addressing. A heron loomed out of the mist like a pterodactyl and her startled eyes followed its slow-motion flap until it was once more swallowed in cloud. It was something Kate tried not to think about, that reticence of Daniel's. Maybe she imagined Daniel avoided talking about it. The whole issue, his whole life it seemed, had been consumed by the loss of Roz. That was all he would talk about, if you could call it talk. *I've lost Mama* had become a kind of mantra. He used it to excuse getting up late, being late home, and doing bugger all in between.

It was a huge relief to be with normal people. The fog was thinning now as they came into the outskirts of the town. Lisa slowed down. Vanessa was giving directions. There was something to focus on.

'Whose idea was it to come to Sheerness in February?'

The cold hit as Kate stepped out of the car, and the movement caused a painful thundering in her head. She hunched further into her coat as the three women left the car park and stepped through into a scruffy street with shoppers and buggies jostling on the pavements. An icy wind funnelled off the sea and knifed through her.

'This is it. This is the High Street.' Vanessa held the street map and peered at the buildings, a jumble of Georgian, Victorian and Edwardian, many masked by modern plastic shop fronts. 'Number forty-one. Even numbers must be on the other side.'

Lisa pointed down the road. 'There's a pub, just down there. I bet that's it, next door.'

'It's a far cry from Gibraltar,' said Kate. She pulled her polo neck up over her mouth.

'Don't rub it in. I drew the short straw, coming on this trip instead of Gibraltar. Trust you, Sis. Hey, are you okay? You look grim.'

Kate was in too much pain to protest. 'It's the wind. Sinuses. Agony.' She spoke though aching teeth.

'Here, have my scarf. It's really long and you can wrap it right round.' Lisa pulled off her black pashmina, wrapped it around Kate's head across her nose and tucked it in at the back. She giggled. 'Can you see where you're going?'

Kate nodded, regretted it and gave a thumbs up. It did feel better.

Vanessa was already setting off across the road.

Kate dropped back, covertly checking her mobile for a message from Daniel. On the journey Vanessa had kept on about Daniel looking after the children and whether he'd remember everything, wanting Kate to phone and see how things were going.

'He'll be at work.' Kate had tried to keep a brittle edge out of her voice. 'Interrupt a meeting to ask if he managed the porridge? I don't think so.' She didn't want the others to know that she, too, had doubts about Daniel coping. He was just so vague these days. Forgetting to tell her when he was going to be late home. A glazed look would come over him. Like when she was telling him how well Jack was doing with his reading. Worried about a deal, he'd say, sale might fall through. And somehow she didn't quite believe him.

Now she followed her mother and sister towards the pub, dodging puddles. In the census of 1901, Henrietta's next-door neighbour was listed as a publican. What had once been a separate dwelling for Henrietta and her family, had since been taken over by the pub. There were notices in the porch about drug-dealing, warnings that the police would be called.

'I don't think Henrietta would have liked this one little bit.' Vanessa took photographs of Lisa and Kate in the doorway, and of the window through which Henrietta probably surveyed the comings and goings on the High Street.

Kate said nothing. Here she was again, imagining her ancestor in a new location, feeling nothing, thinking that Henrietta would have had too much dignity to be a twitcher of net curtains.

'The library's down on the left.' Lisa led the way and Kate followed.

Mum was still taking photos of the pub, said she would catch up. The pavement was uneven and dirty and crowded, mostly with mothers and small children. Kate tried to pull the scarf clear of her eyes but didn't want to uncover her nose which was better for breathing in warm, recycled air.

She'd narrowly missed an elderly couple carrying heavy bags, when a woman dragging a child came straight out of a doorway across her path and nearly knocked her off balance. Kate turned and was about to do the usual English thing of apologising for someone else's mistake when the woman shouted, 'Murdering cow!' and spat on the ground at her feet before pushing past, still dragging the child.

Kate stood still while the crowd surged round her. It was all over so quickly, but people were staring, making comments. Then Vanessa's arm was round her.

'What was that all about? Must be off her head.' She felt her shoulders squeezed and Mum was moving her along, steering through the shoppers until they caught up with Lisa who was waiting outside the library.

'Was there something? What kept you?'

She heard Vanessa describe what had happened.

'Oh, shit!' Lisa gave a short laugh. 'I did think, when I'd tied you up that you looked a bit Islamic. The woman must have thought it was a headscarf. As in *headscarf*, hijab, veil. Whatever you want to call it.'

'Bloody hell.' Vanessa turned to look again at Kate. 'I see what you mean, what with the black coat as well.'

'But why? What?' Kate still felt dazed.

'Who knows?' said Lisa. 'There's a lot of it about and there doesn't have to be a reason. Not a logical one, anyway. Fear, prejudice. People get a bee in their bonnet. Especially since 7/7 – you know, the London bombing?'

'Yeah, yeah. Or something in her life, perhaps. A personal grudge. As you say, who knows. But what a horrid thing to happen. Poor darling.' Vanessa opened the library door. 'Let's get inside in the warm and unwrap you.'

The librarian was helpful. She showed them newspapers of the period and records of the Wesleyan Methodist chapel. These yielded some grainy photographs of the teachers' group, among whom there were some dark faces. Vanessa fell on them and swore she could recognise Henrietta, but, as Lisa pointed out, the picture quality was too poor to make any positive identification. The building itself had been demolished to make way for the car park.

Kate made her way back to the car through a cold drizzle that had sluiced away the fog, while the other two queued for fish and chips.

So the Wesleyan chapel had been right here. She tried to imagine being Henrietta, living her life in the town. Black skin, black headscarf. Both highly visible identifiers. If it was that bad today, in the twenty-first century, and so bad for Thea in Portsmouth in the 1920s that she carried her secret to the grave, what chance had a woman in Edwardian times in a backwater like this? Not funny, thought Kate, shuddering at the memory of the hatred in that woman's eyes.

'I was wondering what it was like for Henrietta,' said Kate unwrapping her parcel of fish and chips. 'I mean, if I got that sort of treatment today. I don't imagine the Edwardians were any more enlightened.'

'Pretty awful is my guess,' said Lisa. 'I don't think I've seen any black faces this morning. Shouldn't think the demographic was much different back then. So, at the very best, people would have stared.'

'Victorians, actually,' Vanessa corrected. 'It was still Victoria when they got here from Gibraltar. 1894 it was.'

Lisa waved a chip to cool it. 'And it was probably a dump then, like it is now. Lots of poverty. Competition for jobs. That's when outsiders get scapegoated.'

They munched in silence, the windows steaming up.

Then Vanessa again. 'So Daniel's coping with the children this evening?'

Kate sighed. 'Morag's giving them tea. He's only got to put them to bed.'

'I just wondered.' There was that doubt again in Mum's voice.

'What did you wonder?'

'He just seemed so, kind of, cut off when we came over at the weekend.'

'Oh, that's just the medication.' Kate didn't believe it was the drug at all. In fact Mum seemed to have put her finger right on the problem.

Lisa raised an eyebrow. 'What's he on then?'

'Oh, some anti-depressant, stuff the doc gave him. Supposed to help him get over Roz.'

'And does it?'

'Not that I notice. Anyway, he's still functioning, going to work and so on. He'll be fine. After all, he coped when we went to Gibraltar. That was three nights.'

'But Morag had them sleep over for two, you said.'

'And that was before he lost his Mummy.' Lisa made a face. 'Sorry. But, you know... Time Danny-boy got his act together.'

Kate rolled her eyes and grunted. The truth was that Daniel had lost his compass when Roz died. Kate had fondly imagined that she herself was the centre of Daniel's world and it hurt to admit how important Roz had always remained, how critical she'd been to his stability. All those phone calls, often four or five a week, they hadn't been duty calls at all. He'd been the one relying on them. He'd never grown up, still needed to prove himself to his mother. Daniel reported every deal, the commission he'd earned, every bonus he was due. He basked in her praise, fell into a sulk when it wasn't forthcoming.

Lisa gathered up the detritus of the fish and chips. 'I'm sure he's coping fine. Kate, why don't you have some aspirin? You're still looking pretty rough.' She handed Kate a packet, along with a bottle of water, and pointedly changed the subject. 'When did the family move to Plymouth? Do we know?'

'No idea. They were still here, obviously, when William died in 1909. Then we have nothing until that letter from the daughter, Ada, with the Plymouth address in 1926. Nothing in between.'

'And why did they move to Plymouth?' said Kate. 'Mind you, anywhere would be an improvement on this place.'

'Right, what's next on the agenda?' asked Lisa.

'How about we head for the cemetery now? I've got the plan and the plot number.' Vanessa waved the photocopy of the layout of graves given them by the helpful librarian.

'But she did say the plots weren't all numbered.' Lisa was unenthusiastic about this part of the trip.

They drove round by the sea wall, a massive defence showing just how fierce the winter weather must be, and took a road through suburbs to Halfway Cemetery.

After trying in vain to match the plan with what was on the ground, they separated to cover the whole area, constantly bending and peering to decipher inscriptions that were half-obliterated by weather and creeping plants.

They met at an intersection.

Kate held her still-aching head. 'Is it time to call it a day?'

Lisa was shivering and eager to abandon the search. She was convinced Henrietta had been too poor to mark the grave.

But Vanessa was reluctant to abandon the search. 'Poor William. He has a good military career and ends up working for a brewer and being buried in an unmarked grave.'

'Come on, Ma. We're going to die of exposure.'

As Lisa spoke, Kate felt a sense of conviction coming from behind her, as if pulling at the small of her back. She spun round and walked towards a moss-covered cross. 'We haven't looked at this one.'

'Oh, I think we have.' Lisa turned away, taking Vanessa's arm.

'This is it!' Kate dropped on to her hands and knees, scraping at the moss on the inscription with a twig.

'How did we come to miss that? It's huge,' said Lisa.

Vanessa pulled out her camera. 'But how did you know?'

'It was her. Henrietta,' said Kate, looking up at them. 'She just pulled me over here. It was like I was on a lead. Weird.'

Vanessa exchanged looks with Lisa. 'You know I told you about what happened in Gibraltar?'

'Yes, yes.' Lisa shook her head vigorously as if to dislodge any superstition that might want to take hold there. 'Weird is certainly the word.'

'I can see your scientific mind is having a problemette, Sis. Sixth sense, extra dimension, call it what you will, but it's been forced upon me in the last few months. Like it or not, there is something there, something we can't see.'

'Imagination. That's what I'd call it.'

Kate shrugged. 'I'm not going to argue. But just because you can't prove it, doesn't mean it doesn't exist.'

Lisa drew breath to reply but was interrupted by Vanessa.

'"In Loving Memory, Late 1st Class Master Gunner",' she read. 'I'm so glad he wasn't forgotten.'

'It's quite grand. And the stone surround is all intact,' said Lisa.

'No sign that Henrietta was buried here too.'

'I'm sure she'd have moved to Plymouth, to live with her daughter. After William died. It's what people did.' Vanessa stepped back to photograph the grave.

'Maybe she went back home. To the West Indies.' Kate picked two celandines from the bank and laid them at the bottom of the cross.

Kate stepped out of the taxi. Any minute now she'd be crawling into bed in a dark room. She turned towards the gate and blinked at the blaze of light from the house. No curtains drawn. And the light still on in Flora's room over the front door.

Jack's wail greeted her as she opened the door. He was sitting hunched, halfway up the stairs, face streaked with dried on tears, fresh ones welling up as she ran to meet him.

'What happened? Where's Daddy?'

It was some time before Jack was coherent. 'Couldn't wake Daddy up. And I tried, I really tried. I rocked her and I rocked her, but Flora wouldn't go to sleep and she wouldn't stop crying for ages and ages and ages.'

Kate leapt up the stairs two at a time. Toys and clothes lay everywhere. The toilet roll had been unravelled across the bathroom floor and on to the landing. A favourite attention-seeking ploy of Flora's. It always made Daniel particularly mad. She found Flora in a snuffling sleep, her sheet soaked, face a mass of snot, the room thick with the smell of dirty nappy. Kate bent and felt her forehead. She was all right. Dirty but okay. Kate's stomach returned to its normal location.

'I think she done a poo,' said Jack from the door.

'Yes, I think so too. But she's sleeping now, so we'll leave her for a little while.'

'Daddy wouldn't come.'

'Where is Daddy?'

'In the living room on the floor.'

Kate's stomach lurched again. What had happened to Daniel? Was he unconscious? She slid down the stairs again thinking hospital, ambulance, 999.

'Daniel?'

No response. He was lying on the floor as if he'd fallen off the sofa. An empty bottle of Scotch and a glass stood on the coffee table. His tie snaked on the floor. The smell of alcohol in here was as strong as the stench of nappy upstairs. Kate knelt and shook him by the shoulders. He snored. Furious, Kate heaved his weight towards her. He belched and flopped back. She tried again, noticing how much she disliked the fleshiness that had gathered on his once lean body. After three attempts she managed to drag the sofa cushion down and wedge it behind his back, so that he was turned onto his side. That was what you were supposed to do, wasn't it? In case he vomited.

Her head was pounding with the sinusitis and with rage. How

could he? Blind drunk, unconscious, when he had the kids to look after? It was beyond belief. She could understand why people murdered each other. With him in this state, it probably wouldn't be that hard to strangle him with his own tie. She stood up slowly and held her head.

'Come on, Jakey. Let's get you a hot drink and get you to bed. How about some of that special chocolate?'

32

I'm twenty-five years old and I'm a widow, and not even a rich one.

I'm mad with Clive for dying. For abandoning me. I'm mad with Lily for giving him the cancer. And I'm mad with him for giving in, for letting it kill him, for going to join her. Suppose he's passed it on to me? They say that's not possible, but I don't believe them. I shall die too, and I don't even care.

Apart from the rage there is total blankness in my mind. Clive has gone and I am alone. I loved him. I am paralysed without him. I cannot believe how quickly the disease took him, once it got a hold. He seemed to waste away in front of my eyes. Hardly eating, of course, and what he did have went straight through him. That was the nature of the illness. It just ate him up until he was like a skeleton, a skull on legs.

I pace the flat keeping the curtains drawn, this horrid, pokey flat. It's close to *Milady's*. That's all you can say for it, except I never expected to have to go back to work. But with no inheritance and no pension I'll have no choice.

That was another lie. Not that he ever said in so many words that I'd have a naval widow's pension. I just assumed it. But I have no entitlement, because he'd already retired before we got married. He never told me that. He kept on going to work. How was I to know it was a retired officer's job? Of course, none of that mattered until he got ill. But he lay there in that hospital and told me I'd be provided for. How dare he? Sometimes I have to sit very still to hold on to my rage. I'm afraid of what I might do if I walk about.

There were signs and signals, of course, but I only noticed when I looked back. All the obstacles he put in the way of me going to meet his parents. The fact that none of his family attended the wedding. It was always too far, his father's business was too demanding or somebody was ill.

I was taken in by that newspaper cutting. Clive even showed me pictures of his "father" in his mayoral robes in the company of the King on the royal visit to Sheffield.

Then these people turn up at the hospital. Somebody must have sent for them. Nobody told me.

'Clive's parents.' A grey-looking man extending a podgy hand. 'Pleased to meet you at last.'

I stare from him to the mousey woman at his side. 'Sir Arthur, Lady...?'

The man frowns. 'I doubt they'll be coming down. My brother's always so tied up with the business. No. Clive's parents,' he repeats as if I'm deaf. 'George and Aileen Atkins.'

I recover quickly. 'Of course. I just wondered.' And I rattle on about how sad it is we haven't met sooner. Anything rather than let them know how Clive had fooled me.

Near the end he showed a spark of his old self, the Clive I fell in love with. He grabbed my hand with a twist of a smile and said, 'You're driving me crazy. You always did.' It took me right back to that garden party where I suppose you could say it all started. I leaned forward to kiss him and he said something that took my breath away. 'My beautiful mistress.' He whispered it into my ear and sank away into sleep. I could have hit him.

I won't go to the funeral. Everyone will be shocked of course, but I won't tell them why. I can't sit beside those vulgar people and pretend to be the devoted widow. I cannot go. I will not go. I will not have people point and comment. I will not cry in public, whether from humiliation or grief.

I refuse to open the door to anyone. Lucy has sent me a flowery card – in the post, I notice. So she couldn't cope with coming round. Mum rings and rings that doorbell. I can hear her fiddling with the letterbox down in the hallway and calling out, 'Coo-ee!' In the end she pushes a note through. It's written on the back of a shopping list.

Flour
Margarine
¼ tea
Suet

I turn it over slowly.

Dear Marge
Must talk to you about the funeral. Your father will come tomor-
row. Mind you let him in.
Mum
P.S. Hope you are all right.

When Dadser comes I do let him in. Partly because I know he'll need to sit down. But mostly because suddenly I long to see him.

Dadser gives me a hug. Then he sits down and says, 'Well, little maid. What's all this about? They say you won't go to the funeral.'

I tell Dadser everything.

He shakes his head. 'Well, well, well. Poor little Marge. Best thing is, then, I go as the representative of the widow. That's how it's done, I believe.'

Oh, bless you, Dadser. He doesn't even say I told you so. I don't think he even thinks it. He just looks very sad. I hug him.

When he's leaving he looks round the room and says, 'Any time you want, you can come back home. You know that, don't you?'

Winchester, Oxford, Banbury, Northampton, Leicester, Derby, Sheffield. I've got the main towns written in big letters on the back of a big envelope on the passenger seat and I set off in the Lanchester at six in the morning. Clive always said I was hopeless at reading a map. But I can pick out a route and read a signpost. Auntie said I couldn't do it on my own and wanted Lucy to come with me. What a terrible thought. When I said I needed to be alone, she clacked her teeth and Mum tutted. Dadser said why not, and to let me get on with it. I had no intention of letting anyone stop me.

The letter came about a week after the funeral. Headed notepaper, beautifully embossed. I ran my finger over the address – Oak Villa,

Mapperton Park – and read that Sir Arthur and his wife would be delighted to make the acquaintance of the widow of their esteemed nephew whom they remembered with such affection. Apparently Clive wrote to him from hospital. Dear Clive. He did make sure I was provided for, after all. Sir Arthur's invited me to stay, and so here I am heading North on the open road. I stop just south of Oxford for breakfast, and strip off my warm jumper and scarf. Marmalade sandwiches taste so much better eaten sitting on a fence beside the road. There's a lark singing miles up in the blue sky above me and I drive on full of optimism, practising how I will accept Sir Arthur's offer. Will it be a lump sum or a yearly allowance I wonder, and decide an allowance would be best. I might even be able to go back to art college.

The house is grand. It is just as Clive described it, except he always let me imagine he was describing his parents' house. I am shown to my room by a butler and invited to meet Sir Arthur in the library at six.

Clive's uncle is a large, florid, blustery man who looks me up and down very rudely. 'So that's why we never met you, lass. I never knew our Clive married a darkie. Well, I never did. He kept that under his hat. Where do you come from then?'

I can hardly believe what I'm hearing. 'Portsmouth,' I say icily.

He laughs heartily at that and tells me he won't hold it against me. And here was I, expecting a man of culture. He proceeds to tell me that, as well as the butler, they keep a cook-housekeeper, a housemaid, a kitchen maid and a gardener. In this day and age, when hardly anyone has servants any more. Even when Lily was alive, she only kept Rosie on because she was ill. I can't help but be impressed. But I'm shocked he is telling me all this. It's nothing to do with me and I find it very vulgar. He keeps calling me "lass" and patting me on the knee. Eventually he tells me to go and dress for dinner and that we will "talk business" in the morning.

Dress for dinner. I hadn't expected that. Thank goodness I brought my black cocktail dress as an afterthought. I hope it will be suitable. I think allowances will be made because I am in mourning, after all.

At dinner I meet Sir Arthur's son, Richard, and his wife, Lottie, who have been invited to meet me. I immediately like Lottie, who makes a great effort to involve me in conversation while the men talk motor cars. Lady Atkins is dining in her room. There is much exchange of glances about this information, which sets me wondering. Halfway through dessert, Sir Arthur's hot hand arrives on my knee and stays there. I must have look startled because Lottie catches my eye and winks.

When we ladies retire to the drawing room she says, 'I feel quite cheated. Clive was such a dark horse! He would never let us meet you. There was always some excuse. He obviously wanted you all to himself. We have to make up for lost time!'

I dare not say anything for fear of giving away how duped I was. It's a relief to get to my room. They all make me feel uneasy.

Next morning Sir Arthur introduces me to his wife. 'She likes to be called Lady Alice,' he says, his hand on the morning room doorknob. 'Not strictly correct as I understand, but who's bothered so long as she's happy?' He greets his wife with a peck on the cheek and guides her forward to take my hand.

She stares at me with watery blue eyes and he motions me to follow her. Every time I speak she seems to have forgotten who I am. She shows me the Orangery, a huge greenhouse with trees growing in it. Peaches, a vine and orchids, which Lady Alice strokes and speaks to as if they are friends. When Sir Arthur reappears and invites me for coffee in the library, she looks startled and tearful and drifts away towards the stairs.

Sir Arthur sets out his proposal as if he were selling me a motor car. I am to come as Lady Alice's companion and live as a member of the family.

'Not as a servant, mark you. We've got plenty of those. So no housework, not even light duties.'

Now I understand why he was so careful to describe the household the evening before.

'We wouldn't want to see Clive's widow in any kind of difficulties. And you're a good lass.' He pats my knee with the merest suggestion of a squeeze. 'My wife has taken to you, I can see that.' He winks. 'Fancy that. Well, well, good old Clive.'

A number of things begin to fall into place, the hand on my knee, Lottie's wink.

'And it comes at a time when Alice, bless her, is beginning to need a little help about the place. She's become very forgetful, you may have noticed. Not the woman she was – in all sorts of ways.' His eyes linger over my legs. 'You'll be a godsend, just what we need.'

He doesn't even ask whether I agree to his proposal.

I write to Auntie before lunch and the next day a telegram arrives for me. It summons me home because my mother has been taken ill. Good for Auntie. Just as I asked. I don't care if I have to go and ask for my old job back. I don't care if I have to give up the flat and move back home. I've never wanted to see Mum in the scullery in her overall so much.

When I get home my downstairs neighbour stops me on the stairs. She's taken in a box for me.

'A Petty Officer on a bicycle… He had such a problem…' She follows me up the stairs with the box because I'm carrying my suitcase. It's obvious she's angling to come in, but I don't want to hear any more about the Petty Officer and his bicycle.

In the box are the contents of Clive's cabin at the School of Navigation and a note of apology from his commanding officer. Apparently it was packed up when he went into hospital and then got forgotten in the stores. I decide to go through it and get it over with.

I'm shocked to find a painted miniature of Lily in a leather case, love letters from Lily and an album of photographs of Lily. There is no photograph of me. It's as if he kept a shrine to Lily, hidden from me. And, all the while, I was not permitted to utter her name.

There are studio photographs of Clive in his grand dress uniform complete with cocked hat, taken when he gained his officer's commission. I remember he was very proud of these at the time. They had one displayed in their drawing room in a silver frame. I believe Lily was a little embarrassed by it. At first glance he looked like at least an admiral with all the gold braid and epaulettes, until you noticed the single stripe.

At the bottom of the box are three buff exercise books, like the ones Clive used to use for his accounts. Two are flat and new looking and have 'Beginning' and 'End' printed on the outside. The third is labelled 'Middle'. I open it expecting to see columns of figures in Clive's neat hand. Instead I read: *Lily's Diary of Dying*.

It makes the hairs on my arms stand on end and I shut it again quickly.

33

2007

Kate was doling out porridge next morning when a bleary-eyed Daniel appeared in the kitchen doorway, trailing a blanket and steadying himself on the doorframe.

She raised an eyebrow, watching him sideways as he started in a jocular tone, his voice thick with sleep. 'I really don't know what happened... Decent of you to cover me up. Did...?'

'Don't ask,' interrupted Kate through gritted teeth. 'You clearly have no idea.' She ushered him into the hall and pushed him towards the stairs, out of earshot of the children. 'I actually cannot bear to look at you, let alone speak to you. Just get showered and get out.'

Daniel held up his hands with an exaggerated expression of hurt bewilderment.

'Go!' Kate shoved him in the back and turned on her heel as he groaned and stumbled up the stairs.

When she got back from taking Jack to school, Daniel's coat and keys were gone and the phone was ringing.

'Morag! I was about to ring you. I need to talk, wondered if you could get round here in your lunch hour?'

'Well, I thought as much. I was in the next check-out queue. I saw it all.'

'All what? Check-out? What are you talking about?' As Kate asked the question, she remembered a remark of Jack's at breakfast, that Daddy was "naughty in the supermarket". She'd been rushing to get his school bag ready and didn't take much notice, assumed he'd bought them all chocolate or something. That kind of naughty.

Morag was silent and drew breath. 'Oh, so he didn't tell you. Got in an argument. Bit of a scene. Look, I can't talk here. I'll be round soon after twelve.'

What was Morag talking about? Kate cleared the breakfast things and the whisky bottle. At least he hadn't vomited.

'Well,' said Morag. 'This is what I saw. It was the children I felt sorry for, poor lambs. Especially Jack, but wee Flora too. She was watching, taking it all in with those big eyes of hers... By the way, where *is* Flora?'

'Morag! Tell me. What *happened*? Flora's at Charlotte's for the afternoon. Now get on with it!'

'Well, Daniel's boss – you know, the tall one with the heavy glasses?'

'Keith Reynolds. Came from the Midlands six months ago.'

'Yes, that's the one. He came up behind Daniel at the check-out. And they were doing a bit of the male-shopping banter type stuff and Flora was in the trolley seat, and this guy was watching her. I'd finished emptying my trolley and I was just trying to remember who he was. And I was waving to...'

'Morag, get *on* with it.'

'As I said, I was waving at Jack, but he hadn't seen me. When suddenly this guy says to Daniel, "I didn't know that you'd adopted". And he nods towards Flora. And Daniel says, "We didn't".' Morag paused for dramatic effect.

'Go on.'

'Well, the guy makes a face and he says, "So you *both* play away from home, then? Nice arrangement." That was the phrase. You can imagine I'd got my ears pinned back by this time. And in a trice Daniel's got him by the lapels of his jacket and is leaning him back against the counter. The check-out girl must have pressed some button or other, because in seconds the manager appears with a heavy in tow and Daniel's asked to leave. His stuff's all gone through the till by then, so they stand over him while he pays and then they escort him to the car park.'

When Morag stopped talking, Kate stared down the garden to

the black branches of the apple tree. She knew the story she'd just been told contained the key to what was going on in her relationship with Daniel. But which part of it? How? The sense wouldn't come. She felt like the prince in a fairy tale who is asked a riddle. What he says next will either admit him to paradise or condemn him to death. How to set about solving the riddle? Her eyes followed the pattern of drizzle as it slid down the glass.

'Kate?'

Kate moved her gaze from the window to her friend, saw the concern on her face. 'Just trying to make sense of it all.'

'Be thankful the police weren't involved. And at least he did it defending your honour.'

'*My* honour?' Kate gave a short laugh. 'I rather doubt that. And anyway that's only the half of it.'

'Meaning?'

Kate shook her head. 'Not sure myself yet. But I'll tell you when I am. It's the beginning of the end, that I do know.'

Morag frowned a question.

'We can't go on. Not any more. He's not staying.'

'Oh, now, I hope I haven't exaggerated. I mean…'

Since when was Morag so keen to defend Daniel? Kate spoke in a monotone. 'What you don't know is that he was unconscious with drink when I got home, Jack was up crying, waiting for me. Flora had cried herself to sleep.'

'I see. Even so, is it such a sin, Kate? To lose your temper or get drunk?'

'*And* get drunk,' corrected Kate. 'And not just drunk. Unconscious. *And* in charge of the children. You didn't see how distressed Jack was, or the state Flora was in.'

'Poor wee things. If only I'd known.'

'If only *I'd* known. I'd have asked you to have them, but you're always…'

Kate waved aside Morag's protests. 'I thought it was time he did something for them for a change. It's nearly six months since Roz died.'

'I suppose the alcohol reacted with the drugs. He is still on…?'

'Oh, yes. But he absolutely knows he's not supposed to drink. I mean, a glass of wine with food's okay. But not a whole bottle of

Scotch. There's no excuse. And anyway, like I said, that's not the whole story.'

'But you won't do anything hasty? Think how it would be for those wee ones.'

'Morag, you know me. Don't you think I haven't agonised over it? For weeks, months. On and off for years, actually. You know I think the world of my kids.'

'I know, I know. But it's all a bit of a shock. Andy's never going to believe it. Let us know if there's anything...'

'Sure I will. And thanks, Morag, thanks for coming round. Now I guess you need to get back to work and I think I need to get out. I need the sea, to walk.'

Morag looked suddenly concerned again.

'It's all right. I'll be fine, but I need to think. Before I pick them up.'

Kate walked, pounding her heels into the shingle and pushing away fiercely from the pebbles that sucked the energy out of each stride. The physical effort felt good. She lifted her face to the rain but it wouldn't wash away the image of Jack sitting on the stairs, nor that odd sighting of Daniel a few weeks back. She'd been pushing the buggy past a car park in town. He was with a blonde woman. And Kate recognised her immediately from the bouncing walk, the tilt of her head. The girl, Mitch, of Daniel's first fling. Could you really identify someone on such slender evidence? Her gut said, yes. Not that they were "doing anything". But there was something about the way he had his hand in the small of her back as she opened her car door, how he leant down to the window and laughed.

She pushed the pictures away, shouting into the wind and tide all the obscenities she could think of. Which wasn't that many, but she still looked over her shoulder to check for witnesses.

When her throat was sore she picked big smooth pebbles and lobbed them into the water, watching the fat plop they made. *Mad, screaming woman, 29, arrested on beach. Father of two assaults boss in supermarket.* How come she'd got into a state where her life lent itself to tabloid headlines? *Father drunk in charge of kids. Neglected children taken into care as middle-class family falls apart.* And just how much of a family had they ever been? A family because she'd been determined they should be one? A family which survived because she held it together? And if she stopped doing that?

She tossed her last piece of shingle towards the waterline and stood listening to the scooch and swish of the little waves as they steadily advanced towards her stone. The rain had stopped and watery sunlight played on the encroaching ripples, bringing them to life with occasional sparks of iridescence. Kate looked at her watch. Time to pick the children up.

Kate was cooking when she heard Daniel's key in the lock and firm steps across the hall.

'Ta-da!'

She turned to see him standing in the kitchen doorway for the second time that day. Now he was wearing a new black trench-coat, belted at the waist. He looked like a TV detective. He even did a twirl to show it off, producing a bunch of red roses from behind his back. Tight little buds that would never open. She made no move to take them and he dropped them on the table.

Flora waved a crayon at him, said, 'Da-da! I's drawring,' and returned to total absorption in making swirls of colour on sheets of newspaper.

He ignored Flora. 'What do you think? Closing-down sale. I thought...'

Kate dropped her jaw at him. 'What do I think? You seriously ask me that? After what happened yesterday, you come home with roses and... Ask. Me. To. Admire. A. New. Coat?' She turned back to stir the pot on the stove.

'Ah well, yes. Last night. A bit of a miscalculation that. Mixing the Scotch and the anti-depressants.'

'And beating up your boss in the supermarket?'

'Ah, you heard about...'

'And leaving your kids to fend for themselves?'

'Now, come on, Katie...'

'Now, come on, Daniel. You have repair work to do. First with Jack. He ran away up to his room when he heard you on the path. Tea in half an hour. Then bedtime and stories. When they're settled, we talk. Now get on with it.'

Daniel made an exaggerated play of walking backwards out of the kitchen, pulling his forelock, which each time bounced back into the little quiff she had once found so sexy. 'This is not a game,' she muttered into the chilli.

After a few moments she walked to the bottom of the stairs to eavesdrop.

'Hey, Jack,' she heard Daniel begin. 'I'm sorry about last night. I'm sorry if you woke up and were scared.'

There was no response from Jack, who she guessed was doing Lego.

Daniel persevered. 'You know these funny pills I'm taking that I told you about? Well, Daddy had a bit too much to drink last night and it disagreed with the pills.'

Kate heard Daniel's knees thud on the floor. 'I'm really sorry. Will you come here and have a hug to show we can be friends again? And then maybe I could help with the crane?'

There was a pause, then the sound of Lego scrunched underfoot, a grunt from Daniel, a giggle from Jack. 'Were you drunk as a skrunk, Daddy?'

She turned away. Daniel had done a good job and, as always, Jack was generous in forgiving, glad to have his Daddy back. She was glad too, glad for Jack, she really was, and buried the shameful part of her which wished it otherwise.

'Drink?' Daniel waved the corkscrew.

'No thanks. You neither.'

'Could be tea?'

'Just sit down. You've got a lot to tell me.'

'Yes indeed. I'd had a bad day and then again I had bad luck, Keith being behind me at the check-out. I didn't realise he hadn't met the children. And there was Flora, looking as alien as ever...'

Kate winced.

'Well, she does. She can't help it, but I find it hard. You never seem to understand how hard I find it. And Keith goes and puts his finger on it. Or, as one might prefer to say, his foot in it. How did you hear about it, anyway?'

'Morag was at the next check-out.'

'Oh, she just would be. I never saw her.' He seemed about to attack Morag, but thought better of it.

'And Jack told me you were naughty...'

'Did he now? Anyway, I was insulted. I wasn't about to stand for someone saying that to me. How dare he imply she wasn't my child?'

'So you weren't defending my honour, then?'

A look of genuine surprise passed across Daniel's face, a look of such clarity that Kate nearly laughed. For a moment it swept away all his other carefully contrived expressions of protest, indignation, concern, showing them for what they were.

'Of course. Your honour. Goes without saying. You reputation is beyond reproach.'

But not yours, thought Kate. And how would Keith Reynolds know that? Which he clearly did. *So you both play away from home.* If the last affair Daniel was supposed to have had was two-and-a-half years ago, before Flora was born? Two years before Keith joined the firm?

Aloud she said, 'And so then you came home. And...?'

Daniel's face took on grief and wetness round the eyes. 'First thing I wanted to do was ring Mama. And then of course I realised I couldn't.'

'Poor Daniel. I know how hard that is for you.' And she did. She meant it. At the same time as it drove her crazy with impatience. 'So I had a drink instead. Just one, felt a lot better. Got them off to bed, stories and so on. They were settled, Kate. They weren't fending for themselves, as you put it.'

'So you had another drink. Or two, or three, or a whole bottle. And at some stage, of which you were totally oblivious, Flora pooed herself, woke up Jack and he couldn't rouse you. That's what I mean by fending for themselves. Jack trying to look after his sister and totally distraught.'

For a moment Daniel was silenced. 'Oh. I see. I didn't realise any of that. That bad.'

'What was really going on, Daniel?'

Daniel sighed. 'I told you. You know. I cannot abide it. This fact that, wherever I go with Flora, people think I can't be her father. It attacks me right here.' He patted his heart.

A bit lower down, I'd say, thought Kate. 'Male pride. Your precious identity. I. I. I. That's all I've heard this evening. Have you for one moment stopped to think what it was like for our children in the supermarket? What it was like for Flora lying in her own mess? For Jack, trying to cope, frightened about what had happened to you?' She raised a hand as Daniel started to protest. 'Okay, you did a good job with Jack tonight, made your peace. But those times will stay with him. And did you for one second think what it might have been like for me, coming home to all that? And, thanks for asking, my sinusitis is quite a lot better, but last night I felt like death.'

'Mea culpa, mea culpa. I apologise…'

From all positions, completed Kate silently.

'From all positions. I'm sorry about Jack, I really am. And Flora, well, I struggle there. She's a great kid, but I admit I don't feel the same way about her. For obvious reasons. As to you, dear, dear Kate, you're so wonderful at coping with everything. You take it all in your stride. You always have.'

'And you take that for granted. You always have.'

Kate got up and walked round the table. She placed her hands on Daniel's shoulders.

'Oh, Daniel. When I married you, we were both young and mad. You were a Jack-the-lad. No. You were more of a one-off than that.'

Daniel twisted round and gave her his best smile. Even now it had the potential to melt her, but she let it slide off her, let it go.

'You were Daniel-the-lad. And I thought you and I would grow together and you'd become Daniel, the man. But you didn't. You stayed Daniel-the-lad. And there's something very lovable about that. I've fallen for it again and again.'

Another radiant smile, full of confidence. Daniel seeing the home straight ahead. He's expecting to have sex in the next half-hour, thought Kate. Ten minutes even. She'd lay money on it.

'But as a grown-up and a parent I simply cannot continue to live with a person who makes the kind of choices you made last night.'

Daniel banged his fists on the table. 'Not "choices", Kate. I was overwhelmed. Humiliation in public. Grief, feeling deserted, no one to turn to. The prospect of this going on and on for years and years.'

Years and years is right, thought Kate. Neither of us can do it.

She returned to her seat so that she could see his face. 'And this has nothing to do with Mitch?'

The second genuine expression of the evening arrived on Daniel's face. Sheer, naked shock and horror. His ears turned red. Kate knew she'd hit the spot.

'Your face tells me everything. Okay, you probably did want to ring Roz. But then you wanted to ring Mitch, who was unavailable. And that put you in an even filthier mood. I'm right aren't I?'

She watched for his protest, but he just dropped his head onto his chest. An attitude of defeat. 'And today you saw her and you feel a million dollars, and you buy a new coat and think I'll forgive and forget if I get a bunch of tacky roses.'

She gestured towards the rose stems sticking out of the top of the bin and burst into tears. Shit! This was not part of the plan. There was satisfaction in being vindicated, in being right. But part of her waited in vain to hear Daniel deny it. The last thing she wanted was for Daniel to see that part of her.

'How the hell did you know about Mitch?'

'I saw you together. And, after what Keith said, I've been putting two and two together and making four every which way I looked at it.'

He grabbed her hand across the table.

'Get off me! And don't say, "I can explain" or "Mea culpa" or any of that effing rubbish. In fact don't say anything, if you can't say something you mean for once.'

Daniel stared at her for a long moment. 'I'm sorry,' he said eventually.

'Really?'

'Sorry I'm not the person you want me to be. Sorry... I should never... Oh, I don't know. Just sorry.'

Kate nodded. For once, no excuses. He even seemed to mean it. Not that it changed anything.

'It only really happened because of Mama.'

'I don't see how...'

'Mama not being there. Needing someone to turn to.'

Of course, looking for someone else to mother you. 'I thought the Mitch girl got married? Left the area? Not that...'

'She did. But it didn't last. She got divorced six months ago.'

'And came running to Daniel-the-lad.'

'She came back to work. She's in the Old Portsmouth office.' There was actually a smirk on his face. 'She…'

'I don't wish to know any more.'

'I'll pack it in, Kate.'

'You can do what you like. It will be no concern of mine. Because you won't be living here. I won't throw you out, but…'

'But Katie…'

'I'll give you to the end of the month to find somewhere else. In case you're thinking of it, I wouldn't advise moving in with her, for the children's sake if nothing else. I hope we can be civilised and stay friends, again for the children's sake. You can see them plenty. And I mean both of them. You're Flora's father and you're to behave like it, even if you can't bear to be seen with her in public.'

Daniel's jaw was flapping. He'd never heard her talk like this. In spite of her earlier tears she was surprising herself. Nothing he could do or say would budge her. A small internal voice was accusing her of acting out of jealousy and pique, but it was easily silenced. Of course those feelings were present. But she was perfectly clear that, in the whole scheme of things, Mitch was not important.

'Katie, you're tired. We'll talk again tomorrow. I'll be good. Promise.'

'You're right, I am tired. But no talking tomorrow. I've said all I have to say.'

'And me?'

'All the things you'll have to say, I've heard before. It may sound harsh, but I'm bored with them, Daniel. So let's not put ourselves through it.'

'Since when have you been so high-handed? You can't make unilateral decisions like this. I've a right to be heard. What about Jack?'

'What about Jack?'

'He's my son. What will he think? How will he…?'

'Don't forget you've got a daughter. Like I said, you'll see them both. Oh, Daniel, don't think I haven't been thinking of all that. I'm the last person on earth to want to cause upset to the kids. You know that. It keeps me awake at night. But I can't go on. Holding it all together. And I honestly think we'll do them more damage in the long run if we try to stay together.'

'You mean, I will. Do them damage.'

'Yes, I suppose I do. Well, no, not just you, but how we are together. You must know what I mean.'

Daniel nodded.

'And Daniel, I'm sorry if I was high-handed and unilateral, like you said. But it was the only way I could do it. It hurts. It's scary. But I know it's got to happen. I just can't carry on holding it all together.'

Daniel nodded again. 'I don't know what to say.'

That's a change. She gave him a little smile. 'Well, I suppose it frees you up, doesn't it?' She took a deep breath and tried not to picture him with Mitch. 'But apart from that I hope we can stay friends. And not just for the sake of the children?'

'I hope so, Kate. I can't imagine you not being there.'

'Oh, I'll be here all right. But now I am just too tired to go on with this tonight.'

He stood up from the table. 'Where do you want me to sleep?'

'I really don't care. It makes no difference to me.' Which she realised was more of a slap in the face than if she had cared. Half an hour ago that would have given her some satisfaction. Now it just made her sad.

She walked towards the back door. 'You go on up. I want some fresh air.'

She stepped outside, sniffing wet garden smells: leaves, earth, wood smoke from next door's fire. The sky had cleared and pinpricks of stars were visible. As she tipped back her head to look, she realised that her head had cleared too and took a long deep breath, feeling the cold air rush through her nostrils with unaccustomed clarity. Willow thumped down from the fence and trotted neatly towards her, tail held straight and high. She scooped the little cat into her arms.

'It's just you and me, Wispy Willow, from now on in. You, me and the kids. As for that Mitch-bitch, good luck to the woman.'

34

1938

Once I have recovered from the shock of the title, *Lily's Diary of Dying*, I find I cannot resist it. I slowly open the notebook and start turning the pages.

> *Brittany, 8th September 1933*
> *I brought these little exercise books with brown covers. I wanted them to be unobtrusive. Something I can slip under a book when someone comes in.*
>
> *I called them Beginning, Middle and End but I'm starting in the Middle one. I'll go back and fill in the beginning later. The trouble with beginnings is that you only know about them in retrospect, when it becomes clear there is something to have a beginning, middle and end. Like an illness or an affair.*
>
> *There is something now. That is certain. What do I call it? Lily Atkins' illness? Or, if I am honest, Lily Atkins' cancer. I have to write that very small because people don't like to see it written or to hear it spoken in case they catch it. Or in case they have to look you in the eye at the same time.*
>
> *I said I'd write about the beginning and it's difficult because all I can think of is that first look he gave her. That first time he saw her in the hall when she brought the hats. It pierced me. It might sound melodramatic, but it pierced my heart. My heart, my breast. But you see, already I'm confusing the two. Which is why I can't put it in the "Beginning" book. It would be too bald and obvious.*

And it wasn't like that at the time. Just a pain. People would say, it's very sad but Lily was insane, quite mad. She went mad with jealousy, which is not the case at all. I became extremely sane and rational. I decided if he was going to have one of his infatuations, here at home, then I was going to be in control.

But of course I wasn't in control at all. The disease was in control. But I didn't know it then. I was too busy falling for that extraordinary girl myself.

Which is why the Beginning is where beginnings always truly belong: buried in the confusions of the Middle.

A passing thought – I wonder what it will be like to write in the book called End? Will it be frightening? Or will I be peaceful by then? Or in pain? For make no mistake. I am going to die. There! I have written it. Even Mr Britten wouldn't say it quite like that. It was difficult enough to see him alone. How ridiculous it is a woman can't easily see her surgeon alone. He wouldn't tell Clive, which is right. But I was firm and eventually he said he could see I was a strong woman. He said it was rare to survive such a condition, but medical science was moving all the time.

I find I am holding my breath and I'm feeling quite sick but I have to keep turning the pages.

10th September 1933

Of course I know now that really I am writing for me. I don't imagine "other women" will see this, although "the other woman" might. It is to unburden myself partly, as to a friend. Given that no one will talk about it.

Also to let them know I was no fool.

To show them my anger.

And to wish them well.

To tell him I still love him, in spite of everything.

To tell her I really was her friend, that I loved her too – in a different way – for who she is.

I see I move into the past tense. This really should be in the End book, perhaps.

You have such life, Thea. I thought at the beginning I could

286

control you. But I couldn't. And after a bit I didn't want to. You have such spirit. But I fear for you. You put too much store by social position. Just concentrate on being yourself.

'Oh, it's all very well for you,' I say out loud to myself. 'You were comfortably off, you were white, well-educated. You could have become a teacher.'

11th September 1933
Thea may, of course, be quite innocent of Clive's attraction to her. Innocent, because she did not invite him, or innocent because she hasn't noticed? I'm not sure what I mean. Innocent. It's a strange word to use of Thea – who has an air of mystery, never innocence. Her eyes flicker sideways under those long lashes more often when Clive is in the room. That much I've noticed. Like a cat on the alert. Maybe he just makes her nervous.

Of course, there were others. That woman in Malta, for instance. Rosamund. All that partying, and his friends making out he was drunker than he was and distracting my attention. And then his ship was leaving to go on exercise and I had to come home, knowing he'd be back in Valetta in a few weeks and she'd be there waiting for him. Laughing at the dowdy wife who'd gone back home.

That makes me stop and think. "Rosamund". But there were no other women when Clive was married to me. I'm sure of that. I gave him what he wanted. And very painful it was, too. I remember Charlie's remark – *I never thought he'd marry you.* Huh! They thought I was mistress material. How wrong they were. I was never going to settle for that.

12th September 1933
Love is supposed to be blind.
I'm resting again on the sofa in this grey-panelled room at that lost time of day when invalids and people who live in hot countries take a siesta. Clive calls it "taking a nap" and is scornful of healthy people who do it. He used to nod off on the terrace

with his trilby tilted forward and the newspaper collapsed on his lap. But that was different.

He's very solicitous of me now, but that's different too, in another way neither of us can speak of.

He won't be sleeping now and nor will Thea. I don't have to search the sands from my balcony to know they will be walking together, discreetly separate, but flinging those glances between them like shuttlecocks in a game of beach badminton.

On buoyant, relaxed days I can't decide which of them I love the most. On days like today I know I hate them both equally. My love isn't blind. I've always known what was going on between those two, sensing it probably before they knew themselves. The shift of focus in Clive's eyes, that degree less warmth in his touch, and an unmistakable tension when Thea visited, as if his skin tautened at her approach.

Their love is blind of course. For they are "in love" which is presumably what Shakespeare was talking about. They commit "pretty follies" all the time, unaware of how transparent they are, of the hurt they inflict. Even on bad days I truly believe neither of them intends to cause me pain, that they are sincere in the love and care they each show me. Or is that where my blind spot lies? Do I merely imagine they are as joyful in my company as I am in theirs? Sometimes this journal seems the only really true friend.

I fetch a handkerchief, blow my nose and wipe my eyes. All that stuff about love. It reminds me of that evening at the beach house in Gibraltar. I feel sick, but I have to read on.

16th September 1933
I'm happy here on my sofa. I allow my body to sink into the pillows. The soft mushroom colour of the room soothes me and the vertical planks of the panelling remind me of the beach huts at Southsea. I try to let my tiredness drain into the cushions, to imagine it ebbing through the floorboards into the earth and being sucked into the ocean which flows back to me beyond the windows. But my energy seeps away with the fatigue. I can never shake off the grey weight of exhaustion.

I'm reminded of Devon because the pink-striped curtains are the colour of the underside of the creamy field fungi I used to pick in September. Holidays with Clive, especially in that healing time after the war. Staying at the Wakehams' farm, being spoilt with country cooking. I'd wander up the hillside before breakfast and bring in those mushrooms for Mrs Wakeham to fry because I knew Clive loved them. Wonderful it was, watching him come back to life, losing the rings under his eyes and that gaunt, haunted look.

I have slept for a while. Now the tide is right out and two small dogs are racing along the sands putting up flight after lazy flight of gulls. They remind me of Whisky, left with my parents back home, and I hope he isn't missing me, at the same time as hoping he is.

Clive doesn't understand how I can't bear to hear some things. This morning, for instance. He came in after breakfast and kissed the top of my head, as he always does. Then he said it was chilly, autumn was in the air.

It made me shudder. I try not to see the upturned collar of the man strolling after the dogs, the browning leaves of the little hornbeams that shade the hotel terrace. I don't want to be reminded. Clive went on about lighting the fire, having crumpets for tea.

It's true, I used to love autumn, but now... I don't want crumpets. I don't want to see the bare silhouettes of the trees in the garden, when I probably won't see the green buds and primroses following on.

Clive is so predictable. I love that. After he'd kissed my hair he sat down in the chair opposite, hitching his crisp grey flannels at the knees and took the The Times *from under his arm. His eyes flicked up and down the personal column, a routine perusal. I can always predict the moment when he will lean back, cross his legs and open the paper, leafing the thin edges of newsprint between finger and thumb and peeping into the news pages as if illicitly, then shaking it out vigorously at the Leader section.*

But then the unpredictable happened. There was his immaculate deck shoe rocking like a boat at anchor and dark hairs curling over the edge of his navy blue sock. I felt an unaccountable yearning at the sight of those hairs. It was nostalgic rather than sexual, a longing for times that once were and never will be again. But it was unsettling. I know those times would not be repeated, even if I were healthy.

Is it love I feel or self-pity, self-indulgence? I can't imagine Clive resenting the spring without me. He will share it with Thea, whose youth and beauty will rival the cherry blossom. He will be released by my death and the task I have set myself for this week is to be happy for him, to let go of that possessiveness that demands Clive be inconsolable at losing me. I want to be glad he will have someone to look after him.

I wake up cold and stiff, still sitting in the chair, my cheeks taut with dried tears. I fill a hot water bottle, even though it's August, and crawl into bed. In the morning I eat toast in the kitchen, trying to avoid the diary. But it pulls me back. I pick it up from where it fell the night before and take it back to bed.

20th September 1933
I want to believe our marriage is as special as it ever was. Shall I tell Clive I know? Are we still capable of being generous with each other? Would that make it easier for him? Or for me? Or would it muddy our last months together with guilt and recriminations? What of my friendship with Thea?

If only I hadn't tumbled to the truth about those two. I love them both separately. But I can't cope with them together. Immediately I bring them together in my mind I feel excluded, bereft of each of them. Sometimes sadness and self-pity predominate, sometimes anger, a debilitating fury that leaves me more exhausted than tears. My jealousy nauseates me and gnaws as painfully in my heart as the cancer that is killing me, so sometimes I wonder if I would still be well if Thea had never appeared in my life.

That bit takes my breath away. What does she mean? How dare she think such a thing? It's horrible. I thought she was my friend.

Sometimes I'm occupied with which jealousy is the stronger. Am I jealous of Thea's hold over Clive? Or of Clive's desire to possess Thea? I shock myself for thinking this, but there is no point in suppressing my feelings. Not now my body is incapable of following them into action. I'm tempted to shock Clive, too. When he asks if he can get me anything. I want to say things like, just a glass of passion, or Thea's breasts on a plate, or a lethal dose of morphine. But I just smile and say I don't need anything.

I know I should be finding it in my heart to forgive them. I want to, I suppose. "Forgive them, for they know not what they do." Except they do know what they do. Don't they? But they can't help it, I suppose. I don't want to be bitter. Somewhere I read that being wronged is an opportunity to practise forgiveness.

Suddenly I am disappointed in Lily. Why on earth should she forgive Clive? Or me? And what was she forgiving us *for*? What did she think was going on? We were so chaste. If chaste is not touching. It didn't feel chaste. "Forgiveness", indeed! Forgiveness is for fools. Phoney, pious stuff. The bit about my breasts on a plate – that's more like it. Would she think I should "forgive" Clive? Would she see the way he deceived me as an "opportunity to practise forgiveness"? Opportunity, my foot! It teaches me not to be so naïve and trusting.

21st September 1933

I have been avoiding writing about the main thing.

Having my breast removed. "Removed." What a puny word that is. Like removing the smut on my nose. "Removed" is for things that shouldn't be there in the first place. Not for parts of yourself, parts you expected would be there forever.

It is a kind of irony. People say of women "Her nose is her best feature" – or her eyes, or whatever. My breasts were my best feature. Not that anyone ever said so. Breasts are not in the category of features to remark upon in polite society – and our society is, of course, very polite. Hardly anyone ever saw them anyway. Just Clive. And one or two girls at school in the changing room before they were fully formed. And Mr Britten of course. Before, during and after the "removal".

I cannot begin to describe how it feels to be so disfigured. In one way it is nothing. In another it is everything. Clive can't bear to look at me. He doesn't say so. He would tell me it is to spare my feelings. I know it is to spare his. I wonder if he gets to see Thea's breasts? I think by now it is probable. They look so decorous when they are with me but I'm sure they find ways.

Thea, of course, has seen my breasts.

22nd September 1933

Thea was scared that day when I hugged her on the beach in Gibraltar, her nipples erect with fear. It never occurred to me before that moment to want another woman. I know of such things, of course, but they belong in another world where people are painters and poets, drinking absinthe and smoking substances I've never heard of in Soho or Montmartre. It doesn't happen in the naval quarters or in middle class Southsea. But for a moment I actually wanted to taste them, to see if it would be like sucking a toffee. I wonder if Thea felt it too? Really, I've no idea – she gives nothing away. She'd probably think I was disgusting.

Losing my breast brings back all the pain and sadness of not conceiving. Another thing I could never talk about. Oh, the ache to have a little baby, a child to raise and love. My breasts were never used. Well, I suppose Clive used them for his pleasure, and it was a pleasure for us both. A delicious pleasure. I wonder how it would be if he were to use the one that is left? I don't think either of us could face finding out.

They were never used for feeding a baby. I would have loved babies. I would have been a good mother. I have enjoyed being an Auntie, but it isn't the same. I wish I could say Clive would have been a good father. But I don't believe he would. He is too attached to me mothering him. He pretended otherwise. He thought having a child was the thing to do. But I always knew he was relieved when I didn't conceive.

A barren woman. A barren women with only one breast. You don't get a bleaker prospect than that.

No wonder he has needed Thea.

23rd September 1933

Today I'm going to remember the happy times. Just married, in love. Oh, that funny little car he got. He taught me to drive it up and down his uncle's driveway. And the holiday in Devon. Walking on Exmoor and picnicking by that river with all the big boulders. We were happy then. A whole world to each other. I was quite stylish then, too. I remember the day he made me pose for photographs all over the garden. On the stone seat, under the rose arch and by the sundial. What fun it all was. I've still got those photos tucked away somewhere.

I was no beauty, even then. I'm sure lots of people wondered how I snapped him up. Clive, the ladies' man, and little Lily. I wasn't pretty or attractive even, certainly not alluring. But I wasn't ugly, either. "Pleasant-looking" that friend of mother's said. Mrs Astley-Jones. I overheard them talking under my window. If Mrs A-J said so, then it was true. "Pleasant-looking." She might just as well have said "Homely". And it was right. That was it for Clive. I was reassuring. His anchor, the person he always came home to.

The last entry is quite short. It's dated the day before we came home from Brittany. I remember because it was Dadser's birthday.

29th September 1933

Every day and all day I lie on the day bed watching the grey-green sea. Whether the tide is ebbing or flooding, it always seems to be flowing past me, in towards the land, as if it will slowly and steadily inundate the hotel, the town, the whole of France, the entire continent of Europe. "Washing away the sins of the world" is the phrase that echoes in my mind as the tide drains out of the bay, leaving the sand smooth, unmarked. Rinsing the trivia out of my mind. I imagine lying on the sand washed by the sea, rolling over and over, drifting away on the current.

I blow my nose and run a bath. I even crumble a bath salt into the water. It's the last of the box Clive gave me at Christmas. I've been saving it as a memento, but I don't want to save it any more. I do too much thinking in the bath. I get dressed and open a tin of soup. I hack into the tin with the point of the tin opener as if I was killing someone. As I saw away and lift the jagged edge of the can, I wish I could see into Clive's head as easily.

I have to get out of the house. I can hear Clive's mocking voice saying, "She knew all the time". He's even saying, "And I knew that she knew. You were our little conspiracy." But I don't believe that.

It's ridiculous. Lily wasn't like that. I don't really believe he knew or that they talked about me. But then again, who knows? What of my friendship with Lily? What was it really? Was she an innocent, a victim? Or was she manipulating me, lining me up to take care of her husband's needs?

I'll drive to the sea. Blow those voices away.

35

2007

'I'm so worried about Kate.' Vanessa bent and picked up the stick that had been dropped at her feet. 'Do you imagine there's anything we can do?' She made a series of throwing motions, sending the waiting dog on a number of false chases, and then flung it in a great arc down the hill.

She and David watched the retriever thunder after it and disappear into the bracken, the pale frond of her tail flagging her progress.

'We ought to come up here more often. Puts things in perspective.' David clipped the dog's lead onto his belt. 'You can see for miles. We don't need a dog to do this.'

It was a crisp February day and they'd brought their neighbours' dog up to the Down.

'Did you hear what I just said?'

David nodded. 'Thinking about it. I don't really think so, for what it's worth.' He turned up a steep chalky path.

'I just feel so helpless. I can't bear to think of Kate struggling with it all. But I don't want to interfere. She'd hate that.'

'So how was she – when she came over?'

'She actually said she'd given Daniel his marching orders. I did tell you. I knew you weren't listening.'

'I did hear. Wondered about it. But it must have been music to your ears.'

'Hardly.'

'But you've never liked the man.'

'No, but I've kind of got used to him.'

David turned and waited for her at the top of the path making an exaggerated expression of surprise.

'Anyway, that's not the point. It's breaking up the family. We may not go a bundle on him, but he's still their father. And Jack adores him. Flora too, come to that.'

David took the stick from the dog and threw it in the other direction, down the hill and out of sight. 'And you say it's all because of that night he got drunk? The day you all went to Sheerness?'

'Well, that was the last straw. Maybe she won't go through with it. It seems a bit harsh... One drunken evening...'

'"The last straw."' David repeated the phrase. 'I understand that. The thing about the last straw is not that particular event. The last straw just makes you take notice of the rest of the load, all the other straws that have been piling up on the old camel's back.'

They walked on in silence, Vanessa considering this.

'She's been everything to that man,' continued David. 'Stuck to him through thick and thin. Mostly thin.' He paused. 'You know those old windows I was talking about? In the sitting room?'

Oh, David, thought Vanessa. Just when we were beginning to get somewhere, and now we're back to house maintenance. She sighed. 'Yes? What have they got to do with the price of eggs?'

'Quite a lot, actually.' David eyed her over the dog as it leapt to reclaim the stick. 'It just struck me. I said the putty had gone, right? Perished. I just thought, Kate's like that. She can't do it any more. Keep out the draughts. Dried out, like the putty.'

Vanessa rolled her eyes. 'You're a wise old thing sometimes. You don't say much, but it all goes on, in that head of yours.'

'What she needs is a holiday. We could take them all. In the spring maybe. A cheap flight to somewhere hot, live on the beach. Kids would love it.'

Vanessa couldn't see that a holiday was going to save Kate's marriage. 'Can't see Daniel living on the beach.'

'He wouldn't be there. After he's gone, I mean.'

'But David, it's by no means certain. I don't think she will... No, you're jumping the gun.'

'I know Kate. Once she decides, she decides.' David took the spitty stick presented by the dog, threw it again and wiped his hand on his trousers.

"Oh, I hope you're wrong. Anyway, she hasn't decided. I'm sure she hasn't. But I do wish she'd let me know sooner. You know, how bad things were getting. I mean, she was a bit quiet at Lisa's and in Sheerness, but I just thought it was her cold.'

'At least she came over when she did. It's not so surprising. She probably didn't want to admit it before – even to herself, let alone to us.'

'I suppose so. But it makes me feel kind of sad. Left out, I guess. Silly really. And then...'

'What now?'

'I keep thinking. I mean, what did we do or not do for this to happen?'

David was whistling for the dog and gave her a sideways look.

'I mean, did she rush into marrying him just because I didn't want her to? And then, there was always Lisa coming up behind at a great rate, being career-minded. Did she feel she couldn't compete? So she took the home-and-family route? A sister always more extrovert, more obviously attractive? And competitive in a way she never was, and...'

'And Daddy's girl, you're thinking?'

'Well, that too. Lisa was always such a tomboy, but I'm not blaming...'

'Good. Because searching around in the past for reasons to feel guilty isn't helping anyone. I thought Thea taught you that much at least. You're always going on about how she was such a guilt merchant, how guilt's totally destructive stuff.' He put an arm round her shoulder. 'Kate's an adult now – and, in case you haven't noticed, she has been for some time. The pickles she gets in are her responsibility and it's their problem – they've got to sort it themselves.'

'Lecture over?' Vanessa detached herself from his arm and walked away down a side path. "Pickle" indeed! This was more than a pickle.

She reached the ancient beech tree with its accommodating lower branches, where she'd always brought the girls when they were little. Sitting on the smooth seat it offered and swinging her legs, she remembered their shouts as they clambered up, and how she'd tried not to look as Lisa climbed dangerously high. To hell with David's logic. Part of her fondly imagined that if she searched hard enough she'd find a magic wand. As a mother, she should be able to locate it. Of course no such magic wand existed, but surely... Surely what?

She caught up with David on the way back to the car park.

He looked up from fastening the dog's lead. 'Okay?'

'Sure. I just needed to... You know me. Of course you're right – *but, and...*'

'I know. *But, and*, you do realise don't you, that we probably don't know the half of it?'

'Parcel for you,' said David when they got home, handing her a re-used Jiffy bag with a handwritten label.

Vanessa ripped it open. 'It's from Geoff. You know, the second-hand book guy?' She tipped out a folder of snaps, some postcards and a packet of cigarettes wrapped in a note.

'More stuff from Mead End?' David rolled his eyes. 'It never ends.'

'Actually, this looks good. Says he found them in amongst the books and thought they might be of interest. That's so kind, he didn't have to bother.'

'Good chap.'

'Look, postcards to mother from Clive. Dated 1934. That's the year before they were married. From Whipsnade and Gretna Green. That's weird – a chimps' tea party. At least Gretna Green's a bit romantic.'

She handed David the two cards and sorted through the rest. 'But these are obviously from Clive, too. Same handwriting. Postmark 1932 to Mrs L Atkins in Gibraltar. Signed "C". They're to Lily! Picture of his ship, sent from Palma, saying he'll be in Gib in the next few days. How strange for Mother to have kept these.'

'That is pretty strange. I'll give you that.'

The Kodak wallet design showed a girl with bobbed hair, in what Vanessa thought was a Twenties dress, holding a box camera with a concertina front. The price of the prints was pencilled on the back.

'Three shillings and a penny-halfpenny. What would that be in today's money?'

'About a fiver I would guess.' David looked over her shoulder. 'The wallet's probably worth that – a collector's item. It's the sort of thing people take to *Antiques Roadshow*.'

Most of the snaps inside were of people Vanessa didn't know – partying, sitting in a garden or holding tennis racquets. Then she recognised Lily, wearing a tennis dress and in deep conversation with a young man so like her that he must have been her brother.

'Oh, look! Here's Lily. And another. Oh, blimey. She suddenly looks so old.'

In the next picture Lily was sitting on a garden seat next to a young woman who'd featured in other groups. There was a wind-up gramophone next to them on the bench. Lily stared straight at the camera, looking worn and exhausted. Incongruously, she was wearing a frilled white frock in broderie anglaise and a long string of beads.

'Look David. Isn't that one of the saddest pictures you've ever seen?'

She turned to the cigarettes. A slim black box labelled *Sobranie Virginia Cocktail*. Inside, under thin gold paper, a rainbow of gold-tipped tubes. Bright pastels. Pink, blue, lemon, lime and lilac. And a faint smell – not so much tobacco as moustache-of-retired-colonel. The legend inside the lid described the contents as "gay and sophisticated".

Vanessa giggled. 'Listen to this. Made for "connoisseurs of smoking…suitably dressed for any occasion. Sobranie Ltd. 17 Worship St. London. E.C.2."' Vanessa fingered the cigarettes and sniffed. What a world was conjured up. On the bottom of the box was a stamp: *Duty Free, HM Ships Only*.

Then she noticed another envelope, marked "Enlargements". The images inside transported her to another world. Thea as a beautiful young woman, the same beauty who posed in her elegant lace wedding dress, but less formal, more relaxed. Vanessa guessed they were taken on her first honeymoon.

One picture in particular took her breath away. It was as if a veil were lifted. As if she saw her mother for the first time. Her eyes were luminous and gazed directly at the camera, at the photographer.

They were vulnerable, loving. She was smiling slightly, naturally, as if about to giggle. There was an air of lightness and innocence about her, emphasised by the flower-sprigged white dress with its round, pin-tucked neck and frill. "Thea." For that was how Clive addressed her on those postcards. Gone was "Marge". Gone the defiance of childhood and the sullen stare of the teenage photos. And there was no sign of the masks, the tension of later years. Thea at twenty-two, relaxed and happy. Vanessa could see she must have loved this man who was more than twice her age.

The last two pictures seemed to be taken at another time and a car was very much part of the scene.

'Oh, look!' said Vanessa. 'It's the car we had when I was little. There's the registration: *ALY*.' She looked round, but David had wandered off.

Vanessa stared at Clive standing proudly beside the long bonnet in a pale double-breasted suit and a bowler hat, hands behind his back and half-smiling, a crooked little smile. How dare he stand there, looking so cocky with *her* car? So the car, as well as the cutlery, had once belonged to Clive. She felt possessive, territorial even, about the soft crinkly leather of the back seat, the little patch of crazed glass yellowing in the corner of the window. Her domain, where the voices of her parents used to fade as she drifted to sleep.

Clive was wearing a round white badge on a thread, and the car was lined up with others on the grass, so it looked like a day at the races. In the last photo Thea was also wearing a white badge. Her long stylish coat had two big buttons at the waist and a little row of three small buttons at the elbow. Those little details, the essence of style. Thea was nothing if not stylish. She was staring tensely into the camera, one ankle turned self-consciously, her free hand almost clenched, while the look of determination on her face bordered on the rebellious.

36

It's a glorious afternoon when I emerge from the flat. I packed the diary away in the box and put it out of sight in the bottom of the wardrobe. Then I changed and put some make-up on and felt a lot better. Driving the Lanchester always does me good.

I've just passed the Grand Hotel when I see an open top car coming the other way. It's a crisp blue and driven by a young man in an open-necked shirt and blazer. I slow down. He's very good-looking, tanned, relaxed at the wheel. He slows down too. As we draw level my impressions are confirmed and our eyes meet for an instant. I find I'm smiling. I'm just coming up to the Lady's Mile so I pull in and stop, keeping a watch in the rear view mirror. He slows right down and swings round in a big U, coming up behind me with a growl of the engine. The car's a Triumph, very nice. I take no notice, get out and start to walk along the path. I walk and walk. Is he never going to catch up with me? Maybe he was going to park there anyway. Maybe he's meeting a friend. I will not look round. I'll walk to the end, sit on a bench maybe, if there's one free, and then walk back again and continue to the sea as planned.

Then I hear footsteps. A strong, brisk stride. Here he comes. He draws level. Out of the corner of my eye I see grey flannels, a navy blazer. He doesn't check his pace but passes me without a sideways glance. Just as I think I will have to resort to dropping a handkerchief or falling over, he makes an exaggerated gesture of looking at his wristwatch. Sticking out the elbow and pushing up his cuff. I nearly laugh out loud. Then he exclaims and turns on his heel to face me.

'Excuse me, may I trouble you for the time? My watch has stopped.'

I giggle. It's the look on his face. 'I don't think you'd be much good as an actor.'

The tips of his rather large ears turn red and I regret my outspokenness.

But he's grinning. 'Actually, it's time for tea. Ted Stanley.'

He holds out a hand and I take it. A firm, dry grip. 'Thea Atkins.'

'Would you care to join me for cream cakes at Fullers? Our PMO recommends it, and I do hate eating alone, don't you?'

I bumped into Gwen yesterday. She knew about Clive, but I hadn't seen her so it was a bit awkward. I told her about meeting Ted and I could see she was a bit shocked at first. It is only a month since Clive died, but so much has happened that it seems longer to me. But then she said life had to go on and did I think he was the second Mr Right? I said nothing about how Clive turned out to be Mr Not-Quite-Right. I just nodded in a "Well, maybe" kind of way. Ted and I have been seeing each other whenever he can get away from his ship. The next thing I know, Gwen's dragged me off to Copnor to make an appointment with a fortune-teller for Saturday afternoon.

Mrs Hastie, her name is, and here I am waiting in her back room. Gwen's gone in first, desperate to know whether there's a baby on the horizon, though I can't think why she wants one. The room smells of fried bread and the old dog flopped across the hearthrug. It's just like our room at home, except it's dirty. Crumbs and old egg yolk on the tablecloth, cigarette butts piled in an ashtray on the arm of a chair.

Mrs Hastie isn't any more inspiring. She's got curlers in her hair under the scarf and a baggy cardigan in a dreary shade of pink. The front parlour is chilly and there's no crystal ball, only a folding card table and a stack of cards, which are furry round the edges. She doesn't even put a shawl on. She looks like any of our neighbours queuing for half a pound of shin at the butcher's.

'Got the object, then?'

I produce the signet ring of Ted's that he dropped in my car the other day. I'll "find" it next time I see him.

She takes it in her hands and closes her eyes, rocking very slightly backwards and forwards in her chair. When she speaks her voice has changed.

'This person is a very loyal person. He makes friends for life. He's also very stubborn. He likes things plain and straightforward. Can't abide anything devious or secretive. He's a very fit person, very sporty. He's good at all kinds of sports.'

Silence, while I think how accurate she is. Ted's always going on about cricket.

'I see water, lots of water. And ships. Big ships. Looks like this person will be going overseas.'

She stops rocking and looks up sharply. In her normal voice she says, 'Is this making sense?'

I nod, but not very emphatically as I want her to go on. Ted's in the Navy, a good bet in Portsmouth. She probably says that to everyone. She isn't telling me the thing I really want to know.

'I suppose you want to know whether he's going to marry you? Why do girls always want to know that?' She looks at me fiercely over the top of her spectacles. 'It's not always the most important thing, you know. Not these days.' Then she closes her eyes and starts to rock again.

Once upon a time I would have agreed with her and said the most important thing was to become a painter. But I've grown up since then. That didn't work out and I don't see my way out of North End being a milliner either. I'd have to make hats for the Queen for that. I need a husband.

'This gentleman is going to have a long marriage.' She stops abruptly and looks at my left hand.

I'm glad I remembered to take off my wedding ring. These days I'm learning to take it on and off as it suits me.

'You may not want to hear this. But I believe in being honest.'

'Go on.' I have to know.

'As I say, a long marriage. But it doesn't look as if it will be to you. There's a marriage certificate. I'm sorry my dear. He's marrying a widow lady. I have initials, M D – I think they are. It's fading now.' Her voice tails away and she rubs her eyes and sighs.

She looks astonished when I bounce out of the room with a big grin and call to Gwen.

It's beginning to get dark as we reach the outskirts of Bristol and make our way into St George, where Ted's family live. When we turn into Jubilee Road I give a little sigh of relief and recognition to see terraces of Victorian houses like the one I grew up in. True, the street is wider and the houses on a larger scale, but I know I'll feel at home in the narrow hall and find my way through the scullery to the privy out the back. So it's a shock when Ted says, 'That's it, that one there,' and points to the sore thumb of a building which I've ignored: a red brick cube with razor-sharp edges set in concrete and separated from the pavement by a low brick wall, and from the other houses by a higher one. You wouldn't want to walk round that corner without a cardigan. I laugh to myself, having such silly thoughts. I'm glad I haven't said it out loud, but I can just feel those bricks grazing my skin. The four square windows glare out at me and I shiver.

I edge the long bonnet of the Lanchester between the gateposts and come to a stop alongside the front door, which is at the side of the house. When I get out of the car my footsteps echo as if we're in a tunnel. They must have been looking out for us. By the time I walk round the car and join Ted on the doorstep, the front door is open and I face five pairs of eyes. His whole family are standing in a semi-circle in the hall. Nobody smiles. Nobody speaks. This is an inspection rather than a welcome. All my instincts tell me to turn on my elegant heel and drive back to Portsmouth and poverty. But I make myself look right back at them.

I've never seen such a plain collection of people in my life. It isn't that they're ugly. How could they be, when Ted's so good-looking? But I'd hardly have chosen him for a fiancé if he looked like any of these. It's how they stand, awkward in lumpy old-fashioned clothes, flanked by closed brown doors and a dark oak cupboard. We might not have had any spare money, but me and Nora always refashioned last years dresses or ran up something new in material we got from the market. Even Edna wouldn't be seen dead looking that frumpy. The younger brother and sister are still only children, but they look old-fashioned too. It makes me want to giggle. Somebody say something, please! I nudge Ted hard in the ribs. Then something very strange happens. As he clears his throat to speak, his mother comes forward. She is short and severe and seems to have her dress belted to stop her bosom falling any further. As I say, she steps forward and shakes hands with Ted, with her son. I can't believe what I'm seeing. He doesn't seem to think it odd. He carries on clearing his throat and says, 'This is Thea.' And she shakes hands with me too.

The tea and home-made fruit cake are welcoming, but by the time the children are sent up to bed I need a stiff drink. The sherry I brought has been placed on the sideboard with barely a nod of thanks. I keep glancing at it meaningfully as the evening advances and try to catch Ted's eye. It's Christmas Eve, after all. I find myself thinking of the living room at home with Mum and Dadser and Binnie putting up the decorations, which always ended up with all the same old things in the same places. *They'd* be having a glass of sherry and Dadser a nip of whisky. There's not a paper chain to be seen here, not even a Christmas tree. I never thought I'd wish myself back there, but I have to stop thinking about it because my eyes start to prick.

Ted's elder sister, Ethel, looks at me earnestly through her round spectacles and asks me what sports I like. When I say, 'None if I can help it,' the specs fall down her nose with shock. She doesn't laugh. I can't believe she's the same age as me. Her mousy hair's plaited into earphones, which makes her look about forty, although she behaves more like fourteen. Ted said she's a mathematician, and I can well believe it. Ted's mother passes on family news – Auntie Blanche this and Uncle Frank that. She doesn't chat. She lays statements on the air as if she's slapping them down on a table. Everything she says seems to imply "That's that, like it or not", although those words are never said. She serves food in the same way.

I get confused by her flat Bristol accent. She pronounces "Auntie" like "Anti" and vice versa, so when she refers to the outbreak of flying ants they had back in the summer I get the giggles because I hear, 'There were aunts crawling all over the verandah'.

Ted's father puts in a word from time to time and Ted asks the odd question, but nobody else says anything. Ted's father looks at me a lot. I can see out the corner of my eye. Then Ted's mother notices and looks back at her knitting, twitching her mouth into puckers as if there's a lot she isn't going to say.

305

I'm glad to be given a hot water bottle which I put in the bed while I get undressed. But when I go to get in, the bed is steamy. I put my hand down and it comes out wet. I can just imagine what Mum would have to say about that. I put my coat on and lie there shivering, listening to the house becoming quiet. Ted's mother came up at the same time as us. Not like Mum, who's up half the night on Christmas Eve doing last minute things. When I hear a steady snoring coming from Ted's parents' room across the landing, I creep out and down the stairs. I've just grabbed hold of my bottle of sherry when I hear the creak of footsteps. I shrink back behind the door. Ted's mother remembering something she hasn't done? Please, please go to the kitchen. The door opens and Ted's head appears.

'Phew! I thought I was getting caught red-handed.'

He grins. 'Ah! You got there first. They wouldn't eat you. It's your sherry after all.'

'I was *soo* cold!'

'Your bed as damp as mine? I forgot to warn you. They're always like that.'

He opens the bottle and passes it to me. I take a swig and pass it back.

'Here, let me warm you up.' He puts his arms round me and I snuggle into the smell of him, coal tar soap and the damp wool of his dressing gown.

'I also forgot to say they don't drink.'

'What, never?'

Ted shakes his head. 'Never. Chapel people. Wesleyan Methodist to be precise. Drink is evil, of the devil.'

My eyebrows shoot up. What am I doing here? I know people like Pansy Best's family who don't often have drink in the house, but everyone I know has something at Christmas. Thank goodness I wasn't caught with the sherry. They've already been looking at me strangely. I don't want them to think I'm "of the devil", whatever that means. Really. How ridiculous.

When we've warmed ourselves up I suggest he comes to my bed so we can keep each other warm. Ted jerks his head back in shock. You'd think I'd hit him. He says, 'Not here!' I nearly ask if that's something else they don't do, but maybe Ted won't be amused.

In the morning it becomes clear Ted's father is jealous as anything of the Lanchester. We came in it because the hood of Ted's Triumph leaks and it's freezing in winter. Mr Stanley's eyes are out on stalks. He doesn't know what to make of the fact that it's mine, can't make up his mind whether to like me or whether I'm of the devil. I'm pretty sure Ted's mother's made up her mind. Her lips twitch every time she looks at me. When we're alone in the kitchen and I'm set to peeling potatoes she talks about my first marriage. She doesn't ask questions, just makes statements in that flat voice: 'So you were married before.' Is it a crime to be a widow? She looks like she just got a whiff of incense in her precious chapel.

We get through Christmas Day somehow. Too much to eat and not much else. We have turkey, which is a treat, but I'm shocked that Ted and his father are given a whole leg each as well as some breast. I'm glad Mum's not here to see it. Ethel and Ted and his father want me to make a four at bridge in the evening, but I won't. They're all so humourless, and Ted seems like a different person with his family. Absorbed in crosswords and talk of cricket, being competitive at cards and hardly noticing me. But I've grown so fond of him. You should see him in his uniform, so tall and handsome. Funny, good company, and absolutely straightforward. I don't think Ted knows how to lie. Above all, he's respectful. And so trusting. As wholesome as his mother's cooking. If he were a cheese he'd be a tasty Cheddar, while Clive was a Stilton. All those tricky blue bits. I never can decide whether I like it or not. Ted makes me feel safe, but his family bores me rigid and the thought of becoming part of it is almost too much to bear. I don't want to make another mistake.

I've never felt so alone as I did in that church.

Charlie and Eric put me up the night before, and Eric drove us all here. They live near Exeter, so when I knew I was getting married in Dartmouth I got in touch. Binnie came with me to Charlie's and Eric's to help me dress and everything. I don't know what I'd have done without her. Charlie's been good to me, too. I thought she might be huffy about me getting married again so soon, but she was really understanding.

It's actually St Clement's Church in Townstal we're going to.

Not even the main Dartmouth town church, but the one nearest to the naval college where Ted's stationed. It's a long drive and all the way there I can't get the words of the rhyme out of my head:

Oranges and Lemons,
Say the bells of St Clement's
You owe me five farthings,
Say the bells of St Martin's
When will you pay me...?

When we arrive at the church, the vicar comes out and tells me to wait. He takes Charlie and Eric in with him. Eric's going to take a part in the service, so I suppose they have things to sort out.

When I grow rich,
Say the bells of Shoreditch...

Then a strange man comes out and introduces himself as the Best Man. There seems to be a problem, but he's not saying what it is. He tells me that Ted says we're to go ahead. But where's Dadser to give me away? I ask Binnie to go and fetch Dadser. The best man looks embarrassed and says my father isn't there. I'm worrying Dadser has been taken ill, when Eric comes out and says he will give me away. But he's supposed to be marrying us.

'They haven't turned up.' Eric looks pitying and pulls my arm through his. 'The vicar won't wait any longer.'

Sure enough, when we get inside there's only Charlie and Binnie sitting on my side. I'm so angry. Why didn't they tell me? Why can't we wait?

Here comes a candle to light you to bed,
And here comes a chopper to chop off your head!

It's all very well for Ted. He's got all his dowdy family lined up behind him. I can practically hear his mother's lips twitching. They must think my family are the sort of feckless lot who don't bother to come to their daughter's wedding. And Eric. Why did he use that phrase "haven't turned up"? Why didn't he say, "They must have been delayed"? Just because they haven't got a smart motor car. I worry about what's happened to them. Probably Len's motorcycle's broken down. I imagine them on the side of the road somewhere. I hope they're all right.

Am I'm making another awful mistake? If my knees weren't like frogspawn I'd turn and run. Ted told me St Clement is the patron saint of hatmakers. What a coincidence, but he hasn't been doing a very good job so far. If only Ted could put his arm round me – but he's all stiff and formal, just like me, both of us staring straight ahead. Is it a bad omen that Mum and Dadser aren't here? I keep reminding myself of what that fortune-teller said, the long marriage, not knowing my name, but seeing my initials. Even my bouquet isn't what I ordered. I wanted sweet peas, but they all went in the storm and I've had to make do with scabious instead. I wanted it all to be different from the first time, but not in this way.

That's the real reason we're getting married here and not in Portsmouth. Not where people know me. Not the same church as before. I couldn't bear that. I told Mum and Dadser it was because Ted couldn't get away. Now they aren't here and it feel likes a punishment.

I think of that first immaculate wedding day, all faultlessly organised by Clive. What a contrast with this shambles! And Clive's prestigious funeral which Dadser described to me, the honours accorded him by the Navy, the mountains of wreaths. I was astonished he was so well regarded. To think that was only a year ago. Not quite a year in fact. I did tell Ted a little fib when we first met. It was Auntie's idea, for Ted's sake. She thought it might unsettle him if he knew the truth, that Clive was "hardly cold in his grave", as she put it. So I told Ted we were only married for a year and that it was a year since Clive died. I thought it best.

The whole service goes by in a blur. Before I know it I'm Mrs Edward Stanley.

When we get out to the porch as husband and wife, there are Mum and Dadser with Edna and Len.

And all Mum says is, 'We got held up by lions and tigers.'

I think she's gone stark staring mad. But then Dadser explains they got stuck behind a travelling circus all the way from Exeter. 'Then the mist came down, thick fog. It was a bit of a journey,' he says. Dadser's looking grey, and I can see he and Mum are as upset as I am.

All I can say is, 'They said it didn't matter who gave me away. But it did.'

Dadser says, 'Hush. You're married now. That's all that matters.'

I look round at Ted, and he squeezes my arm and smiles down at me and looks so proud I think maybe Dadser is right after all. My dress is fine, the scabious are really quite pretty and my headdress is still in place. Maybe St Clement *is* looking after me. I'm an elegant bride, after all.

The scene on the pavement outside the church is attracting attention. Villagers have gathered at the gate, as people do for weddings, but they are not looking at me. Len is tightening the belt on his big coat. He sets his cap straight, adjusts his goggles and begins to pull on his gauntlets. Meanwhile, Dadser is easing himself into the sidecar and Edna is standing by to help Mum into the make-shift seat in front of him and close the lid. I cannot bear it. They've come a hundred odd miles squeezed in like this. It's a horrible reminder that, after all, I'm only Marge from North End.

I let go of Ted and turn to Eric, who has just emerged from the church carrying his cassock. 'Can we fit an extra one in the car with us?'

Eric looks dubious but takes charge of the situation. He strides over to where Ted's father is already revving his engine. He's not long had this new car, a big saloon, a Flying Standard, I think Ted said it was. Ted's mother is sitting in the front looking straight ahead and Ethel and Jean are in the back, peering through the rear window to watch the motorcycle and sidecar fiasco. Eric talks to Ted's father who gets out of the car and makes an expansive gesture. Now Mum must be helped up out of the sidecar but absolutely refuses to travel in the car. 'Oh my, oh my. No, no, no. Not me. You go Dick.'

So Dadser tries to get out by himself and Eric goes to his rescue. Finally Dadser is settled in the back of the Standard with Ted's sisters, Mum is in the sidecar and Edna climbs onto the pillion seat behind Len. Two little girls stand on the pavement waving at Mum who waves back at them like the Queen in a goldfish bowl. I'm in the back of Eric's car between Ted and Binnie, with my dress all squashed up, and I am mortified. We all wait for Len, who kicks the cycle into life at the third attempt, and then Eric pulls away to lead the cavalcade.

The little crowd cheers and waves as we move off.

37

2007

Kate met Vanessa on the doorstep. 'Thanks for coming, Mum. He's gone. I thought I'd... But I feel all at sea. And flat... Not what I...'

'Can we go inside? Can I just get through the door?'

'Sorry, Mum.' Kate stepped aside, wiped her eyes with the back of her hand, pushed the front door shut.

'Did you say he's gone?' Vanessa was already in the kitchen filling the kettle. Which was a bit odd for Mum.

'Like I said, yes. Gone. But there's still lots of his stuff here. Well, our stuff really, but things he needs to take. I want to box it up so it's easy, well quicker, when he comes to collect it. And I just found I couldn't make myself do it. Not on my own. I mean, I suppose it would be best to do it with him. But I couldn't do that either. I just thought...'

'Hey! Slow down, will you. I'm still catching up. He's actually gone, you say?'

Kate nodded. 'Yes, I thought it was going to be...'

'The wretched man has actually walked out on you?'

'No, Mum. It's not like that at all. I told you. I told him he had to go. And, as I was saying, I thought it was going to be hard, that he'd refuse to go at the end of the month. But Wednesday, he just came home and said he'd found a place, and yesterday he went.'

'But you didn't really mean it, did you? Surely he knew that?'

'Mum! I did mean it. And he knew it.'

'But you're regretting it now. Obviously.'

What had got into Mum? This was more than she could cope with. 'I am absolutely not regretting it.'

'But look at you. You're all over the place. Not yourself at all. It's not too late, you know.'

'Mum, stop it. If you'd seen me when he actually went.' She recalled the relief, the sudden rush of euphoria that had her dancing in the living room, dancing to Sibelius, of all things. 'I was dancing, Mum. I was ecstatic.'

Vanessa raised her eyebrows. 'But not any more?'

'Well, no. Couldn't keep that up. And, anyway – reality has to kick in. Like Jack and Flora. Jack's really upset about Daddy not being here, really thrown. Well, of course he is. I knew he would be. It's the first time he's ever been nasty to Flora. She...'

'Where is Flora, by the way?'

'It's her day at nursery. You remember? I set it up so I could start painting again. That's why I thought it would be a good opportunity... Anyway, as I was saying, she doesn't understand of course, and keeps asking where Daddy is. And Jack can't stand it, he's started smacking her. So it's all a bit fraught. But nothing you wouldn't expect.'

'Oh, Katie. Poor little Jack. My poor girl. Can't we work something out? He'd come back, wouldn't he?'

Kate moved sharply away as Vanessa tried to put an arm round her. What sort of support was this? Certainly not what she expected from Mum. Not support at all, actually. 'What's going on Mum? Can't you hear what I'm saying? I don't *want* Daniel back. End of story. You never thought I should marry him in the first place. I'd have thought you'd be putting out the flags.'

'That's what your father said. But once there's a family it's different.'

'So Dad isn't taking this line?'

'"Line"? I don't know what you're talking about. I'm not "taking a line", as you put it. I'm just trying to help.'

'Well, you're not. I didn't realise... I shouldn't have asked you.'

'But I want to help.'

Kate looked out at the garden. She bit back the urge to shout. 'Well, barging in being bossy isn't helping. I don't know what's got into you. I just wanted someone to listen to me and help me with a job I'm kind of scared to do by myself.'

There was silence behind her, then the sound of Vanessa thudding into a chair.

'I'm so worried. About you and the children. I love you, Katie. I feel I've let you down. Gone wrong somewhere along the road. And I can't help and you don't trust me, and you won't let me anywhere near any more.'

She turned slowly to see Vanessa with her head in her hands. So that's what was up with Mum. So edgy. So uncharacteristically busy with so-called help.

'Oh, Mum, you silly old idiot.' She put an arm round Vanessa's shoulders. 'Of course I trust you. Why do you think I asked you to come over? I couldn't do this with anyone else. What I can't cope with is you trying to tell me what I think, what I should do. It's not like you.'

Vanessa sighed. 'I just thought maybe I should have done more of that. Failed as mother. That sort of thing. And wanting to make up for being so blind – over Nan and her colour.'

'Mum! Ridiculous woman. One, we left all that behind. Not your fault. Two, it's my life. I have to sort it. But I need you to...'

'That's what your father said, too.'

'Well, then. Here, have some kitchen paper.' Kate tore off a sheet for herself and passed the roll to Vanessa. 'What a pair! Now, I'm going to make some strong coffee and maybe we can start again?'

'Oh dear. Sorry, Kate. The last thing you want is a whinging mother on your hands. You need me to be strong, so I was doing my...'

'Mum, just stop telling me what I need, will you? I don't need you to be "strong".' Kate made exaggerated quote marks in the air. 'I need you to be you. Not rushing in all directions pretending to be someone else's mother and bossing me about.'

'Oh.' Vanessa gave a watery smile. 'Didn't really pull that off, did I?'

Kate put the pot of coffee on the table.

'Shouldn't we be doing boxes?'

'Forget the bloody boxes. Plenty of time for that. Look, I'm sorry you felt left out. But I knew I had to work it all out for myself, by myself. Like I said – my life, my mess.'

'Of course. I know that, really. I'd be just the same.'

'And I do know it's right. It was a huge relief. Which doesn't stop it being shitty as well. I don't want to have to pretend, put on a front with you.'

'Good.' Vanessa blew her nose.

'Now, are you absolutely clear, Daniel has gone, and gone for good? Because I'd really like to talk about it all, but not if you're going to keep going on about him coming back.'

Vanessa nodded slowly. 'I can see now how sure you are. And I was only saying what I thought I ought to say. Stupid really. You'll be much better off without him. After all, I've seen him dragging you down over the years. And you, always so loyal, holding it all together. Anyone could have seen it coming. Except me.' Vanessa sighed and tapped her head with two fingers. 'But what was it that tipped you over? It wasn't just him being drunk, was it?'

'No, not at all. Though that was bad, very bad, especially for the kids. It's this business about Flora. He just can't get to grips with it. Can't get beyond obsessing that people are thinking she's not his child. I've told him till I'm blue in the face that people don't think like that, and then that prat of a boss of his demonstrates that he was thinking precisely that. Nightmare.'

'But he'll still see her, won't he?'

'Oh yes. I've told him he must. He's her father, and how would she feel if Jack went to stay with him and she didn't? But she won't be living with it all the time. And nor will he.'

They both fell silent while Kate poured coffee into mugs.

'Oh, Mum! You don't think I'm ruining their lives, do you? I lie awake worrying myself sick.'

'They'll be fine. With you for a mother. Really, Kate. You'll manage it. And they won't be the only ones. At school and so on, I mean. Kids are resilient.'

'But Jack thinks the world of Daniel. That worries me.'

'Maybe he'll see a better side of him if you aren't together. It's possible.'

Kate gave a harsh laugh. 'He might turn into a paragon. And pigs might fly. No, actually, that's not fair. He's a good father to Jack. Normally, that is. They do all sorts of stuff together, get on really, really well. And then there's Flora.'

'Well, like you say, there was going to be a problem there anyway. I wouldn't worry about her. She's a strong one. She's got her great-great-great grandmother's genes, remember.'

Kate smiled. 'I bet Henrietta's watching over her.'

'But I do find it extraordinary that Daniel should be so hung up on her colour.'

'It's not really about colour. Male ego, really. Which doesn't help Flora, of course.' Kate paused and sipped her coffee. 'But that's not the only issue. It's all been very challenging. You see, I always thought I was the centre of Daniel's universe. Even when he had other women, he always came back. Then Roz died and I discovered that she was really his rock, not me. And I never thought the affairs were that significant. More fool me. It's all come out over the last ten days that this Mitch...'

'Mitch?'

'You know, the first one, is actually the love of his life. Or so he says. They're soulmates, he says, always were.'

'Really? Oh, Kate! Oh, shit. And yet, didn't she get married to someone else?'

Kate nodded. 'He did the "right thing" by me and Jack. Broke it off, told her to get on with her life. Mind you, I think that probably had more to do with the fact that Roz would never have coped with him getting divorced. Roman Catholic, remember.'

'Aah, it's beginning to make sense. So have they been seeing each other all those years?'

'No idea. He says not. He says only recently, since she got divorced. But I don't know what to believe any more. Those other women might have been Mitch substitutes. Or they could have been a smokescreen. Who knows?'

'So it was a combination of things that tipped the balance.'

'Exactly. Isn't it always? If Roz hadn't died he might still be here. If Flora had been white, he'd almost certainly still be here. If he hadn't met Mitch, he'd still be here. If he hadn't got blind drunk... You can't say it's one thing or the other. I mean, when does a marriage start unravelling? And what finishes it off? I don't think you can really be sure. Certainly not at the time. It's not like it's one event. Now I love you, now I don't. It's something that erodes over time, a gradual thing.'

'You're right. Yes, of course it is.'

'I was thinking it all through, down on the beach. And I got a picture of one of those waves you make with dominos. It was like I could see our whole marriage as a series of dominos, all set up, ready to fall. And that evening, when we had THE conversation, I said this one thing and it was like the trigger, the finger tipping the first domino. And I could see them all frilling away with a soft little clicking sound. Beautiful really. Not that the rest of it was very beautiful.'

'What a metaphor! You do think of things in the most amazing way. In the middle of everything.' Vanessa paused and sipped coffee. 'So what was it? The one thing that you said?'

'I confronted him about Mitch. He had no idea I knew. And I didn't really. Just a glimpse of them in town and the rest was gut feel.'

'Gut feeling. Never lets you down. And yours is particularly strong.'

'And, you see, if there'd only been one domino – Mitch, say – it would just have fallen flat. It wouldn't have flattened the whole marriage. Maybe.'

'What about you? You've changed. Obviously.'

'Just a bit.'

Kate remembered the smell of Daniel that night when she came home from Sheerness. She shuddered. She used to positively like the smell of his sweat. A trivial thing, but so basic. Another domino moment.

'Once upon a time I couldn't imagine surviving without Daniel. Even when he was being a bastard. And okay, it's taking a bit of getting used to, but I suppose that's inevitable, that's transitions for you. I just can't wait for the next phase. Being independent, getting on with my life.'

'That's *so* good to hear. And I must say, I look forward to it too. Seeing you without him. I did try to get on with him, but it never really got any easier.' She made a face and they both laughed. 'Now, boxes?'

'I guess we can't put them off any longer. But it was good to talk, as they say.' Kate took a deep breath.

'I've got something to tell you, too,' said Vanessa as they started stacking Daniel's vinyl collection into the first carton. 'I've at last found out where Henrietta died.'

'I thought you couldn't find her death?'

'No, that's right. It's thanks to your father and Broadband that I have. It's a laborious business, you see, when you don't have a date.'

'Uhuh. God, these shelves are dusty. These haven't been touched in years.'

'I'd only gone up to 1930. I mean, I thought she was highly unlikely to have lived beyond eighty-five. Especially in those days. But your father challenged that, so I had another go.'

'And?'

'There's no doubt, this new Broadband thing is amazing. Instead of having time to go and make coffee while the screen loads, the stuff's up there in seconds. I just couldn't believe it. Anyway there she was. She was actually ninety when she died. 1935.'

'And where was she? Does it tell you that? Plymouth, I suppose, not abroad.'

'Yes. I've ordered the certificate. That will tell us exactly where. And what she died of.'

'Old age? I would have thought.'

'Mm.' Vanessa held out an early Beatles album. 'Are you sure all these are Daniel's? You used to know these all off by heart. You don't want to…?'

'Yes, I did, but this is no time for nostalgia, Mum. They are *all* going. They are supposed to be his pride and joy, regardless of the fact that he hasn't got anything to play them on.'

'I can't think why you don't go out for the day and let him come and do all this himself.'

Kate shrugged. 'Doesn't feel right. Don't want him in the house.'

'But surely he wouldn't take stuff?'

'Oh, he can take all he likes. Well, within reason. No, it's not that. I suppose really I'm afraid he might bring a helper. Can't you just imagine? Mitch being curious? Nosing round the house. Going through my paintings. Can't stand the thought of it.'

'See what you mean. Hey, look, Carly Simon! I used to have a shirt just like that.'

'Same colour, as I remember. That was always your ironing music.' Kate took the album and turned it over. 'Omigod! This is the one with "You're So Vain".' She clapped a hand over her mouth.

Vanessa broke off from singing the refrain. 'What's the matter?'

'It was on one time, when I came round to see you. When I was living in the caravan. You were ironing and listening to that song. And I instantly thought, that's Daniel. He probably would have thought the song was about him, yeah? And just as instantly I stamped on it and pretended I hadn't thought it.' Her eyes filled with tears. 'Oh, Mum. You see, I knew, somewhere inside me that it wasn't right, even then. I couldn't bear to hear it after that. What a waste, what a bloody waste.'

Vanessa hugged her. 'Not entirely a waste. Think of Jack and Flora.'

'I know, I know. Of course. God! How right I was to think I couldn't do this job on my own. Let's get it over. Just this last shelf and then it's his books from the bookcase on the landing.'

They had reached the last few LPs when a card fell from a record sleeve and landed on Kate's lap.

'Someone knew him well.' Kate laughed and held up a Batman card, saying "3 Today" in sparkly letters. Next to the figure 3 a zero had been inked in. She opened the card and her insides went into free fall. She looked away quickly, thought for a moment she might throw up.

'Well?' Vanessa was looking up, expectant. 'My God! What's up? You're as white as a sheet.'

She let Vanessa take the card. 'Read it, Mum. Read it out loud. Then I'll know I'm not seeing things.'

'"Darling Daniel, Happy 30th Birthday. You're such an old man now, exclam. All my love, Mitch." Bloody hell! Mitch!'

'Go on.'

'"PS. Saw your Mum yesterday. She said how much she misses you." I don't get it. Daniel's thirtieth. When was that then?'

'Daniel was thirty the year I got pregnant with Jack. We had a barbecue, remember? The chicken was burnt on the outside and raw inside, and everyone got food poisoning.'

'How could I have forgotten? It was dreadful. But that means...'

'Yes. It does mean. He knew *her* before me. Knew her from home. Hell, she even knew his sainted mother.' Kate stopped and took a deep breath. 'Fuck! Fuck! Fuck!' The word echoed round the room. 'And I always thought, whatever happened later, I always thought that time was special, that time in the caravan. Our summer of love. What a fool I was. I should have listened to you. You always said he didn't add up. But I was convinced he was just as besotted with me as I was with him. And all the time...'

'He *was* besotted. Anyone could see that. I'm sure it must have been all off with her. You don't even know it was ever on. They might have been just good friends.'

'I don't think Daniel and "woman" and "friend" belong in the same sentence. It's a bit too much of a coincidence, anyway. Plus a birthday card with "Darling Daniel" and "All my love". And if it was all so innocent, why did he hide it in the record cover? No. You know what that means, don't you?'

Vanessa shrugged. 'Well, lots of things, but...'

'It means *I* was a Mitch substitute. While she was off at college or something. And then he got trapped. Something like that.'

Vanessa was frowning and shaking her head.

'No, really, Mum. I've just remembered something that Blake said. On the day of Roz's funeral. He said it was girl trouble that made Daniel leave home. I took no notice at the time...'

'Blake said that?'

Kate nodded. 'That was probably Mitch. And remember how he went AWOL when he heard I was pregnant? Bet that's where he went. To see Mitch. Decide which way to jump.'

'Well, at least he did the decent thing. And he did care about you, Kate. That I have always been able to see.'

'I bet she sent him packing. Then regretted it. Who knows? And I'm not sure I want to. I could ask him, of course. But maybe not. After all, what difference does it make? When all's said and done?'

'I'd say you have a right to know.'

'Oh, I'm sure he'd tell me. But do I really want to have that conversation?' She stood up and dusted off her jeans. 'Let's talk about something else.'

Kate could see Vanessa swallowing the things she wanted to say, desperately trying to focus on something harmless. Between them they dragged the cardboard boxes into the hall and lined them up along the wall.

Vanessa straightened and rubbed her back. 'There was something I meant to ask you. When I found out where Henrietta was when she died I emailed Josie – you know, the Plymouth cousin? The one who's my age. Gave her an update. And when she replied, she said some of the family are planning a visit to Sussex to visit some aunt. I think she'd like to call in en route and meet up. I wondered if they might come here? Meet you all? What do you think? Or maybe it's all too much to cope with just now.'

'What the hell! Actually, it would be great to have something else to think about. When are they coming?'

'I'll find out. She mentioned Easter but I can't remember whether it was before or after or what it was. Plus I've no idea when Easter is this year.'

'Oh, we'll be a lot more settled by then. I hope.' Kate made a face. 'I'll have had time to get used to this latest – *thing*. And with any luck Jack will have stopped beating up his sister. Yeah, go ahead. Invite them for lunch – soup and bread and cheese, or something.'

38

1944

With this child I have truly escaped my skin, for her paleness spills onto me and I bask in the glory of that reflected light. It was a dark time carrying that unknown being inside me. I fought against the birth, against the moment of knowing. I made it hard for myself. They had to get me out of the way, I fought so hard. They put me into the total darkness of anaesthesia. But out of the darkness came a great light. A child so like her father that the nurses recognised him when he visited. An April child, blonder than daffodils.

So now I sit smiling, elegant in my suit. See what I have achieved! I am simply the slim, dark mother of a dimpled blonde child with chubby legs. A fair-skinned child with pale golden hair I must roll up in rags to make it curl. And the curls I create in this way are not tight and frizzy but loose bubbles and silky waves.

I will not go through that chancy business again. No need. Why tempt providence when the one perfect child is enough? Indeed I am told I cannot go through that again. The doctors say it will not be possible. I am too damaged.

I am a naval officer's wife, a role I am careful to fulfil, whilst holding in scorn those who take it too seriously. Always the loner who doesn't suffer fools gladly, I never kow-tow or sign up to the activities which absorb those other wives. I will not conform. Since I could never conform as a child, I have made not conforming into an art form. I know precisely how far to go, dancing the knife-edge between being outrageous and being outcast, knowing how mystery attracts.

The Navy suits me of course. The moving on every two years. No time to get too close. An ever-changing circle of friends and no intimates. And months and years of being alone while the officer is at sea. That gives me a solitude I can enjoy. For among people I am always lonely. That is the price of secrets and I guard them well.

It was awful getting the telegram to go to Nora's. Mum and Dadser moved in with them in Rayners Lane when Portsmouth was bombed. Dadser was dying. The journey was terrible, all soldiers and delays on freezing platforms. I was too late. The thing that was worse than malaria destroyed him. That word again. Cancer. A hidden presence for years, the symptoms masked by the malaria. Not that it would have made any difference if we'd known. I stayed for the funeral and I didn't want to go home. Nora's house is bigger than the North End one, but it was crowded with all of us there and it felt like home again, even without Dadser.

Mum asked if I wanted to take something of Dadser's, and I don't know why, but I chose his prayer book. I didn't ever see him read the prayers but he used to cut little sayings out of the newspapers, things he thought were wise, and he kept them inside the cover, held in with a rubber band. He used to leaf through those and then just sit holding the book, looking thoughtful.

When I got home from Rayners Lane I sat down after breakfast one day, catching the pale winter sun in the bay window and took off the rubber band. Underneath the clippings was the flyleaf and on it the inscription, *To Frederick from Almira, in remembrance of Gibraltar, September 29th 1894. "Love one another"*. Where had I heard that name before? Of course. The wide smile, the tears in her eyes as she whispered to me on the street in Gibraltar. Dadser's mystery.

I remembered how he was when I passed on the message about being in Almira's prayers. Tears welled up and he turned away.

Then he said, 'We have a little secret here, you and I. Almira and me, it was love at first sight. It does happen. But it didn't work out. Her family were proud. Couldn't accept my mother's colour. I bowed out. Maybe that was cowardly, but I didn't want to cause her pain.' He blew his nose. 'All such a long time ago. And I'm much better off here with your mother and all of you. No regrets. No regrets at all.' And he squeezed my arm.

323

I was glad I took the prayer book. He wouldn't have wanted Mum to find it. A never was for "Amor" after all.

The war years were difficult. I wondered what I was doing all on my own in that house in Dartmouth with so much space. A drab house with eighty-four steps up to the front door and thirty-seven down to the back. Those steps and picking the apples ruled my life. But spring came and I started gardening, growing things to eat. When I'd been digging all day I would sleep in spite of the worries. And there were plenty of them: lack of money, lack of news from Ted, fear of being a widow again. And always the danger that when, if, Ted did come home, there would be the making of a baby.

I put my energy into my home. A house doesn't let you down and furniture stays where you put it. Walls may have ears, but they don't talk. I do my painting on to ceilings and walls these days, not on to paper. And I was right about Ted. He'll never set the world alight but I do truly love him. Sometimes he can be obstinate and moody but he always admits in the end that I'm right. And he's perfectly happy with our one little golden girl.

I was the poor little darkie baby left for dead, the half-sister, half-caste, with skin that wasn't clean and hair that wouldn't comb out. The chubby brown girl, spoilt at home, pointed at on the street. Big sisters fussing me like a doll, playing with the funny hair, other children nudging, giggling, chanting. They all made me angry so I bit and spat and scratched. "Get off me!" My eyes would blaze, the sisters would laugh, "Naughty Marge!" They thought I was funny and also frightening. Little wild thing. Little coffee-coloured savage. I made up my mind to get away from the stroking, poking, hitting hands. To get out of the house, out of the street, out of my skin. I'd show them.

And I did show them.

And now I can show them my blonde child.

39

2007

Kate stared round the room, from the elderly Brenda in the high-backed chair to Brenda's daughter, Josie, to *her* daughter, Lynn, and finally to Lynn's two children, Freddie and Amber, sitting cross-legged in the doorway. There were four generations of cousins gathered in her sitting room.

Not a blue eye amongst them. Pair after pair of Flora's eyes met her gaze. Flora was napping so they hadn't met her yet, and Jack, of course, was at school.

Vanessa was recounting, as if for Kate's benefit, how she had made the first contact with the family. 'I was having a piece of toast and the phone rings, and David says, a lady who says you sent her mother a letter.' Kate had heard it all before of course. Vanessa was doing it to break the ice. These people were family, so there was something that said they should all be relaxed and at ease with each other. But they had no shared history, no common ground, so it was hard to know where to begin. Good old Mum.

'My heart sank. Such a quick response. I was so afraid you'd be angry, or your mother might be upset?'

Josie laughed across at Brenda, shaking her head.

What Vanessa had actually said to Kate was, she thought Josie's mother might be dead and Josie highly indignant.

'I tell you, my hand was shaking when I took the phone. And then there came this wonderful warm Devon voice, and you said – do you remember?' Vanessa looked over at Josie. 'You said, "We are so excited!"'

'Oh, we were. And when you said on the phone that your great-grandmother was West Indian! Well, we always had this bit of a mystery, that there was "colour" in the family somewhere. But we never knew where.'

Brenda chipped in. 'At my wedding one of the great-aunts recognised Ada. She said...'

Josie interrupted and spoke to Kate. 'My father, John, was Ada's grandson, you see. Just so you keep track.'

Kate nodded.

Brenda gave Josie a look, as if her explanation had been quite unnecessary. 'As I was saying, my great-aunt recognised Ada. She used to see her walking round Plymouth with a dark-skinned woman, two tall, elegant ladies who both wore hats. That woman with Ada must have been your great-grandmother, Henrietta. Mother and daughter, going shopping. I can believe it. Ada dressed well. She was tall, but she had very small feet.'

What a fascinating thing to know, thought Kate. 'I wonder whether Flora will have small feet,' she said, more for the sake of saying something, rather than just nodding and smiling.

Vanessa was laying out photographs of Thea, starting at four years old right through her life. 'These are all of my mother. You can see how she changes.'

Josie and Lynn knelt at the coffee table to examine the pictures and pass them to Brenda.

'Look,' Josie nodded towards the doorway. 'In this one she's got Freddie's hair, the really tight curls, only his are blonde. Now Lynn, here, you're always being taken for Indian, aren't you?' She lifted the black curtain of Lynn's hair and let it fall, straight and smooth down her back.

Josie picked up another photo. 'Oh, she looks very dark here. And yet not so dark in this one. None of our family is what you might call "coloured", but, put it this way, we all take a tan very easily!'

Lynn turned to Josie. 'Tell them about when you were born, Mum.'

'Oh yes, Ada was very concerned when I arrived. The first thing she asked on the phone was "What colour is she?" And you have to admit that is a very strange question. You expect, boy or girl?

How heavy? Has she got any hair? But what colour! Isn't that right, Mum?'

'Oh yes,' said Brenda. 'And she had to come and see for herself. She was very overweight by then, but she heaved herself up those stairs. Said she had to hold John's child. She was besotted with my John.'

Josie turned to Vanessa. 'My Dad only died two years ago. Very fond of Ada, he was, devoted to his Gran.'

Kate was struggling with the number of generations being described, even more than in her own family. 'So Henrietta was your great-*great*-grandmother,' she said to Josie. 'Which means, there's an extra generation down your branch. You must have all got married younger.'

Josie nodded, grinning. Looking round the room Kate could see this was a continuing trend. Josie didn't look old enough to be a grandmother and Lynn looked far too young to have a ten-year-old.

Vanessa now produced Henrietta's death certificate and passed it to Josie. 'This is the latest thing I've got. 'It gives us another address in Plymouth.'

'Look, Mum. She lived at number seventy. That's only two doors up from Ada and Bert. Dad used to go there, didn't he Mum?'

Brenda nodded emphatically. 'Oh yes. He used to go every Saturday afternoon. Visited his Gran every weekend without fail.'

Lynn studied the certificate and passed it to Brenda. 'Look, Nan. She didn't die until 1935. Ninety, she was, Nan.'

Brenda frowned. '1935, you say? Now let me see. Oh, that can't be right. My John would have been ten years old in 1935 and he never knew her.'

'But look, Mum.' Josie moved over next to her mother and pointed out the figures. 'June 1935. 90 years.'

Brenda stared, then covered her mouth with her hand. 'Oh my. That's terrible. You see what that means? He went there all those years. And all the time there she was, living two doors away and he never knew it.'

The room went quiet. Even the children in the doorway looked up from their PlayStation. All those eyes watching the old lady.

Josie was shaking her head and frowning. 'Why would they do that?'

'There can only be one reason. To my mind, anyway. Her colour. That's criminal. That really is. He would be so mad, so upset, my John would, if he was still here.' Brenda's eyes filled with tears.

Josie handed her a tissue. 'Maybe she had dementia, something like that.'

Vanessa shook her head. 'If she had, it would be on the death certificate. It says "cardio valvular degeneration". Basically she died of old age. Her heart wore out.'

'Then Mum has to be right.'

Flora chose this moment to wake from her nap and Kate heard a yell of protest from upstairs and the padding of feet overhead. She'd been slightly worried that Flora would turn into an exhibit among Vanessa's research findings and wondered how to introduce her. But Flora herself took control, running into the room and stopping dead at the sight of so many strange faces. Just as Kate thought she might burst into tears, she did a twirl and sang her version of "Twinkle, twinkle little star" which she'd been learning at Nursery earlier in the week.

Everybody clapped, Flora turned away, suddenly shy and spotted the photographs on the coffee table. She picked one up. It was a picture of Thea as a young woman.

'Charlotte,' said Flora and carried the frame to Kate to show her. 'Mummy, it's Charlotte,' she said again. 'Picture of Charlotte.'

Vanessa frowned, watching Flora. 'Who's Charlotte? Why does she think it's Charlotte?'

'Charlotte's my Jamaican friend. She thinks it's Charlotte because she's black, Mum. Very black, actually. You play with Kevin at nursery, don't you, Flora?' Flora nodded. 'And sometimes you go and play at his house.'

But Flora had lost interest in Charlotte and was already busy pulling her furry rabbit out of the toy box to show the other children. Kate watched the expression on Vanessa's face as she re-examined the photograph of Thea.

'Talking of photographs,' Brenda was saying. 'I'm still thinking of how my John was stopped from knowing his great-grandmother. It makes me so angry. He would have been mad. I remember he told me, once when he visited Ada, there was a photograph on the window sill and he asked who it was. He never really got an answer. But he noticed it was gone the following week. It would have been of her. I'll bet you anything it was. It could have been the very photo you've got there. My, oh my. What a terrible thing.'

Vanessa recalled the road of houses she'd seen on her visit to Plymouth with David. 'They're built in pairs aren't they?'

Brenda nodded.

'So Ada would have lived in the downhill half of one pair, and Henrietta would have lived in the uphill half of the one next door? That is so close! Imagine her sitting there every week, longing to see her great-grandson!'

Vanessa was burdened all the way home with that image of the old woman watching and waiting and wishing.

As she got undressed she said to David, 'Now I know why I'm doing this research. It's to recognise Henrietta, acknowledge all she achieved in her life. Think of it. Coming all the way from Bermuda. Raising that big family in Gibraltar. Adjusting to England and that dreadful Sheerness. Moving to Plymouth and then – to cap it all – being shut away at the end of her life. They made her invisible. I'm making her visible again.'

'You realise you're doing it for Flora, too?'

'But of course. She'll want to know. At some stage. And it's got to be different for her, different from Thea's experience.'

'I don't think you need worry about that. It's a very different world.'

'You realise that to get to Henrietta's roots I'm going to have to go to Bermuda? Bermuda and Barbados.'

'Barbados?'

'I used that email network I told you about. Got a response form an archivist in Bermuda. It looks highly likely Henrietta's mother came as a slave from Barbados.'

'Wait till Flora's a bit older. Take her with you.'

'We could all go. There's an idea.'

David gave a non-committal grunt. 'Come and get into bed.'

Vanessa leaned out of the bedroom window. 'Good stars tonight. Oh, David, it was so good to see the three of them today. The children didn't seem any different. And Kate so much more relaxed. They're doing okay, you know.'

'Of course they are. Now, you're not going to leave that window wide open, are you?'

'You know, that family today...our new cousins. So refreshing. They couldn't react more differently from Thea. To the "colour in the family", I mean. No defensiveness. No secrets. Just curiosity, interest, noticing. One person's curly and fair, someone else is dark with straight hair, and so on. I do wish you could have been there.'

'I wish too. They sound a sensible bunch. But you know I couldn't get out of the conference. Anyway, it sounds very much a women's sort of day.'

'Well, yes, I suppose it was. I told you about Flora and that photo of Thea, didn't I?'

'Just a few times.'

'I still can't cope with how I didn't notice. I've been dealing with it by saying my mother was a black child and a white adult. Which can't really happen.'

'Not really.'

'And then along comes Flora. All clear-eyed and innocent. Talk about, out of the mouths of babes and so on. I felt such an idiot. And I could feel Kate looking at me as if to say, *now* do you get it?' Vanessa kicked off her slippers and slid into bed.

'An *Emperor's New Clothes* moment.'

'I suppose it was. Thea as emperor. Huh. Makes sense. It's like stages of waking from a dream. I slept for a hundred years, well sixty-five, and Flora woke me up. Again.'

'You're mixing up the fairy tales.'

Vanessa laughed. 'Interesting though, how relevant they still are. Everlasting.'

'What would have happened, I wonder, if Thea had been there today? If she'd met them all today? Would she have liked them? Got on with them?'

'Perish the thought! How embarrassing would that have been! Actually, she wouldn't have allowed herself to even speak to them. She'd have shut her ears and decided they were beyond the pale for even talking about it. Especially for talking about it.'

'But from what you said, they must have looked a lot like she did.'

'Ah yes, but unlike Thea they were calling themselves mixed race, exploring the various combinations. For Thea, you were either black or white, and she was white. She had a very black-and-white view of the world, generally. No shades of grey. Or brown. Whether or not it was about skin colour. You could say, a very racist view of the world.'

David grunted. 'You're not going all PC on me I hope.'

'No, listen. That's exactly what political correctness is all about, that phrase, using "black-and-white" in that way.'

'But *black* and *white*. We're just talking about the presence or absence of light. It's a neutral concept.'

'For about a nanosecond! How would you feel if you were black and people talked about "black humour" and having a "black day", and the "black sheep" of the family? White's okay and black's not okay. It's in the language. Black people use it too...'

'I know, I know. No need to rant. I don't disagree, as you well know.' David yawned.

'And another thing, Thea hated herself. It occurred to me on the way home. I've kind of half known it, but it became so clear. Those people today, our new cousins, they were all so at ease with themselves as a family. They always suspected there was what they called "colour in the family", but it didn't make them twitchy and defensive. They just laughed about it. Maybe it's a generational thing. But even Brenda, the old lady, accepted it. I can't imagine her chucking Flora on the floor. Or Lynn's husband wanting a DNA test. They were curious, but happy to be who they are. Thea never was.'

'But she thought she was better than everyone else – at pretty well everything, always. *Anything you can do, I can do better.* That was her motto.'

'Overcompensation. It's so obvious.' Vanessa watched the shadow of leaves on the ceiling, mentally rehearsing her next remark. 'And the other thing was, she hated me.' She hadn't said it aloud before. It wasn't that difficult to hear after all.

'Oh, come on. That was the dementia.'

'No, not at all. It was entirely logical. She was either loving me or hating me. Imagine when I was born. I was one of those white-blonde children. I proved she was white. So I got put on a pedestal and all the time I was there on the pedestal she was okay. But I kept falling from grace. So it was like a seesaw. Love me. Hate me. Her up, me down. Me up, her down. It was so rare we were level together.'

'No wonder she lost her mind. If you're right.'

'It was almost inevitable. Something had to give. And all that sulphurous stuff came seething out. I only hope she made some kind of peace with herself at the end.'

'Can you make peace with her?'

'Not sure. I'm not angry with her, at least only sometimes. But I still don't know about forgiveness. I'm not sure what it means. But I do feel I've reached some kind of understanding now. Acceptance. Is that forgiveness? Is it not being angry anymore? I really don't know. But just now it feels good enough.'

'Sounds pretty good to me.' David's voice was sleepy.

'Was she a monster? Sometimes she'd be just an ordinary mother, glad to see me, worried about the rabbits eating her bedding plants. How does that happen? Sometimes I think I make it all up. Then it feels like I'm the one going mad.'

'Nonsense. 'Course you're not. Come on, snuggle up. And, for the record, I don't think Thea was ever an ordinary mother.'

'I'm glad you said that. It's hard when everyone else thinks she was wonderful. But it was all hidden, that love-hate stuff. For most of the people most of the time.'

Vanessa thought of all the people who turned up for Thea's funeral, the tributes in letters, so many, all so admiring. 'People said it was sad that the illness changed her. But I never thought it changed her. It was just, other people saw what I'd always seen.'

No comment from David. He'd heard all this before.

Vanessa smoothed cream into her face and was struck by another thought. 'I wonder how she'd have been different if she'd known Henrietta properly. Bet she was a pretty feisty woman. I can't see Thea growing up hating herself if Henrietta had been around.'

She screwed the lid on the jar and switched off the bedside lamp. 'Think of it, that long line of women stretching over two centuries, from Henrietta in Bermuda and her mother in Barbados. They must have had such strength, such spirit. Then there was Ada. And Thea.

Now there's me and Lisa and Kate and Flora. And all those strong women in Plymouth.'

She sighed. 'It felt good today, making links, following the line down the years.'

A snore came from beside her and Vanessa realised she'd been talking to herself for some time. Talking to herself, and to Thea and Henrietta, making sense of it all.

As she lay in the dark images of Thea slotted through her mind: Thea in the later stages of her illness before she became bed-ridden, on the attack, spitting, scratching, biting, hissing venomous accusations. Another slideshow followed on: Thea in her twenties, the innocent in the sprigged dress; Thea elegant and groomed in her peep-toe shoes; Thea in the garden, brown as the earth, soaking up the sun. Vanessa drifted into sleep.

When the children were in bed Kate took a glass of wine into the garden. The air was chill and there was no moon, but she was drawn to sit under her apple tree. Insects rustled, and a bat flitted across the back wall. She was too tired to think. She just needed to be there alone with the tree and the sense that she was in the process of making a new beginning in her life.

She'd had more time since Daniel left. More energy too. Not just when the children were with him, but all the time. Amazing how much effort had gone into "managing" him, watching his moods, keeping him happy. There was no doubt, her creative self was growing into the space that Daniel left. She'd exhibited in an open show at the Arts Centre, even sold a picture, and as a result a local gallery was taking an interest. She'd been invited to be part of a three-woman show in the autumn, and she was going to have to come up with a coherent body of work.

Today, watching the family studying those photographs and talking about Henrietta, she'd known what she would do. First thing tomorrow, she would get out those "dream paintings" of Henrietta's life and start working them up. They had real potential, strong and vibrant. A new direction for her art. And there'd be an added bonus. What better way for Flora to learn about her ancestor? What better way to bring Henrietta out of the shadows?

Visit www.jilltresederwriter.com to find out
more about the author and her work

Lightning Source UK Ltd.
Milton Keynes UK
UKOW04f2349260917
309929UK00001B/160/P